D0554128

Song of the Vagabond Bird

MERCER
UNIVERSITY PRESS

Endowed by
TOM WATSON BROWN
and
THE WATSON-BROWN FOUNDATION, INC.

Song of the Vagabond Bird

Vagabond Bird

A STORY OF OBSESSION

TERRY KAY

MERCER UNIVERSITY PRESS
MACON, GEORGIA
35 YEARS OF PUBLISHING EXCELLENCE

DISCARD
CARLSBAD CITY LIBRARY
CARLSBAD CA 92011

KAY,
T.

MUP/ H888

Published by Mercer University Press, Macon, Georgia 31207
© 2014 by Mercer University Press
1400 Coleman Avenue
Macon, Georgia 31207
All rights reserved

9 8 7 6 5 4 3 2 1

Books published by Mercer University Press are printed on acid-free paper that meets the requirements of the American National Standard for Information Sciences—Permanence of Paper for Printed Library Materials.

Library of Congress Cataloging-in-Publication Data

Kay, Terry.
  Song of the vagabond bird / Terry Kay.
    pages cm
  ISBN 978-0-88146-481-8 (hardback : acid-free paper) -- ISBN 0-88146-481-3
(hardback : acid-free paper) -- ISBN 978-0-88146-497-9 (ebook) -- ISBN 0-
88146-497-X (ebook)
  1. Group psychotherapy--Fiction. 2. Self-realization--Fiction. I. Title.
  PS3561.A885S58 2014
  813'.54--dc23
                                        2014015641

DEC 2 9 2014

For Tommie

Author's Note

I put the first words of this story on paper in 1992, and then filed it in a folder tagged *Notes for Books*. But I've often done that, knowing that one day I'd likely give them another reading and hopefully would discover something worth chasing after. I think it is the same of all writers with fidgety fingers at the keyboard.

A few years ago, I read again those words from 1992 and came across this expression: *Men ache.*

And in that expression I discovered a story worth chasing after—for my interest at least: a tale of five men who ache, who suffer from near-debilitating obsession over their relationship with women.

For ten days they meet on an island off the South Carolina coast to seek healing from intensive sessions of group therapy, led by a psychiatrist whose methods are alarmingly unconventional, and whose own obsession has left him as unstable as any of his clients.

I am not sure when I realized it, but I had personally known each of the men in one degree or another—a pinch of an edgy disposition from one acquaintance, a fear of failure from another, anger and scorn and confusion and hatred and self-denial from others. I had listened to their weeping over women they worshipped, only to learn that their women were carriers of pain, either by intent or by circumstance. And I discovered in each of them—in their range of bravado and despair—a fragility that men struggle to hide in the name of manliness.

The same was true of the women characters. I had personally known each of them, also from fragments of their persona, and I had some sense of their nature as they wiggled up from the pages—from guile to goodness, from abused to abuser. I had seen them flare in neurotic temper and bring calm to chaos. I had watched them collapse in agony and stand strong with unwavering faith. I knew their storm and their seductiveness, their madness and their majesty.

Because I believe that everyone has multiple personalities—some faint, yet some strong enough to invite diagnosis and treatment—it was as though all the men of this story were from one man and all the women were from one woman. That is how tied together the story seemed to me as it made its way through the filter of my imagination.

I discovered, too, that one man's obsession is another man's shrug, which is probably the reason the phrase "Get over it..." is so often uttered. But obsession is akin to blindness and it is hard to see what should be gotten over in a midnight world. I think that is what good counseling is supposed to do—bring light to darkness, put a name to the it of "Get over it." To those who shrug, it might seem an inconsequential—even silly—experience, but to the obsessed, it is revelation from the magic of miracles.

During the writing, I was surprised by the way things played out. As a story of the brittle nature of the psyche, it took on the same tangle of discovery that writers of fiction find invigorating.

One day, while following the vagueness of a what-if scene, I found a ghost at the front door of Cabin 18, and that ghost would connect dots that needed connecting. In another scene, I stumbled onto a quick, intense romance born of deception, but holding promise. And there, in the background, driving a Mercedes, was a woman of wealth and tease, and a California poster boy wanting to make a television show out of gossip. Because the men being counseled were engaged in confession, there was a penis reference that made me smile. A toothless gateman who watched soap operas had a great knowing of secrets on the island. And, always, there was Carson X. Willingham, counselor, who insisted that the men of his seminars tell lies about themselves.

Writing is a stitching of scenes, using the thread of possibility. In this book, there are many threads of many colors, yet all make one garment. I hope it wears well with the reader.

Acknowledgments

Only the arrogant writer claims total authorship of his/her work. If he/she forgets the careful urging of family and friends, he/she is engaging in selfishness. And what of the people who provide the thread used to stitch the story together—the barber, the neighbor, the doctor, the mechanic, the waitress, the priest, the politician, the addict—all who speak the words and act out the scenes that the eavesdropping writer subconsciously steals. Most are nameless, yet many are so instrumental, the story would not exist without them, for they supply both information and inspiration. Dr. Ronald (Ron) Bloodworth of Macon, Georgia, is such a person for me. He is a psychiatrist, as is the Bloodworth of my story. I appropriated his name with his permission because we became friends a half-century ago in the beginning days of our careers. However, none of the descriptions or actions attributed to the Bloodworth of my story refer to Ron. I selected his name simply because I like him and because I know he has rescued many who were confused and fearful in the handling of their life experiences. Also, I would never have explored this story without the friendship and kind guidance of Jessie Greene, LCSW, of Athens, Georgia. A dear and cherished friend, she has listened and corrected and cautioned and, most important, she has encouraged. The abuses of protocol that appear in the story are of my doing, schemed and committed without her knowledge or agreement.

SONG OF THE VAGABOND BIRD

PROLOGUE

Morning of the Day of Leaving

When I think of Neal's Island in the years left to me, I want to have pleasing memories of the five of us and of the fragile, yet revealing, ten days we were together.

I want to remember the hurts we shared, each from his own hell.

I want to again hear our voices in song, the lusty noise we made as a choir of off-key bellowers caught up in the emotion of a moment so charged with energy it permitted us to be temporary fools.

"A-a-MEN, a-a-MEN a-MEN, a-MEN..."

I want to imagine the portrait we drew of Miss Perfect, for I know the image will cause a smile.

And, yes, I want that. I want to smile.

I want to listen for the echo of Barkeep again telling us the pretzel was created by a psychiatrist trying to make a biscuit.

I want the gift of seeing his face when he said those words, comically furrowed as it was, like an actor in a put-on of heavy drama from a classic mobster movie—a sneering Humphrey Bogart or a growling James Cagney.

I want to remember that we laughed, as we usually did when Barkeep offered an opinion, for Barkeep was funny in an edgy, often uncomfortable way, especially for a man who, like all of us, had wrestled with demons and ghosts.

Still, after our times with Dr. Carson X. Willingham, counselor to troubled men, we would learn there was something profound in Barkeep's rant about psychiatrists. If we each had carried medieval shields to protect us against insanity, his declaration could have been the reading of our escutcheon.

The Pretzel was Created
By a Psychiatrist
Trying to Make a Biscuit

But that is in the past.

Today, we are leaving Neal's Island, and if there is any truth in what we have experienced, and in what Carson X. Willingham has promised, the demons and the ghosts will not travel with us.

None of us talked about it when we made our goodbyes at breakfast, yet we all knew the first twenty-five miles away from the island would be a risky and melancholy drive. After the first twenty-five miles, we would be in Beaufort and the highway would divide and we would each choose a route to follow, returning to our homes. We would be alone, far enough away to resist turning back for the comfort of whatever healing—real or imagined—we might have experienced.

Still, we were also eager to leave the island and to test our understanding of a truth each of us had discovered: Love and Sorrow are such look-alikes they could well be mutant twins conjoined at the chest, forced to stare—unblinking and forever—at one another.

I ache from the searing, overwhelming power of this truth, yet I also ached from my confusion about it on the day I arrived here, annoyed and stubborn and convinced it was nothing more than expensive street theater performed in the name of therapy.

Ten days ago, I believed being on Neal's Island was a Bloodworth trick. Nothing more. Bloodworth's last act of desperation before he insisted on something as primitive as electric shock treatment, or before he had me surprised at work one day by men who would wrap me in the arm-hugging restraint of a straitjacket and then drag me away to a sterilized institution for an old-fashioned radical lobotomy.

There must have been days in the past year when Bloodworth would have liked that. He would have wanted a high-definition video of surgeons pulling sheets of brain from my skull, like tissue from a box.

Frankly, I wouldn't have blamed him, even if part of what I must work out in the future is Bloodworth himself. There is something in me, some irritating presence that tells me Bloodworth was part of the pain. But perhaps I am still too conditioned; perhaps I still need someone to blame if the healing I have accepted is an illusion.

I know the men from our breakfast only by the name they have chosen to call themselves—Godsick, Menlo, Barkeep, and Max. These are pseudonyms, of course. It is part of the program that Dr. Carson X. Willingham has designed for his FullLife Foundation. He does not believe in absolute truth, does not think it is possible. Carson X. (as we have called him, on his instruction) is convinced that men are relatively truthful only if they are able to maintain the dignity of some secret. Thus, he wrote it into the program: No one could offer his real name, or his real profession. Other than these required lies, everything else must be the truth. He admits that he catches hell from many of his colleagues over this practice of deliberate deception. His colleagues say a person's name is his badge of honor, the signature of his history, his culture, his status. They say a person's profession is the heartbeat of his public experiences. They call Carson X. a charlatan, a street preacher, a showoff—or so Carson X. gleefully claims. He also declares he is not bothered by the charges. He believes passionately in what he is doing, and, though there are things about him that I pity, I also believe.

I do now, I mean. At first, I didn't. But I do now.

Carson X. made a believer of me. Not the pseudonym me, but the *me* me.

The pseudonym I chose was Bloodworth. My profession was psychiatry.

When I introduced myself ten days ago as Bloodworth, psychiatrist, the group—Godsick, Menlo, Barkeep, and Max—raised their eyebrows in unison, like members of a violin section hoisting their bows. Barkeep laughed a loud, thundering laugh. He said, "Jesus, I wish I'd thought of that."

It was a cordial breakfast, our last gathering. Pleasant good-byes, and other such courtesies among men who are reasonably civilized and have been forced together for an intense involvement. No one offered to reveal his real name or his actual profession, however. No one suggested a reunion, or said, "Hey, I live in So-and-So. Why don't you guys look me up if you're ever around?" That, too, was part of Carson X.'s offbeat philosophy: You can take group dynamics only so far. Too much group leaves too little person. It is why we had so much free time during the ten days we were together. Carson X. is a confident man. He believes that after ten days with him, you will be able to bite the bullet, or you will, at last, swallow it. He proudly boasts that no one has ever left his program and swallowed one, though I wonder about that. Carson X. could be the leading cause of suicide among needy clients in the United States. In that regard, he could be a serial killer.

Yet, it would be wrong to say we left the breakfast without some regard for one another. We had a few heart-in-the-throat moments of memory, quietly shared. We embraced at our leaving—a gesture that had become natural with us. Godsick even kissed me on both cheeks, like a Frenchman. But I knew he would. I had Godsick figured from the first day. He told us he was a house painter, but, of course, he wasn't; he was a priest, probably an inept one assigned to a small, stable parish. His chosen name— Godsick—and his story gave him away. And his fingers. His fingers were forever making the sign of the cross, but not in the traditional way. His hands rested always in his lap and his fingers made the sign over his navel, like a nervous tick. Godsick was a broken, sad man when he came to Neal's Island, and I am sure he was convinced that God was sick of him —thus, his offered name of Godsick. When we began this ten days ago, Godsick would have been an appropriate nom de guerre for all of us.

I did not know the hidden truth about the others, and I did not believe they knew about me.

It doesn't matter. Carson X. was right about that. It simply doesn't matter. We were all there for the same reason, or illness. We were all diseased by obsession.

And we were—as Barkeep observed in the first session of the first day— "...a certified, in-the-flesh, mucked-up covey of semi-insane men."

To which Carson X. replied, "Well, I hope so, or it wouldn't be any fun for me, and your description, though amusing and perhaps a bit crude, is actually a good beginning, and I'm glad you know who you are, Barkeep. I hope all of you do."

And it was.

A good beginning, I mean.

It got the ball rolling, so to speak.

Then.

Ten days ago.

But, today, there is another beginning and, somehow, I know it has to do with the first twenty-five miles of the drive away from Neal's Island.

I think—no; I know—the same is true of the others. I could tell it in the eager way they glanced toward the road when we gathered at our cars to leave Menlo's cabin. There was joy in their look. And apprehension.

I wanted it to be a lovely drive, those twenty-five miles. I would go slowly along the narrow, tree-lined lowcountry road, over the bridges that link the chain of islands together, like a tightly laced steel stitch. I wanted to watch the egrets and the great blue herons playing air-tag, and I wanted to see Lucifer, the giant alligator that suns on the bank of Stillwater Lake. I wanted a last glimpse of Billy the Kid and his family of deer that has a browsing route as regular as a postman. I wanted to bid goodbye to Old Joe—Old Joe Bonner—who works at the security gate and collects oyster shells and paints the face of Santa Claus on them to sell to tourists.

I wanted to remember the letter I have left, slipped under a doorway after leaving Menlo's cabin.

It was important that I would be conscious of all these things, these leaving-behind experiences. If I did not see the egrets and the great blue herons, or Lucifer, or the deer, or Old Joe, if I did not remember the letter, it would mean I have not used the brave man's sword, as I believed I had, and she has reached out with the

6

powerful grip of her soft, begging hand, and is holding on to my soul.

It would be easy for her to do.

I never wanted to leave her, or for her to leave me.

Yet, if I let her consume me, Carson X. has warned, I will swallow the bullet.

The same is true of Godsick, Menlo, Barkeep, and Max.

1

The Beginning

I will offer only part of the truth I did not share with Godsick, Menlo, Barkeep, and Max: my profession.

I am an account executive for an advertising firm in Atlanta. The name of the firm doesn't matter. It's a big one. Many clients, a lot of money. I will admit, sincerely but with modesty, that I am good at my work. There are awards to prove it. Once or twice a year, I am offered a position with higher pay from competitors, but I never accept. I like where I am and the people I work with. They know me; I know them.

The owner of the firm is a man I will call Spence. He is my closest friend, and he is the reason I began seeing Bloodworth and the reason I agreed with Bloodworth to attend Carson X. Willingham's seminar for Men with Obsession Disorders, or the MOD Mob, as we would call ourselves in the need to avoid anonymity by becoming acronymic.

"You're going," Spence said bluntly when I told him of Bloodworth's suggestion. "You're damned right you're going, and when you come back, you're going to be smiling and healthy, well enough to say her name and be glad you knew her, but that's going to be the limit of it. You're going to get on with your life. Period. End of statement."

Her name is Kalee.

"Do you understand me?" Spence asked.

Close friends are the only people in the world who can beat up on you, reduce you to pulp, and make you listen. Or perhaps that is a man's thing. Friendship among men is always part-war, something learned from childhood.

But Spence also had a right to be forceful.

Spence had suffered my madness patiently, from the very beginning of it, before it became madness.

Spence knew. He knew from the first day he met Kalee. She and I were having lunch in Jilson's Café and he saw us through the window. He smiled his pleasant, easy-going grin-smile and came inside on the invitation of my wave. After introductions, he gave me the quick eye-glance, and the nod. The nod said, "Good choice." Later that afternoon, he admitted he knew who she was before names were exchanged. Her ex-husband was a partner in a conglomerate that owned a chain of hotels. At one time Spence had campaigned unsuccessfully for the account. "I didn't think she would remember me," he said. "She didn't like being in that crowd."

"I barely know her," I said. "We're on the United Way Committee together."

"Well, here's some advice," Spence offered. "Watch your back. She was married to a first-rate bastard, one of those preening good-old-boy assholes with an aversion for losing. Word on the street says she got hammered pretty hard in the divorce. I know her attorney. He told me it was as close to a courtroom assassination as he'd ever seen."

"I wouldn't know," I said. "All we did was have lunch."

Spence pulled himself from the armchair he had occupied. "She seemed a little shy," he said.

"She is, I think," I told him.

"Good," he replied. "After your track record, shy is an improvement. I like shy." He laughed again, a smug kind of laugh, and then he wandered away, whistling.

9

I have not asked him, but I think Spence recognized the same thing in Kalee that I sensed when I first met her. She had a beggar's need for gentleness. Childlike is an expression that comes to mind. Childlike. Fragile. She seemed to be eternally on guard against disappointment, or pain. A friend once said of her, "She wears a pale aura."

When I think of her now, I know the meaning of that statement. It is how I think of her, how I see her. A pale aura has the color of thin, silk clouds.

We were introduced by Abby Hemingway at a meeting of the United Way, and when Abby told her of my work, she awkwardly volunteered she had taken a few courses in advertising in college and had considered pursuing it for a career.

"I still think about it," she said. She added with a small, nervous laugh, "But there must be a thousand things I've wanted to do, if only I had the nerve to try them."

We sat together during the meeting, a dull lecture on projections, accented with dull charts. I watched her. She seemed to be hearing the speaker speaking of his dull projections and dull charts, yet I knew she was not listening to him. Her eyes betrayed her. Her eyes were seeing some other thing in some other place. At the end of the meeting, I gave her my business card and told her I had enjoyed meeting her. And for a reason I still do not understand, I invited her to call me if she ever wanted to talk about getting into advertising. It had the sound of a poor pick-up line, and it was exactly that, even if I did not know it at the time.

To my surprise, she called the next day and asked if we could have lunch. She had some thoughts about the United Way campaign, she said.

Sure, I told her. Lunch would be fine.

"Tomorrow?" she asked. "Are you free tomorrow?"

"I am," I told her without looking at my calendar, knowing I would cancel whatever appointment rested on the page.

That was the day in Jilson's Café, the day Spence happened by and came inside to speak to her, the day he saw what he called The Look.

Oddly, my memory of that day—as life changing as it was—is surprisingly vague. I know we talked briefly of an account I had been working on, a restaurant chain, and we talked about a few people we knew in common, but we did not mention the United Way. Chatter, mostly. I saw she had a quick, flashing smile, yet was not comfortable with looking directly at me. Her hands moved constantly, her fingers playing the air like a pianist. She was the one who made mention of her divorce, calling it, "Painful, but necessary." She added, "I wouldn't recommend it to anyone."

"I know," I told her. "I've been on that journey."

"You were married?" she said with surprise.

"For a couple of years," I answered.

"What happened?" she asked.

"Realization," I told her.

"What does that mean?"

"It means we both realized we weren't ready for the adventure," I said.

She smiled, looked away. After a moment, she asked if I knew of any entry-level positions with an advertising agency. Anything, she said. Receptionist. Secretary. Researcher.

"It's time I made use of my education," she added.

I told her I would make some inquiries for her.

And that was when Spence walked by and I waved him inside the restaurant.

.

11

When the lunch was over, she thanked me for the time, saying, "I enjoyed this so much." And then she repeated softly: "So much."

Funny how words can bore into a person's soul. "So much," said twice, said softly, caused a shiver across my shoulders.

I know it is absurd (Bloodworth has told me as much in his more aggravated moods), but I fell in love with her from the force of those words. I think of them now as code words carrying secrets.

So much.

So much to have.

So much to lose.

When we met again, two weeks later in a bar at Lenox Square, we talked for a long time. The words came easily, eagerly. The words were coated in gladness. I touched her hand across the table, and she did not pull away. Her hand was damp and warm. After the drinks, I walked her to her car.

"Where are you parked?" she asked.

"On the other side of the mall," I said.

"I'll drive you."

In her car, in the isolated dark of a parking space, we kissed—at first an awkward, tentative touching of lips. Touching and pulling back. Then with holding. Mouth gently searching mouth. And then with passion that came from blood.

"Will you go with me to my place?" I asked in whisper.

The answer trembled in her throat: "Yes."

The taste of her mouth from that night was heat and mint, and when we made love in the bed of my apartment, she was wondrously free and giving, the slender muscles of her thighs bracing her legs against the flat of the bed, her body raised to me.

When my fingers touched her, her body opened like an exploding flower.

The first time we made love was astonishing. And all the times after. Astonishing.

Six months after our first meeting at the United Way campaign luncheon, I asked Kalee to marry me. Her answer was given in sobs, in a clinging to me, in a rapid nodding of her head.

I said to her, "Are you sure?"

She nodded again.

And then she became quiet and rested her face against my chest.

"We won't rush it," I told her. "We'll take our time."

"Yes," she replied in whisper.

Two days later, Spence insisted on arranging a surprise dinner for Kalee. It would be an announcement party for our engagement, he said. A few friends and co-workers. Some merriment. Champagne. Caviar. Chocolates. Maybe even a small band for the dancing. Details would come later, he said.

I protested, arguing that Spence did not know Kalee well enough to put her in the center ring of a circus.

He smiled his I've-got-it-handled smile. "Here's what you do," he instructed. "Tell her it's going to be a dinner for a potential client. Make up something. Give it a good name, something French. Tell her she'll need to get involved in these things sooner or later. Tell her people like to see stability when they're doing business, and nothing is more stable than a happy couple."

"Spence, you're doing too much," I said.

Spence leaned back in his chair and lifted his feet to the edge of his desk, crossing his legs at the ankles. "Well, my friend, think of it this way. When I die and you give the eulogy, it damn well better sing."

When I told Kalee of the dinner for the important French client, an importer of perfume, she frowned. "Is this what I have to look forward to? Ozzie and Harriet?"

"I want to show you off," I said. "I want the whole damn world to know you are about to be my wife."

"I'm not sure the whole world will be happy about that," she whispered.

Spence was like an older brother who is foolishly proud of his awkward, younger sibling. He assured me he would take care of all the details for the dinner—from invitations to dessert. "All you need to do is show up," he told me.

The dinner was held at the Ashford Country Club, where the agency had a membership. It was a small group—a few of my associates and friends who were good-natured and caring. They gathered early, bringing gifts of humor and nonsense, and they said, in a collective voice, that they were eager to set the record straight with Kalee: if she took up with me, she would be inviting misery into her life.

They drank wine and talked and laughed at the brief comic sketches of people improvising an evening of good foolishness. And they waited for Kalee, waited to spring out of the darkness of a room, yodeling "Surprise!"

Kalee did not appear.

When I finally traced her by telephone, I discovered a message on the answering machine in my apartment. She apologized for missing dinner, but had decided to go to Florida, she explained. A spur of the moment thing. A need to visit an old friend. "I'll tell you about it when I get back," she said. "I knew if I called your cell, you would try to talk me into staying," she added. She promised to call later. "I'll make it up to you. I just sent you a text. Read it. Have a good dinner. Bring me a bottle of perfume."

My friends made a joke of my embarrassed announcement about Kalee's decision to skip off to Florida. They circled me like taunting demons, and they chortled, "Surprise! Surprise!"

No one said it was a case of cold feet, though everyone thought so.

I spent the night pouring out false energy, fending off jabs about my conquest of women. I laughed when laughed at, raised my glass in toast each time someone offered one. "To bliss," they chortled. "Through thickness and thin, for richer or poorer," they sang. "To death do we part," they bellowed.

There were many such toasts. I lifted the glass many times.

That night, I got as senselessly drunk as I had ever been. Spence drove me to my apartment and promised to stay with me until I fell asleep—"To know you're not going to hit the bottle again," he said.

"I'm all right," I slurred.

"You're a wreck," Spence said. "You're a pissed-off wreck."

I flared at him: "Wouldn't you be?"

"Maybe," he admitted, "but I know this: It's not the end of the world. She went to see a friend. Get over it."

"Friend?" I snapped. "How the hell do you know it's a friend? Maybe it's an old lover she's never talked about. Maybe she wants one last comparison, for God's sake."

"And maybe—just maybe—you're an idiot," Spence countered. "My God, I've never seen you this angry."

"Well, buddy, you don't know me," I snarled. "I don't like being laughed at."

"You're drunk," Spence said in a sad, tired voice.

"Yeah, I am," I told him. "Feels great."

I fell asleep on the sofa, with Spence sitting in a lounge chair across from me. When I awoke the next morning, there was a note from him on my coffee table: *Don't rush to judgment. Remember, she thought it was a client meeting, and who in their right mind would want to waste time at one of those? She's already been married to an ass as we know, so don't judge her. She's a good lady.*

There was no reason for judgment.

Anguish obscures judgment.

At ten o'clock, as I was dressing for work, I received a call from the Georgia State Patrol informing me that Kalee had been killed in a car accident on her way to Florida. She apparently had been driving too fast in a rainstorm. Her car had hydroplaned, left the highway and plunged down an embankment, striking a tree.

It was then that I read the text message she had sent to me the night before. It said: *I will never leave you.*

After that, the madness began. The great need, the great loss. Anguish as torture. Unbearable pain. Anyone who has known the death of someone deeply loved understands it.

Spence watched it, endured it. He coached me through meetings that had no meaning for me. He spent hours rewriting the gibberish I was submitting for clients. He forgave the days I missed appointments and he covered for me when I returned mid-afternoon from martini lunches, unable to work. In one conference in New York with a European carmaker, a video segment on safety featured the danger of driving too fast in a rainstorm and as I watched it, hearing the sounds of rain and the tearing of metal in the crash of the test car, I began to sob uncontrollably. Howling sobs. Frightening sobs. I was transported by ambulance to a hospital where doctors plunged needles into blood vessels and dripped unpronounceable medicines into me. A week later, Spence sat beside me on a flight back to Atlanta. He said nothing of losing the account. He talked instead of the two of us taking a holiday to Ireland, or maybe New Zealand. "Just to get away," he said. "To some place beautiful. We deserve it."

Spence was not my brother, not by blood, but if caring had any DNA, he would have been the good half of my life, split from some ethereal mother's egg.

And then one day, after witnessing a shouting exchange I had with a co-worker, he called me into his office, and he said, very calmly, "All right, I'm taking over your life for a while." He opened his billfold and pulled out a card and punched a number on his telephone. He said, after a moment, "I'd like to speak to Tyler Bloodworth." Spence did not ask my permission to make that first appointment with Bloodworth; he simply made it, and he told me I would be there. "He'll help you," Spence insisted. "I know. He's helped me." It was an admission I have never asked about and one he has never explained.

And, God love him, Bloodworth tried to perform the same magic with me that he must have performed with Spence. I have to give him that. He led me through a maze of questions that would make Alice's trip to Wonderland look like an afternoon stroll through a park with cotton candy trees. He chased me down imaginary corridors and into secret rooms of the mind, where the password was a blithering cry. He gave me maps of my behavior that could be the terrain of an alien planet—from the surprise of having Kalee and not deserving her, to the paralyzing shock of losing her. If there is a medicine he did not prescribe for me, it was because they were still testing it on mice. A few helped, or I believed they did until I began to obsess over whether or not they were placebos. Most left me festered with so many side effects I was afraid of going to sleep and terrified of waking up.

I am grateful to Bloodworth, even with the reservations I have about him. He's a professional, but he has a weakness that his profession does not comfortably tolerate: he becomes too involved. I think he can never decide if he wants to be a psychiatrist or, like Godsick, a priest, and maybe the difference between the two is not so great. Still, the more time (and money) that I spent with Bloodworth, the more I believed he would rather hear confession than perform healing. Or, if he did heal, he would want it to be an exorcism. And that's all right. I have nothing against exorcism. If, early on, I could have spit between my fingers and mumbled some mumbo-jumbo and tossed around some chicken bones, and if that had worked, I would have done it gladly, and I would have paid Bloodworth whatever he wanted.

But such miracles are only in stories of hearsay.

Or, maybe Bloodworth believed Carson X. was a worker of the miracles of hearsay, and maybe that is why he put me on the path to Neal's Island.

The people who play with the mind are impossible to understand.

2

The First Day

When I think of the first day on Neal's Island, I think of meeting Old Joe Bonner at the security gate, and of writing the first letter to Kalee.

Old Joe took the paper that gave me permission to enter the island and he checked it against information on his clipboard. He bobbed his head and smiled a sunken-mouth smile and said, "Number eighteen. That's a good one. I remember when they put it up." He looked into my car, scanning it. "You one of the doc's boys, ain't you?" he added.

"Excuse me?"

"Doc Willingham. You one of his boys, ain't you?" Old Joe repeated.

"Well, yes, I guess you could say that," I admitted.

Old Joe cackled. "Doc's crazy as the day is long," he said.

"Is that right?"

"But he's all right," Old Joe replied. "Yep, he's all right. Once in a while he brings me by some of that soft cheese they make somewheres up north, and hangs around to talk. Talks a lot, Doc does, but I like that. He's like me, but he don't let you put a word in edgeways. Me, I talk and let-talk. Anytime you feel like listening and being listened to, come on by. I love to do both. Yes, I do."

"So do I," I told him. "I hope we can do that."

"Like I said, anytime you feel like it," Old Joe assured me. "I just sit here most of the time. Got me a little tee-vee. I watch them soap operas. I love them things. Lots of people think they a waste of time, but not me."

"I'll remember that," I told him.

"You be careful of the deer," Old Joe warned. "They's everywhere. You kill a deer on Neal's Island and it'll follow you around the rest of your life, just like it was a cloud floating on the back of your eyes."

I told him I would watch for the deer, and thanked him for being friendly, and then I drove away to find the cabin—Cabin 18—that had been marked at the end of the green highlighted line on the island map. Old Joe's snickering laughter stayed in the car with me.

Because I had arrived early, and because it was a cool and overcast Sunday afternoon and I had nothing else to do but occupy time before the scheduled six o'clock meeting at Carson X. Willingham's home, I wrote the first letter to Kalee.

Writing the letter was part of my therapy—a conspiracy between Bloodworth and Carson X.

Bloodworth suggested it, and Carson X. endorsed it in his pre-seminar telephone consultation with Bloodworth.

Bloodworth instructed me to take my laptop (I think of it as my word-maker) and my printer with me to Neal's Island, and he told me I should sit at the word-maker every day and write a letter to Kalee, write it as though she would take it from her mailbox and read it, write it as though she were still alive. In that letter, I should say precisely how I felt. No mincing of words. "Say it, say it, say it," Bloodworth repeated like an excited parrot.

Though I enjoy disagreeing with Bloodworth, I did not object to his instructions. I am comfortable at the word-maker. It is an extension of me. At the word-maker, I feel free and in command.

At the agency, I am regarded as the fastest writer on the planet. My fingers easily find the keys I am to strike. Sometimes, I marvel at my fingers. They are like intense athletes in an intense game. I think if I were a concert pianist, I would play those selections that make the fingers work frantically and leave the audience dazzled by the music.

This is the letter I wrote on the afternoon of the first day on Neal's Island:

Dear Kalee,

This is Bloodworth's doing, this letter.

I am writing this because Bloodworth ordered it.

I think it is supposed to be a way of removing me from you, or you from me. A form of closure.

Yet, now that I think about it, Bloodworth has never used that word with me. He has never said "closure."

Still, that is what it is about: closing out the moments we had together, putting a ribbon around them and storing them in some dry, protected place, like a time capsule that will be discovered a thousand years from now and the discoverer will be startled by the great love that once existed between two flesh and bone people, people so long gone there is no trace of flesh or of bone. Yes, that's why I'm here, writing the letter Bloodworth said to write.

But, of course, I could be wrong. Perhaps it's Bloodworth's way of conducting sessions from afar. Makes sense, doesn't it? All I did was talk about you, anyway. Writing to you is pretty much the same, I think. I will know for certain if Bloodworth sends a bill.

This, then, is a letter of duty, lovingly touched together by the fingertips of your correspondent.

I like that. Your Correspondent. Big Y, big C. Cap Y, cap C. Forgive me if it seems arrogant. I don't mean it that way. I simply need to believe in myself, and I need a little distance, a little detachment to achieve that.

I have mentioned being here, and you should know where here is. Neal's Island, they call it. South of Beaufort, South Carolina. It is an island shaped like a fat comma not quite attached to anything, but is held to a string of other islands by a long concrete-and-steel bridge. From the air, I think it must look like a fisherman's net that has been twirled into the water and is still floating on the surface. It is really a very beautiful place. Once we talked of a weekend together in such a place—remote and romantic. You told me of a week on a sailing ship off the Gulf of Mexico with your parents when you were thirteen. Your face glowed when you talked about it. You said you had thought of us together on such a sailing ship, with the sea spraying its glitter of sun bubbles over us. Do you remember that? I do. Yes, Kalee, I do. It is a sweet and sad memory.

Forgive me. I really don't mean to dwell on the sadness.

Still, it's there.

Before I sat at the word-maker, I took a weak scotch (I promised Bloodworth I would not drink alone, but I needed a harmless lie to maintain a little independence, so I lied) and I went out onto the deck, but there was a storm nudging in from the west and I hate cold weather, as you should remember, so I came back inside and put the word-maker on the dining room table in front of the bay window and began this letter. Besides, I wanted a cigarette and that's an urge I haven't had in years. What do you think caused that, Kalee? There's a line from a poem I like. Has to do with a man in love with a woman named Lillian. In the poem he smokes to check the jitters. Jitters is one of the great words in all the languages of the world.

And maybe that's what I'm really doing with the writing of this letter. Checking the jitters. Yes, I think so. To please Bloodworth, of course. I think if I don't do it, he will suffer a career lapse over my stubbornness, and his depression will only heap more guilt on me. Frankly, Kalee, I'm not up to that sort of responsibility. I am already the King of Guilt, thank you. Enough is enough. My crown is heavy and tarnished and my subjects have all deserted me because no one likes serving the King of Guilt. Anyway, I thought: What the hell. Knock it out. Do it.

So I am sitting here at the word-maker, this processor of the alphabet, with its clickity-click sounding keys (I know, I know; they're silent, but I like saying clickity-click) and I am looking out of the window at sand mounds and at the grass they don't want you to pull—sea oats, I think it is called—and beyond the sand mounds and the grass, there's the ocean. It's white-capped at the moment, little spits of foam curling off the blade of the waves. The wind is up. The tips of the sea oats are swimming in the wind.

What's wrong with me? That's a lovely scene, a pretty sight. It is, Kalee. It really is. So I can't get by with blaming the place, can I? You wouldn't buy that. Bloodworth wouldn't buy it. I don't buy it. The blunt truth is this: I have been flippant, and, with it, slightly off-color, for so many years, it is now the instinct of my personality. I don't like that about me, but I must acknowledge it. I know why, though. Flippant is the name of my shield, my wall, my fortress. Hurl an insult at me, or even a compliment, and I will deflect it with a flippant, obscene swipe. I think I learned it in the business. No one can stay in advertising without becoming a punch-line personality.

I'm sorry. I'm doing it again. Setting up a defense for myself.

Bloodworth said I would most likely write nonsense, if, indeed, I wrote anything at all. He said I would ping-pong from

God to absurdity, and that I would want to retract everything I said about either extreme, but not to. Bloodworth believes in the polarized soul—the yin and yang of things. Everyone has a gene or two from Rasputin, according to Bloodworth, and damned if I haven't begun to believe him. He said the idea of writing the letters was to get it out. Gut-spilling is the layman's term. He wants me to gut-spill, and he wants me to do it by saying whatever enters my mind and flies off my fingers before I have a chance to stop it. Free association, they used to call it, before free association became a party game that led to pitiful jokes about mammary glands and penis envy. But it's not Bloodworth's term. He would never use it. Never in a million years would Bloodworth open his mouth and in his silky, placating voice, speak the words, "free association." It's a term for amateurs, and Bloodworth is most definitely not an amateur. His rates are too high.

My God, I just scrolled back and realized that I've been writing for only a short time and this thing is already longer than War and Peace. *Flying fingers fly on. Clickity-click, clickity-click.*

Actually, I should have finished by now, and the letter should have been signed, sealed and delivered to the post office (in this case, my briefcase). On the drive here, thinking about it, I decided to write only one letter, and it would be no more than three or four sentences long. I thought a lot about what I should say to you. The drive down I-16 takes forever and when you're on the road alone, you've got time to think. I fashioned a few words in my mind and memorized them. They said:

Dear Kalee:

Please leave me.

I love you.

And that is the way I meant for the letter to be, even ending that way: I love you.

24

Simple. Direct. Honest.

It sounded so right and absolute when I said it aloud in the car—especially with the Brahms CD playing—that I stopped for coffee somewhere below the Dublin exit, and I wrote the words on a paper napkin, and when I read them, I wanted to gag. So I folded the napkin and placed it in the coffee saucer and poured coffee on it and watched the ink of its words blot over the napkin until the words disappeared.

This is going to be an adventure, I believe. Yes, Kalee, an adventure. I'm not sure I will survive it. And perhaps that is what it's all about. If I don't survive, I will be with you. That would be a plus, my love.

Your Correspondent

3

Late Afternoon of the First Day

The drive to Carson X. Willingham's home from Cabin 18 took ten minutes. His house was well hidden among those odd, ancient trees one sees on beaches, the kind with the shaped and scissor-trimmed look of bonsai on coffee tables. Off-the-ocean winds twist their limbs until the limbs can only grow the way the wind wishes them to grow.

Carson X.'s home was large and spectacular, which I had expected, and, yet, it seemed misplaced. It had a Mexican influence, like homes in Santa Fe. There was a feeling of stone and heavy timber, of streams of light burning into white, antiseptic walls through small, high windows. It was comfortably, but not lavishly, decorated—except for the art hanging from walls. The art was bold and colorful and dominating.

I was surprised by Carson X. Willingham. Meeting him, I knew instantly why he was the founder of the FullLife Foundation. He was tall and lean-muscled. His skin was sun-brown, with the first swipe of age feathering in thin lines at the corners of his eyes. His short-cropped hair was dark grey, his eyes a rich green. Shallow dimples cut into his cheeks. When he smiled, his face became a sign—not gaudy, like neon, or oversized, like a billboard, but a small, simple, eye-catching sign. Good advertising, we would call it at the agency. The message in his dimpled smile-sign declared: You are special. It is amazing to be blessed with such a gift. Without a word, without communication except from a smile and the eyes directing that smile, Carson X. told me I was special.

He said, standing in the doorway of his home, "Let me guess. You would be Bloodworth."

"Yes," I replied.

"Younger than I thought," he said. "What are you? Thirty-eight? Thirty-nine?"

I knew it was a compliment intended to make me relax. I was certain Carson X. knew all that was to be known about me, from childhood diseases to birthmarks. "Forty-one," I told him.

"A great age," he said with enthusiasm. "I envy you."

I apologized for being early, though I knew I was not the first to arrive. Two other cars were parked in the driveway.

"Not a problem," he said. "Come on in. A couple of the others are already here."

I followed him into the house, into a great room that was recessed by a single step. The recessed area was crowded with a three-quarter circle of sofas facing a large stone fireplace. I saw two men sitting uncomfortably on the sofas with a wide space between them. They smiled awkwardly as we entered.

"Gentlemen, this is Bloodworth," Carson X. said easily. "Bloodworth, meet Godsick and Max."

The two men stood. They were wearing an adhesive nametag on their shirts.

The one tagged MAX was tall and muscular, with the proud, fierce look of the Germans. He was red-faced under a thick crop of rusty-red hair. His eyes were a startling blue. I wondered about his pseudonym. Max was a simple name, yet it fit him so well it might have been his real name. I thought of Max Schmeling, the great German fighter, who lost a famous fight to Max Baer of Omaha, Nebraska. Baer was wearing trunks embroidered with the Star of David; Schmeling was Hitler's example of Aryan superiority. Something about that odd moment—Max vs. Max—in the history

27

of a brutal and violent time has always intrigued me, and I wondered if MAX of the rusty-red hair and startling blue eyes had even a fleeting moment of such a history. Intuitively, I thought: Yes.

The other man, GODSICK, was handsome in a handsome Italian manner. He had dark, doubting eyes and dark hair, graying at the temples. His face told me he was uneasy. His face told me he regretted his decision to attend the sessions, and if any of us bolted in the middle of the night, it would be Godsick.

Max, I believed, was younger than me, and Godsick a few years older. We shook hands and exchanged greetings.

"And this is just to keep things straight until we get to know one another," Carson X. said, handing me the peeled nametag with BLOODWORTH written on it. "Please, sit. Be comfortable. Would you like something? A glass of wine? I'm sure it violates some professional counselor-client pledge of conduct to offer it, but it's my house and I enjoy good wine."

"Yes," I told him. "Wine would be nice."

"Chardonnay?" Carson X. asked. There was teasing in his voice.

I smiled. I wondered how much he knew about Kalee and me. We always drank chardonnay. Always.

"That's good," I said, and Carson X. left the room. I sat on the circled sofa, between Godsick and Max, leaving space.

"This is some place," Max said, after a moment, forcing a smile. He glanced around the room.

"Yes, it is," I replied.

"We were just talking," Godsick said, "about the art. Dr. Willingham—ah, Carson X.—said it was from the painter, Jose Rainier."

"He's good, whoever he is," Max added obligatorily.

I admitted I was not familiar with Jose Rainier, but his paintings were interesting.

"Full of energy," Godsick said awkwardly.

"The perfect room for them," I suggested.

Max merely nodded.

We sat for a few moments, examining the paintings, waiting for Carson X. to return with my wine.

It is curious about men in such surroundings, under such circumstances. They behave as strangers, even to themselves. Women, I think, are different. Women can leap forward in conversation. They will sidestep the absurd and will be peeling back layers of anxieties before the cork is popped on the wine. Men are good face-to-face, one-on-one, in a bar, or at an airport, or sitting on a park bench. Two men, that is. Strangers. Two men—strangers—in a bar, or at the airport, or sitting on a park bench, will tell the absolute truth to one another. If a third man joins them, they become liars, or they stop talking.

There were three of us waiting for Carson X. We had nothing to lie about—not then, not in that uneasy moment. We stopped talking.

When he did return with my wine, Godsick spoke again of the paintings, and Carson X. began to tell us of Jose Rainier, son of Maria Gonzalez, a Cuban refugee from the Castro take-over, and Edward Rainier, an American minister whose church had sponsored the Gonzalez family's escape to America. He paraded the room like a curator of a gallery, giving the history and the humanity of each painting. If he noticed we were uncomfortable, he did not acknowledge it. His behavior was that of a pleasant host, a man who cared to share those things he enjoyed. His voice was deep, but soft. It was not a voice you only hear; it was a voice that invades you, a voice you want to see. I was so taken by it I realized I was staring at his throat.

By six, Menlo and Barkeep had arrived, and Carson X. had introduced them and tagged them and served them wine and had placed a plate of soft cheese and fruit and crackers on the large glass coffee table that was in the center of the ring of sofas. Carson X. then sat on the edge of the stone fireplace, facing us. He smiled warmly.

"Gentlemen, let us begin," he said.

I could hear an intake of breath.

"You know who I am," Carson X. continued, "and you know that each of you has selected a pseudonym and a profession unrelated to your actual work. It's a little game of mine, if you want to call it something.

"But what I'd like to do, if you don't object, is to have everyone re-introduce himself—not your real identity, of course, but that identity you have chosen for yourself. We'll have a bit of a laugh and get that out of the way, then we'll get started."

Because it was the first session, with first-session anxieties, I am not sure we would have laughed at the names and the professions we had chosen if Carson X. had not given us permission by the casual nature of his own conduct.

But the stories were funny.

Menlo, the only black man among us, had a shaved head and a medium mustache and intense, dark eyes peering from an intense, walnut-brown face. He had about him an air of accomplishment. He was stylishly dressed, yet, the clothes were meant for Menlo, and Menlo for the clothes. He was handsome and he knew it, but he did not flaunt it. He may have been a corporate lawyer, but said he was a teacher. "My name is Menlo," he said in a rich baritone, then he cut his eyes to us and a boyish smile perched on

30

his lips. "That was the name of my high school. I was Mr. Menlo, but you fellows don't have to be formal about it. Menlo's fine." He said it with such ease and humor, we all offered a smile in return.

"Damn," exclaimed Barkeep. "I like that. If I'd thought of that, you guys would be calling me Sister Mary Francis."

Barkeep, who was beefy, with heavy jowls and thick fingers, had the rumpled appearance of a backyard beer drinker and the personality of an obscene comic on the strip-club circuit. He claimed he was a lawyer. "You see, I hate the bastards," he said with affected intensity. Then a flash of anxiety crossed his face and he added, "I hope to God none of you guys do that, but if you do, I need to talk to you about a loan because your cohorts have taken me to the cleaners." He had chosen the name Barkeep, he explained proudly, because he had kept plenty of bars in business.

The way Barkeep looked—like a man who slept in his clothes and combed his hair with his fingers—and the cocky way he stormed into the middle of the group with his presence, made all of us begin to relax. We knew instantly that Barkeep would be the talker among us, the rabble-rouser, the one who commanded center stage. We knew we would laugh at him and with him, and we knew he would embarrass us and irritate us. We had all known a Barkeep, and we were all glad he was in the group. We needed a Barkeep. All groups do.

Godsick announced that he was a painter, but insisted it meant he painted houses, not portraits or landscapes. I saw him glance at the paintings of Jose Rainier and do the sign of the cross against his navel. Godsick did not like even the humor of a pretended truth.

Max told us he was a manicurist. He said it calmly, seriously, and he got a good laugh from the group. Max might have been a

31

bouncer in a nightclub, or a professional wrestler, or a bodyguard for a rap singer, but not even God could have made him a manicurist. He would have crushed fingers just by holding them. He would later confess to us he had chosen the profession to please a sister who owned a nail salon in a large east coast city. The sister was the one person who had never abandoned him.

And, of course, they all raised their eyebrows, as I have said, when I announced that I was a psychiatrist.

Carson X. only smiled. He said, "You're not a spy, are you?"

"Nor an expert," I replied.

The smile stayed on Carson X.'s face, but it seemed unnatural. He said, "There are those who would say the same of me." Then he moved his eyes from me to scan the others. "Well, gentlemen, we now know something about one another, even if we know that none of it is true. But we do know one thing that is true, don't we? We know all of you are suffering from the same malady: an obsession with a woman, or because of a woman."

He stood and rubbed his hands together eagerly, a subconscious gesture we would quickly learn was a signal that he was in command.

"But a lot of men can say that, can't they?" he continued.

He paused and looked at Godsick, and then he tapped his hands together, forefinger-to-forefinger. "The difference between them and you is simple: they've learned to live with the obsession, learned to handle it. You have not. That's why I accepted each of you, out of dozens of applications, most of them from small-minded whiners." He inhaled, held the breath for a moment, and then he said in a strong, vibrant voice, "Of course, you will discover there are similarities between each of you. Your ages are close to the same. Only one of you has been married, but amicably divorced. None of you have children and, frankly, that pleases me because it makes my work less complicated. Men with children tend to feel guilty over a sense of being unfit, or sad over giving them too much or too little, and that becomes a first class distraction.

"But here is the nub of the matter," he added. "Each of you has suffered pain. Some of you because of loss and some of you because you believe you were treated badly by women who were selfish and mean-spirited and probably deeply disturbed by their own demons." He looked at Menlo. "And all of you have been betrayed to some degree, either by design or by fate. That is what you have in common."

The room became suddenly solemn, and Carson X. paused.

"Flashbacks, right?" he said gleefully.

I could feel my head nodding shamefully. I thought: Yes, damn it. I looked up. Everyone was nodding, their faces clouded with the dread and the disaster of memory.

"It's all right," Carson X. told us. "When you leave here, ten days from now, you will leave those flashbacks on this island. You will drive away from here as free men, knowing you have choices you've never considered.

"And you do," he added emphatically.

He paused again. I saw Max pick up his wine glass and drink the contents in a smooth swallow.

"In fact, I can tell you right now that what you must learn is as simple as that: you have choices," Carson X. insisted. "You also must realize that you have the right, and the capability, to make those choices. When you choose to let go of your past and to get on with your life, you will be astonished at how splendid living can be."

A mischievous grin grew on his face. "You will find that I do things somewhat different than those good people who have been

33

attempting to guide you back to health. I have been accused of breaking the rules, and I admit guilt to that charge. I can only offer this advice: trust me."

I glanced at Godsick. He gazed intensely at Carson X.

"Now, I want to try something with this group that I've never done before," Carson X. said. "Something I thought of a few weeks ago while reviewing your cases." His eyes scanned us and settled on Max. "How about giving me a hand, Max."

"Sure," Max said.

"We'll be back in a second," Carson X. told us. He and Max left the room.

"Boys, I think we'd better make a run for the door," Barkeep said in a low voice. "I've got some advanced experience in this, and I can tell you this guy's nuttier than a Christmas fruitcake. He's crazier than I am."

Menlo smiled calmly. "At least it's different," he said.

"Yeah, well, a bird's different from an elephant," Barkeep mumbled, "but that don't mean both of them won't piss on your parade if they get a chance."

Menlo laughed. Godsick frowned in disapproval.

When Carson X. and Max returned to the room, they were carrying a flip chart on a metal stand, and at Carson X.'s instruction, they placed it before us. He thanked Max for his help and Max sat again on the sofa.

"This is what I want us to do," Carson X. said, pacing like a lecturer. "I want us to draw a portrait of the woman of our dreams."

"Sure," Barkeep said derisively

"No, I mean it," Carson X. said. "I want to see her, to know how she looks."

"Anybody got a picture of Julia Roberts?" Barkeep mumbled.

A quiet gurgling of laughter fluttered across the group. Even Carson X. smiled.

"How about Halle Berry?" Menlo added easily.

"Good choices, both of them," Carson X. agreed, "but we're not talking pin-up, we're talking ideal." He took a marker from a box. "I'm going to start it," he added. He paused, mugged comically, and then drew the outline of hair covering a head. It had the look of a hairdo that would be curled over the shoulders. He turned and smiled proudly. "See. Nothing to it." He held the marker up, toward us. "Everyone does one thing. Who's next?"

"We just doing her face?" asked Barkeep, "or can I put some knockers up there?"

Carson X. smiled again. I saw his eyes narrow on Barkeep, saw his eyes hold Barkeep for a moment, and then he blinked Barkeep away and looked at Menlo. "What do you think, Menlo? First the face, or the body?"

"The face, I think," Menlo said.

"Good, would you like to add your touch?" Carson X. asked.

Menlo glanced quickly at us and then stood. He took the marker from Carson X. and lingered before the flip chart from a moment, studying the outline. Then he began to draw an eye. It was a large, dramatic oval, like the eye of a woman who makes people uncomfortable with her stare. He drew an eyebrow above it and feathered in an eyelid in quick strokes. He stepped back and studied it, and then he handed the marker back to Carson X.

"Jesus, is she blind?" Barkeep said. "You didn't give her a pupil. She looks like a one-eyed Little Orphan Annie."

Menlo looked again. His brow furrowed in thought.

"It's fine," Carson X. said quickly. "Here's a rule I just made up: once you hand over the marker, you can't add or take away anything. How's that?"

Menlo shrugged and returned to his seat.

"Who's next?" asked Carson X.

"I'll do it," Max volunteered.

Max drew the other eye, matching its size and shape to the eye that Menlo had drawn, but he added the pupil, a large, single bubble.

And then Barkeep added the nose, clowning as he drew it, explaining that it was the nose of a Greek goddess. And then he changed his mind and said it was copied from the nose of an old girlfriend named Daisy. The nose was a caricature of noses, overlarge and crooked, with the appearance of being smashed against the face. Barkeep touched a dot to it and called it a beauty mark. It looked like the wart of a witch.

Godsick drew the lips. They were thin and pinched and severe. "I meant for them to be more dignified than that," he said, surrendering the marker to Carson X. "Like I said, I'm just a house painter, not an artist." The lips did not belong to the eyes or to the nose.

I was the last to make a contribution. I drew the outline of the face inside the boundaries of the hair, giving the woman a slender, almost anorexic appearance, with a neckline that curved into a V below the throat. As I drew, I remembered Kalee's throat and the blush on it and the racing pulse-beat hidden in it when she was happy. I handed the marker back to Carson X. and returned to my seat on the sofa.

"Gentlemen, there she is," Carson X. announced. "The woman of your dreams."

"Boys, that is one ugly broad," Barkeep snorted. "Half-blind, thin-lipped, giraffe nose, skinny-faced, and no tits. If that's the broad in our dreams, it's no damn wonder we're sitting here."

Menlo laughed easily—a gentle, good-natured chuckle. I saw Max lean back on the sofa and bite a smile.

And then Barkeep delivered the assessment that described us perfectly: "Doc, judging from that little example, you've got yourself a certified, in-the-flesh, mucked-up covey of semi-insane men."

Carson X. chuckled. He said, "Well, I hope so, or it wouldn't be any fun for me, and your description, though amusing and perhaps a bit crude, is actually a good beginning, and I'm glad you know who you are, Barkeep. I hope all of you do."

"Doc, I hope you know it," Barkeep retorted.

"Oh, I think I do," Carson X. replied confidently. He turned to the chart and the grotesque drawing we had created. "She is a bit unattractive, isn't she?" he said. "But when we finish, this woman will be so beautiful you'll think she's a goddess. You'll believe she's waiting somewhere out there just for you. And she is. She can be yours if you make the right choices, and you're going to learn that choosing is an adventure, not a chore."

Godsick leaned forward on the sofa, his elbows balanced on his knees. He said, "You make it sound so easy."

Carson X. beamed. "Oh, it is," he replied. "It is. But like any wound of the body, the spirit must be cleansed if it is to heal. What we are going to do over the next ten days is to cleanse the spirit and heal the wounds."

"Do you promise that will happen?" Godsick asked in a pleading voice.

Carson X. looked at Godsick warmly. "I promise you it can," he said softly. "Only you can choose if it will."

Then he said it—the sentence that made me want to leap up and leave. He said: "I believe that health is in the healer and the healer is in the injured."

37

My mind reacted. My mind said, "Nonsense." I could visualize Bloodworth staring at me with his annoyed, all-knowing gaze.

I think I did not speak my objection aloud because of Godsick. He lowered his head and stared at the floor. I could see his lips moving in a repeat of Carson X's philosophy. After a moment, he mumbled, "Yes."

"I don't think I know what that means," Menlo said politely.

"It means you can heal you," Godsick told him.

"Bullshit," Barkeep snapped. "I would have done that already, if I could have."

"Me, too," Max said in agreement.

Carson X. raised his hands to us, palms out, as though to ward off debate. He said, "It does mean you can heal yourself, but anyone can say that, can't they? I know you've tried, Barkeep. You, too, Max. I know all of you have tried. I know you've spent considerable amounts of money in counseling to find the relief that you want. And, yet, you're here, spending more, an obscene amount, in fact. What you must understand is this: you have to trust and believe it can happen. If you don't trust and believe, it won't happen. What we are going to do is work on that trust and belief."

I am not sure that any of us, other than Godsick, left the home of Carson X. that night with abundant enthusiasm. For good reason, I think. Each of us had listened to friends tell us the same thing—in different words, of course, but still the same message: heal yourself. But Godsick, being a priest (likely) instead of a painter, would not have had such discussions. Because he was in love, and tormented by it, Godsick would have suffered alone, having only his prayers.

And there was another reason Godsick would have been encouraged by Carson X.'s admonition: he was a man accustomed to the power of trust and belief.

For the rest of us, trust and belief was not so easy to accept.

4

Morning of the Second Day

At early morning, a gray, overcast sky was hanging on the lip of the ocean, over the whitecaps. I knew it was early morning by the fluorescent dot of light where the sun would have been, if clouds did not have it covered.

The group would not meet again until after lunch. "Rest," Carson X. had said to us. "Walk, if the day's fit. Read. Do whatever you wish. Settle in."

I made an omelet, the kind Kalee favored—mushrooms, bell peppers, a shaving of cheddar cheese. And I had coffee to counter the wine I consumed before going to bed.

It began to rain when I was cooking the omelet. Nothing is as desolate as rain in the off-season of the Atlantic. Against the ocean, rainwater has a color. Gray, I would call it, though Bloodworth would despair over such a description from me. Gray-colored rain. It's the sort of phrase he writes in his little book and draws a box around—as though caging in curious alphabet animals—and later tells me there may be a subconscious meaning to it, suggesting I am being symbolically metaphoric, or maybe metaphorically symbolic, or something equally revealing. I do not understand why Bloodworth refuses to accept a thing as it is, or as it appears to be, without complicating matters.

I wondered if the rain that fell on Kalee the night she died was gray-colored.

I picked up the letter I had written to her and read it again, and I realized it had been years since I had written a personal letter to anyone—something other than emails, I mean. The last one was to my mother, on the anniversary of my father's death. It made her cry uncontrollably, which surprised me. I never believed their relationship was at all special. They lived together, but apart. They seldom laughed, seldom touched, seldom did anything that appeared remotely romantic, yet my mother cried when she read the letter I had written to her. She called me, crying that way, crying torrents of pain. I have never been sure she cried because of my father, or because I had written a letter to her. So unlike me, she said.

And I suppose it is unlike me. I write advertising copy for a profession, and that has always killed the urge to write anything else, though I have played with sketches for theater. I had never written a letter to Kalee, not before the first day on Neal's Island. Emails, yes. Hundreds of them. No, thousands. Once, we got into a competition—which would send the other the most emails in a 24-hour period. I won. It was no contest. She sent forty-five; I sent one hundred and twenty.

I have saved those emails in a large box stored in the attic above my garage.

Oh yes, I wrote emails.

And poems.

Poems to Kalee, or about Kalee, or because of Kalee. A collection of them. Yet, it is boasting to think of them as poems. Poems—great poems—are crafted ballets, words on tiptoe. I have words on flat feet, words that move like a clumsy square dancer. My words are just that: words. Little erotic notes remembering a sudden, good moment, notes scribbled on the backs of envelopes in bars or typed out on the word-maker when I should have been writing copy for health insurance or organic foods. But I did not keep those words in a computer folder. I printed them out, then deleted them from the word-maker, probably because I did not want anyone accidentally finding them and exposing me for being sappy. I knew they were sappy. It's how I felt when I wrote them. Sappy is among my favorite emotions. I had them with me in another folder—a paper one—marked K-for-Kalee. For no reason, I had them.

I never told Kalee about them, mostly out of embarrassment, knowing they were sappy and sentimental, though I had planned to present them to her as a wedding gift. Too late. Too late. The gift not given is not a gift at all. It is just a thing. And maybe that is why I had them with me: still wishing to make a gift of them.

But I am wrong: I did give her a poem once. We were in a bar in Buckhead and I wrote it on a napkin. She read it and laughed, believing I was merely playing the fool, but I wasn't. I was as serious as I ever was with her, or with anyone. In fact, that poem may be the most profound writing I have ever done. It read:

Roses are red,
Violets are blue.
Clouds need rain,
 And I need you.

It was not so simple as it appeared. And as metaphor for love, it was far better than some of the other drivel I have read, or written.

Rain gives life.

Clouds are rain.

Clouds without rain are nothing, not even clouds.

When I wrote it, I believed that without Kalee there would be nothing in my life. And that has been the seed of my agony. Without her, the only rain in my life has been the rain in my heart, misting from clouds of memory.

But the other poems—those word-rambling scribblings— were out of reach, across the room.

I put down the letter I had written to Kalee and turned on the word-maker and began a second letter.

Dear Kalee,

This morning I am trapped by gray-colored rain—down-straight rain, as my grandmother called it, meaning the way it fell—and gray-colored is how I feel. It would be perfect if you were here with me. Yes, it would. Nothing is better than love-making under the sound and the mood of rain.

So, what should I say this dreary morning? Did I describe this place to you? I don't think so.

The room I am in is a living/dining room, or a dining/living room, depending on your perspective or your needs at the moment. It has a sofa, two armchairs, an ottoman, two straight back chairs (out of place for such a room), a coffee table, some bookshelves along the wall, crammed with old books bought, I am certain, at a garage sale from someone named Nelson Harvey. His name is seal-stamped in each book with one of those devices that Notary Publics use for verifying your signature. And, across the way from where I am sitting, is a small but new-looking television set on a television-set table. I am sitting, by the way, at the dining table, which is in front of a bay window. It is one hell of a bay window, Kalee. You would love it. Yes, you would.

But this is not a one-room place, not at all. The other rooms are: two bedrooms, one with a king bed (the kind for two athletic people), the other with a queen bed; a bathroom, with all the things you find in a bathroom—sink, commode, tub/shower (the shower has one of those detachable massage gadgets, like the one we used in the hotel in Savannah with great, playful happiness: remember?); and, last, the kitchen, featuring a tiny, four-eye gas range, an oven, a refrigerator from the first century, a dishwasher, a microwave, a few inexpensive, but adequate, cooking utensils, and four-of-everything table service. The kitchen, to me, is the size of a closet, and of closets, there are three.

That's about it for the cabin, except for the outside. It sits off the ground on sawed-off utility poles. For the tide, I suppose—if the tide gets angry. The utility poles make the cabin appear to be jabbed into the sand. There is a covered deck shaded by trees— water oaks, I think. It has a couple of plastic-strap lounge chairs and a small table. Earlier, I noticed some initials carved into the railing—A B + P R—and I remembered carving my initials and your initials into a beech tree in Piedmont Park on one of our walks.

Memory. When I pick at it, it bleeds. It does, Kalee.

And how are you in that Mystic Place where your spirit drifts (in my dreaming of it) as aimlessly as a cloud?

I have been told by physicians and psychics and psychologists and rabbis and priests and barroom drunks (who are often amazingly profound) that a dead person no longer feels pain or distress. I hope that is true. No, I believe it is true, therefore I'm glad you are not in pain.

They told me when you were killed that you did not feel any pain, or, if you did, it was quickly gone. I do not know how they understand such things, but I trust their verdicts. Still, there must have been some terror for you. I know there was for me. When they told me you were dead, I thought I had been struck by an assassin's bullet. I could feel it exploding in my chest, pulverizing bone, turning muscle into puree, causing a volcano of blood to spew up through my throat. I could not breathe, Kalee. I could not. I've thought a lot about that sensation and I wonder if it was a moment of sympathetic horror, the same as a person having sympathetic labor pains.

Enough.

Yesterday, at our first meeting, we began to explore the reasons we are here, and it was, for me, a revealing experience. We are all suffering loss, but for different reasons. I am, I think, the only person who confronts death as an issue, though I may be wrong. We really haven't done that much sharing.

There's little reason to detail my group-mates—Max, Barkeep, Menlo, and Godsick. They're men and, as such, have little need for description if you go along with the mindset of a lot of people I know. Each of us has been assigned a cabin deliberately isolated, meaning none of us are close-by neighbors and we have not shared locations or cabin and telephone numbers. Carson X. does not want us fraternizing outside our sessions. He wants us to do some serious personal reflecting.

Anyway, we did this odd exercise. We all contributed to a drawing of a woman, starting with the face. An eye here, a nose there, etc. I drew the outline of the face, copying it from your face. (Arrogance aside, it is the most wonderful part of this part-person we are creating on a sheet of flip-chart paper.)

That was something I enjoyed about our time together— touching your face.

Your face was as slender as a model's face. Smooth. Warm. There were times when you would take my touching fingertips into your mouth and the heat of your tongue would surge through me like electricity made by God.

Do you remember the book by Walter Benton, the one called This is My Beloved? *We read from it one night, by candlelight, in bed. There was a line in a poem noted as* Entry, May 11 *(I remember that date because it was your birthday), and the line read: "But I see you unrelated...with not a metaphor to your name: / your hair not like the silk of corn or spiders but like your*

45

hair, / your mouth resembling nothing so wonderfully much as your own mouth."

It's a beautiful poem, really, as are all the poems in the collection. (Now that I think about it, I'm sure that book is the reason I wrote the K-for-Kalee scribblings, and the reason I am ashamed of them. I've always believed you were more like the Lillian of those poems than anyone else.)

And now—for no reason other than the joy of it—I am remembering you on the day we went for a walk in the country and made love in a field of grain, on a quilt of wheat stalks and our own discarded clothing. You were as golden as the wheat stalks, golden where the sun had tinted you from the summer. Your mouth was as sweet as ripe, sweet fruit. Your mouth took me in the fields of grain.

The thought of you is trembling in my chest.

You would laugh over our flip-chart rendering of the ideal woman. Frankly, she is ugly enough to cause blindness. She did not look like you at all. But, then, I didn't think she would. How could five men—or five hundred men—draw you?

I wonder: Does Carson X. Willingham really believe I will temper my love for you by helping other men draw an ugly woman?

If he does, he is wrong.

I do not want to ache any longer, but I cannot put you aside.

I do love you. Oh, my God, I do love you.

I would gladly give up my soul to be with you.

Your Correspondent

There was a thick smell of the sea in the after-rain air, leaving me with a longing for shrimp sautéed in lemon butter and wine, served on a bed of spinach or escarole. It would be a good dinner, I thought, something to anticipate during the inquisition I was certain we would hear from Carson X. in the afternoon session. The thought of it—of the shrimp—was enough to send me to a small grocery I had noticed near the security gate.

I surprised the woman in the grocery. She looked up from the book she was reading, and smiled pleasantly, as though she knew me, but was too uncertain to ask. Still, she offered a greeting and said she would gladly answer any questions I might have.

I thanked her and told her I was there for shrimp and maybe a couple of steaks and for a few other items I had failed to bring with me from Atlanta.

"I'll browse," I said.

"Let me know if I can help you find anything," she replied. "I'll get the shrimp and steaks when you're ready to check out."

She stayed close to the cash register, reading, or pretending to read, as I shopped. I believed she was watching me, still wondering if we had met. As she rang up the purchases we began to talk casually. I asked about escarole and she said the store had never carried it. Too little demand, she explained. She had a warm, friendly voice, and when she asked if I was on vacation, I volunteered that I was there to rest and to catch up on some professional study. She nodded and smiled, but she did not ask what my profession was.

"I have to let the body and mind heal occasionally," I said.

The woman's expression changed immediately. She became sympathetic. She said, "Yes, that's important." She added, as I was leaving, "This is a great place for healing. Just give it time."

She had the voice, and the look, of authority on the subject of healing. And that was something else for me to wonder about. Why was this woman—in her early 40s, I guessed, with a faded,

47

bright-eyed prettiness about her—so knowledgeable about healing? I saw her name on the little plastic tag pinned to her blouse: INGA. What had happened to Inga? Where was the scar I could not see on her? Or did she have a scar?

"I'll keep that in mind," I told her.

"We're open until eight," she said, as though she needed to change the conversation.

"Good," I replied. "I'm sure I'll see you."

5

Afternoon of the Second Day

Bloodworth had said little to me about Carson X., only that he had a celebrity-type reputation for helping men suffering from obsession to resolve their problems and to heal from pain.

"He's unorthodox," Bloodworth had emphasized. "Very unorthodox. Supposedly, he pays little attention to protocol and, for that, he stays under scrutiny by his peers. I don't know of a single practicing professional who agrees with him, or would adopt his methodology, yet a lot of men say they owe their life to him. So prepare to be surprised. Rumor has it the man sets his schedule by his mood. You might meet for five hours or for thirty minutes, or you might go for a couple of days without seeing him. He's not at all predictable."

Bloodworth did not overstate.

When we arrived at Carson X.'s home at one o'clock to continue our sessions, we found him pacing eagerly on his lawn, enjoying the weather's mood—rain to mist to sun. He was like a vacationing child impatient for the beach, but leashed to the tagalong command of parents—the child wanting only to splash in the in-and-out skim of water that wiggled tamely on the sand.

"Well," Carson X. said cheerfully, "let's go do the bonding thing."

"Let's," said Barkeep in a sarcastic whisper.

The bonding thing was as simple as the imagination can make it. We had all done it as children.

We followed Carson X. to the beach, where we were told to remove our shoes and socks and to tuck our socks inside the shoes.

"Sorry that the sand's still damp, but there'll be towels at the house," he said.

He instructed us to form a circle and hold hands.

"A good grip," he urged.

Then he told us to bend backward at the waist, until our arms were extended and there was strain on our hands and wrists.

"If one of you loses your grip, or if one of you releases your grip on purpose, the rest of us will fall, won't we?" Carson X. intoned.

No one answered.

"Barkeep, is that true?" Carson X. shouted.

"You bet your sweet ass," Barkeep bellowed.

"You are right, Barkeep. It is true," Carson X. cried gleefully.

And then he released his grip.

And we fell.

When we looked up, Carson X. was holding his hands above his head, clasped in a sign of victory like a boxer taunting his knocked-down opponent.

"Now, you have learned all you need to know about depending on one another," he said. "From now until you leave, you must remember that you are responsible for everyone else. You must think of truth as being the grip. If you do not share the truth, you will lose your grip and you will cause the rest of us to fall."

We got up and slapped the wet sand from us.

"Son of a bitch," Barkeep grumbled. "I just got these pants out of the cleaners."

Carson X. stood looking toward the ocean. He said, after a moment, "It's really magnificent, isn't it? All that water. It's magnificent."

We exchanged questioning looks.

He walked toward the water. "I love it out here," he cried. "I love the wind and the shrimp boats." He threw open his arms and began to sing in a lusty, operatic voice: "Shrimp boats are coming, their sails are in sight. Shrimp boats are coming, there'll be dancing tonight. . ."

He turned to us. "I have seen whales out there, gentlemen. Great, marvelous whales. They looked like tanks, bobbing in the water. And sailing ships that pass by, the ones that belong to the outrageously rich. Some of them you wouldn't believe. Once, I saw a yacht with a naked woman standing on the bow, leaning into the wind, like a figurehead carved and painted by some talented, drunken artist in love with pale skin and huge breasts. I watched her through my binoculars. She was beautiful, out there in the sun and the sea mist, saying to anyone who saw her, 'This is who I am, the sea whore! The man who owns this yacht worships me. He would kill to take his pleasure with this body.'"

Carson X. laughed, a great high cackle and then he strolled back to us. He said, quietly, as though revealing a conspiracy, "And I have seen the ghosts that wander this island." He paused, looking back at the sea, then back to us. "Do you know? Did they tell you? Have you read about it? This is an island of ghosts. They're everywhere. I have felt them walking beside me on this beach. I've watched them slipping through the trees—creatures made of fog. They're like children playing games. Ghost-tag, maybe. Captain Jeremiah Neal is one of them, I am told. The pirate, Blackbeard, killed him here in a raid. There is a legend that storms from the west are not storms at all, but the raging of Captain Neal. Go to the lighthouse at night if you want to see him. Sometimes, he visits the lighthouse."

51

Carson X. whirled on his heel and picked up his shoes and began striding back to his house. We picked up our shoes and followed.

"I was obsessed with a woman once," he said in a glad cry spoken to the wind. "The same kind of woman you are obsessed with, Barkeep, and you, Godsick. She played the field with me. Pretended she was doing nothing wrong. It was her favorite word 'Nothing, nothing, nothing. . .'"

He paused and yelled in a screaming voice, "Nothing!" And then he again began his strong stride, leaving deep footprints in the sand. We followed in quickstep, as though we were commanded to do so.

"She became friends with a pilot for a corporation in Charleston and every time he flew somewhere on his own, he would ask her to go with him," he added. "Do you know what she told me, Barkeep?"

"Not the foggiest," Barkeep said.

"She told me she would have gone with him if it hadn't been for me. When I expressed a little displeasure over that, she smiled sweetly—and all of you know what I mean by that—and she said, 'Every woman needs a back-up.'"

Barkeep laughed. "I think I know her," he said.

"I loved her so much, I wanted to kill her," Carson X. confessed easily.

He turned to us like an actor about to leap to center stage.

"Have any of you wanted to kill the woman who causes your obsession?" he asked merrily.

We again exchanged glances. None of us spoke.

"Of course you have," Carson X. declared. "At least, all but one of you. You're men. All men either want to rescue women or to kill them before being killed by them. But you can't bring yourself to admit it, or if you admit it in your soul, you can't say it aloud. You will. You will. Come. I've got coffee brewing, a wonderful bean from Costa Rica."

We cleaned the sand from our legs and trousers with towels Carson X. provided, and then we took the coffee from Carson X.'s kitchen and went into Carson X.'s large den, to the circle of sofas. The flip chart with the sketch of the woman of our dreams was standing beside the fireplace. Carson X. had written across the top of the pad, in large letters: Miss Perfect. It was a humorous reminder of our first session.

"I dreamed about that woman last night," vowed Barkeep. "You boys think her face is ugly, you ought to see her naked. But she's not bad in bed, with the lights off. No sir, not bad at all."

We chuckled obligatorily, knowing Barkeep needed the attention, and then we found places to sit on the sofas. Carson X. took his seat on the edge of the raised fireplace hearth.

"It is true that I had an obsession for a woman," he said in a quiet, even, story-telling tone. "I loved her more than I thought it possible to love anyone, and I know that each of you feel that way toward the woman who has driven you here. It's an unbearable kind of passion, isn't it?"

It was not a question meant to be answered, but Godsick whispered, "Yes."

Carson X. did not look at Godsick.

"There are all kinds of women," Carson X. continued. "Angelic women. Givers. Women with soft, caring natures. Women who are goddesses. And there are women who are bitches, takers—selfish, whorish women. Imposters. The woman I loved was an imposter. She could give material things, but she could not give of herself, her soul. A great lover, yes, but an imposter. I did not understand that. I did not understand how someone could say they loved you and then dismiss you without a flicker of emotion."

Again, only Godsick spoke. Again, in a whisper. Again, "Yes."

And, again, Carson X. ignored him.

"I'm going to let you in on a little secret," Carson X. said in a lowered voice. "My practice is crowded with men tolerating wives who have become wild in their thirties and forties. We've always accepted that men were the sinners, the bold ones, the cheaters, and that's been true historically, but, gentlemen, the tables are turning with a vengeance. Take a trip to a bar. You'll see what I'm talking about. Wives and young mothers on the prowl, tattooed and body-pierced women, druggies shopping for a one-night man like they're living in a cheap novel. They're no better than whores looking for a quick trick in the backseat of a car, a wet tryst for a dry martini. Maybe they're worse. They don't want money; they want a thrill." Words were now spilling from him. He squirmed nervously, and then he sprang up so suddenly, we all recoiled. "Do you know of Gandhi's *Seven Dangers to Human Virtue?*" he asked. "You should, if you don't. The second one on his list is this: Pleasure without conscience. Do you hear that, gentlemen? Pleasure without conscience."

He began pacing. His face was flush with anger. "Have any of you ever known a woman who went to bars with the sole purpose of getting laid? I have. I've had them in my practice. They laugh about it. It means nothing. They have no remorse. Gentlemen, you have no idea how much women have changed in the past ten years. Not all of them, of course, but enough to seriously affect our culture. Trust me." He paused. A muscle twitched in his face. "The woman I loved had a lover who lived in a cheap mobile home. She had sex with him two or three times a week. When I learned of it, I thought it would kill me. I finally found the nerve to ask her about it. Do you know what she told me? She said, 'It was just sex.' There was absolutely no shame about it. None. Later she said she had changed. Matured was the word she used. Credited me for it, but, of course she lied. She had an obsession for quick, stunning sex. That obsession will never leave her."

He whirled in his pacing and retraced his steps. "And this," he added over a sarcastic laugh. "This is what she said: 'Be patient. Give me time. I just need time to think things out.'" He wagged his head side to side, an exaggeration that caused Barkeep to subconsciously mock him. And then he said, "Gentlemen, no words from the tongue of the female sex are more deceiving. This is what they mean: Get lost. It's over, buster. Over. I've found another toy. And then they begin to get you confused with the new interest in their life. But it's all slippery-slope territory for them. They will say they've shared something with you, some innocent bit of news, but that would be wrong. Wasn't you at all. And when you call their hand on it, they will vow on the sacred life of their parents that you are mistaken, that you are trying to cause an argument."

He stopped his pacing and inhaled deeply behind a sad smile. "I gave her years, gentlemen. Years," he said. He shrugged. The anger flew from his face. "I'm sorry. Sometimes it seems so unfair, I get a little vexed." He paused in thought and then added, "Do you know what the great writer Oscar Wilde wrote about love? He wrote, Yet each man kills the thing he loves, / By each let this be heard, / Some do it with a bitter look, / Some with a flattering word. / The coward does it with a kiss, / The brave man with a sword."

He picked up his coffee cup and sipped from it. He said, "I want you to learn to be brave men. I want you to kill with the sword, not with a kiss. The kissing is over. To kiss again is to commit suicide with your lips."

He sat again on the fireplace hearth and rubbed the palms of his hands together.

"Please understand that I know a lot about each of you from the counselors you've been visiting, and from my own investigation," he continued. "You are here because your counselor recommended that you consider the program, and after we went through the annoyance of applications and permissions, et cetera, I have chosen you to be here. As I told you before, I receive a lot of applications. The men I choose are special men, such as each of you. But there's one thing I know about you that I do not need counselors to tell me: each of you is subconsciously afraid that someone is about to see into you and through you, and then they will know how truly human you really are."

I glanced at the men sitting around me. They were staring at Carson X. with amazement.

"And that is what is going to happen here," Carson X. warned us. "We—all of us—will see into you and through you. That's why you're here. You will tell your stories and, as you do, you will reveal yourself, and when you realize there is nothing wrong with doing that, with revealing yourself, you will begin to heal." He smiled. "Of course, to be fair, we have to understand all of this is a little one-sided, isn't it? There's no rebuttal for what we say, no defense argument from the women who sent us here. Still, we're going to assume that what we say and what we hear is truthful. That's the beauty of having the floor."

Max coughed. He moved uneasily on the sofa, his great, muscular frame tensing.

"Now, let's share stories," Carson X. said enthusiastically. "Share them honestly. Share everything. The loveliness, the bitterness. All of it."

He paused, inhaled, looked into the faces staring at him.

"Who wants to be first?" he asked pleasantly.

Menlo tried to break the tension. He said, "Where's the Talking Stick?"

A laugh erupted from Carson X. He jumped to his feet and crossed the room in long, athletic strides to a cabinet displaying knives. He opened the cabinet and pulled a Bowie knife from its case and returned to the group.

"How's this for a Talking Stick?" he said in a jubilant voice.

Menlo was embarrassed and irritated. "Hey, I was just making a joke," he said defensively. "I've heard about these groups and the Talking Stick."

Carson X. nodded agreement. "That's right," he said. "The Talking Stick is famous. But it's just a ritual. Nothing more. The man with the Talking Stick does the talking and the truth telling. But remember what I told you about the brave man with a sword? The poem doesn't say, 'Brave man with a stick,' does it? So let's use the sword, or something that could pass for a sword." He handed the knife to Menlo. His eyes scanned us. "How about it? Do we use the Talking Knife?"

There was a pause—an awkward pause.

"We don't need it," Max said suddenly and firmly. I could see the blood pumping in the jugular veins of his large neck.

"I don't know. Why not?" Barkeep said.

Carson X. leaned toward Barkeep. "Are you certain?"

"I really don't give a shit," Barkeep said.

Carson X. smiled warmly. "You're a classic, Barkeep. I knew you would be." He turned to Max. "But I think this should be your call, Max."

Max ducked his head. He sat for a moment, controlling his breathing—slow in, slow out. Then he nodded. "It's all right," he said quietly. "Use it."

"All right," Carson X. said. "We'll think of it as the blade of truth, the scalpel that cuts away the disease." He looked back to Barkeep. "But, remember: it's sharp. Don't play with it."

"Excuse me," Godsick said tentatively, "but don't you think that's dangerous? I thought a psychiatrist would never endanger a—a client."

"Ah, yes, they did tell us something about that," Carson X. said in a bright voice. "But without risk, how do we ever make any progress?"

Godsick did not reply. He looked away.

Carson X. sat again on the hearth. He picked up his coffee cup and calmly drank from it. "Menlo, you hold the knife. Would you like to be first?" he asked.

Menlo turned the knife in his hand, gazing at the curved shape of the blade.

"I think I'll pass," he muttered after a moment.

"Fine," Carson X. replied. "No one should feel forced." He drank again from his coffee, waited patiently. Then he said, "Volunteers? Or, do we draw straws? Get back to being the little child, before we look for the inner child." There was an edge of cynicism in his voice.

Godsick spoke: "I'll do it."

"Hand him the knife," Carson X. instructed.

Menlo handed the knife to me and I handed it to Godsick. Godsick ran his fingers tentatively over the flat of the blade, and then he leaned forward on the sofa and placed the knife on the floor, between his feet.

"I don't know how this is done," he said. "Not in a group like this. I've never been in a group—not for therapy, I mean."

"You do it openly," Carson X. urged. "Honestly."

Godsick nodded. His hands trembled in his lap. I saw his finger flutter through the sign of the cross. He stared at the floor.

"There is a woman. Anna. Her name is—" He looked at Carson X.

"It's all right to use her name," Carson X. told him. "It stays with the group."

"Her name is Anna," Godsick continued quietly. "She came into my life two years ago. I think I was caught off-guard by her. She was not a beautiful woman, not like movie stars, but I thought she was the gentlest and the most caring…"

Godsick paused. He tried to speak again, but his voice faltered.

"Take your time," Carson X. said.

Godsick nodded. He continued to stare at the floor. "She had come to me for—for advice, and, over time, I fell in love with her and we began an affair. It was not like me, I promise, but it was uncontrollable. And it was more than—than physical. It was everything about her. The more I was with her, the more certain I was that I could not live without her. Nothing on earth could compare to being with her. Nothing. I wanted to do as she willed, anything she wanted, but—"

He stopped talking. He buried his head into his hands and began to weep softly.

"We all know how he's feeling, don't we?" Carson X. said.

None of us answered. There was no need for words.

"But she stopped it. She found someone, or something, else. Is that what Godsick was about to say?" Carson X. asked.

"Yeah," Max answered bitterly.

"And she treated Godsick badly?" Carson X. added.

"Like shit," Barkeep snarled.

Godsick looked up to Barkeep. He shook his head and rubbed the tears from his eyes with his fingers.

"She treated him like shit because she knew damn well she could, and she knew she could get by with it," Barkeep continued in an angry, condemning voice.

Carson X. gazed at Godsick. "Are you ready to tell us?" he asked.

Godsick nodded. And Godsick told us.

Anna was a divorced woman with a small child who came to him for counsel—financial matters, he told us, and if he were a priest, as I believed, his explanation was plausible. As they talked, as they shared their experiences, Godsick became intrigued with her, and in her tender, pleading ways, in her feigning of innocence, in the fragrance of her very presence, she began to seduce him. One afternoon, she called him to her home. "She was hysterical," Godsick said. "Her former husband had called, threatening to send some men to take their child." Godsick left his work and went immediately to her, and there, in the bedroom of her sleeping child, she rubbed him into an erection, and, in the swimming madness of ecstasy he had never experienced, Godsick drove himself into her until he was raw and exhausted and the sheet of the bed beside the sleeping baby was damp with the fluids of their sex.

"It was only the beginning," he said sorrowfully. "After that, I had no power to stop it. She would call, and I would go. She would come to my home or to my office, at any hour, and I would slip her inside and we would make love quickly. I loved her. I gave her money, some of it not mine, I'm sorry to say. Anything she wanted, I tried to give her. I bought her a car. I paid for a vacation to Canada and to Europe, not knowing she was meeting another man. She even accidentally sent me an email photograph of the two of them. They were hiking in Sweden. When I asked her about it, she brushed it off as being with a friend, yet she later admitted he had been a lover, but vowed it was no longer true. Just a friend she said."

"And she was doing nothing wrong," Carson X. interjected forcibly. "Am I right, Godsick? Is that the word she used? Nothing."

Godsick's face furrowed in confusion. Then he said, "Yes, she said that. She used that word."

Carson X. smiled a smug smile, a triumphant smile. He rolled his hand in a signal for Godsick to continue.

"She told me that when she talked to him, they talked of his work, his children, as friends would," Godsick said. "She used that word—'friend'—like a tease. She knew I didn't believe her and that made her say it even more often. 'Friend,' 'friend,' 'friend.' She told me she had asked him to stop contacting her, but I learned she was the one doing the calling." He paused, inhaled suddenly. "Dear God, I loved her," he sobbed.

When he began telling his story, Godsick spilled it out, like the bile of illness. He stood and paced, not knowing he was standing and pacing. His voice rolled, trembled. His breathing was labored. Carson X. watched Godsick's face with intense interest and I thought of him as the exorcist Bloodworth wanted to be, an exorcist trapping a demon. And, in a way, that is who he was, and that is what he was doing.

The rest of us listened to Godsick and remembered our own pain, for our own reasons.

"She said she loved me," he cried, loudly and painfully. "She vowed she did. But no one treats someone they're supposed to love with such evil, unless they are evil."

"Is that what bothers you?" Carson X. asked.

Godsick nodded his head. He began to weep again. "She wouldn't talk to me when I begged her not to leave," he whispered. "She told me to get out of her life."

"Ah, shit," Barkeep muttered painfully.

Carson X. leaned forward, toward Godsick. "She said you were suffocating her," he offered. "Am I right?"

Godsick nodded.

"And you probably were," Carson X. added. He waved his hand in a lariat to cover all of us. "With the exception of one of you, that accusation could be true of everyone here, including me." He laughed lightly. "Oh, yes, I did it. Smothering. That's the word. Women do not like to be smothered, but they also use that word as justification for their own restlessness." He stood and again rubbed the palms of his hands together. He said, "Well, the sharing has begun." He glanced at his watch. "It's a few minutes after three. Why don't we take a break the rest of the afternoon and meet back here tonight at eight. Let me spend a few minutes with Godsick."

"It's after three?" Menlo asked. He checked his watch. "It is," he added in amazement.

Godsick had talked for more than an hour.

"Pain fills time, doesn't it?" Carson X. said.

6

Still the Afternoon of the Second Day

I was inexplicably tired and wanted to nap before dinner, but I could not, not with Godsick's agonized confession echoing in memory. Oddly, I thought of Josie, my ex-wife, and of Bloodworth's attitude whenever we talked about her. He had listened patiently, yet with the detached look of a bartender hearing the lamentations of a mumbling drunk. "She sounds very nice," he had said in a bored voice.

Josie was nice. She was rock-solid, a good person, the perfect friend, and that was why our marriage had ended. She said to me one night, "I really love you, but I like you more than I love you. I'd rather be your friend than your wife." She had been so remarkably calm I agreed without argument. That night we slept together, holding, but without making love. The next day she moved out of our apartment. Occasionally, she called to ask how life was going for me, and to tell me of some wonderful moment she had experienced.

Josie was a good person. Just that: a good person. Bloodworth seemed annoyed with good people. Bloodworth wanted storm, not calm. He wanted to hear stories that made him squirm, not slumber.

Bloodworth wanted to hear of Kalee. He wanted to know how one person—shy, uncertain, needy—could have such command over another person. He believed I had lied about her, that she privately ruled me, the same as Anna had ruled Godsick.

To get away from thinking of Bloodworth, I drove to the grocery and bought cigarettes from Inga.

"You really should give them up," she said in a playful manner.

"Give them up?" I replied. "I haven't smoked in years. I'm starting over. Meant to buy them when I was in earlier."

"Then I shouldn't sell them to you," she said.

"Three a day. No more," I told her. "I promise."

She smiled and handed me the cigarettes. "So, how has the day been?"

"Fine," I answered. "A little damp, but otherwise pleasant."

"You have to put up with the weather, but it's still a good place to get away from things," she said.

"Are you from here?" I asked.

"Oh, no. I'm from Richmond, Virginia," she replied. "But I've lived here for a couple of years."

I tried to be flippant, but pleasant: "Did you come here to get away from the aggravation of the world?"

A blush, like a surprise, swept Inga's face. Her eyes flashed away from me. I could see a splotch burning on her neck, below her left ear. She said, "I guess you could say that."

"I'm sorry," I said. "I didn't mean to pry."

Her eyes found me again. She smiled weakly. "It's all right. We all have our little burdens, I suppose." She paused. "Did you need anything else?"

"No. This is all," I said. "I think I've got enough junk food to survive for a few days."

Her smile deepened. "If you're going to be here for a few days, you need to get out," she advised. "There's a restaurant about three miles off the island, toward Beaufort. Marty's. The seafood's good."

"Thanks, I'll remember that," I replied. I added, "Look, I'm sorry about prying. It's none of my business."

"Don't think about it," she said. "Where are you staying?"

I told her the address. Her eyes did not move from my face.

"I know those cabins," she said. "You've got the best one."

"So the real estate agency tells me. But I think I could have had my pick. When the season's over here, it must really be over."

"Yes, almost everyone clears out."

I felt suddenly awkward. I said, "Well, I'll be running along. I'm sure I'll see you."

"I hope so," she said.

At the cabin, I lit a cigarette and felt its poison run through my body. A damp coating of perspiration covered my face. I crushed the cigarette out and went to the word-maker and turned it on and began to write. For some reason—maybe the cigarette—I could feel a tsunami of energy roaring across my chest, flooding into my fingers.

Dear Kalee,

If you were here, I would tell you a story, one that has been floating in my mind and is begging to find its way to paper. I can feel the words building like the fire pit of a volcano, or of Hell. A lot of them are about to spill from the fingers. Beware. They're headed your way.

The story? It's about the initials in the deck railing that I described in my first letter to you. Remember?

A B

+

P R

Initials have always intrigued me. Whenever I have seen them cut into the smooth trunks of trees, or spray-painted on rocks, or gouged into the cement of sidewalks, I want to know who these people are, or were. I want to know if they are alive or dead, if they are young or old, if they are still attached by the plus sign, or if they have been ripped apart.

I want to know: Do they remember the day of the carving or spraying or gouging?

It is a game of harmless God-playing, but I have always given names to initials, and then given their names a story, and I decided instantly, in a pulse of inspiration that blew into my senses like a sudden storm leaping from a cloudless sky, that A B and P R were Arlo Bowers and Penny Rymer.

Arlo and Penny. Two names that could have been stars on the soap operas that Old Joe watches faithfully. A B and P R. Arlo and Penny. Penny and Arlo. Their names were so wonderful, I could imagine organ music playing sweetly in the background.

I said aloud, "A B, A B...," like a conjurer calling up an apparition.

And then I saw him posing on the stage of my imagination.

Arlo Bowers, thirty-six years old, a paint stroke of gray at the temples of his brown-tinted hair. Not tall—five-eleven at most—but a good build for his age. Legs muscled from jogging, good shoulders. Not Hollywood handsome, nor pitifully plain. A good face, with good Irish-English markings. Rouge-blush coloring. Razor-fine lines at the corners of his eyes, like those marking the face of Carson X. Smiles easily. Blue eyes, with merriment. Yet, his face is also a mirror of his moods—anger, hurt, disappoint-

ment, thoughtfulness. Arlo is not blessed with a same-faced expression, like men of great command. Not Arlo. His face blabs secrets. That is both his charm and his flaw.

Curiously, Arlo, like me, works for an advertising agency. He specializes in financial accounts, not because he understands anything about finance, but because he knows how to take the confusion and make it simple.

And then I saw Penny.

P R.

Penny Rymer, stunningly pretty. Blonde hair that is silver and blonde, hair that gathers like a halo. Aqua eyes—greenish-blue-yellow eyes, with small, swimming dots for pupils. Full lips, but not oversized. White-on-white teeth. A slender and long-muscled body, with proud, perfect breasts—not large, not small, but perfect. Her skin is warm. There is a perfume about her, not something she splashed on, but something that is her.

Arlo and Penny are lovers.

No. They were lovers. The word "are" does not apply here. "Are" is a word of pain.

Anyway, being lovers was something that neither of them sought, nor wanted. It was something that happened. Trite, yes. A little silly, even. The stuff of Twitter romances and rich gossip around the water cooler, but still true. It happened. Like us, Kalee. Yes, like you and me. We were something that happened.

There was a problem, however: Penny is married to a man named Duncan—has been for four years.

Penny and Duncan are supposedly happy, though there's little to recommend the marriage. Penny and Duncan are as differ-rent as the proverbial day and night—which is truly appropriate, since day is light and night is dark. Penny is the day, the light— light so brilliant that it is blinding, light spilling over itself, light

67

over light, brighter that the sun through ice. Duncan is night, as dark as pitch. Dull dark. Dull. He has the appearance of a scowling valet when he is around Penny. He doesn't smile. He does a Duncan. Doing a Duncan means never wavering. Doing a Duncan means control over everyone and everything. Penny? She's a great pretender. She pretends she can take whatever Duncan can dish out. She can do a Penny that would make a joke of doing a Duncan. But deep inside this Penny, hums the heart of a proud lioness—a sweet, beautiful creature that survives by instinct.

I tell you, Kalee, this is startling—how well I see everything. I feel almost god-like, having this gift of seeing. Stay with me. I will tell you all of it.

Where was I? Penny. Yes, Penny. The fact is, Penny is only slightly aware of this other self, this sweet, beautiful creature. Duncan calls it her bitch side. When she resists him, when she locks herself away from his dark self to stand in the light of her light self, he screams at her through the door, and when he screams, Penny's heart trembles.

And that is what happens on the morning that P R meets A B at the firm where he works. Duncan has bellowed at her for taking a job without asking his permission. Penny's lioness heart trembles, but only she feels it.

From the beginning, the affair between Arlo and Penny is inevitable, like a strange and unsettling prophecy. Eyes meet in a conference room—blue eyes and aqua eyes. Muscles twitch across lips. Auras flow together like scented clouds and, slam, bam, alakazam, two weeks later A B and P R are behind the Do Not Disturb sign in room 320 at a nearby motel.

The story of how their initials were cut into the railing of this rent-by-the-week cabin on Neal's Island is both joyful and sad.

For more than a year, they are lovers. Great lovers. Lovers that real operas should be written about. Lovers with baritone and soprano voices. Lovers with an orchestra pit at their feet. Arlo begs Penny to leave Duncan and to marry him. "I don't know," she says. "Could you change your life for me?" Yes, he tells her eagerly. Yes. Yes. Yes.

Yes. Yes. Yes.

It becomes their code of whispers.

Yes, I love you.

Yes, I miss you.

Yes, I want to see you.

Yes. Yes. Yes.

The quick telephone call at night. The whispered three words. Yes. Yes. Yes.

Penny files for divorce.

Arlo and Penny celebrate by escaping to Neal's Island for a weekend. On the first night, as they are grilling steaks on the deck of Cabin 18, Arlo takes his pen knife—a Christmas present from Penny—and carves their initials into the railing.

A B

+

P R

Penny smiles at the act. She tells him it makes her feel girlish. They kiss. A movie close-up kiss, a kiss so gentle, and yet so heated, steam escapes from their tongues.

Nightingales play violins from treetops. The music drapes over the shoulders of Arlo and Penny like warm silk.

After dinner, in twilight, they go for a walk on the beach. The wind is up. It bites at their legs with sharp wind-teeth. The water lashes, pours toward them from the unsteady bowl of the ocean. Kettledrums roll thunder and cymbals strike lightning from the orchestra pit. Penny shouts that the wind and the water, the thunder and the lightning, frighten her. She wants to return to the cabin. Arlo laughs. He pulls away from her and races down the beach, clowning. She cries, "Arlo, come back!" Arlo does a comic U-turn, then sprints into the water. He stands for a moment, waist deep, drumming his chest in a Tarzan yell that is lost to the ocean's roar. And then he is yanked away by the water, yanked so violently that he falls forward. Penny will later report that the last expression she saw on his face was one of surprise as he threw out his hands to break the fall.

A single flute from the orchestra pit cries pitifully under Penny's scream.

Arlo dies in the ocean. His body is never recovered.

And now—as it is told on Neal's Island—there are nights when the wind is whispery and warm, and the waves lap against the sandbars of the beach and the heads of the sea oats purr, you can hear a voice that sighs, "Penny, Penny, Penny. . ." And if the moon is full, you can see a shadow skimming across the water. The shadow looks like a man riding the back of a dolphin.

Do you like my story, Kalee?

I think I will share it with Godsick, and maybe the others. What do you think?

I'm sorry we didn't know Arlo and Penny. We would have been friends.

I do love you.

Your Correspondent

It is odd how the imagination can sprint away. I was only God-playing with names and stories divined from initials carved into a deck railing, yet I had become saddened with grief for Arlo. I had to get way from the cabin and the initials for a few minutes, and so I slipped on the windbreaker Kalee had given me and I crossed the sand mounds and walked the beach. It was soggy and damp from the rain and there were long-legged birds—birds with the strange, crooked-back knees—squawking insanely and pecking at little unseen creatures buried in the sand. I saw a dead jellyfish, looking like a ball of murky rubber that had melted in the sun. And I saw some shells. The wind was strong. Waves whipped against the shore, bubbled over the sand, then rolled back in a sizzling of foam.

Far off, down the beach, I saw someone fishing, saw his arm whipping over his head as he tossed the weighted line into the surf. He was wearing brown waders and a long brown raincoat and a red cap. I thought of Old Joe, wondered if Old Joe ever fished.

I had been on Neal's Island for only two days, yet I was ready to go home. I wanted to be in the city where Kalee had lived, near the cemetery where she forever rested. I wanted to be under the power of her presence, even if it had been removed from me, even if it was killing me.

But two days is not a lot of time—a mere finger snap of time—and I had promised Bloodworth and Spence I would not leave early.

"Don't jerk me around on that one," Spence had warned. "You come back before it's over and I will kick your ass so hard you'll be pissing out of your nose."

The thought of Spence's threat made me smile.

And then I realized I did not know what time it was—the hour and minute of the day, I mean.

That was also Bloodworth's doing—not knowing the clock time of the day. Bloodworth made me promise to leave my watch

71

and cell telephone locked away in my car, and not to spend time surfing the Internet—an easy assignment: Internet was not accessible in the cabin I had been assigned.

He also ordered me to lock away every clock in the cabin when I settled in. I asked him why. "Just do it," he told me. He had a look of arrogance on his face. But I knew what he was attempting, what his trick was about. He wanted me to believe there's something significant about not keeping track of time or using my cell telephone as a narcotic. A phrase he loved was, "Break the habit." He meant addiction. Keeping track of time can be an addiction; the same with constantly blathering on a cell telephone or broadcasting text messages and abbreviated tweets to satellites streaking across space. Certainly, Kalee was an addiction. Bloodworth's theory about it was as basic as breathing: addictions need distractions, because the right distraction is a kind of chemical patch for insanity. But Bloodworth was far too cunning to make it as simple as ridding myself of a wrist watch and cell telephone. He wanted me to stubbornly refuse to be distracted, and therefore apply myself to the tasks that Carson X. had in store for me. Bloodworth was occasionally brilliant.

I did not know what time it was, not in clock hours. I knew that I could go to the car and look, or to the closet, where I had hidden the cabin clock—setting the alarm for warnings about the sessions—but that would be cheating. I knew only that by the sun's tilt it was late, and I thought of the day Kalee and I were in a park during our trip to Savannah. The sun was fading and there was a chill to the air. She asked me to hold her. Her body was warm against mine, and she said, "When you hold me, I think the last piece of the puzzle has been put into my life."

At the cabin, in the K-for-Kalee folder, was the first poem—
no, the first scribbling—that I had written for her. It was the only
one with a title.

taking words from your mouth and putting them into mine
the puzzle that is me (jigsaw cuts,
curvy little nothing-pieces
that pull apart with ease)
is complete because of you.
there in the park, where sun
and wind gather, you embraced
me, body to body, and the
way you fit against me—into me—
i knew that i was whole.
and now that i am whole,
the bits and pieces together,
how can i ever be the
not-quite-finished person
i used to be? how?

The nausea of loneliness swept over me and I could feel my
throat swelling with the ache of memory. I went back into the
cabin and made a sandwich and ate it quickly, washing it down
with a glass of milk.

The clock in the closet rang its alert for the session, and I was
glad to hear it. I needed to be with people.

7

Night of the Second Day

We were subdued at the evening meeting of the MOD Mob, but Carson X. did not seem to notice.

"So, how did you spend the afternoon?" he asked brightly.

Godsick spoke first. "I went for a walk on the beach."

"That's good," Carson X. responded. "The sea air's good for everything. And the rest of you?"

Menlo cooked a carrot cake. Cooking, he said, was his hobby, his balance. He had brought the cake with him for us to have with coffee.

Max drank wine—too much, he admitted—and slept. He had the drained look of a man suffering from hangover.

Barkeep wrote a letter to a sister. "But I won't mail it," he said. "She couldn't take it."

"And why not?" Carson X. asked.

"I told her the truth about how tired I am of her trying to live my life," Barkeep replied. "My sister is a goddamn tyrant."

"I see," Carson X. mused. He turned to me. "Bloodworth?"

"I went to the grocery, and I also wrote a letter," I said.

"To your wife?" Max asked.

"I'm divorced," I answered. "I wrote to the woman who sent me here."

"I'm sorry," Max apologized. "For some reason, I thought you were married."

Menlo asked if I would mail the letter.

"No," I said. "It would be useless." I added, "I think you'll understand later."

"Women, they're all the same," Barkeep volunteered. "Once they grab you by the gonads, they don't stop squeezing."

Barkeep did not intend his comment to be funny, but Carson X. laughed and Barkeep stared at him curiously.

"I mean it," Barkeep said.

"I know you do," Carson X. replied. "That's why I think it's humorous."

We were in the kitchen and Carson X. was pouring coffee and distributing Menlo's carrot cake, which was extraordinary, leaving me to wonder if in his real life he was an executive pastry chef in an exclusive hotel.

Carson X. was dressed in white pants, a white pullover shirt and white shoes. He looked like a photographer's model about to board the yacht he had described to us earlier, the one with the nude woman leaning against the bow. His dimples winked as he talked enthusiastically of his own joy of cooking, saying he and Menlo should prepare a dinner for us before the sessions were over.

"Why don't we sit in here?" he suggested. "Keep the coffee pot handy. Stay near the cake. From this time forward, it's a serve-yourself environment."

We took seats at the kitchen table and on the stools that were pushed up to the bar separating the kitchen from the great room.

"All right, I know what some of you must be thinking—or should be," Carson X. said. "A waste of time and money. Right?"

I saw Barkeep tilt his head and look at Menlo, and I knew they had talked.

Menlo cleared his throat. He said, "Well, now that you brought it up. I am a little curious as to why we've only spent a few hours together."

Carson X. nodded thoughtfully. He sat on one of the stools. "A fair point, and to be honest, my colleagues disagree with me on this, but I believe you need time to yourself, even if you're supposed to be with the group. It's even fine with me if you want to take off. Skip a session. Go fishing. Drive in to Beaufort or Savannah. But you need to consider what you've heard from one another. You need to think about it, ask questions. And that's what we're going to do tonight. We'll do that over the next few days, until each of you has shared his truth."

Carson X. paused and smiled at Menlo. "Believe me," he added, "before it's over, you'll think you've been living together."

"It's not a complaint," Menlo said. "I was just curious."

"Good," Carson X. replied. He looked at Godsick. "This is what we're going to do," he said. "We're going to talk with you. We're going ask questions, and you are to answer them truthfully. When you answer, please use the pronoun 'I.' Tell us, 'I believe,' or 'I think,' or 'I felt.' All right?"

Godsick nodded tentatively.

"Just a moment," Carson X. said. He left the kitchen and we waited. He returned with the Bowie knife and handed it to Godsick. "To cut to the truth," Carson X. told him. Godsick placed the knife on the table.

Carson X. took his seat again. "And who has the first question of Godsick?"

Menlo responded quietly. "I do." He was sitting opposite Godsick and he leaned toward him. "Did she ever give you a reason for leaving you?"

Godsick looked away. He shook his head.

"Put it in words," Carson X. said.

"No," Godsick mumbled. He swallowed. His voice grew stronger. "She said she didn't want to see me any longer, that's all. I thought it would kill me."

"Did you tell her how you felt?" Menlo asked.

"Yes, I did."

Barkeep spit the word: "Bitch."

"That's not a question," Carson X. said.

Barkeep's face flooded red with anger. "It's a goddamn feeling," he snapped. "And that's how I feel."

"Ask Godsick," Carson X. said patiently.

"All right," Barkeep said. He looked at Godsick. "Is the bitch a bitch?"

"I can't say that about her," Godsick whispered. "I love her. It's a hard word for me."

"Not for me," Barkeep countered.

The coffee had spiked Barkeep's energy and he was listening intently. He said, "What do you miss the most, being around her or being in her?"

"We made love," Godsick replied quickly, defiantly.

"You made love, she screwed," Barkeep hissed. "My God, man, admit it. That's what she was doing. She was screwing you, and screwing with you. Ask me. I can tell you a thousand stories about it."

Godsick did not answer. He looked pleadingly at Carson X.

Carson X. said, gently, "He may be right, you know."

"I don't like the way he says it," Godsick argued. "I don't like what it implies."

Carson X. smiled at Barkeep. "Maybe it would help if we kept things a little more civilized."

"Sure," Barkeep mumbled. Then, to Godsick: "Sorry."

"It's all right," Godsick said meekly.

A pause swam through the kitchen. Quiet. Awkward. Brittle. Carson X. sipped again from his coffee and waited for someone to speak. He seemed preoccupied with some pleasant, distant thought. I recognized it as a technique Bloodworth had often used with me. The waiting game. Force me to break the silence with babbling. I had learned to out-wait him, to pretend that I, too, was preoccupied with some pleasant, distant thought. After a few minutes of silence, Bloodworth always broke, always had his question to ask. The question was always the same: "What are you thinking?"

Carson X. was not Bloodworth. He would not break easily.

It was Menlo who ended the pause. "Did she ever hit you?" he asked.

"No," Godsick answered. "No. Not physically."

"Did you ever hit her?" Max asked.

Godsick closed his eyes. He said, softly, "Once. I hit her once."

"Tell us about it," urged Carson X.

Godsick inhaled deeply. "It was when she laughed at me, when she called me sick, when she said I was a joke of a man, too old for her. She said making love to me always made her sick. I was begging her to stay with me, and she laughed. I hit her before I knew what I had done." He looked at me. "Not hard. I didn't hit her hard, but I hit her and I'm sorry I did. I had never hit anyone before—ever. I've never been so sorry about anything. I don't believe in violence. I love her and I hit her."

"That's what she wanted," Barkeep snarled. "Don't you know that? She wanted something to hold over you."

Again silence invaded the room. The only sound was the click of coffee cups being raised and replaced on saucers.

78

And then Carson X. asked the question: "You wanted to hurt her as much as she had hurt you, didn't you?"

For a moment, Godsick did not respond. The question seemed lodged in the space separating him from Carson X. Then his head moved, dropped in a single nod. "Yes," he whispered. "God forgive me, yes."

"Good," Carson X. said.

ও

As we were walking to our cars after the session, Menlo said in a whisper, "I think we've got a sadist as a leader."

"Yeah, I like him," Barkeep announced, grinning. "He's a lot different from that eunuch I go to back home."

Menlo laughed and shook his head. "You white boys amaze me sometimes. You surely do."

Barkeep paused in his walk. He glanced over his shoulder toward the front door of Carson X.'s home, and then he leaned to Menlo. "Let me tell you something, pal, something I know about all of these guys," he said in a low, affected stage voice. "The pretzel was created by a psychiatrist trying to make a biscuit."

A look of delight waved in Menlo's face. "That's funny," he said, chuckling. "Damn, that's funny."

And we laughed easily, all of us.

And Barkeep beamed. "It's the greatest single thought that's ever rolled off my tongue, and, son, it's got so much truth packed in it, it ought to be one of the commandments," he declared. "I think I'll go write it down. Send it to the Pope, or somebody."

We drove away, five cars going in five different directions to five different cabins on Neal's Island, each of us hearing the echo of Barkeep's proud moment.

79

Still, I too wondered about Carson X. The talk of Godsick's striking back at Anna appeared to invigorate him. It was in his voice as he closed the session.

He took the Bowie knife from Godsick and led us into his great room to stand before our sketch of the ideal woman. "Behold, Miss Perfect," he cried. Then he held the knife above his head like a Shakespearean actor and turned to face Godsick. "Behold the Talking Knife," he sang. "The Killing Knife. The Brave Man's Sword. We will use it to kill the demon that has haunted our friend, Godsick. We will use it to cut the heart of the demon from its beautiful body." He whirled and jabbed the tip of the knife into the sketch, below the neckline that I had drawn, where the heart would be, and then he picked up a red marker and quickly drew a single drop of blood coming from the tear in the page.

"What are you doing?" asked Godsick. There was fear in his voice.

Carson X.'s head snapped back to Godsick. His eyes were shining, a smile quivered across his face. "You will wash your hands in the blood of the demon," he said happily. "And then you will dig a pit and bury the demon and its beautiful body."

Barkeep stared at him in disbelief. "Jesus," he muttered. "Are you nuts?"

And Carson X. laughed. "No," he answered. "I'm sane. My killing is over. This is a declaration of liberty." He laughed again. "Repeat it after me," he said.

"Yet each man kills the thing he loves..."

He paused and looked at us, urged the chorus from us with his motioning hands. We answered, tentatively:

"Yet each man kills the thing he loves..."

He nodded vigorously and continued:

80

"The coward does it with a kiss..."

We repeated:

"The coward does it with a kiss..."

Carson X. lifted his arms, like someone seized by ecstasy. His voice rose:

"The brave man with a sword!"

There was a beat. We stared at him, and then, in timid voices, we said:

"The brave man with a sword..."

"Say it! Sing it!" Carson X. shouted. He thundered the line again: *"The brave man with a sword!"*

We lifted our voices to match him:

"The brave man with a sword!"

I could hear Carson X.'s ringing cry swimming inside my head on the quiet side streets of Neal's Island. It was a cry that trailed me like a haunting music, and I wondered if Barkeep knew something the rest of us were only learning. It was possible that he was right. It was possible that the pretzel really was created by a psychiatrist trying to make a biscuit.

At the cabin, I took a scotch—neat, strong—and went onto the deck and sat in one of the plastic-strip lounge chairs and watched the tilted cup of the quarter moon as it spilled a cluster of stars into the velvet of darkness.

The sensation of Kalee rolled through me like a sickness.

And I took more scotch.

And more.

Carson X.'s voice cried again: *"Yet each man kills the thing he loves. The coward does it with a kiss, the brave man with a sword."*

I did not want to raise the sword against Kalee. Not even to kill the anguish of being without her.

I wanted to feel the heat of her living nestled against my chest.

Instead, what I felt was the scotch coating my brain.

8

Morning of the Third Day

Dear Kalee,

Good morning.

If you knew about the late night that I had and the drinking and the dark mood, you would wonder if I survived. I did. You should know that I feel tip-top. Zippidy-do-da. I could be a model for one of those before/after ads that I used to create for multi-vitamins (today, I am the after). The surge of the Force is in Your Correspondent this morning.

I don't know why it is so, but sometimes I do feel invigorated the morning after too much drinking, too much stupidity. I'm beginning to believe there is something religious about it. Instead of God driving the Florida A&M Marching Band through my head, with cymbals a-clash, and rather than poison my stomach with the acid of illness, I think he allows me to realize how magnificent things are, or can be, and that causes me to wonder why I would ever want to drink, to abuse myself. Reverse divine psychology, you could call it. Someday, I must ask Bloodworth about that. Maybe the priest in him has an answer. Or maybe it's a question for Godsick.

Sun out this morning. I watched it rise up from the ocean like the fireball of a distant rocket slowly lifting into space. The water from the Atlantic seemed to drip from it, sizzling into steam. I was alone on the beach. Alone and cool and exhilarated. I even jogged a few yards. The tide had sloshed in and slithered back out, leaving in its wake a sticky film of water and little sacrificial offerings of fish life. More shells than I saw yesterday, but not as plentiful as on other beaches. I always wonder about the shells. Something, some pulp of life, made them and used them and then got ripped away from them. The shells look like empty hulls. On one stretch of the beach this morning, there were so many of them in a line, I thought of a delicate shell necklace I saw in a gem shop in Atlanta when you and I were shopping.

Bloodworth was right. This morning I am in the ping of the ping-pong, the yin of the yin and yang. If I were Rasputin, that mad, merry Russian monk, I would heal the blind today, make the lame to walk, the deaf would hear, the dumb would sing operas.

I sensed God on the beach this morning, watching the sun lift its fierce face from its ocean bath.

I wanted to return and destroy everything I had written to you, but I will not. I do not know if I will read it, but I will not destroy it—not now. I will accept that I have struck the keys that click-clicked the words together and whatever those words say, so be it. I cannot interfere with Bloodworth's fling at exorcism, even if I don't wholly believe in it. I'm not a complete fool, Kalee. I know that all of us are pulp, residing in shells that we build up and hide in. I think that Bloodworth wants to help. Nothing more. I think he cares.

Okay, on to business. I am in the mood for this. My hands were actually clammy with anticipation, my fingers twitched before I started. Bloodworth would be ecstatic. I think I will write with blinding speed today. What a magnificent place to work, sitting before this bay window, looking out. If I were John Steinbeck or William Faulkner or Wendell Berry, I would win the Nobel Prize for Literature today. Yes, I would. I feel it. It is like being alive in a dream, soaring effortlessly through rainbow skies.

Should I do that, Kalee? Should I do a Steinbeck or a Faulkner or a Berry, or even a Zane Grey?

Should I write a book of fiction about us, disguising it with names I have picked out of obituary notices, obfuscating the what-is and the what-has-been until it is unrecognizable?

Could be interesting.

So, here is my diary—my blog—of this day, to this moment. Pancakes for breakfast, with real maple syrup. Two glasses of orange juice. Coffee. The walk on the beach. A shower. And I threw bread crumbs out for the birds that keep looking south with longing, but are not quite sure the weather is yet right for flying. They do test the wind a hell of a lot, though, flying from the trees to the railing on the deck.

Point is, I am fine this morning, this splendid morning. Fine. Better than I've been in years. Maybe it's the sea air. Maybe the sea air has a healing property, like taking a whiff of smelling salts when you feel faint. I miss you, yes. I will always miss you. If things—you know, circumstances—were different, we would have a splendid time here. You would be in awe. The look on your face when you are in awe is the look of a child. Your laughter would decorate the room like great paintings.

* * *

Forgive me. I had to get away. If I had not heard you laugh then—up there, above the ***—I would not have had the jolt of sorrow that stabbed me. But you did. You laughed. And as one sound leads to another sound to another, so, too, does memory. Your laughter became your voice and your voice became your whisper and your whisper was against my face. Then you were in the room with me. I had to get away. Rush away.

That's one good thing about the word-maker, I suppose. Whenever you pop up with such force that it weakens me, I can click the *** and get away from the screen that blips you to life with each keystroke. But I must be careful. I write your name—

Kalee—and the words on the screen whirl about until they become you. My fingers rake the keys and I watch the letters build your face. O's make your eyes, the parenthesis keys ( ) make your mouth—open in gladness—and the dash I put within the parentheses (—) is your tongue. Your tongue leaps from the screen like a visual trick in a teenage horror movie and enters my mouth and fills it with the mint and sweet heat I remember from kissing you.

* * *

Where was I? On a high. Yes, that's where I was. I can read that. Funny, I was that way only a few minutes ago and now I cannot remember it clearly. Now, I remember only that I walked on the beach as the sun was rising. I do not remember its color or the feeling I had. I cannot see the delicate necklace of shells. They must have been there. I don't believe I could invent that.

* * *

The fingers of Your Correspondent feel suddenly sluggish. The click-clicks of the word-maker have no beat, no rhythm. There is a bitterness in my mouth, not the sweetness of maple syrup. I must have been mocking God.

So, what else is new?

I'm human.

I could be in a monastic order and mock God. That's how human I am.

This is what I did when I broke off at the ***: I took another cup of coffee and went onto the deck and smoked a cigarette and again got ill from the taste of it. I saw again the initials of Arlo Bowers and Penny Rymer, and I had this sense of embarrassment that I have become preoccupied with the notion that I can read carved initials. (Do you think it's part of the madness, the same as someone in an asylum seeing angels in wallpaper?)

Anyway, this is my take on it: the knife tip leaves histories as certain as the lines of a palm, tells stories of events that have happened, or are about to happen, as clearly as images in a crystal ball. I am beginning to believe I should open a roadside business in a doublewide trailer and advertise as a mystic. Bring your initials craved in a piece of pine and have your life revealed. Yowsir, yowsir, yowsir.

People may be skeptical about A B and P R, but I am not. I have read their initials and I know. Besides, it's a very famous story here. Yes, it is. Very famous. Everyone talks about it. They've got brochures about it. There's a summer drama called "Arlo and Penny," performed on the beach by a wandering summer stock theater company. It replaced "Romeo and Juliet," because it is a more tragic love story. I would guess that, someday, Arlo and Penny would have a bronze marker unveiled in their honor. Tragic love stories should never die, Kalee.

Oh, a word about last night's session with Carson X. I think he's a maniac, and I'm quite sure he'll wind up one day in an asylum somewhere (with Bloodworth, I hope). I'm not sure how he is as a psychiatrist, but I think he could give a good pep talk to the warriors of the Mafia. Last night, he plunged a Bowie knife into the heart of the ideal woman we had all drawn (you remember the drawing, I hope), and he sketched a drop of blood from the wound. With a red marker, no less. The man has style. Today, I expect to see buckets of blood flowing from that heart-nick.

Got to close. We have "reflecting" time this morning. Orders from Carson X. We're to think about what we've heard and said in the sessions we've had, and we are to be prepared to "shine the blade of the sword," as Carson X. put it.

He has a way with words. Yes, he does.
I love you.

Your Correspondent

෨

I was consciously exhausted when I pushed away from the word-maker, the kind of fatigue one suffers from hard yard labor, or from intense mental gymnastics over something too complex to understand, and without reason I thought of Inga at the grocery. I looked up the number in the Neal's Island phone book and called the store. Surprisingly, she knew my voice immediately. "Cabin eighteen," she said pleasantly. I lied to her. I said, "Inga, you mentioned a restaurant earlier, but I forgot the name. You mind telling me?"

"Marty's."

"That's it. Sorry to be a bother."

"You're not," she replied. "I wasn't doing anything. It's been so dead around here this morning, I'm thinking about calling the undertaker."

"Sounds like boredom to me," I said.

"A good word for it," she admitted. "And how is your day?"

"Lazy," I told her. "I'm making a weak attempt at work."

"Really?" she said. "What do you do?"

The question threw me. I laughed to fill a moment, then I told her I was a psychiatrist, taking my own good advice about emotional healing. She was impressed. I could tell by the short pause and the lowered voice of her response: "Are you, really?"

"I don't want it advertised," I cautioned.

"Of course not," she said. "I rarely talk to anyone, anyway. At least not to strangers. I don't know why I started a conversation with you. Maybe it's because you know how to make people talk, doing what you do."

I said, casually, "I doubt that. I have a theory about why people talk to one another."

"Really? What is it?"

"Are you sure you want to hear this?" I asked.

"Yes. It sounds intriguing."

"Well," I said, "it has to do with a complex chemical makeup. There are people who give off something like musk, or maybe it's simply vibes. But it's not telepathy, not at all. It's a chemical reaction, a little like magnets attracting other magnets."

Her reply was serious. She confessed she had never heard of the theory, and I immediately regretted the foolishness of it. "I've never tried to prove it," I said, wanting to wiggle away from the topic. "It's just something I believe."

"Interesting," she said.

"Are you sure I'm not keeping you from something?" I asked.

"Nothing," she answered, then her tone changed quickly and she said, "Oh, I'm sorry. You're busy and I'm keeping you."

I laughed as I thought Bloodworth might laugh. "Oh, no, it's nothing serious. I'm just making notes for a lecture."

"Well, I don't want to interrupt," Inga said. "I'm sure I'll see you around when you run out of cigarettes."

"I'm sure you will," I said. "I'm becoming addicted again."

I felt relieved talking to Inga. I also felt guilty. I had lied to her, a perfectly decent human being, as far as I knew. I had lied because I did not want her to know about me. Yet, if she wanted to know my name, I knew I would lie again and tell her I am Tyler Bloodworth. I had paid him enough for such a small deception.

But I did wonder about Inga, the lady in the grocery. There was something about her, something in her voice that reminded me of Kalee in the first days that I knew her. I thought: Who knows? Perhaps I will find happiness with Inga, talking about the evils of smoking. Or perhaps we will walk the beach together like old people looking for the footsteps of their youth in the sand. Or perhaps I will perform a miracle and heal her in the name of Bloodworth. Dominus Bloodworth.

9

Afternoon of the Third Day

I am never late for an appointment. It is a habit drilled into me by my father, whose history of failure in a dreamy life was always balanced precariously between hope and sadness. He achieved only a series of jobs in his life, none of them with great responsibility, none of them critical for the success of the companies he served with enthusiasm and devotion. He countered his failures with homilies that anyone could attain. Two of his favorites were, "Keep clean" and "Be on time."

I was clean for the meeting with Carson X. and the MOD Mob, but I was not on time. I had lingered too long in the cabin after the warning of the alarm in the closet and it was 1:07 on the car clock when I arrived. Seven minutes late. It would have prompted a lecture from my father: "Son, it may not seem like much to you, being late like that, but the point is..." My father always had a point. He often failed to express it in the complexity of his argument, but it was there. The real point was simple: he wanted me to listen, to believe he was wise and that his wisdom was the most valuable thing he could ever give me. It was. My father's homilies were embedded in me like nursery rimes. As a boy, they annoyed me; now, I longed to hear them.

"I'm sorry," I said to Carson X. when he opened the door.

He waved away the apology. "For what? You haven't missed anything, other than some Barkeep merriment."

I followed him into the great room. Max and Godsick were seated, Barkeep and Menlo were standing before the flip chart, before Miss Perfect, holding markers. I knew there had been laughter in the room. It was on the face of everyone except Godsick, and it was hanging in the air like a scent. I had missed something special. I took a seat beside Max.

"Well, Bloodworth, you finally made it," Barkeep said. "Damned if you're not taking that head-shrinker role serious. They're always late." He looked at Carson X. and mugged a smile. Carson X. mugged a shrug.

"What we're doing here," Barkeep explained in a pontifical voice, "is improving the woman of our dreams. We're going to give her some knockers." He turned to Menlo. "Left or right?" he asked.

"Your choice," Menlo told him.

"They all look the same to me," Barkeep countered. He wiggled his eyebrows like Groucho Marx.

"Not to me," Menlo said.

"Let's have at it," Barkeep said.

The two turned to the flip chart and began to draw, their bodies obstructing our view of what they were doing. After a few moments, they stepped aside.

Barkeep made a sweep of his hand. "Tah-dah," he sang.

Menlo grinned. He shook his head. "You're a crazy man," he said to Barkeep.

"Of course, I am. We all are. That's why we're here," Barkeep crowed.

The drawings of the breasts on Miss Perfect were a contrast, as they were intended to be.

Barkeep's breast, a drooping loop like a capital U, was sketched around the spot where Carson X. had plunged the knife. He had colored in a low nipple, giving it the illusion of being old and sagging.

Menlo's breast was round and firm, with a perfectly drawn nipple that was as long as a fingertip. Menlo had also streaked the breast with fine, black lines, shading it.

"What's that?" Barkeep asked of the lines.

"That's the breast of a black woman," Menlo answered confidently.

"I didn't know she was black," Barkeep said with honesty.

"I didn't know she was white," Menlo countered.

For a moment, Barkeep looked puzzled. An argument worked on his face, but he did not argue. Instead, he laughed. "Well, now, it doesn't make much difference, does it? They're still broads. Broads, pal. Women. Females. Friends to the snake. And in their hearts they're all alike. Full of the blood they've sucked out of some good, hard-working man."

Barkeep turned to the flip chart and picked up the red marker and quickly dotted a string of blood drops below the drop that Carson X. had drawn.

"What are you doing?" Carson X. asked casually.

"Being brave," Barkeep answered.

Carson X. chuckled. He stood. "All right, how about some coffee?"

We followed him into the kitchen, joking about the deformity of Miss Perfect. Barkeep confessed he would like to meet the woman who had been the model for the breast Menlo had drawn.

"I'm sure you would," Menlo said. "That's why I'm here."

"Should have known," Barkeep crowed. He added with a headshake, "Broads. Boys, we are lucky we're still standing."

We poured our coffee and returned to the great room and took our seats. Carson X. again faced us from his position on the hearth. He crossed his legs at the knees and balanced his left arm over the thigh of his right leg, and he leaned forward, holding the saucer of his coffee cup in his left hand, the cup in his right. It was the picture of a delicate man in control of his environment.

He said: "Gentlemen, before we begin, let me thank you for our last session. It did you no good at all, I suspect, but it was wonderful for me. I needed it, yet I think it might have left you wondering about my professional credentials." He smiled—almost mischievously—then added, "Because I know each of you have counselors who go about their work with dignity and sincere concern, and with unwavering civil behavior. As I investigated you, I also investigated each of them. I mean it when I tell you that I envy their allegiance to ethical conduct, but I don't want to be them. It's really an odd way to make a living, to be honest. I have Shylock's attitude about it. Shall not a counselor bleed when you prick us? Or die when you poison us? And shall not a counselor fall in love with a client, or yearn to rid himself of his own agony?" He paused again. The smile stayed, but had gently faded. "Yes, gentleman, we are human."

And then he blinked and his eyes blazed. He put his coffee down on the hearth beside him and uncrossed his legs and picked up the Talking Knife.

"And who would be next?" he said.

Barkeep stood. "I'll do it," he said, and there was energy in his voice. He moved to take the knife from Carson X.

I could see a flash of delight in Carson X.'s face, but he did not say anything. He handed the knife to Barkeep.

Barkeep turned the knife in his hand, gazing at the razor edge of the blade. He began to pace in front of Miss Perfect, his eyes fixed on the knife. I could see his mood change.

"I've thought a lot about what Godsick told us," he began quietly. "He didn't say anything I haven't heard before, but I've never heard anybody say it the way he did, and, damn it, that matters to me—to know there's somebody out there who's gone through the same thing, who feels the same way."

Godsick ducked his head and stared at the floor.

"Lilly, that's her name," Barkeep continued. "As you might guess, I met her at a nightclub. I'd gone there with a bunch of buddies after work, because we'd worked late and the boss was treating us. There was a birthday party at the table next to ours. A group of pilots and stewardesses. Lilly was one of the stews, and it was her birthday, and I promise you, I had never seen a more beautiful woman. She looked like a model, or one of those women you see in *Penthouse*, for those of you who subscribe for its literary value. Flawless. God, she was flawless."

Barkeep put the knife on the coffee table. He looked at Godsick.

"Anyway, we were all a little high, a little too happy. I sent a bottle of champagne to her table, as a birthday gift, then the band started playing and she came over to me and said the champagne wasn't enough, she wanted a dance."

Barkeep laughed sadly. He tugged at the back of his shirt.

"Now, boys, take a good look at me. I'm not exactly Paul Newman, or Tom Cruise, or George Clooney. Jesus, I'm not even Don Knotts. A beautiful woman giving me the time of day comes along about as often as Halley's Comet." He waved his hand at Menlo. "If I were as good looking as Menlo, I'd expect it, but I'm not." He smiled at Menlo. "I swear, God's unfair sometimes."

He began to pace again. "It was a dare, she told me when we were on the dance floor," he added. "One of her friends playing games. Me? Why should I care? I was dancing with the most beautiful woman in the place, and, God, could she dance. I asked for her phone number and, to my surprise, she gave it to me. 'It's not a fake, either,' she said. She told me she had just broken up with a married pilot and was eager to get on with her life.

"We started dating. It was on the sly at first. I was practically engaged to a woman I'd known for four or five years, one of those 'good' women. Karen. She even had a good name, for God's sake. Karen. You know what I mean? Wanted the family and the picket fence and the hybrid car. Pretty as a flower. Everything a man should ever want, and I'll go to my grave feeling bad about how I treated her, but I couldn't help myself."

Barkeep paused and cocked his head in thought. "Believe me, boys, I don't know about the rest of you, but I'm pretty damn sure I deserve the misery I've been through, the way I treated Karen. Makes me wonder why men are such fools," he said.

He shook away the thought. "Anyway, I blew it. Broke off with Karen. Hell, it wasn't even a contest. As good as Karen was in bed, she was still a virgin compared to Lilly. I felt like I was walking around in a dream. When we first started dating, she'd pull it off for me to fly free to places like Paris with her. I don't know how she did it, but she did. My God, it was something. Paris. Rome. London. Brussels. You can't believe how it is to make love in some of those places." He paused. His eyes blinked memory. "Brussels," he whispered. "My God. Brussels." He shook away the memory. "I was spending a fortune on her, but I didn't care. She was worth it, even when she was trying to get me to clean up my act and be a gentleman."

Barkeep chuckled derisively. He reached for his coffee and took a sip and then set the cup back down. "And this is what I got for all of it," he said.

It was a story of surprising violence, though somehow it perfectly described Barkeep's passion and temper.

Two years after they began to live together, Lilly met a baseball player on a chartered flight from New York to San Diego. He was a man who carried a layer of muscles that made Hulk Hogan look like Beetle Bailey, Barkeep vowed. Muscles and the scars of the game. "He had this scar over this left eye that made him look like he'd been in a fight with a goddamn gorilla. I guess it turned her on. Who knows? Anyway, he asked her to go to dinner with him, and she went.

"Dinner," Barkeep added in a sneer. "Dinner. Sure, dinner. Good pink meat served in a buttery lather of passion."

Barkeep did not know it—would not learn of it until weeks later—but the night of the dinner was the end of his relationship with Lilly.

It was also the beginning of his pain and his anger.

"I decided if she loved scars, she would damn well be crazy about the man I'd make of him," Barkeep hissed. "I was born in Arkansas, where, by God, a fight is a fight."

Barkeep purchased a baseball bat and then he went to New York, where Superstud (as Barkeep called him) was living with Lilly. For three days, he took notes on Superstud's schedule, getting the routine down. He discovered that Superstud went for a jog every evening in Central Park, at the same time. Barkeep found a spot in the park that was relatively dark and deserted, and he hid behind a clump of shrubs, waiting. When Superstud came huffing along, his great muscled legs springing high off the ground, Barkeep stepped out, called a greeting, smiled, and swung the bat like Hank Aaron chasing Babe Ruth. The handle caught Superstud on the shoulder and careened off his face. It broke his nose and his cheekbone and left enough scar tissue to inspire a new issue of Friday, the 13th.

"I mailed her the bat," Barkeep said bitterly. "It had his signature on it. And blood. No name, but she knew who it was from."

"That was you?" Max asked with surprise. "I remember that."

"Me, too," Menlo added. "There was talk that one of his ex-teammates did it. I saw some pictures of him in the hospital. It was brutal. Could have ended his career."

A wide smile—a smile of pride—flew across Barkeep's face. "Hey, I did it during off-season," he said. "He didn't miss any time, but he was never the same. Couldn't take one inside and high."

I asked, "Didn't you worry about her telling him?"

"No," Barkeep said. "I knew she wouldn't."

Menlo leaned forward on the sofa. He asked, "Would you have felt better if it had been her you hit?" There was a tone of meanness in his voice.

Barkeep wagged his head. "I don't know. Damned good question. Maybe." He shrugged. "Maybe I'll still do it."

"Of course you won't," Carson X. interjected. "You don't kill that way. That's the same as a kiss."

"Great fucking kiss, if you ask me," Barkeep snapped.

Carson X. again laughed at Barkeep. Barkeep again flushed in anger.

"It does bring up an interesting situation, however," Carson X. continued. "Do we really know what obsesses us?"

Godsick cocked his head with interest. "I don't understand," he said.

"Think about it," Carson X. replied. "What does obsession mean, anyway? You may think of it as madness, and, yes, there's good argument for that position, but, gentlemen, there are two kinds of obsession. One is sweet, the other bitter. Over the next few days you'll hear stories of both types, and you'll be amazed at how different they are, yet, how each has a common trigger."

"I still don't understand," said Godsick.

"You," Carson X. replied, looking at Godsick. "Were you obsessed by Anna, or were you obsessed by the evil that Anna represented to you?"

"It's the same, isn't it?" Godsick asked in a weak voice.

"Is it?" Carson X. asked.

Godsick's face pinched in bewilderment.

"It's something all of you must consider," Carson X. said. "Are you obsessed by the woman, or by the thing that caused you to have the obsession?"

No one spoke. Barkeep picked up the Bowie knife and rolled it in his hand, watching its blade glitter in the light.

"I had to learn that good lesson," Carson X. said brightly. "And it was a very, very great revelation. The woman I loved—who had promised to marry me, by the way—began seeing a colleague. Not a handsome man. He was Greek, but certainly not a Greek god, as the ladies like to call those fellows. Not even a pleasant man. But he had something that, apparently, I did not have. Some unseen quality. It took me months to realize that my anger—my obsession—had to do with him, and not the woman. What did he have that I didn't have? That was the issue, the thing that cut into me."

Barkeep leaned forward, toward Carson X. He said in a slow, blunt voice, "Doc, let me tell you what he had. He's Greek. He's hung like a racehorse in the Kentucky Derby."

A flush of embarrassment waved over Carson X.'s face—the only time we would see it, and then he let a smile build. "Of course, I consider myself fortunate," he said, dismissing Barkeep. "I learned this about marriage—for me, I mean: I could have handled the thick and the thin, the better and the worse, of it, but I would have had a lot of trouble with the in-between. Better to let the other man experience all of that."

"Is he still around?" Menlo asked.

"He is," Carson X. said. "Not on the island any longer, but he's still in the profession and I occasionally see him at conferences, that sort of thing. We don't have dinner together, but we are civil."

"The woman?" Menlo pressed.

Carson X. smiled. He let the pause build. Then he said, evenly, "She never married. She even tried to get back in my good graces, but it was too late. I was cured, healed, washed clean of her. When I accepted that I was obsessed by her lies, and not by her, I was over it. I am a brave man, gentlemen, as you will be, each of you." He stood and dusted his pants where he had been sitting. He looked for a moment at Godsick with kind, understanding eyes. Then he blinked and looked at Barkeep, and his eyes were bright and cheerful. "Gentlemen," he said forcefully, "we're getting there, don't you think? Can you feel it?"

We nodded—not because we agreed, but because we didn't disagree.

"I like this group, I really do," Carson X. said. "I knew I would."

"This was good—today, I mean," Godsick offered.

"So was last night," Carson X. said. "As the rest of the sessions will be. You'll see." He paused. "Now, do any of you sing?"

I think all of us smiled. Only Godsick answered: "A little."

"Do you know the song, *Amen*?"

We muttered, "Yes," like reluctant children.

"Then, let's sing it," Carson X. intoned. "But bear down on the 'men' in amen."

He began to sing in a rich, powerful voice, his hands conducting us with broad, emphatic gestures. We joined him timidly, then with joy.

"A-a-MEN, a-a-MEN a-MEN, a-MEN. . ."

&

"A-a-MEN, a-a-MEN, a-MEN, a-MEN. . ."

I could not stop singing.

I had forgot how wonderful the song was—bright, jubilant, a song of celebration.

In the car, driving away from Carson X's home, the song stayed with me. My voice was not meant for singing, but it did sing, and it filled the car with a-MENS.

I felt good, better than in a long time. It was comforting to be with men who had loved and suffered.

I wondered: Could Bloodworth be right? Did the son of a bitch know what would happen to me on Neal's Island?

"A-a-MEN, a-a-MEN, a-MEN, a-MEN..."

&

The telephone was ringing when I arrived at the cabin, but I was too late in answering. The click hit my ear before I could say hello. I'm always aggravated when that happens. I wonder who has called and why, especially at a place like Neal's Island. With no call identifier, it could have been anyone.

Odds favored Bloodworth, I thought. To my knowledge, he was the only person from Atlanta who had my cabin number—

Spence had refused to take it, vowing he wouldn't need me—and Bloodworth did say he would check on me. If it was Bloodworth, he must have wondered why I did not answer. In my last session with him before leaving for Neal's Island, he said to me, "Don't do anything foolish." The way he said it, with a touch of kindness, I wondered if he meant suicide. Perhaps. I think he believed I was a borderline candidate for that sad surrender.

Still, maybe the call wasn't from Bloodworth. Maybe it was from Carson X., wanting to sing another chorus or two of *Amen.* He had the number to my cabin, of course, and he would not have shared it with Barkeep or Godsick or Menlo or Max. It was one of Carson X.'s rules: none of us were to contact the others when not in session. Fraternization was for college fraternities where boy-men drank imported beer and boasted of conquests of squirmy virgins.

A. . .MEN...a-a-aMEN...a-a-aMEN. . .

If it was Carson X. who called, I hoped he would call back. I was in the mood to sing.

And then I did the foolish thing, the idiotic thing. I lifted the receiver and punched in Kalee's old number—all but the last digit.

One finger-touch from where her voice used to be.

I had done the same dozens of times. Once I even touched the last digit and a woman with an older, quaking voice answered. I apologized, explained that I must have misdialed. She asked in a loud voice, "Who you calling for?"

I gave her Kalee's name.

"Well, this is the Brinson's home," the woman said.

Still, I touched the buttons to make the calls, except for the last digit. I could not stop myself. Bloodworth told me it was my way of reaching for her. "Find something else to do," he suggested irritably.

The scribblings in the K-for-Kalee folder became that something else.

I replaced the receiver and picked up the folder and opened it and read from one of the pages:

i dreamed of you last night
(again). we loved, slept,
loved. your body was warm,
curled. your breasts were
quiet in sleep, like small,
closed eyes. i touched the
matting of your dark,
feathered hair, still damp,
still heated, still soft.

in my dream you were
kneeling over me, like
a supplicant at prayer,
gently guiding my body
into your body. your mouth
was open, filled with
whispers, and i could feel
the muscles inside you
tighten and then release,
and the flow of you (and
of me) coated us.

love has never been so grand.
nor dreaming.

10

Night of the Third Day

Bloodworth could, and should, take lessons from Carson X. Carson X. is a most unpredictable man.

We were sitting in the great room, with wine and a tray of hors d'oeuvres on the coffee table that contained crab pâté and lobster pinwheels. The hors d'oeuvres, Carson X. told us, were from a friend who had hosted a small party with too much food. "It's our system of bartering on the island," he chirped. "I give her worthless advice; she occasionally feeds me. Share and share alike." My father would have loved the expression.

Miss Perfect was still on the flip chart, still staring down at us with one blank eye and one stabbed and bleeding breast. The drawings of her breasts by Barkeep and Menlo still caused light jesting. Barkeep wanted to finish her, to draw the rest of her body. "She's got to have a body that's better than her face, boys," he insisted.

"Why don't we leave that for later?" suggested Carson X. "There'll be time. Why don't we get back to the real thing now? Spend a few minutes questioning Barkeep about the story we heard this afternoon."

"Fine with me," Barkeep said enthusiastically. "I can tell you, it helped getting some of that off my chest—with you guys, I mean. I've said the same thing a thousand bloody times back home, but it never felt as good as it did this morning."

"See? Progress," Carson X. enthused. And, then to us: "Ask away. You've got thirty minutes."

We asked a few questions, but they were mostly lame.

Did he enjoy hitting Superstud?

"Damned right, I did. It felt great."

Did he see Lilly after that day?

"Once. Ran into her in a grocery store. She told me I was a freaking maniac, and she got that one right."

Did he still miss her?

His tone softened: "More than anything in my life."

Had he dated anyone after Lilly?

"I tried. I hated it. Who wants a hamburger after he's had sirloin?"

None of the questions excited any possibility of revelation. None equaled the energy of Barkeep. All were forced—something to say in a placid effort to belong to the group.

And then Carson X. said, "All right. Enough. It's obvious that Barkeep's aggressive, and that's good. We all have to be aggressive if we're going to move forward." And then he slapped his hands together, like a teacher calling for attention. He asked, "Did all of you play sports?"

We all admitted that we had. Yes. At one level or another, we had all participated in sports.

"Do you remember any single, magnificent moment from those experiences?" Carson X. asked.

For a moment, no one spoke, and then Max said, "A football game in high school. I played in the line. On offense. Right tackle." He dipped his head, as though embarrassed. "I guess you could say I was pretty good. Anyway, I was playing against this guy, a middle linebacker. If I said his name you'd know him. He went to one of the SEC schools. Made All-America. He was that good, the biggest I ever played against up to that time. He talked a lot of trash, and he kept bad-mouthing me all night. Said he was going to whip my ass in front of God and everybody in the stands, and, to be honest, he almost did."

Max was sitting forward on the sofa. His face was rosy with his remembered moment. "Then he made the mistake of calling my mother a whore."

"Isn't that rather common in sports?" Carson X. said.

"I guess so," agreed Max, "but nobody had ever said it to me. Nobody ever had the nerve. My mother might not have been an angel, but she was my mother."

"And?" Carson X. asked.

"I broke his leg," Max answered calmly, without emotion. "It was a guard-pull and Joe—Joe Wakefield, the left guard—caught him high, in his chest, and that held him up, and I got just below his knee. I could hear the bone snap like a stick."

I saw Godsick's body jerk involuntarily.

Barkeep laughed. "I like it," he said.

Menlo wagged his head and frowned. "White boys," he muttered.

"Interesting," Carson X. said thoughtfully.

Max shrugged uncomfortably.

Carson X. rubbed the palms of his hands together. "But what interests me is—what was his name? Joe?"

"Joe Wakefield."

"Yes. You did it with Joe helping out. Teamwork. Men waging war together, finding the enemy, defeating him," Carson X. said. He stood and began to pace before Miss Perfect. "Haven't all of you known that sort of thing in sports?"

We all nodded agreement—not at once, but nods that fell like dominoes—and Carson X. urged the stories from us.

The stories were of the sort that boys tell in bragging sessions.

A squeeze bunt that a boy named Cal Hemphill executed perfectly to allow Barkeep to score from third base to win a Little League championship.

The rebound by Spider Reynolds and the pass back out in order to give Menlo a shot for his thirty-fifth point in a high school basketball game. Menlo made it.

For me, it was an intimidating doubles partner named Gene Bradshaw in a tennis tournament. We won in an upset and almost caused a fight on the courts because of the excess of our celebration.

Even Godsick had a memory of athletic glory.

"It was in a track meet," Godsick told us. "I was put in to run the hundred yard dash at the last minute because the regular runner injured his ankle in the broad jump. I've never been that terrified. I could run pretty fast back then, but not like some of the others. Then, just before the race, Jabbo Coleman—he was our star, the one we were all in awe of—came over to me and took his lucky necklace off—it was a rabbit's foot his father had given him—and he draped it over my neck, and he said, 'You're going to win. You're running with Bugs.' And I did. I won."

Carson X. did a pirouette of joy when Godsick finished his story. "Bravo!" he shouted. He stepped to Godsick and pulled him from the sofa and embraced him, and we applauded.

"See," Carson X. cried. "It works. Togetherness works."

He began to stride the floor again, rubbing his hands, his head bobbing. Energy radiated from him.

"But," he said, "it's not always possible to have a teammate throw a block for us, or pull down a rebound and pass it back out." He paused and looked at Godsick. "And very few of us ever get to wear the rabbit's foot around our neck, and that leaves us alone, doesn't it?"

We were watching him, waiting for his voice, knowing something unexpected would leap from his mouth.

"What we must learn is to be our own teammate, to carry our own rabbit's foot," he said. "And that is both simple and difficult. Simple to say, difficult to believe."

"Now, this is what I want you to do," he continued. "I want you to think of yourself as more than one person, think of the parts of your body as being separate individuals, and those individuals, together, make up the team that is you."

He turned his back to us. We could hear him unzip his pants. When he turned back, he was holding his penis in his hand.

"Gentlemen, meet Oscar," he said proudly. He wiggled his penis. "Oscar, meet the group."

"My God," whispered Menlo in amazement.

Barkeep began to laugh and all but Godsick picked up his laughter. Godsick sat, stunned.

Carson X. looked down at his penis.

"Oscar, they're laughing at you."

He cocked his head, as though listening to his penis, and then he twisted the head of his penis and aimed it at us.

"What's that? Oh, they're laughing at me," he said. "My apology, old man."

"Damn," Barkeep exclaimed. "That's funny. Oscar? You call your pecker Oscar?"

Carson X. ducked Oscar back into his pants and pulled the zipper up. He looked triumphantly at Barkeep. "The Best Actor award," he said. "Bestowed on me by a lady of questionable virtue who had dreams of being a movie star. And what's the name of yours, Barkeep? And don't tell me you don't have one."

Barkeep fought a smile. He pushed his chin forward dramatically and he said, drawing out the word, "Buck."

"Buck?" Carson X. bellowed. "And you laugh at Oscar?"

Barkeep beamed.

Carson X. paraded before us, his eyes sweeping us. "The rest of you," he said. "What do you call yours?"

It startled me, but every man in the room, other than Godsick, had a name for his penis. A joke from childhood locker rooms. A giggled response from a girlfriend. Their own vanity.

To Godsick, it was an uncomfortable discussion, and it was also an invitation for Barkeep to push the envelop with him. "Well, pal, we've got to change that," he said to Godsick in a voice hinting of mock kindness and mock pity. "We've got to give it a name, something worthy of you. You're lucky you're with us. We'll handle this with some dignity. That's a promise, and if I have to, I'll whip everybody's ass in here to keep it that way." He paused and cocked his head in the pretension of thought. "Well," he amended, "everybody except Max. I'm not a complete fool. Max can do whatever he wishes."

Godsick blushed. I thought I heard a whine of regret trapped in his throat.

Barkeep aimed his look at the rest of us. We all wore smiles, but none of us spoke. We knew it was Barkeep's game to play.

"I'd say Ernest," Barkeep continued after a moment, his head bobbing slowly, seriously. "Yeah, Ernest," he repeated. He leaned toward Godsick. "Let me give you another little tidbit about that good Irishman, Oscar Wilde, the fellow who kills with a brave man's sword," he lectured. "As an Oscar, Mr. Wilde was only slightly more noble than Dr. Willingham's Oscar." He paused and preened over his jab at Carson X., and then he added, "That Oscar—Oscar Wilde, I mean —was a drunk and a druggie. Yes, indeed, a questionable character of the highest order. Even went to prison for being homosexual. But he also wrote a very funny play called *The Importance of Being Earnest*. Big hit in its time. Still is. Great title. Best play on words in the history of theater. Ernest—without the 'a'—is a character trying to be earnest—with the 'a'—in the tomfoolery of his life. But, hey, it sounds the same when you say it, so I say Godsick's pecker should be named Ernest, without the 'a'." He punched Godsick's shoulder gently. "Because, my friend, you've got to face the truth, and the truth is this: being Ernest is important, and it's okay to admit that among friends. We're your friends. We're men. Men. And to that, I say a-MEN."

We sat, stunned, all slack-jawed. Barkeep sounded like a contestant on *Jeopardy*, or a professor pontificating on classical literature. Even his voice was different. The only person who did not seem surprised was Carson X. He merely smirked.

"So, how about Ernest?" Barkeep asked.

Godsick shrugged. A smile began to bloom in his face.

"All in favor of Godsick's pecker being named Ernest, say 'Aye.'" Barkeep said.

We answered: "Aye."

"And so it is," said Barkeep.

And there we were: five grown men playing boys, honoring our aliases.

Buck (Barkeep)

Junior (Menlo).

Rocky Balboa (Max).

Alfie. Alfie belonged to me, or I to him.

And Ernest (Godsick).

The laughter was robust from all of us, even Godsick. Its sound echoed in the great room of Carson X. Willingham's home. We wiped tears from our eyes.

"Tonight, when you go to your cabins, I want you to have a conversation with your penis—*mano a mano*," Carson X. said. "I want you to sit back in a chair with the beverage of your choice, remove your penis, call him by name, look him seriously in his eye, and ask him to tell you what's been on his mind lately.

"Let him talk to you. Let him tell you if he's lonely, or feels mistreated, or is embarrassed being associated with you. Mostly, let him be truthful."

"Are you serious?" asked Menlo.

"Absolutely," Carson X. told him. "You may find it very revealing."

"Doc," Max said solemnly, "you'd have a hard time living in my neighborhood."

The roar of the evening followed us from the house, into our cars and into the cabins we occupied.

Dear Kalee,

I had not intended to write, but this is too good to keep to myself.

Let me begin by saying that tonight you are as embedded in my soul as you have ever been, and part of it is because the loneliness I feel (that need for you) has been assuaged somewhat by the warmth of erotic memories. (Okay, I know it's a stretch in reasoning, but I don't care. It is my letter and I will write it as I wish—with or without Bloodworth's interference or Carson X.'s pontifications.)

The erotic memories were inspired by our session tonight. Carson X., who is probably insane, as Barkeep has judged, unzipped in front of us, removed his penis (named Oscar) and

111

proceeded to instruct us to have a face-to-face, sit-down meeting with our own member.

It was hilarious, Kalee, the kind of thing boys do when they're coming out of the cocoon of babyhood and are discovering (with urging from their older playmates) the first elementary impulses for sex. I do not know if girls have the same rituals. I don't think so. With boys, it must go back to the Cave Dwellers. Dark corner of the cave, boys huddled in a circle around the dim light of a fire, pointing, grunting, laughing, amazed by the sensations rising in them.

Anyway, I did as Carson X. instructed.

I poured a weak scotch and water and sat in an armchair and propped my feet across the ottoman and unbuckled my belt and unbuttoned and unzipped my pants and gently removed Alfie. (You never knew I had a name for it, did you? I was too embarrassed to tell you—not embarrassed over telling you, but over the fact that it—he—even had a name. You would have wanted to know: Why Alfie? Truth is, it came from the movie, the one with Michael Caine. I think I was impressed with the line from the song. You know. "What's it all about, Alfie?" Or something like that.)

Sitting there, feeling foolish, I wondered if Godsick and Barkeep and Menlo and Max were in their own cabins at that moment, beverage of choice in one hand, penis in the other.

And then, Kalee, I thought about you, how grand you were as a lover. As shy as you were among people, you were always free and uninhibited with me. The heat of your body could have been from steam, the blood-pulse in your throat and abdomen had the sound of thunder, your mouth tasted of strawberries. Yet it was more than sex. Sex is a muscular giving and taking, an emptying and a filling, high moment for high moment. Love is different. Love has tenderness. Your tenderness. After love, we always embraced. Remember? The way your face fit into my shoulder, your breathing moist on my skin, was always the most remarkable part of our lovemaking.

A quiver just struck me. My chest filled with sadness.

I think I am losing ground in Bloodworth's assault on my sickness.

Where was I?

Oh yes, Alfie.

He did not speak to me, Kalee, not even in imagination. Perhaps he thinks I am a snob, or a bum, and having a conversation with me would be a waste of time.

Carson X. will be disappointed.

Perhaps it would be wise to invent something to share with the group.

Lloyd Seaborn. Did I ever tell you of Lloyd Seaborn? He worked at the firm and was a brilliant think-man. You know—a conceptualizer. He had this wonderful philosophy: always start with extremes, then work your way to practicality. If you did it vice-versa, you were never bold enough. Regardless of the project, Lloyd always started his creative thinking with an image of Dolly Parton's naked breasts in his mind. I think it said a lot about him.

Anyway, Lloyd was in his mid-60s when I met him. He died on the job at age 71. Fell over one morning in the break room, pouring a cup of green tea. The reason I mention him is because he, too, had a name for his penis: Rip Van Winkle. Said it had been asleep so long, it had forgotten how to snore. We all laughed at Lloyd. He was a card, he was. Yet, one morning, in a depressed mood, he confessed to me that he and his wife had had sex—real sex—only once in more than 30 years. More than half his married life. He said, "You know what I miss? I miss being held." And I said to him, "That sounds like Rip Van Winkle talking." He smiled a faint, tired smile. "Maybe it is," he mumbled.

That's a sad story, Kalee, and I wish I had not thought of it. Putting it on paper has soured the earlier spirit of the night when a group of men reverted back to their boyhoods. Not our doing, of course. Blame it on Carson X. I think he was trying to get us to consider the difference between love and lust, but in his clever, pretzel-twisting way, he wants us to reason it out on our own. His little penis-chat exercise was nothing more than a ruse to get us to talk to ourselves. He even told us he had lifted the idea from a book on group therapy. I believe he was afraid of the ridicule of being an idea thief.

I know I should hit the logout icon and quit this blithering, but I am awake and jittery and it helps to sit here, thinking of you, touching the keys that sculpt your name. Kalee. Kalee. Kalee.

There are things you did not know about me. Why didn't I tell you? None of it seemed important at the time. At the time, only you were important to me. You. Now, I want you to know about the other things. It matters that you understand who I have been, as well as who I am. (Sadly, the person I have been is probably a far better person than the one I am now.)

Believe it or not, Kalee, there's more to Your Correspondent than a wink and a smile and a soft-shoe shuffle.

I was a hell of an athlete. You didn't know that, did you?

Oh, I was, Kalee. Yes. Tennis was not my only game. I had some swagger in my gait on the playing fields of my neighborhood. Once, I kicked a field goal in football to win the region championship for our school. My teammates carried me off the field on their shoulders, and Kathi Wemmers, who was the captain of the cheerleaders, kissed me with a tongue hot enough to melt steel. I pitched a no-hitter in a sandlot baseball game, using a *curve I had discovered the day before. With proper regard to Godsick for his rabbit's foot victory in track, I won the 100 AND the 220 AND the long jump in the county track meet when I was a senior. (If you think I had fast hands, you should have seen the feet.) And, of course, you know about winning the city doubles three years ago with Spence.*

My mother has trophies of my adventures as an athlete. They're on the top of an entertainment center at her home. She thinks of them as miniature statues of me, when I was a very special boy-man. (Mothers can be funny and wonderful and silly at the same time, can't they? My mother once took pictures of my trophies—the little, flimsy-metal copies of me, with little flimsy-metal muscles—and mailed them to me. I think it was to remind me that I used to succeed at something.)

What else?

Oh, a sad moment. Once I drove all night, across Tennessee, to be with an old friend who had lost his wife in a hunting accident. He had pulled the trigger, thinking he had seen a deer. He had no idea it was his wife, surprising him with a thermos of coffee. He cried, Kalee. He cried for hours and I sat holding him like a baby. I stayed for the funeral. A day after I came home, he pulled the trigger again. Goodbye, friend. And then I cried.

Crying. That's another thing. But you did see me cry, didn't you? To be honest, Kalee, I'm glad you saw me that way. Crying with you, around you, has been one of the most joyful things of my life. Since your death, I have cried rivers thinking of you. No. Oceans. The Atlantic shore of Neal's Island would be at tsunami if it had all the tears I have spilled.

And here's one that would truly surprise you, Kalee. I used to keep the nursery in the church I attended during my freshman year in college. (Yes, I went to church regularly, a habit I enjoyed during my youth and one that I need to adopt again.) Anyway, I kept watch over the babies. I did. I loved it. I rocked them and sang "Jesus Loves the Little Children" in my off-key voice, and I wiped little rumps and plunged bottles into mewing mouths. I bathed them and I burped them. They loved me, Kalee. God, did they love me. And I loved them. Some of them used to cling to me when their mothers came for them. Their mothers would say in their Southern way of saying things, "Why, I don't know what on earth's the matter with you. It's embarrassing as all get out, how you don't want to leave this nice young man."

Anyway, I'm sorry I never told you about keeping the nursery. If we had had children, you would have been pleased with my fathering.

Enough.

It's all trivial stuff, anyway. I've never said anything to Bloodworth about any of it.

I'm sorry. I didn't mean to ramble so much. At night, alone in this cabin, I have moments of desperate need to be with you. Jittery moments. I can hear you breathing, can sense your presence.

Memory is more powerful than armies.

I love you.

Your Correspondent

11

Morning of the Fourth Day

On the morning of the fourth day, I awoke early and showered and dressed in blue jogging sweats, and then had coffee and a cream cheese bagel and went out to walk along the beach. It was at the sunrise hour, and the sunrise was of the kind that lifts up, bright and clear, on cool days. Such sunrises are found only at the perfect hour of early mornings and on postcards in roadside stands.

In the distance, I saw Inga.

She called from across the beach, "How are the cigarettes holding out?" Her voice was light and cheerful.

"I quit," I said. "Threw them away." It was a lie, or part-lie. I still had them, but I did not think I would smoke again. I added, "You're out early."

"It's a great time of the day," she answered, approaching me. "I always try to walk early on my day off." The chill of the air had flushed her face and there was a tint of red on her cheeks, like powdered rouge. She wore jeans and a yellow sweater over an oxford shirt.

"It's a good habit," I told her. Then I remembered my ruse of being Bloodworth. "I tell my clients that walking is good for body, mind, and soul."

"I hope they listen to you," she said. She smiled easily.

"So do I," I said. "Personally, though, I prefer walking at night."

"And is that where you were last night?" she asked.

"Here, on the beach," I lied again. "How did you know?"

"I called your cabin," she admitted. "I have to go into Beaufort this morning and thought I'd pick up some escarole if you still wanted it."

"That's kind," I said. "Thank you. Yes, I would like that."

"I believe they'll have it, though I could be wrong," she said. "Anyway, after I called, I realized it's been years since I've done anything out of the ordinary like that."

Knowing Bloodworth well enough to be his twin, I imitated him: "I'm glad you did, and I'm sorry I was out. It's a good habit, obeying your impulse. Too few people do it."

She laughed lightly, a pleasant laugh. "It just surprised me, when I thought about it. Calling a man and not knowing that man's name. Not like me at all."

"Well, let's get that out of the way," I said. "I'm Tyler Bloodworth."

Inga extended her hand. "Dr. Bloodworth, I'm Inga Pressley."

"Please," I begged, "it's Tyler. I left the diploma on the wall."

"Tyler," she said. She said it well, like a friend would say it.

We were nearing the stretch of beach leading to my cabin, and we began to slow in our walk.

"Your cabin has the best view of any on this part of the island," Inga said.

"I think so," I said. Then: "Could I offer you a cup of coffee? I've got a fresh pot already brewed, unless being at the cabin with a man whose name you just learned would make you uncomfortable."

Inga glanced in the direction of the cabin, then back to me. I saw a frown flash and then disappear. "Uncomfortable? No, it's not that," she said. "But I do need to be on my way to Beaufort."

118

"Then let me walk you to your car and we can chat on the way," I suggested. "You can give me the life history of Inga Pressley, Escarole Lady."

She smiled comfortably. "It's too early to be bored," she said.

"And shouldn't I be the judge of that?" I replied.

We began the walk toward her car, the lone car in a small public parking lot. The sun was floating on the ocean, a bobbing, bright buoy. Inga began to talk and it startled me how direct and unguarded she was, the same as I had been in my first meetings with Bloodworth. Once I asked him why that was so—why I would say things to him that I would not say to anyone else. "Because you know it's all right to do so," he answered in his pontifical manner. "Because you know that I am trained to listen."

In her rushed-up summary of her life, Inga told me her name was Inga Case Pressley. The Case was her maiden name, the Pressley her married name. She had been divorced for two years from Frank Pressley. She had an eighteen-year-old son—Frank, Jr.—studying finance at the University of Richmond. Frank, Sr. worked with the government, something to do with the Department of Agriculture. She had not spoken to him since their divorce.

She seemed relieved and yet still bothered by talking about her husband and her divorce. It was as though she wanted to say more, but held back the words.

At her car, she said, "Thanks for the walk and for letting me babble. I think this is the best morning I've had all year."

"And to that, I say 'ditto,'" I said. "Thank you for being up and out so early. I am a great believer in splendid accidents."

"Do you want me to call you if I find the escarole?" she asked.

"Sure," I replied. "I could pick it up tomorrow, or, better yet, if you're not promised elsewhere for the evening, would you like to show me the restaurant you mentioned? Marty's, I think. I could meet you there and get it then."

She paused. "That would be nice," she said. "I'd enjoy that, but I'm not sure when I'll get back, and Marty's is a few miles off the island."

"Then here's an alternative," I told her. "Late dinner at the cabin. I'm a so-so chef, but the grill looks to be in great shape."

She hesitated a moment before answering, before saying, "Yes. That would be nice." There was a glint of yellow, the color of her sweater, in her eyes. "And late would be fine for me. I plan to be gone most of the day. However, if your schedule changes, call me. I'm in the phone book, and it switches to my cell."

There was only one thing Inga did not explain before she left: why was she on Neal's Island? It would be something to ask at dinner.

☙

Dear Kalee,

I am rushing to write this letter before the after-lunch session with Carson X. and the MOD Mob. (Did I tell you? MOD is an acronym for Men with Obsession Disorders, which is something of a MODern disease, or a MODern discovery of an ancient disease.) Anyway, I hope you understand the hurrying-along of this epistle. The day, the evening, has become unexpectedly crowded with things to do.

There is this lady—Inga Pressley—who works in the local grocery, and I have invited her to dinner, simply because she is very pleasant and because (I am ashamed to admit) she believes I

120

am Dr. Tyler Bloodworth, psychiatrist, and it is my guess that she needs to talk about her world and all that is in it, and that's fine with me. I will do what Bloodworth does: I will listen and nod and draw smiley faces on a pad. Of course it's a risk, but not as serious as it could be. If she goes to social media she will find Dr. Tyler Bloodworth, but not his photograph. I think counselors have an international agreement to keep their faces hidden, or obscured in some photo-shop fashion.

How did this happen? I took a walk early this morning with Inga (nothing planned; we ran into one another on the beach) and she told me something of her life. Pretty normal stuff, from my view of it. Married, divorced, a child who's probably annoying— those daily things that lead to depression, a condition I certainly understand. That's why I'm here, isn't it? The reason Bloodworth had me exiled.

As I write this, I realize I'm uncomfortable about inviting her for dinner. For some reason (I'm sure Bloodworth knows why) I feel the guilt of betraying you. My instinct is to call Inga with some excuse for canceling the invitation, yet I know eventually I will have to face the fact that you are gone from me. Still, I am feeling foolish about my ruse, and I regret the lie I told to Inga. I'm sure there's a prison sentence for impersonating a psychiatrist (if not, there should be). I will tell her the truth tonight, and we will have a good laugh together—or a great wailing.

And what should we discuss, Kalee? I could tell her about Arlo and Penny, my own private soap-opera lovers. Since she has lived here for two years, Inga may know things about them I have not yet been able to divine from their initials. (That's another thing about the art of reading initials: it's perfectly all right to get assistance, something the palmist would never do.)

121

I will dress for the occasion as you would have me dress—my stone-washed jeans, the sky-blue pullover you like, tennis shoes, but with socks (it is too cool to be cool). I want to look comfortable, yet professional. I will smear on only a finger-dab of my Clubman's after-shave along the ridges of my neck and I will flip up my hair in the front, over my forehead, to give it the look of little-boy unruliness.

That should about do it. I must remember that I am Tyler Bloodworth, psychiatrist. There's a book in the cabin titled A Study of the Precocious Child, *and I will have it open on the desk. It will impress Inga that I find stimulating reading matter wherever I go. And I will put on some background music from the collection of CDs I brought with me. Someone with a voice like Luther Vandross, I think. A voice that could send erotic shivers through a flea. Do you remember the night we made love in Savannah, where we really did burn black candles? It was a joke, but you played a Harry Connick, Jr. disk. I well remember what happened during "The Night I Fell in Love." You wore black net stockings and a black transparent negligee and when you opened it, I could see your heart drumming against your abdomen. It was one of the most remarkable moments of wonder that you added to my life.*

I can still see the black candles, flickering dimly. I can smell the cooking of the slightly scented wax.

I'm sorry. I was drifting. I do that often when you brush against me, leaving the perfume of yourself.

Back to Inga and the dinner.

You will be proud of me, Kalee. After dinner—and before I have revealed myself for the charlatan I am—I will speak in grave tones about the stress of hearing stories of despair from fragile people. I may even tell Inga about the case of an advertising executive who frequents my office, blathering woefully about a goddess he loves and cannot forget.

Yes, Kalee, you will be proud of Your Correspondent.

Excuse me. I must conclude this and prepare for my session with Carson X. and the other MOD Mob sufferers.

I do love you. Inga will never cause me to forget that. You are deep in my soul.

Your Correspondent

P.S.: You will be pleased to know that I did throw away the cigarettes. I think the reason I bought them was because you once told me you liked the taste of smoke on my tongue when you kissed me. Do you remember? When I quit smoking, you told me you missed that taste, even if you were happy that I'd quit.

I marvel at how much command you have over me.

12

Afternoon of the Fourth Day

The one o'clock session began in gaiety.

Barkeep declared that his evening conversation with Buck was the most revealing experience he had ever had. Buck, he said, was a smart-ass, as he had expected.

"You know what he told me? He said he was tired of just hanging around, waiting for me to get on with my life. He said if I couldn't do better, he'd prefer to relocate and quit standing up for me. Forgive the pun, boys, but he just can't get it straight: he doesn't carry me, I carry him. Lord, I hate a holier-than-thou pecker."

Barkeep was strolling in the kitchen, performing his comedian's routine. His eyes swept us and again he did his Groucho Marx face-wiggle. "Anybody want to trade?" he asked. His eyes paused on Menlo. "Menlo, what about you? Buck for Junior? I've got a notion Junior's the strong, silent type."

An easy smile spread across Menlo's face. "I'm afraid I'd get short-changed," he said pleasantly.

Barkeep hooted. He began to nod vigorously. "Yeah, yeah," he roared. "That's true." Then, to the rest of us: "Why do I have the feeling that if our five whackers were a basketball team, Junior would play the low post and Ernest would be the point guard?" Barkeep said.

Menlo chuckled. "White boys," he said.

"Well, you're talking to a power forward," Barkeep chirped. "In case you wonder."

Carson X. sat on one of the kitchen stools, listening, enjoying the bantering. Energy poured from him like a light. He was restless, intense, vibrating with enthusiasm.

Surprisingly, he did not require a report on discussions with our penises. It was as though Barkeep's comic rant was enough. Also, we all knew it was not over with Barkeep. Good material begets good material.

"Today, we're going to sit on the patio," Carson X. announced. "It's too lovely to be inside. Bring your coffee, or tea, or whatever you want, and let's get started."

We followed him to the patio, which was beautifully appointed with clipped shrubs and colorful patches of hardy, fall flowers. Carson X. had placed garden chairs and the flip chart of Miss Perfect in a circle. The Talking Knife was on a small oval coffee table that was in the center of the circle. The day was warm, a re-run of summer. Barkeep kissed Miss Perfect on her thin lips and we settled into the garden chairs. The mood was relaxed, comfortable.

"Ready, gentlemen?" Carson X. asked.

We nodded.

Carson X. did not ask for a volunteer. He picked up the Talking Knife and handed it to Menlo, and then he sat in a chair next to Miss Perfect.

We all knew immediately that it had been arranged for Menlo to tell his story, perhaps in a late-night emergency telephone conversation with Carson X., something to calm the shakes. "Tell it tomorrow," Carson X. would have instructed. "Get it out."

Menlo was dressed for the occasion. He wore a pale orange collarless shirt with sleeves that billowed slightly at the wrists, tan trousers, tan deck shoes, with tan socks. He had the dress and the look of a catalogue model. If Menlo had to talk, Menlo would be presentable. It was in his nature, in his presence.

For a very long time, Menlo did not speak. He leaned forward in his chair, his elbows braced across his knees. He was holding the knife in both hands, gazing at it as though mesmerized. It was impossible to read the mood hiding behind his eyes.

Then, he began. In a calm, almost casual voice, he said: "I am not here because I love a woman, or have need of her. I am here because I want to see one suffer. The truth is, I want to see her dead. That is my obsession."

Barkeep whistled softly and leaned back in his chair.

"I wish I were more like all of you," Menlo continued. "When I'm here, when I listen to all of you, I think I am. Then I go to my cabin and everything's different."

He paused and rolled the knife in his hands.

"Perhaps I should say something," Carson X. suggested. "The truth is, I deliberated a long time before I agreed to accept Menlo into the program. In the classic sense, he doesn't fit. Of the lot of you, women would find his experience unforgivably chauvinistic, and given the chance, most of them would gleefully claw his eyes out and relieve him of his manhood with a straight razor. But I was so intrigued by his—well, his situation and his story—I decided what we're doing would help him, and perhaps help all of us."

Menlo placed the Talking Knife on the table.

"Tell us," Carson X. said quietly.

Menlo nodded.

It was a brutal story, one that easily could have been tailored for a television drama of sensational madness, one with oiled flesh and puddles of blood, of dark nights and jazzy music in neon-lit juke joints, or one that might have played out in high-rise condos or elite restaurants managed by men in tuxedos and ladies in silk gowns.

There was a woman—Regina, her name—who had been the wife of Menlo's younger brother, Victor. Because of her, said Menlo, his brother had committed suicide, but to Menlo it was not suicide. To Menlo, it was self-murder. Victor might have pulled the trigger that sent a bullet spinning into his cranium, but he did not point the gun. The gun-pointer was Regina, even if she was not present when Victor died. She had goaded him to do it, to squeeze the trigger. Self-murder. Murder by anguish.

Still, there had been questions, suspicions, a looming possibility that Regina would be charged with something. It was only idle talk. The circumstances were too murky, the evidence too flimsy.

"None of that mattered," Menlo said bitterly. "If she had been tried and found guilty before the Supreme Court, it wouldn't have mattered. I didn't want that kind of justice. Not that way. Not by some judge and jury." He paused in his telling, inhaled sharply, reached for the Talking Knife, touched it, then pulled his hand away and folded it into a fist. "I want payback," he added. "Eye for eye. I want to see pain."

No one pressed Menlo for details but still he offered them, fragment by fragment, rambling thought by rambling thought.

His brother had met Regina at the place where both worked. She was beautiful, sensuous, brilliant, energetic, ambitious, and she knew a good thing when she saw it. Victor was a good thing, an up-and-comer, a man with a degree from Stanford and a vice-president's position in a Silicon Valley software company that was as up-and-coming as Victor. The Governor attended the wedding, trailed by luminaries from sport and entertainment, arriving from

New York and Los Angeles. The wedding cost was more than $70,000. It was a gaudy, pretentious affair.

Menlo's toast as best man, spoken over a raised crystal glass filled with champagne the color of pale amber, had been: "To perfection. Hold to it as long as you can."

Perfection was short-lived. Within a year, Regina was maneuvering her way through the company, picking off board members and officers like an assassin, using the heat of sex as a weapon as deadly as a drone armed with nuclear explosives.

"There wasn't a man in the company with the power to resist her," Menlo said. "Not one. She once told Victor she'd had sex with the night security guard—just to see the shock on his face. She was a drug. If she breathed on you, you were addicted." He paused and looked at us with a calm, almost sad expression. "None of you could have resisted her. Believe me. Not one. Not you, Godsick. Not you, Bloodworth. None of you."

He turned his gaze to Carson X. and held it, waiting for the question he knew Carson X. would ask. I think all of us had the same sense of it: a staged scene, rehearsed for perfection.

"And you?" said Carson X. "Did you resist her?"

The answer was quick and blunt. Again it sounded rehearsed. "No. No, I did not."

"Would you share that with us?" Carson X. said.

Menlo stood and moved outside the circle and began to pace. When he talked, he flicked fingertip touches to his face like someone batting away gnats, a gesture none of us had seen from him before.

She had seduced him, he told us. In the guise of happy adventure, she had seduced him. A single, wine-soaked time, sex so soaring in its intensity, it still haunted him, still made him weak, still left him in anguish over the shame that followed. Yes, he had shame over it, unbearable shame, shame that had institutionalized him for six months.

When he paused, Carson X. asked the question that was resting with each of us: "Did you have any deep feeling for her?"

Menlo swallowed hard. A frown of pain waved across his forehead. Then he said: "No. I loved my brother. She was sex. I'm sorry for what I did, and I will go to my grave aching over it."

"Do you think it bothered her?" Carson X. pressed.

"Bothered her?" Menlo snapped. "Bothered her? Not for a moment. If anything, it was one of the great thrills of her life. She had both of us."

"Son of a bitch," Barkeep hissed. "You hit the nail on the head, brother. You're damned right it didn't bother her."

For a moment, a net of silence fell over the room. I saw Max staring at his hands. His face was pale and I knew demons were screaming at him. Finally, Carson X. asked of Menlo, "Do you want to take a break?"

"A break?" Menlo said. "I don't need one. I'm finished. I simply want all of you to know that I spend my life trying to put her out of my mind and the only way I think that will happen is when she's dead, and when that wonderful moment happens, I will have only one regret: that you guys will not be with me to celebrate."

Another pause settled in the room, and then Godsick asked in his gentle manner, "Was there anything good about her?"

"No, Godsick, no," Menlo answered evenly. "I know you think what I have said is evil—that I want her death so I can have my life—but I mean it." He looked at Carson X., then turned to the rest of us. "Let me tell you what I've learned," he added. "Not from here or from some padded room or from any single person or any book, but on my own. If you want to find some peace, get pissed off. If you get mad, you won't go mad. It's that simple. I have my own axiom about all of this: The more pissed off you are, the healthier you are." He moved behind Max and patted him on his massive shoulder and then he returned to his seat.

Carson X. cocked his head in thought. "There's some truth to what Menlo has said," he admitted. "I've had something of that same experience. Temper is a great motivator. You will learn that. Menlo will help teach it."

Carson X. leaned back in his chair. He drank slowly from his bottled water. His face wore a pretentious frown of thought. "I want to talk more about that, but later," he said after a moment. "Right now, I'd like to hear the other stories. I think this is a good day for it." He looked at me. "Bloodworth, why don't you take the knife?"

I was sitting next to Menlo. I reached for the knife, touched its handle in agreement, but did not move it. Its blade was still pointed toward Miss Perfect.

"Remember when I talked about two types of obsession?" Carson X. said. "Sweet and bitter?" He smiled. "I think you will find sweetness in Bloodworth's revelation."

"I don't know," I said. "But it is different."

"How?" asked Barkeep. "If there's a woman in it, you're as wasted as the rest of us."

"The woman in my life is dead," I answered quietly. "She was my fiancé. She was killed in a car accident."

At first, no one spoke, and then Barkeep threw back his head and moaned, "Aw, man, I'm sorry. Jesus, I'm sorry. I'm a fuck-up. Forgive me."

"It's all right," I told him.

Godsick whispered, "I'm sorry, too." His fingers flashed over his abdomen.

Max looked away. Menlo kept his gaze on me.

"No, I mean it, it's all right," I said again. "My problem's simple: I can't bury her. I can talk about her. In fact, I'm glad to share her. I just can't bury her."

"Tell us," Carson X said.

And I told them of Kalee. Everything I could remember. The joy of her, the little girl shyness, the giving lover. I told of our getaway trips, of phone calls and emails, of the secret poems, of childish gifts.

I told of the night of the surprise dinner to celebrate our engagement and of the message from Kalee about her trip to Florida. And I told of the accident that killed her. I told them of her text message—*I will never leave you.*

They listened without interruption. I could see on their faces an expression of sadness, of shared pain, or perhaps it was an expression of regret—not for me, but for their own lives. Spence once said to me, "Every man I know wants a woman like that. Yes, they do."

Carson X. echoed Spence when he said, "By the way, he's telling the truth about her from what I've learned, and, as all of you will find out, I'm pretty thorough in my research." He rubbed his hands together—his gesture to move ahead in the conversation—and then he added, "But I'm curious. To follow up on Menlo's philosophy, did you ever get angry with her?"

"No," I said. "Never."

I saw the wiggle of a question cross Carson X's forehead, a sign of doubt, and then it disappeared. He made a single nod. "Not even the night of the party, the night she left you?" he asked, almost as an after-thought.

The question caught me off-guard. I had been annoyed, yes. Had felt foolish and embarrassed. But not angry. Kalee had no way of knowing about the surprise of the dinner. To her, it was to be a business meeting, an obligatory night of clever banter and pasted-on smiles across a table of expensive food and select wine.

"No," I said in answer to Carson X.

"I find that hard to believe," he said calmly. "When she didn't appear for the dinner, did you try to call her on her cell phone?"

It was a question Bloodworth had never asked, one I had never considered. For a moment, I did not remember, and then I did. Yes, I had tried to call her cell, but received only her voice mail. It was why I had called my home number to see if she had left a message for me there.

"I tried," I said. "Her phone was off. I'm sure she was avoiding me, because she didn't want me to talk her out of her trip to Florida."

"And that didn't bother you?" Carson X. said.

I bristled. "I'm sure it did, at that time, but it hasn't been an issue at all, and it certainly doesn't have anything to do with missing her."

"Look, I don't want to make anyone here uncomfortable," Carson X. said softly. "But you need to understand something. Everyone on Earth has a blind spot. Trust me on that. What Bloodworth told us is a touching, beautiful story, isn't it? It's the kind of story that causes us to weep and to ache. For him, everything about the death of the woman he loved is horror, but something's missing, some blocked-out moment, that keeps him from going forward. Godsick's story is a story of deception and, for him, the same kind of horror. Barkeep's tale of betrayal, the same. And Menlo's torment from an act of shame—the same. Gentlemen, the thing common to each confession is this: you've developed a block in your reasoning. You're mired in the quicksand of anguish. What you need is to find the firm ground at the bottom of the slush that makes up the quicksand. Choices. Remember? Get rid of the blocks. Pull them down. Destroy them."

"Are you saying we're holding something over their heads, just to make ourselves feel better?" Barkeep asked in a demanding voice.

Carson X. smiled patiently at Barkeep. He then motioned for the knife, and I took it from the table and handed it to him. He held it up and gazed at the blade. "By holding something over her head, do you mean something like this?" he said.

"If you mean it as a metaphor, yes," I replied.

Carson X. nodded. His squeezed his brow in thought. His fingers wrapped around the handle of the knife. "Yes, I mean it as a metaphor, but it's stronger than that, don't you think? Men are fighters, warriors. It's in our nature, maybe even in our genetic makeup. Fight me and I will fight back. Use deceit and I will use retaliation." He looked at me. "But that is not the cut of the brave man's sword, is it, Bloodworth? That's vengeance, and vengeance and killing are two different things. You can have vengeance without killing, but that's never quite enough, is it? Once you have the taste of vengeance, you want to feast on it."

He turned to Max. He said, "Max?"

Max stared at the knife in Carson X.'s hand. His red face was pale. He shook his head. "I can't do it, not now," he said quietly. "I can't."

"That's all right," Carson X. told him. "When you're ready." He turned his head to the rest of us. "Is that acceptable with everyone?"

We all agreed. Yes. It was all right. Max could talk when Max wanted to talk.

Carson X. stood.

"It's such a beautiful day," he said, his voice rising. "Let's go for a walk on the beach. I'll show you where I saw the whales."

13

Night of the Fourth Day

Dear Kalee,

I first need to say that I understand this is a pretend letter, that it will never be mailed, nor read by anyone other than myself. I say Dear Kalee, as though you are alive, but I am not deceived. I know this is merely an exercise. Otherwise I would not write it, not if you were really alive. (But, then, if you were really alive, I would not be here and none of this would be happening. I would be with you, as I have begged God to let happen since I took the call about your death.) However, I do feel comfortable writing to you, since there was a wonderful friendship between us. We were more than lovers, I mean. You were the one person I could tell anything, and I think I was that person for you. I know it's a cliché—that thing about being lovers and best friends. How faulty the reasoning is, because it happens only in the new, fresh days of a relationship. Yet, I think it would have lasted with us. Lovers. Best friends. But there is no way to know that, is there? Who knows? Perhaps we would have become numb to the joy of that incredible belief. Lovers. Best friends.

It's late, a little before midnight I would guess, and I know I should wait until tomorrow—or daylight tomorrow—to write about the evening with Inga, but I am not sleepy, and my energy is at full throttle.

Tyler Bloodworth, psychiatrist, was on tonight. I mean, snap on the spotlights and aim the beams this way. Hit the drum roll, voice-check the mike. I'm ready to make an acceptance speech.

I know. I know. That's an arrogant way of stating it, but Tyler Bloodworth was absolutely bowled over tonight by what he learned from the woman who appeared at his door.

I will lead you through it.

First, we did not have a session tonight. I suspect that Carson X. decided to spend some time alone with Max, one of the members of the MOD Mob. Max had a bad day, suffered a lot of pain. It was obvious when we all went for a walk on the beach. He could barely hold himself up. He and Carson X. wandered off together for a few minutes and I could see Max trembling, like a man about to have a convulsion. Godsick believes Max is in more pain than any of us. Maybe. I don't know if it's possible, but maybe. Max is the only one in the group who has not shared his story. I think we will hear it tomorrow.

Anyway, because we did not have the session, I called Inga and we arranged an eight o'clock time for dinner. (She had just returned from her day in Beaufort.)

She arrived at seven-fifty. (I stole a glance at her watch.) She was dressed in white slacks, red blouse and white jacket. She wore white canvas shoes. The outfit complemented her. She looked rested and energetic, not faded as I earlier described. She had with her the escarole she had promised to look for in Beaufort, as well as a bottle of wine—red wine, a choice Bordeaux. I was glad it wasn't a chardonnay. I do not think I could have accepted chardonnay.

We did the chatter bit. Hello chatter. You-look-good chatter. Make-yourself-comfortable chatter. Can-I-get-you-anything? chatter.

No reason to go into all of that. It is the kind of ritual that people of all cultures practice in their own way, with their own language—body and verbal.

Permit me a moment of pride: dinner was superb. I grilled the steaks I had purchased on my first visit to Inga's grocery. We had a small bowl of romaine salad, streaked with balsamic vinegar and olive oil, boiled corn cut from the cob, and the escarole, sautéed. She praised my skill at the grill. We laughed comfortably over small talk about the island, the stories of Blackbeard and Jeremiah Neal and of hurricanes that have cut down homes and vegetation like a scythe made of wind. After dinner, we sat in the living/dining, dining/living room—Inga curled on one end of the sofa, while I reclined in a nearby armchair. I thought we were a bit like Dagwood and Blondie, enjoying a pleasing, but unspectacular, evening. The only thing missing was Daisy.

I said to Inga, as Bloodworth would say, but in a better voice, "I know we talked a bit on our walk, but you didn't tell me how you came to be here."

She looked away for a moment, and then sipped from her wine. "That's really not easy to describe," she offered. "It had to do with my divorce." She shifted on the sofa. "It was my doing," she added. "There was another man. Being here has to do with all of that."

I did not ask her to tell me about him, Kalee, but she did, as though she had spoken of him to many people, and each telling was another way to accept blame for her failed marriage. Her lover's name was Evan Hill. He had been the family attorney. The first time they talked one-to-one was on a night when Evan appeared to review the wills he had prepared. Frank, who was supposed to be present, was detained in Washington at a meeting, leaving Inga alone with Evan, and Inga was strangely attracted to the man in her home.

She called it coincidence.

Two days later, she met Evan for lunch at a restaurant in Richmond to review the final documents. Whatever it was that had intrigued Inga about Evan Hill had not escaped Evan. He was, in fact, bolder than Inga. He said to her, "I'd like to see you again, and if you want me to find a reason, I will." Three weeks after that lunch, they made love for the first time in a motel.

"I had never done anything like that, ever," Inga told me. "I know it was ridiculous, but I couldn't help it. I think I was consumed by it from the first few minutes that we spoke, sitting in my house, waiting for Frank to show up, or to call."

She touched the collar of her blouse with her fingers, played with it nervously. Then she made a confession: "I pressured him— Evan, I mean—and he left." It was very much the same confession Godsick had made about Anna, and I remembered something Bloodworth had once said about relationships: "For some of us, love becomes a drug, and we only want it from one source, one dealer. We want it first in small sips, then in deep swallows, then we want it fed to us intravenously. We want to rip open our chests and have it stabbed directly into our hearts."

From what I understood (or guessed at), Inga's love-sickness terrified Evan. Eventually, he left the law firm and moved away. Inga believed he was on the West Coast, but had no proof of it.

Nothing she said bothered me. Such things happen. The MOD Mob is a dramatic testament to that fact. Inga seems to be accepting her experience well enough, though she does confess that memory of that time swipes at her occasionally, leaving little razor nicks of pain.

Yet, she did say one thing that shocked me—the reason she is on Neal's Island: the FullLife Foundation. Carson X. Willingham, founder.

Yes. The FullLife Foundation. And when she says the word, Kalee, it is exactly that—one word, with the cap F and cap L, so designed in order to bring full and life together, a grammatical fusion of two imperatives for happiness

I had to recover quickly. I said, "Oh, really? Tell me about it."

And as I listened to Inga speak enthusiastically about the Foundation, I realized how different she and I viewed the same organization.

To me, being here is a place where I have come to attack a problem, very much the same as going away to Lake Lanier for a week of business planning. I have not thought of it in terms of Life Changing as much as Life Repairing.

Inga speaks of Life Changing.

As she was talking, I remembered Paul Boatwright. I think you met him. Troubled, bothersome, restless Paul Boatwright. Heavy-drinker. Mean-spirited. Anyway, he went off one weekend on a church retreat—drug there by his wife—and returned on Monday morning a changed man. He was like someone who had walked into one of those car-wash stalls and had had his outside scrubbed and waxed to a mirror shine, and then had dropped fifty cents into the vacuum machine and stuck the end of the hose into his mouth to suck out all the trash that had been cluttering his personality. Spence said he believed Boatwright had had a lobotomy and when they were in the general vicinity of his brains, they had cut off his balls. He said that directly to Boatwright. Boatwright only smiled sweetly.

Inga knew by the expression on my face—not at all Bloodworth-like, I am sure—that something was wrong, that I was struggling to respond to her.

She laughed in a little girl's voice, a disarming laugh. "It's not what you think," she told me. "And I do know what you think, especially with your background. So did I, at one time. But it's not a cult. We don't do sacrifices and voodoo and Dr. Willingham's not a god. No one is. It's not that at all. It's just a practice of, well, discipline."

Bloodworth, rescue me, I thought.

Stupidly, I said, "Speaking professionally— "

Inga stopped me. "Please, don't. I've had that experience, also. Several thousand dollars worth. Just because I'm sitting on your sofa, doesn't mean I want to go on the clock."

I tell you, Kalee, I will never understand women. All of you are so beautifully conniving. You have more tricks tucked in your bras than men have up their sleeves, even the ones bearing French cuffs, and that's saying something. It's a wonder men have survived to fight, and die, in the wars that protect their women.

I recovered nicely, however. I said, "Speaking nonprofessionally, I'd like to know more about it."

The gist of what Inga feels about the FullLife Foundation is simple—almost too simple: reside in the center of your own being, or strength.

It was Carson X. to a T and I felt increasingly uncomfortable. I realized as I listened to Inga that I have been trained— indoctrinated, if you will—to disregard my own me. My religion, my belief (and I do have both, no matter how I abuse them), insists that I am a diseased glob of imperfection and that the only relief from the pain of being me is in the magic of the holy creed I am to repeat with fervor and with shame, because I am unworthy of the words. Funny thing: I really believe that. I do. It is as certain to me as breathing.

"All of that's interesting," I said to Inga.

140

She smiled, then pulled up from the sofa and went to the kitchen and returned with the wine. I watched her as she poured for both of us. She said, as she sat again, "I've missed going to my sessions recently. A couple of times a year, Dr. Willingham sponsors a men's seminar and that's going on now."

"Oh, really?" I said. I wanted to cry out that I was a member of the MOD Mob, a patient of Carson X. Willingham, but as you can see, Kalee, I was caught in the web of my own deceit. The web covered my mouth and my good intentions of being a truth-teller went out the window.

"It won't last much longer," Inga said. "I can wait. But it really may be why I've enjoyed talking to you. I've missed having a place to go, or people to be with."

I did not ask Inga about Arlo and Penny. The moment never seemed appropriate. I did catch her staring at the initials as we were on the deck, grilling the steaks. In fact, she was leaning on the railing and she traced her fingertip over the A B. I saw that, but I don't think it means anything. It was merely a subconscious act, something to do with her hands while we talked. (At that particular moment, she was telling me about her son, who must be a bright young man, but something of an ass; he has not forgiven his mother for the divorce.)

And that was about it.

If you're wondering, there was nothing physical between us, other than a brief hug. It happened when she was about to leave. I embraced her at her car, as a friend would embrace a friend. I could tell she was a little uncomfortable, but she smiled what I took to be a this-feels-nice smile, and then she said, "Thank you. I've enjoyed this. I don't have many friends on the island."

I wanted to laugh.

Goodnight, my Kalee, my love, my lovely Kalee. You are very much on my mind, especially after telling the MOD Mob about you. This has now become a night/morning entry in this never-ending search for an answer to my need for you. The word-fix, I call it. What a way to go. A little like breathing exhaust fumes from an idling car, when a bullet would be just as final.

It's time for the meds, the chemical stabilizers, the sleep-makers.

I love you.

Your Correspondent

14

Night/Morning of the Fifth Day

I wanted to dream of Kalee, but I did not. Still, I dreamed.

In my sleep, in the deep, numbing command of the dream, I heard a knocking at the door of the cabin, a monotonous pounding and, still in the dream, I slipped from bed and pulled on my khakis and made a dream-walk to the door and opened it.

A man was standing there. I could hear the wind and smell the odor of the sea. Outside, it was ink-dark. And in the tricky backgroud light of the bedroom lamp thrown against the sheet of night, I thought it was Max.

I said, "Max?"

The man answered in a hoarse voice I did not recognize, "No."

"Who are you?" I asked.

"I need to come in," he said. He did not wait for an invitation. He pushed his way past me and stumbled inside. He looked pale and exhausted.

I glanced outside, then closed the door and followed him. He sat heavily in a straight back chair at the table. Though I had not turned on the light in the room, there seemed to be a glow around him, or coated to him. The glow looked like a silver bruise.

He lifted his face to me. His eyes were dull frost dots. He was breathing in gulps. "You got anything to drink?" he asked.

"Who the hell are you?" I said.

"Anything, anything at all. Something with some alcohol in it," he muttered.

"Scotch. I've got scotch," I told him.

"Pour me one. Please. Straight. I don't need the water. I get enough of that. And pour one for yourself. You're going to need it."

I did as he asked. I do not know why. I have always done things in dreams that I would never do when awake. Still, there was something compelling in his voice. My hands were shaking as I poured the drinks.

"Thanks," he said when I handed him the scotch. He swallowed deeply from the glass and smacked his lips with a pleasing sigh. Then he said, matter-of-factly, "It's cold out there."

"What are you talking about? I asked.

He gestured with his head. "Out there. The ocean."

A chill struck me. "Were—were you on a ship?" I asked.

He laughed softly, a chuckle. He shook his head and took another swallow of his scotch. "Not hardly." He added, casually. "I'm Arlo."

I thought my heart would stop beating. Even knowing I was asleep and dreaming, I had never been as terrified. I stared at him. I tried to speak, but could not bring words into my mouth.

"Have some scotch," he said. "It'll help." He lifted his glass in a salute. I pulled my glass to my mouth and drank. The scotch spilled over my lips. I moved (I do not know how, but I moved) to the armchair and dropped into it.

"You shouldn't be so surprised," he said. "You've known about me all along. I'm amused by that. That's a great trick, that bit with the initials."

I did not speak. Could not.

"I know you think you're dreaming, but you're not," he added. "By the way, I like the scotch." He lifted his glass in a salute. "it's a good brand."

"You can taste it?" I asked.

"I don't know," he replied. "Maybe I only think I can. It's been a long time. I never really liked scotch, but I think this is good. Must be expensive."

"How—?"

"How?" he said. He lifted his arm to look at it. "I don't know. It's very complex. Very. I mean, I can wander around in the invisible state and that's easy, but it takes some doing to be seen. From what I gather, talking to the others—and this island's full of them, a little like Fifth Avenue at lunch hour—you have to start slow, like an apprenticeship of some sort. This is the first time I've been able to pull it off, to tell you the truth. Why? Don't ask me. It probably has something to do with you trying to invent me. One doesn't pry too much when one's on the other side." He paused and cocked his head. "By the way, you've got a serious problem with an overactive imagination. About the only thing you've hit dead center is my name. Arlo. Bowers is wrong, but Arlo's right. Yet, I've got to admit I'm impressed that you came up with that. Good guess."

"Penny?" I said anxiously. "Is Penny right?"

He laughed a short, faint laugh. His frost eyes blinked in memory. "No," he said. "But that's something you'll have to discover on your own." He looked at me. "And you will. I'm sure of it."

"I—don't understand," I stammered. "Who the hell are you? I don't believe in ghosts. Ghosts don't knock on doors in the middle of the night. Who sent you? Bloodworth?"

"Bloodworth? Good heavens, no," he exclaimed. "He's much too clinical to dispatch anyone. I'm surprised he can mail a letter."

"You know him?"

"I didn't until you showed up and started your screwy games and your writing," Arlo confessed. "I think I must be tied into your

145

computer by—I don't know; maybe some electric pulse. Maybe it's like those people who can pick up radio signals from the fillings in their teeth. I always wondered if they could change stations with their tongue." He laughed weakly. "All I know is that every time you write a word, I know what that word is." He drank again from the scotch, then his forehead wrinkled in thought. "But that couldn't be it," he added. "I know what you're thinking, too. You're a very troubled man."

"Carson X.," I said. "He sent you, didn't he? You're from the FullLife Foundation."

Arlo frowned. The light coating his body intensified. He said, sharply, "No. No, he didn't. But you'd better watch out for that group. If you want my advice, pack up and hit the trail. Willingham is one man you want to avoid."

"Why?" I asked.

"Because he's nuttier than all of you put together. It's amazing none of you have figured that out."

"Maybe he's brilliant," I argued.

"Yeah, sure. You don't know him. I do. Trust me, he's a basket case. The ones out there—like me—are always talking about him. He's disturbed."

"Was it Inga?" I asked. "She's in with the Foundation. Did she send you?"

He laughed wearily.

"Inga could have set it up. She was here tonight for dinner," I said, watching him carefully.

"I know," he said somberly, after a pause. He drained his glass and waved it in the air in the gesture a drunk would make for a refill. I got up from the chair and poured him another scotch. He lifted the glass in a "Thank you." A bothered look rested in his hollow eyes.

"How did you know Inga was here?" I asked.

"That's the question of a fool," he said wearily. "I'm a ghost, remember? Ghosts can see through walls, just like Superman."

I was suddenly angry. I knew I was dreaming and I knew the man in that dream, the man sitting before me, drinking my scotch, was a put-on, and I was certain that in the bizarre world of dreams Carson X. was behind whatever was happening, or, if not Carson X., then someone else from the Foundation. I wondered if the other members of the MOD Mob were, at that moment, being teased by an actor pretending to be a ghost, believing they were, like me, in a dream. Drugged perhaps. Maybe from the refreshments Carson X. had fed to us earlier. Time-lapse hallucinations, chemically induced like an alarm on a clock.

Arlo's eyes narrowed. "You don't believe in me, do you?" he asked.

"No, I don't," I said.

"Mistake," Arlo said. "I could teach you a lot." He picked up the glass of scotch and swallowed from it. His gray eyes studied me. A small, jubilant smile played over his lips. He said, "Love can be a mystery, can't it?"

I did not answer.

"Yes, it can," he added. "Yes, yes, yes. Oh, by the way, I like that—the code. You must have used it with her. It's poetic."

"You won't tell me about the P R?" I asked.

Again, he frowned. "No. You're wrong. That's all."

"But you know something about it," I said.

Arlo stood. "I think you'll understand it later," he said. "I have to go now."

"Will you come back?" I asked.

"I don't know. Maybe. But don't worry. I won't pop up at the wrong time, if you know what I mean."

"There won't be a wrong time," I said irritably. "I'm here to get away from something, not to get into something else."

"Don't be too hasty," he said. "Some things you can't control."

"Am I crazy?" I asked. "Is that what this is all about?"

"I didn't say that," Arlo replied. "I don't know. But if you are, you're not as crazy as you're going to be. Believe me."

He left then. I do not remember him leaving, but he did.

In my dream, I returned to my bed and lay there, soaked in perspiration. From the graying of the sky through the window, I knew it was almost dawn. In my dream, I said to myself, "Wake up. Wake up."

And I did.

I got out of bed and went into the living/dining, dining/living room to look for drink glasses. There was only one glass in the room, on the table, but there was another in the kitchen, in the sink.

Then I found the bottle of scotch. It was empty, but I know that I did not drink all of it. At least, I didn't remember drinking it. And I did not remember having a glass at the table, or putting one in the sink.

I was more composed after a shower and coffee and toast. It was still pre-dawn when I left the cabin to walk the beach in search of something, or someone—Inga or Old Joe or even Carson X.—but the beach was deserted and not as wondrous as it is when the sun is making its red-soaked bubble over the water. The night—the visit from Arlo—followed me. Arlo was a dream, certainly. Yet, dreams are not often so real for me. I wondered if I should call Bloodworth and tell him about it. Yet, if I did call him, Bloodworth would probably declare it was an experience of withdrawal, like an addict in a dry-out tank. He would also tell me that my obsession was getting out of hand with my preoccupation over initials carved into a railing.

Still, there was an argument that would not leave me: dreams must be more than dreams. Dreams must also be indicators of what is real, or ought to be real. Was my dream a warning? Was I really so wrong about P R?

I could have proclaimed that P R was Patsy Ragsdale. I could have invented an entire life for her—professional photographer, dancer, artist, a cook at the Blue Spoon Restaurant. I could take a book of names and pick from the As and the Bs and have never-ending possibilities of who A B is. When I saw the A B and P R, their names were clear to me: Arlo Bowers and Penny Rymer. I saw them as adults, as lovers in the last, sad hours of an affair that had been breathtaking. I saw them as Kalee and me. No, that is wrong. Not us exactly. They had their own personalities, their own destinies, and I had become interested in them. I was their creator, and that had to count for something. Isn't that why God is unable to desert mankind? Or have the men of the cloth made all of that up, and use it to bullwhip us back into line?

I went back to the cabin, to the living/dining, dining/living room, and sat in the chair where Arlo had sat in my troubled memory of him. I wondered if he had left some microscopic speck of himself, some ghostly aura that had stayed sealed to the chair, some drop of sea water plump with crystals of salt. I waited, inhaled, imagined.

Nothing.

Until he gave me more than a knowing look from his empty, gray, ghost eyes, I would continue to believe that A B is Arlo

Bowers and P R is Penny Rymer. And if what he told me—dream or not—was true about being linked to me, knowing each word I wrote, or thought, he would know I had issued a challenge: show up again and prove it. Prove that B does not stand for Bowers and P R does not stand for Penny Rymer.

"Are you there, Arlo?" I said aloud. "Are you listening?"

I felt better. The cabin did not shake. I did not sense any ghost eyes staring at me from the ceiling or from the corner. The only thing I saw in the room was a fly left over from the summer. A single fly that buzzed from a lampshade to the top of a picture frame on the wall. If Arlo had returned and crammed himself into that fly, then more power to him. Let him watch. Let him see anything he wished to see. Let Inga return, naked and covered in baby oil or pig lard. Let her attack me. Let our bodies ignite in flame from the friction of our heaving about. I would not care if Arlo watched all of it from his little fly spot on the wall and became so aroused he fainted from lack of blood to his little fly brain and tumbled to the floor and broke his little fly neck.

15

Early Afternoon of the Fifth Day

Dear Kalee,

Bloodworth has tried to convince me that my healing of you boils down to this: time. He tells me that time will soothe the aching, as though the distance of hours and days and weeks and months is a miracle drug.

Time cannot be changed, he tells me. It cannot be rushed. Time is the one thing in the universe that cannot be altered— unless you are Einstein and know something the rest of us don't.

"Be patient," Bloodworth counsels. "Be patient."

It is such smug advice, especially coming from Bloodworth, who says it in such a smug manner. Time. Tick-tock. Tick-tock. As I have revealed, Bloodworth made me leave my watch and my cell phone locked in my car, and he made me vow to hide all the clocks in the cabin. He doesn't fool me. It's his way of telling me to quit thinking about time, that a watched clock is more maddening than Chinese water torture. He wants me to condition my thinking to believe that time is an eye-blink experience. "Look," he says, "ten years from now, you won't even think about this. Ten years from now, you'll be involved in something, or someone, totally different, totally absorbing." Sure Bloodworth, sure. But what? Or with whom?

I have a question, Kalee, though I know it is unfair to involve you: Should I tell Inga the truth? Should I tell her I am not Tyler Bloodworth? As you know—because I've confessed it—I had intended to do so earlier, but lost my nerve.

If I tell her, she will be upset. I'm certain of that. I would be. I sense that she wants—no, needs—to trust me. And I could carry off the ruse. I'm only scheduled to be here for the ten days. I probably won't see her often. At the grocery when I need to restock supplies. Maybe on the beach. Maybe once again for dinner—for her needs, more than mine. I am, after all, taking her time slot with Carson X.—though she doesn't know it—and I'm so much in practice with the disguise of him, it wouldn't be hard to be Tyler Bloodworth during my remaining time here.

Yet, if I don't tell her the truth, I am deceiving her and I am learning this week from my group-mates how it feels to be deceived. All of them talk bitterly of it—at least those who have shared their experiences. We are still waiting to hear from Max, but I have heard enough from Inga to make me think that what she has most suffered from is deception. Evan deceived her, after she had deceived her husband. But that tarnished coin has another side, doesn't it? Her husband also deceived Inga. She married him with faith that she had married a real, live, walking, talking, human-type person—a man who cared for her, a man with passion. He wasn't. He was a bureaucrat, a nodding, yes-ing, by-the-books, policies-and-procedures imitation of a man. An unreasonable facsimile of a man.

So, you can see this is a dilemma for me, Kalee. I'll have to ponder it. Turn the coin around in my mind and study the heads-tails consequences. It's a difficult decision. My nature is to play out the game, stick to the role I have assumed.

I ask you, Kalee: What do I do? Play the role until the curtain falls, or confess that I am only an actor, an impostor?

Though you love me, I know what you would think about all of this. I know what most people would think. I know what I would think if this were someone else and not me.

I would think: What a self-absorbed ass this man is.

Yet, does it matter?

Ten years from now, it won't, or so Bloodworth tells me. I have his word on it.

But ten years from now, will Bloodworth's word matter?

***

The *** fell at mid-morning, or close to it. The sun was easing upward, reaching its high-noon arc, straight up, where the little hand and the big hand would be on a little-hand, big-hand clock if I had one I could see. I had another cup of coffee and then slept for a short time, maybe thirty minutes.

Enough.

I am in a languid mood, which seems strange after the horror of last night. Maybe I am over the shock of the Arlo dream. The longer I am removed from that experience, the more I realize it must have been the scotch, topped off by my medications. Should never mix the two, and I know it. As to the empty bottle, I have no explanation. Maybe I spilled it and forgot. Maybe I had a noble moment, a high-pitch sense of worth, and poured it down the sink. Maybe I drank it in a chugalug. I simply don't know.

Complications, Kalee. Complications. I am beginning to think that exaggeration is the compensation for being alone. Everyone I meet, or think about, assumes exaggerated importance. They become larger than life, or, in the case of Arlo, larger than death. Since I arrived here, I have collected people like a fanatical shopper at a yard sale—Inga, Arlo, Penny, Evan, Old Joe, Godsick, Menlo, Barkeep, Max, Carson X., etc. People are dividing and multiplying like amoebas. If this keeps up, before I leave Neal's Island it may sink from the weight of the crowd.

And here is the thing I most fear: is all of it a conspiracy to pry myself from my obsession of you?

I do not want to be free of you.

Okay. Enough of that. Enough. Enough. Enough.

I will not tell Inga who I am. I will continue to be Dr. Tyler Bloodworth, vacationing psychiatrist, seriously working on a serious paper about a serious malfunction of the seriously fragile self. Yes, it is deception, but it is also my defense against the FullLife Foundation. If I can get away before Inga discovers who I am, and why I am here, I will consider myself fortunate, but I will leave with sorrow for being so cowardly. It is a self-serving strategy that I detest, but intuitively I think it is the kindest way out of a possible trap. If Inga believes I am a psychiatrist, she may believe I am immune to FullLife conversion. I think of my lie as flashing a cross in the face of a demon, or opening a curtain of sunlight on a vampire. If she says to me, "Would you like to join me in FullLife?" she will hear an immediate lecture on Freud, and I know nothing about the fellow, except that he was famous enough to have an ian attached to his name. I will talk about that. I will hold forth on the complex meaning of being Freudian. I may even become Freudian. Surely it can't be any harder than being Fraudian.

Wish me luck, love. Wish me luck.

And don't worry. I only brought two bottles of scotch with me.

I love you dearly, passionately.

Your Correspondent

I was eager for the afternoon session to begin. After Inga and Arlo and (always) Kalee, I needed the companionship of the MOD Mob. The grip among us was still strong. No one had slipped, or released on purpose. We may have been protecting ourselves to some degree—a practice of men—but we had not fallen.

Carson X. was again ebullient.

His first question, after we had settled on the patio, in our circle with Miss Perfect, was, "So, how was your night?" He was looking at me.

"I saw a ghost," I said calmly.

"Really? Who was it?"

"I'm not sure," I lied. "It was late when he showed up."

Barkeep laughed. "Yeah, well, so did I. The son of a bitch was floating in an ice cube in the bottom of my glass. He looked like Captain Hook."

"Don't be so dismissive," Carson X. said to Barkeep. "I told you: this is an island of ghosts. They're everywhere."

"Well, I swallowed mine," Barkeep said. He winked at Godsick. Godsick frowned.

"Do you know why we have so many ghosts on Neal's Island?" Carson X. asked.

"Doc, I don't have the foggiest," Barkeep answered.

"Because people like you—like all of you—bring them here," Carson X. said. "And then they leave them, as each of you will. That is the healing. You leave the ghosts of anxiety behind."

Barkeep nodded dramatically, in a mocking way, but he did not retort. I knew he had a comeback, and I knew it would not be wasted. It was filed in his memory under To Be Used At the Right Time.

And then Carson X. asked, "Have any of you seen Lucifer?"

I saw Godsick recoil in his chair.

"The Devil?" Menlo said easily, and with a little amusement.

Carson X. smiled. "No. The alligator."

155

Lucifer, Carson X. told us, was the largest alligator on Neal's Island, and on warm days, he would pull himself out of the water to sun on the banks of Stillwater Lake.

"You really should see him," Carson X. enthused. "He's a magnificent creature."

He paused in his story. His eyes invited us to question him. No one did.

"Lucifer is probably the oldest living creature on Neal's Island, with the exception of a few turtles," he continued. "He's survived everything from hurricanes to drunks taking shots at him. I have a theory about Lucifer: he knows when to go under water to protect himself, and he knows when the sun is shining and how good it feels to stretch out and be warmed. Lucifer lives because Lucifer has great instincts."

"He also may be the meanest son of a bitch around," Barkeep said. "That'd give him a little bit of an edge."

"Maybe," Carson X. responded. "But I think I'd rather have great instincts than great strength."

"What are you saying?" asked Godsick.

"It's simple," Carson X. answered. "Each of you once had remarkable instincts about the women in your lives. Then, for one reason or another, you lost them, or they were taken from you. You don't know whether to go under water or enjoy the sun. That's something we need to work on, to learn to trust our instincts again." He looked at Max. "Isn't that right, Max?" he added gently.

Max nodded.

"Are you ready to tell us?" Carson X. asked.

Max nodded again.

Carson X. was sitting near Max, holding the Talking Knife. He handed it to Max. "Take you time. Tell us."

Max said, very slowly, very softly, "I killed a man because of a woman."

Godsick's face flew open in shock. I saw Barkeep start to speak, but Carson X. stopped him with a look. I heard Menlo nervously clear his throat.

"Tell us," Carson X. urged.

"He was a dealer," Max whispered. "Drugs."

"Tell us about the woman. Tell us her name," Carson X. said.

"Jenny. Her name was—is—Jenny," Max mumbled. He coughed a weak cry. "She was unbelievable. God...unbelievable."

The story that Max told us of Jenny was a story we all knew well because we all had known someone like Jenny, or believed we had—a fast-life, fast-lane American tragedy that has the making of sensational jabber on television talk shows. They had met in college—Max a football player, Jenny a cheerleader. The way Max described her, she was a goddess, a woman that made men weak with awe and caused women to bristle with jealousy.

"It was the way she laughed," Max whispered. "She was always laughing. Always."

He paused. Seconds passed. He gazed at the Talking Knife. None of us spoke, or moved.

"This is what happened," he finally said in a low, flat voice.

And he told us about Jenny becoming a buyer for an exclusive department store that catered to women of leisure who were married to men of wealth. She must have been a genius at her work, as Max vowed she was. She traveled to the design houses of Europe, to the fashion shows of the major cities of America. And it was on one of those trips—to New York—that she encountered a man, an executive with a de sign house, who plied her with drugs. Heroin, then crack cocaine. A dare, Max told us.

"I knew something had happened," he said, "because of the way she started acting, but I never thought it was drugs. Not Jenny. Later I learned she had an addict's personality. When she had the first taste of it she was hooked, but in the beginning she hid it, and nobody knew."

He swallowed hard, and then reached to touch the handle of the Talking Knife.

"What happened?" asked Carson X.

Max pulled his hand away from the knife. "She got caught," he answered. "A guy offered to sell her a few lines of coke, but he had a badge in his pocket. They took her to jail, and, Jesus, nobody could believe it. Nobody. And then there were the hearings, and she wiggled out. Said the buy was for me."

"Shit," Barkeep exclaimed in a disbelieving whisper.

"They couldn't put me in jail because it was only hearsay and every test I took was negative," Max said, "but it didn't matter. It was her word against mine. The only people who sided with me were my family. Nobody else would speak to me. That's how convincing her story was."

"What happened to her?" asked Menlo.

"She couldn't stop," Max replied. He stood and began to pace, the same as all of us had done when we were telling our stories. "She wound up in Las Vegas," he added in a rushing voice. "One night I got a call from her, begging me to come and get her, and that's what I did. I went there. When I found her, she was out of her head, insane. She was with this sleaze-bag in one of those shit-hole hotels. She didn't even know who I was, but when I tried to take her out of there, the guy pulled a knife on me."

He stopped pacing and turned to us and peeled his pullover shirt up, bearing his stomach and chest. A crisscross of scars covered him, where he had been cut and stitched together. He was trembling.

His personality suddenly changed, darkened. "I killed the son of a bitch," he growled. "I caught him by his fucking throat and ripped it out."

He dropped his shirt and sat. Muscles jerked involuntarily across his shoulders, down his arms, into his hands.

The silence on the patio was oppressive.

"Were you arrested?" I asked after a moment.

Max nodded. "Yeah," he said, "I went through all of that, but nothing ever came of it. Fact is, the police were happy I'd killed him. They didn't say it, but they didn't have to. It was ruled self defense."

He picked up the Talking Knife again and rolled it, hand-to-hand, staring at it.

"And Jenny?" asked Godsick. "Where is she now?"

Max inhaled. "In a treatment center," he whispered. His eyes flicked and tears rolled from them.

"I love her," he whimpered. "Goddamn it, I love her."

He caught the blade of the knife in one hand and squeezed it. Blood began to drip between his fingers.

"I love her," he repeated, sobbing. "I love her so goddamn much, I don't think I can breathe without her."

Carson X. reached for the knife and Max surrendered it.

"Why don't you come with me," Carson X. said softly. "We'll get that cut bandaged."

Carson X. and Max stood and walked away, into the house.

"Christ," Barkeep whispered in shock.

&

159

I wanted to talk to Old Joe Bonner when I left Carson X.'s home.

It was not because of the session. The session was, perhaps, the most healing we would experience on Neal's Island. And the most binding. After Max and Carson X. returned, we went though the exercise of questions for Menlo and for me—nothing prying or disturbing. We did not question Max. There was no reason. When we left, we all embraced—not as an instruction from Carson X, but from something natural, something good. Max held each of us in a grip of power. He did not speak; he simply nodded against us. We understood. All of us understood.

I wanted to see Old Joe Bonner because I had sensed the presence of Arlo as I walked to my car. I even stopped and whispered his name.

"Arlo?"

There was no answer. Yet, I did feel the swipe of a breeze against my face, like the single stroke of a hand-held fan.

I wanted to know if Old Joe Bonner knew of Arlo.

I found him at the security office of the entrance to the island. He was painting Santa Claus faces on oyster shells.

"Yeah," he admitted, "I like doing this. Sell some at the store. Pick me up a few dollars, but it ain't enough to live on."

I complimented him on his artistry.

"Always wanted to draw," he told me. "Even when I was a little tyke, I was always drawing on something. Got my butt whipped more'n once by drawing on the wrong thing." He laughed. "Drawed the picture of a schoolteacher I had one time, put it up on the blackboard at recess time. Had her tits hanging out. My ma almost tore my butt off me."

He laughed again at the memory and put the shell he had been painting on a newspaper to dry.

"How you liking it here?" he asked.

"Fine," I said.

"How's the Doc?"

"Interesting man," I answered.

He nodded. "Ain't that the truth?" Then he said, "You seen any deer?"

"A few," I told him. "I think it's the same group. Five of them. I saw them crossing the road, and then they wandered through my back yard this morning."

"One of them got some missing antlers?" Old Joe asked.

"That's right," I said.

"I know the ones you talking about. I call him Billy the Kid. Last set of horns he growed come out lopsided, like they was deformed. First time I seen him, he looked as much like a goat as he did a deer. That's Billy's group. Got they own territory. Go to the same places, over and over. But you be careful. Don't you kill none. They follow you around, if you do."

"I'll remember," I told him.

"I killed one once," Old Joe confessed. "Hit him with my truck one night. Didn't even see him. He just jumped out of the bushes, right in my lights. Been following me around ever since. Everywhere I go, he's there. Sometimes I can look out of my window when I'm in bed, and there he is, just standing there, looking in."

"A ghost?" I asked.

Old Joe looked at me. "They all over the place," he said earnestly. "Man and animal." He held up an oyster shell and examined it. "They's more ghosts here than they is people—lots more."

"I understand a man named Arlo—I'm not sure about his last name—died here a few years ago," I said. "You think he's one of the ghosts?"

Old Joe frowned, searching his memory. "Seems like that was his name, but I never did see him, unless it was when he checked in, but I never seen him alive after that, and I'm not saying I seen him then. My backup might have been on duty." He paused and grinned. "Maybe I seen him dead, down on the beach, frolicking around with them others, but I never seen his body. Way I remember it—if he's the one I'm thinking about—nobody did."

"What do you mean?"

"It's been a while," Old Joe answered, "but the way I remember it, somebody called the security and said they was a man caught out in the riptide. But they never found nobody. I believe he was wrote down as dead after a while, but that's nothing new. Lots of people get caught by the riptide and they ain't never seen again, unless they wind up in a can of tuna somewhere." He giggled and rubbed the oyster shell clean with a rag.

"Do you remember if it was a man who called the security gate?" I asked.

Old Joe pondered the question and shook his head. "Been a little while since all that happened. Don't think I was on duty."

"He could have been with a woman, then," I said.

Old Joe cackled. "Ain't they all?" He looked at me. "Why you asking about him? You know him? Or was it the woman you know?" His smile was locked across his face.

I think I blushed. "No. Somebody told me the cabin I'm in might have been the cabin he rented."

"Eighteen?" Old Joe said. He picked up a small Santa Claus necklace and blew dust off the shell. "Uh-huh. Could of been. Lots of things have went on out there. There's some what think that was where Captain Neal was buried, right there on that spot. Used to be called the Honeymoon Cabin, but they quit putting honeymooners out there when one of them got drunk and set fire to the place one night." His eyes twinkled. "Must of been a hot time. Almost burnt it to the ground."

"Well, you know how talk is," I said.

"Yeah, ain't it something?" Old Joe replied. He handed me the necklace. "Looks about right for you."

The Santa Claus face painted on the shell was smiling and winking, like a man with a secret.

"I like it," I said. "How much?"

"Free as the talk," Old Joe answered.

Ironically, on the drive away from my visit with Old Joe, I saw Billy the Kid and his nomad band of deer. They were in the woods near my cabin and I stopped to watch them. They stared at me curiously, like beggars on street corners, asking with their eyes for whatever gift I could offer, then they turned and casually vanished into the shadows of the trees.

"All right," I said to the shadows. "All right."

I drove to the grocery.

Other than Inga, there was only one other person in the store, a woman who was pleasingly pretty, with the kind of vibrant, lively face of a young Doris Day.

Her name was Sylvia Reeves.

"Sylvia's been a life-saver for me a few times," Inga said pleasantly after introductions.

"We all need that," I suggested.

"Inga tells me you're a psychiatrist," Sylvia said.

One dinner and I am an item of gossip, I thought.

"A lapsed one the past few days, I'm afraid," I lied.

"And you don't know Dr. Willingham?" Sylvia asked.

I tried to furrow my face as Bloodworth does when asked a question he wants to avoid.

"No. Inga was telling me about him, and his foundation," I said. "I'm surprised I haven't heard of it, but it's a profession with an unending number of programs. That's why I'm here—to work on a paper for one of them."

"You really should meet him," Sylvia enthused. She looked at Inga. "Maybe we can arrange an introduction."

"I don't know," Inga said. "He has his seminar this week, and you know how he is with that."

"Oh, that's right," Sylvia said.

"Must be something special," I suggested.

"It is," Sylvia replied enthusiastically. "No one knows much about it. Carson keeps to himself when the men are here." She glanced at her watch. "I'm sorry, but I've got to run. I'm already late for my hair appointment." She extended her hand to me. "Good to meet you, Dr. Bloodworth."

"Tyler, please," I said.

"Tyler."

Sylvia left, as women such as Sylvia and Doris Day would leave—in a dance-rush, sweeping to the door and through it, pulling her great energy with her, leaving the store suddenly quiet and calm.

"She's nice," I said to Inga.

"Yes. A good friend," Inga told me. "You've been out this morning," she added.

"For a while."

"I tried to call, to thank you for last night. It was a wonderful evening."

"Yes, it was," I said. "We should do it again."

Inga smiled softly. "I'd enjoy that."

"Tomorrow?" I asked.

She did not answer for a moment—long enough to know she had some uncertainty. And then she said, "It would have to be late. I work until eight."

"Perfect for me," I told her. "I have a late conference call—one that was cancelled last night. So, should we say nine?"

"Good," she replied. "I'm a night person. Nine o'clock is my five o'clock."

"Then it's a date," I said. "My cabin. Nine o'clock, but at this moment, I have a serious question: Do you have any apples?"

She smiled. "Yes."

"Do deer eat apples?" I asked.

"Deer eat anything," she said. "They're like a lot of people I know. They only look cute."

At the cabin, I went onto the deck and sat in a lounge chair, deliberately turned away from the A B and P R initials in the railing. I closed my eyes and tried to sense Arlo, but I could not. Arlo was not on the deck with me. Max was. I saw again the ribbons of scars across his massive chest and stomach, and the blood dripping from his fingers, where he had squeezed the Talking Knife, and I remembered how Max had reacted to the knife the first time Carson X. presented it to the MOD Mob, declaring it to be the sword from Oscar Wilde's poem. Max's face had flooded with an angry scream that only Carson X. could hear, because Carson X. knew of the scars. And I remembered too, that Carson X. had given Max permission to make the decision on using the knife as the Talking Stick and Max had surrendered in agreement. To the rest of us, it was a fleeting moment of discomfort; to Carson X. and Max it was a milestone, a breakthrough, a risk that only someone like Carson X. would have taken.

After hearing Max's story, I agreed with Godsick that Max was the one among us with the greatest pain. Max had killed once, and if he followed Carson X.'s advice, he would have to kill again.

"Yet each man kills the thing he loves... / The coward does it with a kiss, / The brave man with a sword..."

The last thing Carson X. said when we ended the session was, "Men ache. Understand that. Men ache. Just because you give, doesn't mean you won't ache."

I thought unexpectedly of a gift—a joke gift—I had given Kalee. It was a small, yellow plastic smiley face from the neck of a bottle of inexpensive wine, a promotional gimmick. She had laughed, had closed her hand over it. "I love it," she had said, and then she had threaded the smiley face onto a thin gold necklace and slipped it around her neck.

That night, she wore it when we made love.

I did not ache that night.

That night I was as complete as I would ever be.

I ached later.

I ached when the yellow plastic smiley face was found around her neck at the scene of the accident that took her life.

When I shared the story of the smiley face with Bloodworth, he told me it was a touching revelation, but also another tale of obsessive behavior. "It's part of the illness," he said. "You must understand that. You don't have to forget such things, but you

166

can't let them rule you." He had said the same thing to me a hundred trillion times. And he wonders why I rail against him when he becomes so damned pontifical. I knew I was obsessive. I knew that before I went to see him. Of course, I knew it: it was my illness. It was why I went to see him.

If only Bloodworth would tell me something I don't know.

If only he would tell me how to become well again.

Bloodworth does not understand that I can hear my brain shattering. It is the sound of dropped crystal—crystal so thin it is barely heavier than air.

I could see Bloodworth sitting in his chair, looking at me with weary disgust, and a question struck me: When I do become well again (I must say when, not if), will Bloodworth miss me? His professional code of conduct prevents him from saying it, I suppose, but I am certain Bloodworth is fascinated by my stories. Other people might mumble and complain with meek embarrassment when they talk to him. I don't. I spit it out. And I am not shy about embellishing a fact or two—here and there, now and then. I want Bloodworth to listen. I want him to wonder what is about to happen when I turn the pages on one of my Kalee stories. I want my money's worth.

I once asked Bloodworth if I was his favorite loony. He shot a rare smile in my direction—not at me, but in my direction—and then he said, "You could have a wing in the Smithsonian of Crazies." I bellowed a laugh. Bloodworth is not always so clever.

I thought: Yes, I will miss Bloodworth when all of this is over.

And he will miss me. Or us. Kalee and me.

☙

After a nap—a short, dreamless one—I went into the living/dining, dining/living room and picked up the K-for-Kalee folder and began to leaf through the pages.

I found a memory from a night of loneliness in Colorado, at a resort in Steamboat Springs. I had been on a skiing trip, a boondoggling business excuse for pleasure, but without Kalee the pleasure had been empty and pretentious. One morning, very early, remembering the night we had spent together in Savannah, I wrote:

> it is still dark, before sunrise. yet there are
> lights in the village, and, in the night sky,
> a glazed, drooping moon, and high on the
> mountain, snow covers the ski runs like
> lovely white thighs.
>
> i awoke to the muted sound of voices outside,
> and i looked from the window and saw them
> walking carefully in the crust-covering of
> new snow from the night, hand-holding,
> balancing their footsteps. i knew
> they had made love. it was in their touching
> and in the steam of their breathing.
>
> do you remember the night of our lovemaking
> in Savannah? the dance of heat? the great
> quickness of it, fitting ourselves easily into
> one another, locked together, holding the lock
> until it erupted like an exploding star, dazzling
> the darkness with crystals of light.
> and then we slept, close, with the sweet,

strong musk of our mixing heavy upon us.

outside it is still dark. i can no longer hear the voice
of lovers warm from their lovemaking.
from the window, i can see the lovely
white thighs of the ski runs. they are yearning
to be touched. i am alone. do you remember
the night of the lovemaking? i do. oh, yes, i do.

I closed the K-for-Kalee folder and put it away in my briefcase. And then I let the loneliness of Colorado fill me with the sadness of loss.

16

Night of the Fifth Day

Carson X. could have made a fortune in advertising, and maybe that is why I liked him.

He is an off-the-wall man. The unexpected is his game. Yet, what he does is certain to command attention.

At the evening session, he had us sit on the circle of sofas and watch a television talk show he had taped during the afternoon. The host was a woman named Rita McGregory. She was tall. She had auburn hair and green eyes that glimmered with delight when people asked embarrassing questions. She was probably twenty-six years old. The theme of the program focused on girls in their early teens selling sex at their schools. Their mothers were with them, lamenting about the difficulties of rearing children who were headstrong and drug-addled and obsessed with sex.

"This, gentlemen, is the world we live in," roared Carson X. "Look at this nonsense."

Rita McGregory introduced a young man, a senior in high school, who had paid to have sex with a number of willing girls, some as young as thirteen—or so he claimed. He was thin and pimple-faced and sloppily dressed in torn jeans and a tee shirt with the sleeves cut out. A tattoo of a smiling snake was baked into his arm. "Damn right," he bragged. "I done it, and I don't see that it's nobody's business." He looked at one of the mothers, an obese woman whose face was blotched from crying. "What's that old bitch butting in for, anyhow?" The "bitch" was bleeped out. He rolled his fist in the air triumphantly.

A howl went up from the audience. The mother broke into a wail. Rita pushed her hand-held microphone into the face of an indignant black woman sitting on the front row of the studio theater.

"You trash," the black woman roared. "How come you treat that girl's mama so bad?"

The young man smiled arrogantly. "What do you know about it? All you got to do is look at her. She ain't nothing but jealous. Put her beside her daughter and you got a pig up against a movie star."

"You ought to have your ass whipped," the black woman bellowed. "I got a good mind to come up there and drag you outta that chair and whip your ass."

"Fuck you," the young man said, though the "fuck" was bleeped.

The black woman leapt from her seat and lunged toward the stage, but Rita caught her arm, and two muscular security guards wearing body-fitting tee shirts advertising the show stepped in front of her and stood like a human wall. Rita's face was blazing in excitement. "No, no, we can't do that," she cooed. Then, to the young man on the stage: "And you can't use that kind of language on television."

The young man smiled. He looked at the young girl sitting beside her mother. The girl had full, puffed lips that were lacquered red. Her eyeliner was heavy and black. She looked whorish. She tipped her lips with her pierced tongue and nodded toward the lap of the young man.

"I wonder what Dr. Eleanor Ragsdale Stewart thinks about this?" Rita said to the camera. "Dr. Stewart is a distinguished psychiatrist and an advisor to young people on numerous issues.

Those of you who have watched the Rita McGregory Show will remember her from several programs. Dr. Stewart?"

The shot cut to Dr. Eleanor Ragsdale Stewart, a handsome middle-aged woman with the eyes of a model set in a face of confidence. A hint of gray, so light it could have been an illusion, coated her dark hair. A teasing smile was posed on her lips.

"Gentlemen, you are about to see one of the great abuses of my profession," Carson X. declared. "This woman is an idiot."

Carson X. was right.

Eleanor Ragsdale Stewart explored the possibility of the mother's jealousy, suggesting that the observation by the young man could have some validity. The audience booed. Eleanor Ragsdale Stewart bristled. "The reaction of this audience is precisely the problem that too many of our disadvantaged young people experience today," she said in a hissing voice. "Instead of understanding the actions of these young people, you are determined to condemn them."

"Well, good God," someone shouted, "why don't we just throw some money up there and watch 'em go at it, right here on national television?"

The audience cheered and applauded.

The young man laughed and leaned back in his chair, spreading his legs. He hunched once. "Suits me," he called out.

Again, the audience booed and yelled lustily. It was the sound of a mob becoming violent. A babble of voices fought for attention.

And Dr. Eleanor Ragsdale Stewart prevailed.

"Don't you understand?" she said to the audience. "The victim here is not only the mother, but also her daughter and this young man."

"Ho!" the black woman shouted. "She ain't nothing but a ho! They need they asses whipped!"

Rita McGregory was ecstatic. She glided to the stage, waving her arms to regain control. She smiled into the camera. "In a minute, we'll meet a fifteen-year-old who has been having sex with—among others—her classroom teachers, and, yes, I mean both male and female teachers. But, first, a word from our sponsors."

Carson X. turned off the television. He whirled to face us. "And we think we've got trouble," he cried. "Gentlemen, compared to that ridiculous Stewart woman, you are looking at a genius."

"Doc," Barkeep drawled, "compared to that little shit who has to pay thirteen year olds to get laid, you are looking at a room full of saints—sane saints."

Carson X. applauded Barkeep. "You're making progress, Barkeep," he said enthusiastically. "Now, why don't we play some games?"

And we did. We played checkers.

Checkers, not chess.

"Chess tires the brain," Carson X. declared. "Checkers frees it."

We were like old men in a reunion of a fraternity. We drank coffee—hot tea for Menlo—and we talked about baseball and antique cars, about the books we had read, about movies we had seen. Menlo insisted that talking of movies always left him with the taste of buttered popcorn in his mouth. Carson X. immediately popped popcorn and drenched it in real butter. "Dangerous living," he announced. "All that butter." The popcorn was delicious.

We talked about women, the women of Barkeep's imagination, women of the one-nighters, women of fantasy, women as strange as Miss Perfect. And we laughed. We laughed easily and often, the kind of laughter than comes from the pleasantness of friendship.

But we did not talk about the women who had sent us to Neal's Island. Carson X. had forbid it. If any of us slipped, if any of us had even the look of thinking about the woman of our obsession, Carson X. snapped his finger and intoned, "Boys, let's talk about opera." That was the code line. It meant to change the subject.

Carson X. used the code twice.

Once with Godsick, when Godsick said softly, "I once played checkers with Anna."

And once with Max, when Max turned suddenly morose and began staring at his bandaged hand.

It worked both times.

At the end of the evening, as we were sitting in the kitchen, with Miss Perfect propped against a cabinet, Carson X. told us a story:

"Once there was a man born without hands or arms," he said, "who, by the sheer power of his own will, grew them.

"He was able to do this because he finally accepted the inarguable truth—that he did not have hands or arms. And that was essential for him. From his childhood, he had accused his parents, his siblings, his friends, of a conspiracy of evil that had caused his misfortune.

"Only when he accepted his reality—that his hands and arms were not taken from him, but he had been born without them— could he rid himself of the burden of that loss, and that is when he was able to perform his miracle."

We listened quietly. The image of a man suddenly growing hands and arms was mesmerizing.

"Too few people know how to rid themselves of the burden of loss," Carson X. lectured quietly. "Too few know how to feel the touch that is healing them."

He smiled and looked at me.

"Don't you agree, Dr. Bloodworth?" he said playfully.

"Unquestionably," I said in Bloodworth's most pontifical voice.

"Do you believe the story of the armless man, Godsick?" asked Carson X.

Godsick wiggled his head. The expression on his face was solemn.

"It's true, absolutely," Carson X. said.

"Yeah, sure," Barkeep snorted.

"Oh?" Carson X. replied in challenge. "You doubt it?"

"Unless it's a lobster you're talking about, I do," Barkeep shot back.

"Is it true, Godsick?" asked Carson X. "Did the armless man grow arms and hands?"

"Yes," Godsick mumbled after a moment.

Barkeep shook his head. He looked up at Carson X. "You know this lobster?"

"Man, not lobster."

"All right. You know this man?"

Carson X. stood. He stretched his arms and hands before him. He said, "Yes, I know him. I am that man."

Barkeep snorted a short laugh. He glanced at Max and rolled his eyes.

"No, look," urged Carson X. He raised his arms and hands to the fluorescent light of the kitchen ceiling. "See how young my arms are, and my hands. They're the arms and hands of a boy. I'm that boy."

175

It might have been the light, or the hypnotic persuasion of Carson X.'s voice, but his arms and hands were younger than the rest of his body. His arms and hands were the arms and hands of a boy or a young man, as he had said. He stood gazing at them in wonder, like a child awestruck by a wondrous trinket. Then he lowered his arms and examined his hands, turning them in the light. After a moment, he said quietly, "Gentlemen, let's not stand on protocol. Please excuse yourself." He wandered away, out of the kitchen, into the back of his house, still gazing at his hands.

For a moment, none of us spoke, and then Barkeep said in a whisper, "Son of a bitch, that's spooky." A nervous smile crossed his face, and he added, "But, boys, if he could do that, he ought to grow a new pecker. Oscar ain't much to brag about."

It was meant to be funny, maybe for relief, but no one laughed. We were thinking of Carson X.'s arms and hands.

By the clock in my car, it was almost nine thirty when I returned to the cabin. The evening of play had been our longest session, and our most enjoyable one. The bonding, at least, was working, and all of us knew it. When we were together, we did not suffer the torment of depression, and though Carson X. had not said it, I think each of us knew the object of the lessons of togetherness: If it was possible to put aside the depression, even for a short time, it was possible to dismiss it altogether.

Carson X. was feeding us in sips of promise, in small, hor d'oeuvre bites of reason. We were like deep-sea divers who must be depressurized gradually after sinking into deep, dark waters in search of treasure.

Before I went into the cabin, I took a walk on the beach, picking my way along the narrow strip of sand near the stone retaining walls, and I listened to the howl of the incoming tide and watched the white caps of the waves, curling in silver strips under the clear light of the moon and stars.

I looked for Arlo.

I could hear him calling in his wind voice, *"Penny, Penny, Penny...."*

I wondered if he would visit me again in the adventure of dreaming.

There was much to ask him, much to learn.

Why had I guessed his name? Was it accident? Did something tell me his name, some presence that I did not understand?

Was it coincidence? Or was it intended, something fixed in my life from the planetary influences at the moment of my birth?

Surely Arlo would know.

Out there, in the Wherever, Arlo would have learned the truth of such mysteries.

"Penny, Penny, Penny..." the waves sighed with their salt tongues.

Dear Kalee,

A few words only—out of habit now, like reaching into my briefcase for the pills that Bloodworth prescribed for me to curb anxiety. I do not know if the pills are real, or are only placebos, but they seem to work (especially when dreams float up). And the same is true of writing to you, of touching the keys that spell your name. Do the letters help, or are the letters only placebos? And I suppose I should take that thought and ask the important question: Were you real, or were you merely a remarkable, beautiful placebo?

Tonight was a good night with the MOD Mob. We did not go on an expedition for our anxieties—at least it wasn't obvious, but I have learned that with Carson X. a mere nod of the head in greeting can be a session. Tonight we played checkers and talked and had coffee and popcorn. It reminded me of the once-a-month poker games I used to play with some of the guys at work. Just men. Men telling funny, outrageous, obscene stories. One-upmanship with no rules. Language that would cause an NFL lineman to excuse himself from the room. We had a grand time on those poker evenings because we never allowed anyone to get serious. No money was ever used. Only chips. None of us wanted the uncertainty of having our earnings wiped out by a straight flush. Nor did we want the uncomfortable feeling of winning by the sheer luck of some wild card popping up from the bottom of the deck.

On the way back from a walk on the beach tonight, I remembered the time I was at Jekyll Island for a meeting and how I longed for you to be with me. I called you. We talked for two hours. Now, at this moment, I miss you as much as I ever have, yet I know I must put away such longing. Conflict, isn't it? But if Carson X. can grow arms and hands (a story from the session tonight), then I can grow a new me, even if I can't grow a new you.

I hope Arlo returns tonight. I think I will uncap the last bottle of scotch and let its fumes spread out. Maybe he will catch a whiff and come calling. It will be good to see someone who understands.

I love you.

Your Correspondent

17

Early Morning and Afternoon of the Sixth Day

I think of it as a fold-over dream, a description given to me by Bloodworth. According to Bloodworth, a fold-over dream is one that continues a previous dream, a sequel, a pick-up from the night before. In the heaviness of sleep (and possibly at the invitation of one of Bloodworth's drugs), Arlo came again from the murky passageway of my subconscious, knocking wearily at the front door, and, again, I took myself from bed and invited him inside the cabin.

He was in a foul mood until he had his first scotch. The tide had taken its toll, he vowed.

"It's tricky out there with the tide sloshing around," he complained. "I don't care how much you think you know about things, you get careless and the tide will rip you apart." He swirled the scotch in his glass and added, "Of course, if you can put yourself back together, as I can, it helps." He looked at me and rolled his shoulders. "So, how are you?" he asked.

"Better, I think," I answered.

"Yeah, I think so, too," he said.

"I wondered if you'd been keeping watch, or eavesdropping," I replied.

He smiled and, I think, winked. His gray eyes were hard to see. "Did you like that little trick today?" he asked.

"Which one?"

"When you were going to your car. That little puff of wind."

"So, it was you. I thought so."

"I know you did," he said. "Calling my name like that. You should be more careful. If somebody hears you, they're going to think you're crazier than you actually are, if that's possible."

"I'll watch it," I replied.

"By the way, that was a touching scene with that old boy who cut his hand," he said casually. "I feel sorry for him. He's got problems. The rest of you have it easy compared to him. He might not make it."

"What do you mean?"

"He might not make it. It's that simple."

"What's going to happen to him?"

"How should I know?"

"You just said—"

Arlo lifted his hand to stop my words. "What I said was an observation, that's all. Don't read anything into it. I just think it's a toss-up with him." There was sadness in his face.

"I wish you hadn't told me," I said.

"You need to know. You need to know there are people who suffer as much as you. Or more."

I thought of Max and of the anguish in his confession—"I loved her. Goddamn it, I loved her." The blood that dripped from his hand, dripped again in a flash of memory. I could feel Max embracing me in his powerful arms.

"Hey," Arlo said gently, "you can't help him. Believe me, you can't. And you know what's tragic about that story?"

"What?"

"I would guess the girl wants him as much as he wants her, but she can't control the thing that controls her. I once knew a girl who was addicted to sex. She couldn't help it, but she wasn't a whore. No, no. That's too easy. She didn't want money. She wanted the dare. Disarm the man with a little charm, a smile, a tongue-flip, a little harmless play. Find some way to get into his bedroom—hook or crook—and then strike. She was a genius, but she also had the addiction. Your Barkeep would have loved her." Arlo paused, swallowed from the scotch, licked his lips to savor the taste.

"So, are you going to tell me about P R?" I said.

Arlo drained his scotch and thrust the glass toward me. "Do you mind? I'm a little tired."

I took the glass and poured another short scotch and handed it to him.

"Well?" I said.

"No, I'm not going to tell you," he replied easily. "Don't you know? You have to discover that one for yourself, but you will. Be patient."

It was the wrong thing to say to me, even for a ghost, dream or no dream.

I stood. "Let yourself out," I said. "I'm tired. I'm going to bed."

He closed his eyes for a moment and tilted his head backward. Then he said, "Be careful, my friend. Be careful."

I turned and went into my bedroom and slammed the door.

I could hear Arlo's voice through the wall: "See you."

Because I want to believe in magic, I want to believe that, before he left, Arlo performed a ritual of magic that only those who exist in the walking-sleep of the dead understand. I want to believe he touched me on the forehead and gave me the blessing of rest.

I slept fully, completely, without dreams of Kalee, or of Max, or Carson X., or Inga, or Arlo, or of anyone else, or of anything. I slept peacefully, wonderfully, and when I awoke my body was pleasantly relaxed.

I had coffee on the deck, deliberately near the railing with the A B, P R initials. I was no longer intrigued by the stories I had invented. Now, it was more than intrigue: I had a need to know the whole story.

I did know Arlo, of course, or at least his first name. And I knew I could snoop about and find more about him, but there would be questions about my asking, and I did not need the questions, not while cloaked in disguise myself.

Too, I was beginning to believe that Arlo was more than a dream, as I had suspected on his first visit. Arlo was real. Or ghost-real. I had found an empty scotch glass on the table, a glass I did not remember using. Yet, he had not frightened me. He had been like a restless neighbor who drops in unannounced, begging in his neighborly way for a few moments of escape from whatever, or whoever, was tormenting him in his own home. I like such people. They bring energy into a place, and when they leave, they leave some of that energy as a gesture of appreciation.

From the deck, I saw the deer. They were moving toward me, single file, with Billy the Kid in front, his antler-deformed head lifted, sending out a radar of suspicion and caution. I went into the cabin and got the apples that Inga had sold to me, and returned to the deck and broke three of them in half and tossed them into the yard. Billy the Kid stood motionless, and then he crept forward, sniffing the ground, until he found one of the half-apples and he took it into his mouth and chewed it slowly.

I watched as the other deer—Billy the Kid's family—found the apples and consumed them. They seemed content and happy.

When they finished, they moved lazily through the yard, only a few feet from my deck, but they did not seem afraid of me. The last to pass, a doe, had small, fragile legs. She paused and looked back at me and flicked her head, and I believed there was a message in that mute signal.

I wondered if it was Arlo, playing his games with me.

కా

Carson X. called at mid-morning. He said the sessions for the day had been canceled. An emergency, he said with apology. He would have to be away from Neal's Island.

"Take the day off. Relax. Go into Beaufort. I strongly recommend it. It's an interesting town," he told me cheerfully. "We're doing great. Believe me, we're far ahead of most groups that I've worked with." He apologized again and hung up.

I called Inga. She sounded as rested as I had been upon awakening. It made me wonder if Arlo had visited her also, touching her forehead with his blessing of sleep.

"You're not calling to tell me that dinner's off, are you?" she said.

"No," I replied. "In fact, I've decided to clear the day. I'm as free as the proverbial breeze. I don't suppose you can close shop for a few hours and show me around Beaufort?"

I could hear her inhale in thought. Then: "I wish I could, but the only replacement I could call on went to Savannah today to see her mother. She's in a rest home."

"My loss," I said. "Maybe another time."

"I'd enjoy that," Inga answered. "But I do have a suggestion."

"What's that?" I asked.

"I know that Sylvia's going in today. Why don't I call her and have her meet you for lunch? No one knows Beaufort better than Sylvia."

"Sounds like a shopper," I said.

Inga laughed. "Professional," she answered. "That's what happens when your father owned half of South Carolina and leaves you with more money that the bank will accept."

I tried to be clever. "Is that right? Maybe I've invited the wrong lady to dinner," I said.

There was a slight pause, a little too long, a little too quiet.

"Bad joke," I added quickly.

Inga laughed again, but with reserve. "You could be right, but I hope you don't change your mind. And now that I think about it, maybe I made a bad suggestion about Sylvia showing you around."

"Not in the least," I said. "I'd like to have lunch with someone, even if they're too rich for my blood."

"I'll make the call," Inga promised. Her voice was again relaxed. "I'll let you know."

The return call came within minutes. Sylvia, Inga reported, would be delighted to meet me. Twelve o'clock. At Gena's.

"You can't miss it," Inga assured me. "It's near the library."

"I think I upset you earlier," I said. "I apologize."

"No, you didn't upset me," she insisted. "Sylvia's my dearest friend here. She's not shy, as you will learn, but she's really a wonderful person."

"I'm sure you're right," I told her.

❧

184

The drive into Beaufort was relaxing and pleasing. On the day of my arrival at Neal's Island, the road—narrow and uneven—had bothered me.

I had not seen the beauty of the lowcountry, the majestic, primitive covering of trees and scrub bushes, the marsh fields, the wind-shimmered ribbons of water, the shrimp boats and the pleasure boats on those waters. On the drive into Beaufort, I thought of the lowcountry as a heart that pumped with an ancient, delicately balanced life.

It angered me that I had not packed my good camera. I wanted to stop and walk along the bridges and take pictures of sea gulls posing on the railings, and of the egrets riding the updrafts of wind. I wanted to pull off at the shrimp docks and wander among the boats and find the shrimp workers at work. I wanted to go into the roadside shops and find an over-priced trinket and buy it, something that had *Welcome to the Lowcountry* printed, or hand-lettered, on it. Salt and pepper shakers, perhaps. Salt and pepper shakers fashioned in the image of leaping dolphins. Or a serving platter with a scene of moss-draped trees against a background of the sea. Or a tee shirt advertising a festival.

On the drive from Neal's Island into Beaufort, I understood why Carson X. had ripped his shingle down in Miami and moved. In Miami, the heartbeat was from the music of the lounges and the wail of police sirens; on Neal's Island, it was from earth and water.

I had driven the twenty-five miles so slowly, I was late arriving at Gena's, and I found Sylvia waiting at a table. She accepted my apology with grace and insisted that I trust her with deciding the meal.

"Of course," I told her. "In fact, I enjoy being taken care of. I need it."

She laughed brightly and I realized I was slightly uncomfortable. I did not know if it was because I had teased Inga about her, or because Inga had revealed the fact of Sylvia's great wealth. People with great wealth have always made me feel a little out of place.

"Then I'll tell Inga you have a weakness," Sylvia said.

"I have lots of them," I replied. "Believe me."

At her insistence, she ordered two gin martinis and when they were delivered, she lifted her glass to me in salute. "To new friendships," she cooed.

I clicked the tip of her glass with mine. "To new friendships," I repeated. For some inexplicable reason, I thought of Kalee.

"So, do you like our little island?" asked Sylvia.

The image of Kalee faded and I remembered the view of Neal's Island from the deck of my cabin. "It's beautiful," I told her.

"Then you should buy a place and settle in with us," she replied enthusiastically. "I promise you wouldn't regret it."

"Maybe someday," I said.

"Why wait?"

"You know: things to do in other places."

"Your work?"

"Well, yes. That and other commitments."

"You're not married are you?"

I smiled at the question and wondered if it was a plant by Inga. "No," I answered. "I'm not. I used to be, but it didn't work."

"I know the story," Sylvia said. "Same with me."

"Want to talk about it?" I asked.

She giggled. "Good Lord, no."

We sat for almost two hours and talked in a wandering, easy manner of easy topics, and we had the lunch Sylvia ordered—a seafood salad created especially for us by Gena of Gena's. As we prepared to leave, I asked the waiter for the check.

"Oh, there is no check," the waiter said gladly. He turned and left.

Sylvia shrugged. "I own the place," she explained casually. "Not paying is one of my privileges."

"But—"

"No arguments," she insisted. "I love to show off. Ask Inga. She knows me well."

"I'm sure she does," I said. "And how well do you know her?"

Sylvia smiled and wagged a finger at me. "She's my friend. Gossip about friends is strictly off limits."

"That sounds serious," I said.

"And that sounds like a psychiatrist trying to worm an answer out of a helpless client," Sylvia replied. "And, trust me, I know that trick. Come on, I'm going to show you Beaufort.

18

Night of the Sixth Day

Dear Kalee,

This is awkward. And embarrassing. I beg you to forgive me.

This is not easy to write, though I know these words have no power to hurt you. How can they? You are a memory, a grand and lovely memory. The pain of you comes from the grandness of you.

All right, let me say it straight out.

Tonight I made love to another woman.

To Inga.

Please forgive me. I never thought it would happen—with Inga or with any other woman. Having loved you, how could I make love to anyone else?

Bloodworth would call it an exorcism without using the word. There were many times when he advised me to re-enter the dating game and become involved with someone. It was his theory—or conviction—that I would never learn the possibilities in other people if I did not take such chances. It was the same advice I received in countless bars from inebriated friends, but, as I've said before, the drunks offered it in more poetic language than Bloodworth.

The exorcism didn't work, Kalee. There is a difference between barroom advice and love.

Still, I needed to test myself. I needed to see if I could live without you—no, to see if I could function without you.

The truth is, I've tried. Yes, Kalee, I have. I have approached women in safe places (not bars; women in bars only want temporary adventure) and I have talked of going to dinner, or to a

188

play or a movie or a concert, and I've accepted their telephone numbers in exchange for promises of calling. Once or twice, I have called, feeling guilty. But I have never been with anyone since your death—until Inga. And that came about in such a curious way, I did not think of it as being with her, but as...I don't know...something. Something unexpected. Truthfully, I was surprised, but pleased, that being with Inga was comfortable. And, of course, it might have been made easier because I was not representing myself, but Bloodworth. Yes, that makes sense, doesn't it? I have borrowed Bloodworth's name and profession, and that provides some protection. I'm certain he would not be happy with me. Or maybe I'm wrong. Maybe he would be overjoyed.

I'm sorry. I really am. I know this is unfair of me. If the roles were reversed—if you were writing this letter, having these experiences—I would not want to know about them. I would become enraged. But this—the letter writing—is what Bloodworth said I should do. It is my medicine, Kalee, the narcotic that feeds me, other than the mind-bending pills in my briefcase. Forgive me for it. I must tell you. I must. Or, I must write it.

***

I needed to *** away before I continued. I needed to stand, to stretch my muscles, to pace the room, to shake away the guilt. I needed to think. I have this oppressive feeling that I am the sinner of sinners, that there is enough stain on me to be the Tattoo Man.

Still, I must write these words, and I will begin at the evening's beginning.

I was not ready with the dinner preparations when Inga arrived at the cabin, because Sylvia Reeves, one of Inga's friends, had kept me too long on a tour of Beaufort. (It's really a fascinating little city, a place you would have liked.) Inga was amused. I told her I'd like to get a quick shower. "Take your time," she said. I showered and dressed, and when I came out of the bedroom, Inga was on the deck, drinking a scotch from my last bottle. She had poured one for me. I apologized again for being unprepared.

"Don't think about it," she said.

But I did have a thought, Kalee: could the drink Inga handed me be doctored? Could that have been the reason for Arlo appearing in his ghost presence, instead of Bloodworth's prescription medicine? Had Inga laced the dinner wine of that first dinner with LSD or some other mind-altering chemical, and, having me under her spell, had she planted the illusion of Arlo showing up, inputting it like a program on a computer? Was she an agent of the FullLife Foundation, on a mission from Carson X?

I do not know why I had that thought, but I did. I also drank only a few sips from the scotch. We talked about her son. She had received a letter from him, asking for money. She told me about his studies. He wants to go to Europe this summer. We talked about Europe. She loves Belgium, has an acquaintance there. The way she said it—with a touch of secrecy—I thought the acquaintance was male and perhaps a once-upon-a-time, but still-thought-of lover.

She asked me casually about my lunch with Sylvia and the tour. I gave her a summary of the day, and told her that Sylvia had been gracious, as she had predicted.

"She had a good time, too," Inga said. "She called me."

"Oh," I replied. "Well, that's nice."

I could go on about the conversation, but it was only light fare—things about Beaufort (the house used in shooting "The Big Chill" and "The Great Santini," for example), the trip from and back to Neal's Island and what I had seen along the way. Light fare. Nothing unusual.

We grilled shrimp and had saffron rice and a salad and drank from the wine Inga brought (this time, a chardonnay, your wine). It was a warm, soft-breeze night, dimly moon-lit, and we took a long walk along the beach and over to Stillwater Lake. Inga showed me where Lucifer, the alligator, suns. He must be huge. The spot was deep and worn.

When we returned to the cabin, we were both relaxed and happy. It was the aura of the night, I think. And the dinner. And the scotch. And the wine.

And then the second part of the night began. The act of healing and the celebration of that act, I believed.

How can I tell you this, Kalee, without it sounding obscene, or ugly?

It wasn't. You must believe that.

It was, in a way, very lovely.

I think Inga understood that she was important, that she was needed, a priestess of the rite of exorcism.

As I closed the door to the cabin, Inga moved against me, as though something in the cabin spooked her. She did not speak. She kissed me. It was a kiss that began gently, then became a happy feeding, a strong sucking nourishment. After a moment, standing there, being filled by a single kiss, Inga stepped back and looked at me. She whispered, "I came from work. Now, it's my time to shower," and she turned and went into the bedroom, leaving the door open.

I think it is important that you understand this, Kalee—that you understand it from a man's perspective.

It is the fantasy of men to be seduced, to have a lovely woman touch them without warning, to press against them, to command

them. (If what I read in romance novels is true, it is the same
fantasy that women have about men, which must prove that we are
more alike than we care to admit.) Still, to be embarrassingly
honest, I was taken aback with Inga's boldness. She did it well.
She did it with drama, with style, with superb timing. The no-word
touch, the growing kiss, the push-away, and, last, the whisper
about the shower. It said to me, to my body, "You need me." I
wanted to leap with joy, Kalee. I wanted to click my heels and spin
around the room like Fred Astaire tap-dancing on walls. I
dropped the Bloodworth face, the on-guard Bloodworth persona. I
watched her go into the bedroom and then I went into the kitchen
and poured another scotch. My hand trembled when I heard the
water running in the shower. I knew Inga would not rush. Not
rushing is part of the beautiful tease of lovemaking.

When she came out of the bedroom, she was wearing one of
my shirts—the blue oxford I had worn to Beaufort and had left
carelessly draped across a chair in the bedroom. It was tugged to
her body, but not buttoned. She had loosened her hair from its
upsweep (I do not know the style; upsweep is how I see it). Her
hair was damp from the shower's spray—damp, but not wet. The
silver of her hair on her shoulders was stunningly sensual. The
shirt hugged her body, her nipples protruding into the cloth. The
shirt reached her thighs. I could see a strip of dark, fluffed hair at
the V of her legs. It, too, was damp.

She crossed to me, cupped my face in her hands, and softly
touched her lips to my mouth—just as the romance novels describe
it. And then she took my hand and led me into the bedroom. Oddly,
I thought she was a little frightened. It was not in the way she
acted, but in something, some aura that was like tension.

I know I should stop this now, Kalee, but I cannot. Please believe me: I must write it. I must. Don't leave me now. You will understand. I promise you will.

I must have misread the aura of Inga. She was not at all timid or ashamed. And she was not clinical or merely accommodating, as many women are (if you listen to the tales of many men). Being with her was more natural than being with anyone I have ever known, other than you. (I wish I could put my ex-wife in that company, but I can't. We were never really close sexually, which was as much my fault as hers.)

She—Inga—let the blue oxford fall from her shoulders and then she began to explore me—slowly, softly. Yes, Kalee, that is the word. That is what she did. She explored me with her fingers and with her mouth and with the nuzzled stroke of her forehead and her closed eyes, like a purring cat. She did not dictate, Kalee. I don't mean that. She gave and pulled back, gave and pulled back. It was like—well, like breathing. A rhythm. An easy rhythm. A rhythm of dancing to some new, wondrous music. When I entered her, I believed I was soaring. The rhythm quickened, the breathing became stronger, faster. We were cupped in heat—heat on us and around us and in us. And then the spasms, the roaring, tunnel-rush of the spasms, white-foamed and flying like tidewater. I closed my eyes and rested my head on the pillow. I wanted to see you leaving me. I wanted to see your face a final time. I could feel Inga riding me, slowing the rhythm—fury to rocking—and my mouth opened and I whispered your name.

Inga's body paused. It did not tense. It did not object. She leaned forward and kissed me on my eyes, then she pulled from me and went into the bathroom. I did not move. I lay on the bed, staring at the ceiling, feeling embarrassed and sad. I could hear the water running. After a few moments, Inga returned with a warm, damp cloth and handed it to me. She did not speak. She smiled, but she did not speak. She showered again and dressed and came back to the bed and sat near me. She took my hand and kissed the tips of my fingers.

"That," she said at last, "was wonderful."

I said, "I'm sorry for—"

She touched my lips to stop my words.

"That's foolish," she said. Then: "Will I see you again?"

"I would like that," I told her.

"Me, too," she said. She kissed my fingertips again, stood, looked around the room as though memorizing it, and then she walked out.

And I am sitting here, at the word-maker, with my fingers that have been kissed by another woman, touching keys that only want to speak one name.

Kalee.

Kalee.

Kalee.

I do love you.

Your Correspondent

I did not go to bed until after midnight and I did not want to dream. Dreaming was Arlo's invitation to appear and I wanted to be alone. I needed to be alone. Yet, I did dream and he did appear.

The first thing he said was, "It's Saturday." His voice had a tone of sadness. He added, "I never liked Saturdays." He sat in the straightback chair he favored.

"Why?" I asked.

"Do you have any good memory about a Saturday?" he said. "I mean, one that stands out?"

"Sleeping late," I replied.

"Yeah, I liked that, too," he admitted.

He seemed wearier than he had been on his first appearance. The light that had been a blush on him was faint and dull. I believed he was losing his energy.

He said, after a moment, "Well, you did it, didn't you?"

"Do you mean Inga?" I asked.

"Of course, I mean Inga," he whispered.

"Yes, and it was grand," I said.

He smiled weakly. "What a word—grand. You overuse it."

"All right. Great. Wonderful. Spectacular."

"Don't make more of it than it was," he said. He tipped the glass to his lips again.

We were quiet for a moment. I watched him stare at his glass. "Did you always drink a lot?" I asked.

He turned the glass in his hand, sloshing the scotch. "No. Not a lot. I don't know why I'm doing this. Maybe it's you."

"Why me?"

"I told you. You think it or write it, I know it. And you don't rest a lot. It's enough to drive a man to drink. How many words a minute can you type, anyway?"

"A lot," I said. Then: "Is that how you know about Inga— what I wrote to Kalee?"

"How else would I know?" he asked, but the question sounded hollow.

"Maybe you were watching," I said.

"Watching?" he replied. "Me? No, I didn't."

"I don't believe you," I told him.

He wagged his head from shoulder to shoulder. A look of loneliness was in his face. "You're wrong. Leave it at that." He paused and looked at me again. "I'm happy for her. She needed it. So let's leave it at that and talk about something else."

"Fine," I said. "Tell me about P R. Who is she?"

The question clearly bothered him.

"I told you: find out for yourself," he snapped.

"I don't know how to do that," I argued.

He pulled himself from the chair. "I've got to go," he said.

"Are you coming back tomorrow night?" I asked.

For a moment, he did not reply. An expression of exhaustion was on his face. And then he mumbled, "I don't know. I doubt it."

"Maybe I need you," I said. "How am I supposed to know if I've got the right answers?"

Arlo smiled a gray, fading smile. His tired eyes closed slowly again, then opened. He said, "That's kind. I like being needed. We all do. I didn't understand back then—you know, before—that someone else could need me. I know it now, but what good does that do me? I need to get on with whatever getting on means. So does she." He shook his head and sighed. "Kalee, I mean. Have you ever thought of it this way? Could be she's trying to separate from you. It's not a one-way street, you know. Maybe she's stuck in her own place, drifting around like me—not here, but some other place. Maybe you're the one that's got her tied to this in-between, not-here, not-there place. Don't you get it? Time moves on. Now is too late. It always is." He looked at me curiously. "We're a lot alike, you and I," he added. "More alike than you know, and because we're alike I can tell you one thing."

"What?" I asked.

"Let it go," he said softly. "Give it up. Leave it alone."

"What do you mean?" I said. "Kalee?"

"Of course, Kalee," he answered irritably. "She'll be fine with it. She wants you to keep bumbling about in that joke you call life. Let me shock you, my friend. She needs her freedom. I know. In fact, I'm an expert on that issue. So free her. Stop holding her back. Let her go."

"I can't," I whispered.

"You can, but you don't know it," he argued. "Maybe you never will. You won't unless you try, I know that." He looked away, across the room, and I had the eerie feeling that he was seeing something out of another time. His face was the face of a man who wants to cry, but does not.

"What is it?" I asked.

He rubbed his face as though rubbing sleep from his eyes, and then he tilted his head back against the chair. He did not speak for a moment, and then he said, "Nothing."

I snapped at him: "Don't say that. I can see it's something."

"You'll understand one day," he said. He stood and moved toward the door. He added, "I like this place."

"Will you come back?" I said. "Will you try?"

"I don't think so," he whispered. "Look, it's not easy, doing this. It's a little like pumping quarters into a parking meter to buy time." He coughed a weak laugh. "And I'm out of money." His frost eyes stayed on my face for a long moment, and then he was gone.

19

Morning of the Seventh Day

When I awoke, I could see the pewter light of morning through the window and I realized I had overslept. I rolled from bed and went into the living/dining, dining/living room, and found the almost-empty bottle of scotch. And I thought—or imagined—there was a distinct odor of the sea in the room, an odor of stale salt air.

I showered and dressed and had coffee reheated in the microwave and a glass of orange juice, and then I left the cabin for a short walk.

On the beach, the sky was again gray, and I knew it would rain before the day was over. I could see it gathering on the horizon, in the clouds of Blackbeard. The beach was deserted and desolate. A large piece of driftwood had washed ashore during the night and was lodged in the sand. It wiggled in the waves that lapped around it, like a huge black fish that had flopped to land to die in the suffocation of air. I also saw a handkerchief someone had dropped, and a beer can that had been squashed with the curl of a fist. The morning was cooler than I thought it would be. I could feel my face stinging from the breeze, and the coffee I had in the Styrofoam cup quickly became unfit to drink.

On the way back to the cabin, I saw Sylvia in the Mercedes that she drove on our tour of Beaufort. She slowed when she saw me and I thought she was going to stop, but she did not. She waved and I waved back, and then she sped away. I could see her looking back at me from the rearview mirror.

I wondered why she slowed the car, but did not stop. And then I sensed a warning from Bloodworth about being paranoid. I thought: that's what this is all about. I am on a strange journey in the ancient city of Paranoia, traveling along a narrow, dark street, crowded with narrow, dark people. The name of the street is Never Can Tell.

And then I thought: My God, I'm losing it.

There could be many reasons, many explanations, as to why Sylvia slowed her Mercedes, but did not stop.

She could have been on her way to the cabin to see me—me being Dr. Tyler Bloodworth—and she hesitated for a beat, for a fraction of a fraction of a second, and that made her unsure of an unannounced visit. I've done that sort of thing a thousand times. And it was early, and I was relieved that she did not stop. The morning session with Carson X. was at ten o'clock. I did not have time for chatter.

But why would she want to see me—me being Dr. Tyler Bloodworth? Perhaps she had need of head-shrinking counsel, and trusted me after our time together in Beaufort. It had been the case with Inga after our walk on the beach, and perhaps Inga had shared that experience with Sylvia. It's something women do, I think—pick up on the doings of other women. Men are not so attentive to what other men think or do.

Or, perhaps she wanted to warn me of Inga. Perhaps Inga had described our night together in glorious detail, and she believes that Inga is casting about for a one-way ticket off Neal's Island. And perhaps that is what Inga was doing.

Or, perhaps she was merely slowing down for a turtle that was crawling leisurely across the road. At lunch, she had talked about the turtles, about the annual crusade she supported to escort hatchlings back to the sea. She had admitted it was an affirmation that her over-indulged life was, indeed, worth something.

I wanted to laugh. I thought: This is what happens, trying to go cold turkey from Kalee. My imagination was in free-fall, hurling toward death from a thousand miles away in space. I did not know the difference between a ghost and scotch. Initials in a deck railing were driving me insane.

I thought of Bloodworth.

Go to Neal's Island, he had advised. Go write a letter, or a thousand letters, he had said. Put it down in words. Or talk it out on Neal's Island with men who might understand the agony. Say everything. Say anything. Say something.

This is something: men ache.

Carson X. was right.

Men ache.

I ached.

Carson X. had lied to us. He had given us the day off not because he had an emergency, but because he had a purpose and, I think, a yearning to prove to us—again—how unique his program could be.

A thin mist—rain that is not quite rain—was swirling when we gathered for the morning session of the seventh day. We met in the kitchen, had coffee and cheesecake that Carson X. swore he had prepared from scratch, but looked identical to the cheesecake on the dessert cart at Gena's. I made the observation aloud, forcing him to confess his deception. He took the teasing with good humor, with laughter, with exaggerations about his talents as a chef. Far superior to Menlo, he assured us.

And for the only time we had been together, Menlo took on an exaggerated black dialect. He said, "White men can't jump, white men can't dance, and white men can't cook."

We all laughed uncomfortably. He sounded like a comic from the days of vaudeville. He even did a couple of steps of the moonwalk, imitating Michael Jackson.

"Damn," Barkeep exclaimed. "Just damn."

Menlo shrugged and pushed the cheesecake aside. "This cake has no soul," he said. He added, "And not enough cream cheese."

We laughed again, but not uncomfortably. We laughed the laughter of locker rooms after a joke or clever remark. In a way not easily defined, Menlo was the most assured and well rounded of the MOD Mob, even with his strong wish to kill the woman who had caused his brother to commit suicide.

And then Carson X. excused himself.

"Relax," he said. "Enjoy. Talk about your off day. Compare notes, but don't believe anything Barkeep says. I'll be back in a few minutes."

We relaxed and enjoyed. We talked about baseball and politics and movies we had seen. Barkeep told us he had gotten into a violent argument with Buck, and that he had choked Buck until Buck confessed to philandering while he, Barkeep, slept in innocence.

"Yep," Barkeep said in mock seriousness, "the little cockroach was pulling a Zorro condom over his head and hitting every bar in town. The boy needs counseling bad. Thinks he's a hero."

Our smiles pleased him.

"You know what? I like you guys," he said easily, proudly. "I'd go to war with any of you." He turned to Max. "Especially you, Max." He wagged his head toward me. "Bloodworth, I have some doubts about, but not you, my friend. I'd take on a pissed-off King Kong with you leading the way."

Max let his smile rest, and we all understood what had happened as we watched: The bonding that Carson X. promised somehow had occurred. Because we were using pseudonyms, we were strangers still, yet we did not feel the distance of separation that strangers might feel.

When he returned to the room, none of us recognized Carson X. He was dressed in a white Panama suit with a white shirt and a bright flowered tie. He had on a white Panama hat pulled down over his forehead. The hatband was colorful, a match for his tie. Large sunglasses covered his eyes. A white beard had been pasted to his face. He had a large camera hanging around his neck, and he was holding the Talking Knife. He looked a little like a middle age Colonel Sanders.

"Jesus, God, and Mary," whispered Barkeep in disbelief. "Is that you?"

"Yes," Carson X. replied, beaming under the beard. "Do you like it?"

"What the hell are you doing now?" Barkeep said.

"It's called an object lesson," Carson X. told him. "And it's for all of you except perhaps Bloodworth. In this, Bloodworth would appear to be an innocent—at least more innocent than the rest of you. Later, you will know why."

"What's the lesson?" asked Max.

Carson X. stood very erect, like an orator pausing for a thought. "Let me begin it this way," he said. "I want to tell you something that I used to be ashamed of. When I was in your place—suffering from obsession, I mean—one of the hardest things for me to do was to pull away from the woman I wanted so badly.

"I found myself stalking her. At first, it was a series of excuses—being where I knew she would be, telling her it was merely coincidental—and then it became fanatical. I followed her car from a distance, sometimes borrowing other cars, or renting other cars. I wore disguises, such as this one. I would sit near her house, where I could see her coming and going, and I made a notebook of all her activities.

"I began to think of myself as a private detective, hired by me, to find something incriminating, something I could shove under her nose and say, 'See, I caught you.'"

He looked at us.

"This was when I was trying to learn the name of the man who was her lover," he added. "I spent a year—longer—investigating it." His voice rose and trembled. "A year of torture," he said angrily. "A year of my life given to one thing because she loved teasing me with it. With her lies, her twisted sense of humor. When I finally discovered his name, this is what she said: 'So, you finally did it. Took some time, didn't it?'"

He paused and inhaled deeply. His body rocked. He looked away. Then he said, "All of you except Bloodworth have done the same thing, haven't you? You've all stalked."

I looked at the group. Godsick nodded. Max bowed his head and gazed at the floor. Menlo's expression did not change. Barkeep grinned. "It was the only pleasure I had," he said happily. "Pure pleasure, and I did find out what she was doing, and she was doing exactly what I thought. Exactly."

ॐ

Carson X. lifted the camera from his neck and aimed it at Menlo. The camera clicked twice. "Did any of you ever take pictures of them?" he asked from behind the camera.

It was an awkward question. There was something perverted about it.

"Well?" Carson X. insisted. He turned the camera to Godsick and, again, clicked it twice. "Did you?"

"Don't aim that thing at me," warned Barkeep. "I don't like having my picture taken."

"You're in for a surprise, then," Carson X. teased. He framed Barkeep, but did not take the picture. Instead, he dropped the camera against his chest and looked at Barkeep. "Did you?" he asked again. "Did you ever take pictures of them?"

"Not me," Barkeep said. "I had a pro do it. Great stuff. Great. I've got a scrapbook full of them."

"No," Godsick whispered. "Thank God, I didn't do that. I followed her, but I didn't take any pictures."

"Same with me," Max said. "I could have, and there were times when I wish I had, but I didn't."

"I thought about it, but I didn't," Menlo confessed. "But with me, there was no reason for it. I stalked her, yes, but I had no need to uncover anything, because I knew what I needed to know. I just had a need to see it taking place." He paused, then added, "For my brother's sake."

Carson X. removed his sunglasses, folded them, and then tucked into the inside pocket of his coat. He pulled the camera from over his head and placed it on the kitchen counter. "So, only Barkeep took pictures," he said. "But each of you wanted to know what such pictures might prove, did you not?"

Menlo and Godsick and Max each nodded. Barkeep shrugged. A smug smile wrinkled across his face.

"Let's say for the sake of argument—and for the point I want to make—that each of you had a file cabinet filled with suspicious photographs, like Barkeep," Carson X. said. "I don't mean engaging in sex. I mean suspicious, the kind of thing that sends your imagination off the deep end. Do you really think such pictures prove anything? And how would you feel if the roles were reversed?"

No one answered, for we all knew there was more to the question than the question.

"Have any of you ever seen anyone who looked like me?" Carson X. continued. "I mean, recently."

We all said no.

"Ah, then, that tells me none of you are very observant," he replied. "And, frankly, gentlemen, that disappoints me. All this time, I've believed each of you to be alert, aware, and inquisitive."

He crossed the kitchen to the counter near the sink and picked up a large envelope and opened it and pulled five smaller envelopes out of it. Each had one of our names written on it in the bold ink of a broad-tipped marker. He distributed them.

"What's this?" Menlo asked.

"Open them," Carson X. instructed.

The envelopes contained photographs of us, taken the day before, on the off day. Mine were of me with Sylvia in the restaurant and in her car.

"What the hell did you do?" Barkeep asked.

"I stalked you," Carson X. answered proudly. "In this costume, which is so obvious it needs to have its own float in a parade. And none of you saw me."

"Jesus," Barkeep whispered in surprise. "How'd you manage that? We must have been all over the place."

"You were," Carson X. said in a happy voice. "But I'm good at what I do, or I don't do it."

We sat for a moment, each scanning the photographs, and then Menlo said in a bitter voice, "I don't appreciate this. My life is private, especially here, where I'm paying a small fortune to try to find some answers."

Carson X. laughed lightly. "Oh, I know you are," he said. "But this is what you're paying for, isn't it? Discovery? Am I right, Godsick?"

"Yes," Godsick mumbled. "I suppose."

"Tell us about your pictures," Carson X. urged.

Godsick fanned the photographs. "I'm in Beaufort," he said, "buying some postcards in a drug store."

"Is there one where you're talking to a woman?" Carson X. asked.

"She was just someone standing at the postcard rack," Godsick explained weakly. "She wanted to know where I'd found one of the cards I had."

Carson X. nodded. The look of glee was on his face. He turned to me. "Bloodworth, what about you?" His voice was calm, but commanding.

"All right," I confessed, "I was caught having lunch with a woman, and then with her in her car. But it was nothing more than something a friend had arranged—someone to show me around Beaufort. She was the one who introduced me to the cheesecake."

"Ah, yes," Carson X. mused. "But could it be interpreted differently? Especially with such a beautiful woman?"

There was something in his voice that made me ask, "Do you know her?"

He smiled behind the false beard. "Of course I do," he replied. "It's a small island. Now, tell me: if someone saw those photographs, is it possible they might think you were husband and wife, or lovers?"

"It's possible," I admitted.

He nodded, stroked his false beard. Then he turned to Max and Menlo and Barkeep. "Gentlemen, tell us what kind of compromising pose you were caught in."

Menlo was on the beach, talking to a woman and a small child.

The child had thrown a ball into the ocean and was crying.

Barkeep was in a bar, laughing with a waitress. "My world," he said. "She was a good lady. Kind of sad, but good."

Max was riding a bicycle. A woman cyclist dressed in a skin-tight cycling outfit was near him. From the angle the picture was taken, they appeared to be together. Max swore he did not remember seeing her.

"Gentlemen," Carson X. said, "I did what I did because I want you to know that stalking is an obsession, and obsession is a sickness, and, believe me, I speak as an expert. I can say with pride that all of you are amateurs compared to me. I may have been the world's greatest obsession maniac—until I understood the sickness of it.

"I don't have to guess with you on this. I know what you have felt, what you have believed. I know the anger, and I know that what you have seen, or imagined, is as damning as anything you've ever experienced, and I also know you can be blinded by it, make something of it totally unrealistic."

He laughed merrily and began to pace, rubbing his hands together.

"There was a night when I saw the woman I loved with another man," he said. "It was dark and I couldn't get a good look, but I did see them go into her house together. Do you know what I did when all the lights were finally turned off? I broke into her house through a window that I knew would not be latched. I knew it because I had deliberately broken the latch when she was away, when I still had a key that fit the lock. I slipped in and belly-crawled my way to her bedroom. She was in bed—alone. I slipped out. The next day, I happened to run into them. The man was her brother, for God's sake. Her brother. I knew him well, but I had been so blinded by rage, that I didn't recognize him, and I should have. Even at night, I should have recognized him. He walks with a limp."

Carson X. wagged his head. A smile spread across his face beneath his false beard.

"I want you to put away the sickness," he said quietly, gently. "I want you to know how painful that sickness can be, how it does nothing but heap hurt upon hurt." His face scanned us. "And this is what I want you to take away from today's session: All of you— including Bloodworth—are still stalking. As long as the woman who sent you here consumes you, you are stalking her, even if you are not following her around like a bloodhound. If she is the focus of your thinking, you are stalking her. If you are living by prescription drugs to hang on to your sanity, you are stalking her. If you have to attend counseling sessions, such as this one, you are stalking her. And it doesn't matter if she's the wife of Satan—as some of you have declared—or a weakling with weak habits, such as Max's Jenny, or an angel, as Bloodworth has described his Kalee, you are stalking."

I glanced at Max. He rubbed at the bandage on his hand. His face was furrowed. He seemed to be mentally repeating what Carson X. had said.

"Do you believe me?" Carson X. asked.

We exchanged glances, waiting for someone to speak.

"Do you?" Carson X. asked again. Firmly.

"Yes," I told him. "I've never thought of it as stalking, but that's what I've been doing. I've been stalking a memory."

"I think you're right," Menlo said.

Max agreed. Godsick agreed. Barkeep gazed at Carson X. as if transfixed. He did not speak.

"You, Barkeep," Cason X. said. "Do any of you have anything to say?"

"Yeah," Barkeep replied. "Part of me wants to kick your ass and get in my car and get out of here while I'm only a little bit bonkers, but part of me admires you. You remind me of me."

"Barkeep, you should see my scrapbooks," Carson X. said cheerfully. "Then you'd know how good I really am." He rubbed his hands together. "Let's have a little fun," he added. "I want to know what sort of fools you've really been. Tell us about the stupid things, and I don't mind if you embellish a bit. Match me if you can."

True or not, the stupid things rolled from the group and we found ourselves laughing again, as we had laughed at Barkeep's story of Buck.

Godsick hiding in poison ivy.

Max locking himself out of his car.

Barkeep bribing a chambermaid and hiding in the closet of the wrong hotel room with a recorder. He had waited so long, he fell asleep. Or so he said.

Even Menlo had a foolish memory and telling it eased his irritation with Carson X. "I was using binoculars," he said, "but it was a summer day, the sun was bright. I saw her going into a hotel, or thought I did, and I wanted a closer look, but I didn't get it. I forgot to take off my sunglasses when I jammed the binoculars to my eyes."

When we left Carson X.'s home at noon, we were still laughing, with good feelings from the fist bumps and high fives and embraces that had become natural with us.

≈

Inga called a few minutes after I arrived at Cabin 18.

She was chatty and friendly, saying she had called earlier, but because I did not answer she presumed I was either in the shower or on the beach. She had learned it was the beach. Sylvia had stopped at the grocery and had reported seeing me.

"Oh, yes," I told her. "I did see her. We waved."

We talked again about the tour of Beaufort. Inga informed me again that I was, in her words, "...a hit." She said Sylvia was eager to know about our dinner.

"I think she wanted to inspect me," she added. "To see if I had the look of gloom or the look of glow."

"I hope it was the latter," I said.

"That was the finding," Inga replied. "But I don't think it was what she saw on my face, as much as what she didn't see on my ears."

"What?" I asked.

"My earrings," she explained. "I always wear the same diamond earrings, little diamond dots, and I don't have them on today. I think I left them in your bathroom. Would you check?"

I checked. The earrings were in the bathroom. Against the white of the countertop I had not seen them earlier.

"I thought so," Inga said lightly. "I'll pick them up later, if that's all right."

"Of course," I said. "If you can make it around nine, I'll offer a late dinner. Something simple."

She protested, then agreed that hamburgers would be good.

"Oh, by the way," she added. "Sylvia wanted me to ask you something."

"Ask," I said.

"She wondered if you would spend a few minutes with her."

The question caught me by surprise. Everything on Neal's Island was becoming more insane by the minute. "Of course," I said. "I'd be pleased to talk to her. All she has to do is call."

"In a way, that's what I'm doing," Inga replied. "I mean, I'm doing it for her. She's a little shy about some things, and she wanted me to make sure it was all right."

It was hard to believe Sylvia Reeves would be shy about anything. Still, I said, "It's fine. She can either call, or drop by this afternoon. I'll be here."

"I'll tell her," Inga said. "I'm sure she'll just drop by."

"That's fine. Any idea what time?"

"In an hour or so, I'd guess," Inga answered. She added, "Aren't you curious about it?"

I thought about Bloodworth, how Bloodworth would handle such a question.

"I'm sure she'll tell me," I said calmly. It was a Bloodworth reply. I even used his voice—calm and smooth.

"Oh, okay," Inga replied. She sounded slightly disappointed that I had accepted a visit from Sylvia without question.

"I'll see you later," I said.

"Good. Nine?"

"Nine," I repeated.

I sat before the bay window, keeping watch for Sylvia. I had no idea what she wanted with Dr. Tyler Bloodworth, even if, in my arrogance, I had experienced the empowerment of clairvoyance when talking to Inga. I knew if I were honest, I would have to concede the only things I have ever been able to see—out of the ordinary, that is—were a few floating worm-lines of astigmatism.

∾

Dear Kalee,

Forgive me for the words that are to follow. If I knew of someone else to share them with, I would do so. I don't. Not Carson X. Not Bloodworth. Not Spence. Not the MOD Mob. Certainly not Inga.

I am dumbstruck.

Inga's friend, Sylvia Reeves, came to see me this afternoon, and this is what she wanted of me: she wanted me to feel her breasts.

Yes, that is the truth, Kalee. She wanted me to feel her breasts.

What's more, I did.

Because I didn't know what else to do.

But, please don't think of it as a come-on. It was purely clinical.

Well, mostly clinical.

You see, Sylvia believes she has a lump in her left breast that shouldn't be there, and she wanted a doctor to examine her, but not just any doctor with a white jacket and a stethoscope. She doesn't trust the locals, apparently because they are among a number of anxious and petty citizens who wish the FullLife Foundation would find other headquarters, preferably a few miles offshore, toward Europe.

I did ask her about Carson X. Why not call him?

"No," she said bluntly. "Not Carson."

I did not press her for an explanation. Her tone warned against it.

I won't go into the preliminaries with you, except to say Sylvia was apologetic for the secretive manner of making her appointment to see me. (I was right about her hesitating while in the car. She told me she had intended to stop, but lost her nerve. And she also wanted to be certain that Inga was not at the cabin.)

She said to me, "I thought about it yesterday, when we were driving around Beaufort. I knew I could trust you."

I protested that I was merely a psychiatrist, not a practicing physician.

"But you had medical training," she said. "You would know enough to advise me."

"I really think it would be best to get someone more up-to-date on procedures," I suggested.

That is when she told me about the local doctors and their snobbish attitude toward the Foundation. "I don't want them to touch me," she said firmly. "Since I started supporting the Foundation, I've been treated like a two-dollar whore. If I have to have any medical attention, I'll go to Savannah, or Charleston, or Atlanta."

Well, there you have it, Kalee.

It was a predicament.

The lump was something she had noticed only a week earlier, but she had worried about it. Her mother had died of breast cancer. *"If there's nothing to it—if it's only my imagination—then fine,"* she said. *"If it's something else, I want to know and get something done about it."*

Maybe it was the story of her mother, but I felt trapped. Finally, I said to her, *"All right, let's take a look."*

The risk was obvious. If she had ever been examined by a real doctor for a lump in her breasts—and certainly she had—she would know immediately that I was a clumsy groper, not an experienced feeler.

She disrobed quickly, without embarrassment. I tried not to stare at her breasts, but I did. She had had implants and they were wonderfully, artistically sculptured.

I said, *"When was the last time you were examined?"*

"A couple of years ago," she replied.

"Where did you feel the lump?" I asked.

"Here," she answered. She placed her finger on the side of her left breast.

I touched the spot gently, then began to knead it with my fingers. I could feel nothing but the firm sponge of implant and flesh.

When she spoke, Sylvia's voice was almost a whisper: *"Do you feel anything?"*

"Not really," I said. *" But that sort of tissue is hard to isolate by touch."* I was surprised and pleased with my selection of words. It was Bloodworth at his best.

"Would you check both breasts?" she asked.

"Of course," I said. And I did.

"You're very gentle," Sylvia said. *"Most doctors think they're working with punching bags."*

I smiled at her humor.

"What do you think?" she said.

"I don't believe there's anything to be concerned about," I answered, "but I think you should to go to Savannah in the next few days and get a second opinion. Just to be on the safe side. I'm not really supposed to do this, you know."

"Oh, I understand," Sylvia said. "I will. I promise."

"Get Inga to go with you," I advised. "Take a girl's day off together."

"I will," she said.

"I wouldn't say anything about this to Dr. Willingham when you see him," I cautioned. "I mean, not ever. He may think it's, well, unethical on my part."

"I know. I won't tell him," Sylvia assured me. "I believe in privacy."

And there we were, Kalee. Bogus doctor and half-nude woman smiling at each other awkwardly. Do you know the thought that leapt into my mind? Should I have washed my hands? That is what I thought. Doctors are always washing their hands, scrubbing up to their elbows with lye soap or something equally powerful.

"Well, I guess you should dress now," I said.

She smiled and reached for her bra and blouse. "I feel much better," she told me as she began to dress. "I'm sure it was only my imagination."

And that is why Sylvia wanted to see me. I have no idea what I will do if she discovers I am not the real Dr. Tyler Bloodworth. Plead insanity, I suppose. It wouldn't be hard to prove.

But there was one other part of Sylvia's visit that interested me. After she dressed, I poured her a cup of hot tea and we sat in the living/dining room and talked for a few minutes.

I asked if she had ever known anyone named Arlo who had stayed at the cabin.

215

Her face clouded, Kalee. I know that's a cheap expression, but that is what happened: her face clouded. She looked away. Then she said, "No, I don't think so." She hesitated, then added, "Maybe you should ask Inga."

"Inga?" I said. "Why?"

Sylvia's clouded face turned to a blush—not a blush of embarrassment, but a blush of discomfort. "Well, she knows a lot of people. Working at the grocery, she meets them when they come in to shop. That's how she met you, isn't it?"

That, of course, was true. And it was possible that she had been invited to a party at the cabin, since she had admitted to me that it was her favorite on the island.

"It's nothing important," I said. "I don't even know why I brought it up."

"Where did you come up with the name?" Sylvia asked.

I half-lied, because it seemed the right thing to do.

"It's ridiculous," I told Sylvia. "I had a dream. There was a man here. His name was Arlo. I suspect it's just professional curiosity. Are dreams merely dreams, or are dreams something else? That sort of thing." I added, "I have a colleague who specializes in dreams. I should call him."

She smiled and changed the subject. She said in a warm, sweet voice, "I really had a grand time yesterday."

"Me, too," I replied. "You were kind to put up with me."

She did not stay long after that. She thanked me for examining her breasts and said that she would like to plan a small going-away party for me, if my schedule permitted it, though she was expecting a guest in a few days. She also said she was glad Inga and I had become friends. Her eyes played across my face when she mentioned Inga. I think she was searching for a

216

confirmation, or denial, of the rumor that must have been on her tongue like sweet candy.

What do you think, Kalee?

Is Your Correspondent suddenly a worthless sex object for the cloistered women of Neal's Island? Is it my Pinaud Clubman after-shave lotion? Or is it the look of injury that hangs on my face like a clown's mask? Or is it because I am pretending to be Bloodworth? My God, Kalee, could that be it? Bloodworth? Does Bloodworth have some Machiavellian spell that he casts on women? Is he seducing them by the dozens on the deep blue sofa where I spill my guts about you?

Kalee, Kalee.

I just realized something: Bloodworth has almost taken over. Bloodworth has me dangling from puppet strings, and there's only one string he hasn't yet pulled. It's around my neck.

I am him. He. Him. He. I am Bloodworth.

Do you know how frightening that is, Kalee?

I must break away now. Inga is coming for hamburgers, and I must prepare before I leave for the evening session. Give the place a going-over with the vacuum. Check out the dishes. Scrub down the grill. Puff up the pillows on the bed. But before I do anything, I want to examine myself in the mirror. I want to see if Bloodworth's face is growing into my skin, like Carson X's arms and hands grew from his body.

I love you.

Your Correspondent

20

Night of the Seventh Day

Carson X. was in a languid, preoccupied mood, the same mood that seemed to swirl in from the Atlantic in little wisps of wind. A wandering wind, he called it as he greeted me at the front door of his home.

"It doesn't know if it wants to be a storm or a breeze," he said, and he stood in the doorway and looked out, lifting his face to test it. "A breeze, I think," he added.

We had coffee and added the outline of a body to Miss Perfect, giving her a thin waist and rounded hips. Menlo blacked in an eye patch to fit over her left eye. He called it exotic. Barkeep dotted in the navel and told a rambling story about an American woman who went to Paris on vacation and met a man named Pierre, who was, in legend, the famous French lover. Pierre's conquest of the American woman—a librarian, according to Barkeep—was obscene and foolish, as we expected it would be, but we laughed, and the laughter again pleased him. He did a little bow and strolled to the coffee pot and refilled his cup.

"Gentlemen," Carson X. said, "I'm curious about what kind of children you were, what might have happened to you along the way."

"Inner-child time?" asked Menlo.

"Something like that," Carson X. replied, "though I'm really more interested in what you actually did."

Barkeep waved his hand for attention. He said, "Doc, I'm curious about something."

Carson X. made one dip of his head, granting permission for the question.

"This going back to the cradle thing, the childhood anxieties," Barkeep continued, "all of it seems like so much bullshit to me. So, here's my question: Does it really interest you? In your soul? Deep down?"

"What a great question," Carson X. exclaimed with exaggerated delight. "No one's ever asked that of me. No one. And here's my answer: Doesn't interest me at all, but it's something of the Hippocratic Oath of psychiatry. You must ask it. I think we all took a vow signed in blood, or something as melodramatic. You simply can't disappoint a client by failing to mention it and that's why I want to talk about it today."

He tilted his head toward Barkeep. "Does that answer it?"

"Doc, you're the man," Barkeep replied. "Let's talk."

Other than admissions of trivial failures that were familiar to each of us, none of the stories—with the exception of Menlo's brush with death from a bicycle accident—were very compelling. Menlo told us he believed he had died in the accident and had been revived, but in the moments of death he had seen a light so blinding it had never totally dimmed in his vision. He called the experience "crossing over and back." He told us he often wondered if his brother had had such a moment before fingering the trigger on the gun that killed him.

To Godsick, the story was riveting. He nodded like a pecking bird throughout the telling, and the way he looked at Menlo, with veneration, gave him the appearance of a child believing that what he has heard was too wondrous to deny. His fingers danced nervously.

Barkeep argued it had been an illusion, saying Menlo never died, that the light was not a light, but the power of suggestion from stories Menlo might have heard as a child. "It's bullshit," Barkeep said. "Just bullshit. Every drunk I know has seen that light." He smiled at Menlo and added, "But I'm glad it means something to you, my friend. A little bullshit's good for a man."

Max was not sure. His grandfather had had such an experience. "It changed his life," Max vowed. "I'd heard stories of how tough, how mean my grandfather was, but after he passed over and came back—as he told it—he was the gentlest person I've ever known. He always said he was waiting to go back to the light. When he finally died and my grandmother found him, she said she'd never seen such a happy smile on his face."

I told them I believed anything was possible. And, at that moment, I did. I had spent evenings with Arlo, and—real or from dreams—Arlo was an impressive experience.

Carson X. tried to relate Menlo's encounter with death, or near-death, to our uncertainties, and our uncertainties to our obsessions, but it was a rambling, vague comparison, and he knew it. He stopped in the middle of his pacing and his lecture and he looked at us. "You know, I sound like an idiot," he said cheerfully. "And I should. That's the way I feel. Why don't we put a stop to this? It's a few minutes after eight, anyway, and I want to take a walk on the beach. Who wants to join me?"

Godsick and Menlo and Barkeep volunteered to go with Carson X.

Max declined. He said he had promised to call his sister immediately after the session.

I explained that I also had prior plans for the evening.

Carson X. did not ask what my plans included. He smiled, letting the smile linger on his face, and then he said, "Good. That's healthy."

Inga arrived at nine or what I assumed to be nine. I did not try to steal a look at her watch. She was casually dressed in green pants and a yellow blouse. She looked rested and relaxed. She was not at all hungry, she said.

"Why don't we just have a salad?" she suggested.

"That's simple," I told her. "It's already made."

We had salad and wine on the deck. We talked. We laughed. We moved inside with our plates and our wine glasses, and she insisted on rinsing the dishes and stacking them in the dishwasher. I think both of us were keenly aware of the bedroom being in such close proximity, yet we did not maneuver to slip through the door and fall across the bed in the blindness of passion. The talking had become easy and relaxing.

We poured more wine and again wandered onto the deck to sit in the breeze, which was cool, but not cold. In the distance, we saw lightning. The rain that had been building over the ocean was blowing in, moving like one of Sylvia's sea turtles waddling across the beach. I could feel the pleasant numbing of the wine spreading through me.

"Oh, I meant to tell you earlier, but I forgot," Inga said. "Sylvia was really pleased with the examination you gave her. She was getting worried. I told her it was probably nothing."

I laughed and said jokingly, "She's well endowed." Then I realized it was something I would have said, but not Bloodworth. I apologized: "I'm sorry. That was crude."

Inga smiled easily. "Men," she said in mock disgust, then she added, "But you're right. They're very nice."

I was surprised. I had never heard a woman speak about another woman's breasts with admiration. I asked, "How do you know?"

"Oh, sometimes we get in her hot tub together," Inga said. She looked at me. The smile had moved to her eyes.

"Well, maybe there's something you want to tell me," I suggested, trying to be clever.

"No," Inga replied. "I'm just being honest with you." She placed her glass on the railing of the deck and stretched out in the lounge chair. "I don't think women have the same inhibitions as men," she said. "It's something I learned from the Foundation. We have to be indoctrinated to have the burden of shame. But I'm sure you know that. You must have had more than your share of distressed women worried over something that shames them."

"What do you mean?" I asked.

"In your practice," Inga said. She reached for my hand. Her fingers were warm. She began to knead my thumb gently. "I don't think you talk a lot about stress in your—private encounters."

I could feel a flutter of excitement. Kalee used to do the same thing. Say something that would be perfectly innocent, but not innocent. Men might be more inhibited, but they love such teasing.

"I have a colleague who never makes love on a sofa," I told her, "and the reason is simple. 'Keep the stress on the couch and the sex in the bed,' is the way he puts it. I don't disagree with him." It was something Bloodworth had sarcastically suggested to me in one of our sessions after I had sarcastically suggested to him that his deep blue sofa would be a perfect place for him to bed his lonely and distraught female clients.

I heard a small, agreeing sound from Inga. Not a word, but a sound. She was still holding my hand, still kneading my thumb.

She turned her face to look out at the night. A strobe of lightning blinked over the ocean.

"I like it here," she said softly.

"Me, too," I replied.

"I didn't think I'd get used to it when I moved here—being alone on an island—but I really never missed the city. Being alone isn't so bad."

"No, it isn't," I said. Then I added, "But I do like company." I squeezed her hand as a signal. "You especially. I think I could do without Arlo."

Her hand jerked, like the involuntary twitch of a muscle.

"Are you all right?" I asked.

She tugged her hand away from me. "Yes," she said. "Just a chill." She pulled her knees up on the lounge chair and wrapped her arms around them. "Who's Arlo?" she whispered after a moment.

"A local ghost," I said. "He's been popping up this week."

I could barely hear her question: "How do you know that's his name?"

"Because I am a reader of initials," I said playfully.

She looked at me quizzically.

"On the railing," I explained. "I found some initials—A B and P R—and I gave them names: Arlo Bowers and Penny Rymer. It's something I've done since I was a child, every time I see initials. It's a little game. I give names to the initials and then make up stories about them. But I must have been close this time. Arlo's been showing up. I'm sure it's just a dream, but with all the stories you hear about ghosts on this island, the mind plays tricks."

She reached for her wine. I could see her hand tremble.

"I'm scaring you," I said. "I'm sorry."

She shook her head.

223

"I told Sylvia about it this afternoon," I added. "I asked if she knew of anyone named Arlo who might have stayed here. She said she didn't, but maybe you would. Do you?"

Again, she shook her head. "No," she mumbled.

"It's nothing," I said. "Like I told Sylvia, I was just curious, that's all."

A few drops of rain began to fall across the roof of the deck and I took Inga by the hand and led her inside the cabin. She sat on the sofa, breathing hard.

I asked if I could get anything for her.

"No," she said. "No, thank you. I'm fine." She tried a smile that failed. A brilliant strike of lightning flashed nearby. Thunder exploded.

She stood quickly. "I think I should go, before the storm really hits," she added.

"I think it already has," I said.

"No, it's just started. I really should be leaving," she replied nervously. "I think I left some windows open." She embraced me, whispered a thank you for the evening, then pushed from me and picked up her purse from the coffee table and rushed away. I watched from the bay window as her car sped down the road.

Because I was a little inebriated, I was confused.

One thing I did know, however: Inga knew Arlo, and that is what Sylvia was telling me. Inga knew Arlo and only Inga should talk about Arlo.

Though it was late, I called Sylvia. I knew the call disturbed her. I could hear it in her voice.

"Hi," she said, trying to be chatty, trying to escape the question she knew I would ask. "How are you?"

"I've had too much to drink," I told her, "and I'm a little baffled about something. You know about Arlo, don't you?"

There was a pause. I could hear her breathing.

"A little," she replied lightly. "Not much at all, really. Why?"

"Because I just frightened Inga, talking about him," I said.

The pause was even longer, the breathing deeper. "Oh," she said, "then, of course, I understand why you called. Why don't we talk about it tomorrow? Could you do that?"

"I'm not wrong, am I?" I said.

"No, no, of course not," Sylvia replied quickly. "We'll go over it tomorrow. I have company at the moment."

"Tomorrow, then," I said.

"Great. I'll call you," she cooed, then hung up.

I wondered if Sylvia would usher her guest out the door and then fly away in her Mercedes to Inga to compare stories, to make plans. Inga knew about Arlo, and Sylvia knew about Arlo, and Inga knew that Sylvia knew, and Sylvia knew that Inga knew. It was a conspiracy worthy of the ancient Greeks, a tangled web that would have sent Barkeep into a rage about the seductive, manipulative power of women—the venom from Eden's snake, as he had blathered in one of his diatribes against Godsick's forgiving nature.

I took the bottle of scotch and sat and waited in the dark of my cabin for Arlo.

Arlo would know the answers to my questions, I thought. Arlo would know and he would tell me. We were men. In a fight, men would not play games. In a fight, men bonded. Bonding was the only good thing ever to come out of wars, and Arlo and I were in a war.

But Arlo did not appear.

Or would not.

Or could not.

In early morning, still dark, I staggered outside into the cold of the rain and the howl of the wind, and I made my way to the beach, holding onto the bottle of scotch, or what was left of it. I was sure Arlo would want the last drink.

I shouted, "Arlo, come on! It's almost gone!"

Waves lashed at me, stinging my feet. Rain beat against my face. The light over the ocean was the color of dark pewter. Streak lightning arched from cloud to cloud like the ripping of a cloth.

And then I saw Arlo.

He was bobbing in the water, or the water was bobbing around him. The water was at his chest.

I called to him, "Swim, Arlo, swim!"

He lifted his hand in a weak salute.

"Swim, Arlo, swim!" I bellowed.

A wave lifted him and dropped him. The water was under his shoulders. He began drifting in the current and I ran along the beach to follow him.

"It's Inga," I screamed. "She knows the answer! Is it Inga?"

He did not answer. He raised his hand again, held it in the air. A spit of lightning hurled across the sky from distant thundercaps, and I could see the dull white of his face and the dark pits of his eyes. Then a wave rose over him and when the wave crashed back down, he was no longer there.

I ran a few steps into the ocean. The water was brutally cold. It slapped me with the opened palm of its curling tips and drove me back.

I called Arlo's name.

But Arlo was gone—if a ghost can ever be gone.

I was sure he was trying to tell me something—there, at the last, with his hand. He was trying to tell me that I was right.

I felt suddenly lonely. I knew intuitively I would never again see Arlo.

I put the scotch bottle in the edge of the water and watched it inch its way into the ocean. Twenty feet out, it disappeared. I believed Arlo had taken it.

21

Morning of the Eighth Day

Dear Kalee,

Good morning.

No, that is not the truth. Not for me.

It is not a good morning. I ache.

You will remember the boast I made before—that I always rebound, lively and alert, from excessive drinking, that God, in his forgiveness, empowers me with such abundant energy that I see clearly the error of my ways.

God must be angry with Your Correspondent this morning.

And I don't blame him.

I did not bounce from bed, Kalee. I awoke with a slight headache and a rash on my chest. The rash is either from the sand and salt water of last night, or my insanity is now beginning to manifest itself in red spots, or maybe Inga had some transmittable infection that she has left on me like a cruel calling card. I hope it's the salt water.

I have had toast, bacon, eggs, coffee, orange juice, and aspirin. I have showered and put cortisone cream on my rash. (I really think the rash is nothing more than sand scratches—from falling like the reeling drunk that I was. I deserve them.)

The storm that passed through during the night left the skies clear and bright. I have not been to the beach, but I did go onto the deck with my coffee and visited with A B and P R. The air was cool and it reminded me that I love the autumn.

I also spent a few minutes scanning the pages I have already written to you, and I'm amazed at how a few innocent letters, written on command from Bloodworth, have become a horror story, a runaway of thousands of words. To be honest, I think my obsession for you is now something of a cancer, and is spreading to my entire environment in a wild rush to consume whatever is left of me that is healthy. Obsession begets obsession, the lesson Carson X. is trying to impart to us.

For example, I am now obsessed with Arlo, because I am becoming convinced that my dreams of him were dreams only in part. Something else has been present. His ghost? I don't know. In my fancy of things, I believe it truly was Arlo, or Arlo's spirit—Arlo, hanging around, waiting for someone (me) to come along and take the burden of dying away from him. It reminds me of a lecture our track coach performed in high school: "Life, boys, is a four-hundred relay. You got to run your ass off and make damn sure you hand that baton off to somebody else without dropping it, and, I got to tell you, that baton don't look heavy, but, ladies, it weighs a ton when you got to carry it with somebody about to run up your ass."

Dreams, Kalee? Maybe. Maybe it's being with the MOD Mob and having my imagination go wild. Listening to Barkeep and Godsick and Menlo and Max, I've certainly become more aware of what an unleashed imagination can do. Still, I would swear that I saw Arlo in the ocean last night, but I had been drinking, and I do know that drunks see things that aren't there. I can't discount that. I just know that my sleeping and my waking moments have been more vivid in the past few days than at any period of my life.

Inga is key to this. She is part of the obsession—not the consuming obsession as with you, but there still. I'm sure that before the day is over, I will know more about Inga, but at this moment, I don't want to see her, or think of her. I had rather spend time with you. (I mean that literally, of course, but in the absence of the literal, physical you, I will take the figurative you, the you that looks at me from the greenish-gray of the laptop screen before me.)

I've also experienced the unsettling sensation of being suspended in time—of completely removing myself from the world. I have no idea what has taken place since last week. Has another foreign country fallen to free enterprise? Has America survived free enterprise? Have more airplanes dropped from the skies to plow into skyscrapers? Have hostages been taken or freed? Has another assassin's bullet penetrated another good heart? How many children have been slaughtered in senseless drive-by shootings? How many have died of starvation in one of those Third World countries scorched by drought and brutalized by armed killers? What in hell is going on in the Middle East? The Far East? The Northeast? The Southeast? How many more people have become homeless? Did California fall into the ocean yet? Did Spence lose the McMahon account with me not being there to smooth the feathers of old man William A. McMahon?

I do not know the answers to any of these questions, Kalee, and, bluntly, I have not worried about them. I have dedicated this time on Neal's Island to my survival, and I have almost mucked up that small task—if survival is, indeed, a small task.

The telephone is ringing. I will not answer. It is Inga, or Sylvia, possibly Bloodworth, or maybe Carson X. I do not want to talk to anyone at the moment. I will lift my fingers from these keys and wait it out.

There. It stopped.

Am I getting paranoid?

Yes, I am.

Perhaps the prescription drugs Bloodworth ordered for me are now working as a poison that has washed into my brain from the blood troughs of my body. It could be that—the red pills and the green pills not happy with their mixing, and the white pills and the orange pills aggravating the situation.

The dreams are particularly disturbing—and if I include Arlo as merely a dream, then you may upgrade disturbing to frightening.

And of dreams, there's one especially haunting. It comes always unexpected, always announced by a white-hot flash that temporarily blinds me, even if I am asleep and my eyes are closed. After the flash, I am standing off the highway, at the spot where you died.

I wish I did not dream of your death-place, Kalee. If I thought it would help, I would drive a white cross into the ground where your car left the road, one with your name carved into it, and I would leave flowers there regularly, as Joe DiMaggio did for Marilyn Monroe—or so goes the story. I see those crosses everywhere. Gaudy plastic flowers are draped over the arms like fake stoles over the shoulders of trashy women.

Each time I have that dream, Kalee, I hear this music: "I can't live if living is without you. . ." Mariah Carey. Remember? We danced to her voice in Savannah.

Silly? Yes, okay.

The music plays and I sing the lyrics, and the lyrics lodge in my throat.

We do cling to songs that bleed, don't we?

But what is that old Chinese proverb? A song of sorrow cannot take the place of weeping.

I like that. I do.

One night, out of that dream, you stood before me and you were pregnant, and you were smiling at me and you whispered one word: "Yes." And your face became round and tender, and you crossed your arms over your breasts in an embrace. In that moment, you became the mother you had always wanted to be, far back in time. It is eerie about women and their children. How they know things. I have heard women say they knew the exact second they became pregnant, as though the sperm that wiggled through the egg's pinkish membrane wall—its fishtail flipping like salmon leaping a waterfall—spoke to them in a telepathic voice. I do not doubt them. If women are stronger than men, and you have taught me that they must be, it is because they can hear sperm voices, and when they do, their bodies shudder a little.

(An aside here. That poetic claim of instantly knowing about pregnancy isn't always true. I know a woman who proudly made such a boast, yet it was a cover-up. She was already pregnant by an unknown contributor when she planned a weekend trip to a motel with her unsuspecting husband. He told me about it on a night of sadness, the kind of night that men have when they are overwhelmed and need a friend who's willing to listen to words of pain. He told me he was suspicious from her first words of the morning—"I'm pregnant." Said it was not so much a sharing of joy, but an announcement of relief. The child of that illicit union had no resemblance to my friend at all. Not at birth. Not as a child. Not as an adult.)

Still, I saw you pregnant in my dream, Kalee. You were beautiful. Women are always beautiful when they are pregnant. There is a butterfly of joy across their eyes and the bridge of their nose. The spreading wings reflect light, like a transparent silk cloth. Dear God, you were beautiful.

When I awoke from that dream, on that night, it was with that image of you, and I remembered the night we talked about having children. It was the same night you said you would marry me.

232

I think about that now, and the loveliness of it is so painful I can feel the blood bubbling in my mouth. If I saw you, if I saw how beautiful you would be with your butterfly, I would shatter.

I do love you. I do.

   Your Correspondent

After I finished the letter to Kalee and printed it, I took the throwaway camera I had purchased in Beaufort and made pictures of the A B and P R initials. I wanted the pictures to prove to Bloodworth that I was not lying, but I did not want to break my vow to him that I would not touch my cell phone during my time on Neal's Island. Not using the cell phone with its amazingly good camera, was, in my thinking, an act of allegiance that should earn high praise from Bloodworth.

I also hid from Inga and Sylvia.

I saw Sylvia's Mercedes from the bay window, and I quickly locked the doors and ducked into the closet in the living/dining, dining/living room. They knocked at the front door and I was sure they peered into the windows, and then they went to the back door and knocked. I could hear their voices, but I could not understand what they were saying. After a few minutes, they left. I sat in the closet and tried to imagine them. They would wonder about my car being in the driveway, but that would be easy enough to explain. I would tell them that I was on a walk, that I had seen Sylvia's car from the distance as it was leaving.

It would be a good, convenient, believable lie.

I did not want to see Inga and Sylvia. Not then. Not so early in the morning.

233

But I did want to talk to Bloodworth, and I called him. He was at his home, and I apologized for the intrusion, though my call did not seem to annoy him.

"It's fine," he said lightly.

"You're not busy?" I asked.

"Just sitting here trying to forget that I know you," Bloodworth replied. I thought he chuckled, but, if he did, it was too slight for a phone echo. "And you?" he asked. "What about you?"

"Holding on," I said.

"I assume that's positive news," he said, and then he told me he had tried to call me the day I was out with Sylvia, which was probably the truth since he does not have the liar's gift for instant story.

"Tell me what you've been doing," he said.

I wanted to report that I had rubbed Sylvia's breasts in the name of medicine (and, for that matter, in his name), and that I was having friendly, if not stimulating conversations with my penis, but I did not. He would not have appreciated the humor in either comment.

"I write a few lines a day," I said.

"Good, good," Bloodworth muttered. "Just take your time. Whatever you're feeling, or thinking, put it down. If you want to send me a few pages, fine. If not, we'll go over it when you get back."

I thought: A few pages? If I dumped what I had written on Bloodworth's desk, he would faint.

"Okay," I said.

"Keep working at it," he advised.

"Sure," I mumbled.

"See you in a few days," he said.

"A few days," I repeated.

When I put down the receiver, the telephone rang instantly, as though the ring was hiding in the palm of my hand.

It was Inga. She said she and Sylvia wanted to see me.

"I called earlier and we even drove by, but you must have been out," she told me.

I lied, as I had planned. "I took a long walk. I thought I saw Sylvia's car from the distance."

"We just missed you, then," Inga said. "Is it all right if we come over?"

"Of course," I replied. "I've got some coffee brewing."

"Good," Inga said. She sounded as though she needed the coffee.

I sat by the phone, wondering why Inga and Sylvia were on their way to see me, though I intuitively believed it had to do with A B and P R. When I last saw Arlo, before the ocean swallowed him, he was not waving goodbye; he was giving me the high sign, the you-got-it-right signal that men use when communicating sudden revelations. Inga knew the truth. That was what Arlo was telling me.

I could use the word anxious for the atmosphere when Inga and Sylvia entered the cabin. It is not exactly the right word, but it is close. Inga especially appeared to be indecisive and a little awkward.

Sylvia tried to be pleasant. She said, "I hope we're not interrupting anything important."

"Not at all," I assured her.

"Good," she said. She looked at Inga and they exchanged a glance that writers of fiction describe as knowing.

"I smell coffee," Inga said.

"Please sit," I told her. "I'll get some."

"That's all right, I'll do it," Inga insisted. She walked away to the kitchen and Sylvia sat on the sofa.

I sat in the armchair.

"I do want to apologize for my behavior last night," I said to Sylvia. "I hate those kinds of calls. And, certainly, I don't endorse such behavior."

"Oh, forget it," Sylvia replied cheerfully.

Inga brought the coffee to us, and then she sat on the sofa with Sylvia. There was a pause, a thick silence, a kind of deadness in the room.

"We—we need to explain something, Tyler," Inga said.

"Yes?"

"About Arlo," Sylvia added easily.

I had a pleasing sensation of being smug. Not arrogant, but smug. I knew I had been right.

I said to them, "You did know him, didn't you?"

"Yes," Sylvia whispered. She looked at Inga, and then she said, "Well, that's not exactly true. I only know about him, but there are times when I think I knew him."

"Could we go outside, on the deck?" Inga said quickly.

"Sure," I replied. "It's nice out."

"Yes it is," Sylvia agreed.

We took our coffee and went onto the deck. The day was bright and the air comfortably warm. Sylvia and I sat in the lounge chairs. Inga did not sit. She leaned against the railing, near A B and P R. Her eyes locked on the initials. It was as though she wanted to say something but was unsure of the words.

"Do you want me to tell?" Sylvia asked gently.

Inga shook her head. She kept staring at the initials. Then she reached out and traced them with her fingertip.

I wanted to ask her what the initials meant. I did not. To ask would have been a question from me, the real me, and not from Bloodworth. Bloodworth would burn in hell before he would show impatience.

"You are right," Inga said quietly. "His name was Arlo." She paused, then continued. "Arlo Boyd."

"Not Bowers?" I asked.

"No. Boyd," Inga answered.

"And P R?" I said, trying to keep my voice even and controlled. "Who is P R?"

Inga turned her face to me. She said, "I am."

I could feel an awkward smile building on my face, an expression of disbelief.

"I am," Inga said again, stiffly. She looked to Sylvia for help.

"She is," Sylvia said.

"The P used to be an I," Inga said in a rush of words. "And the R was a P. P R used to be I P. I changed them after Arlo—after Arlo left. The person you think of as Penny Rymer is me."

I leaned toward the initials and studied them, and I thought: My God, it could be. I had not noticed before, but the looped O at the top of the P was different. Not cut as deep, or as prominent. And the leg on the R was also different.

"I'm confused," I said. "You told me that Evan was the name of the man who left you."

Inga looked away. I could see that her breathing was labored.

"Evan is the name we selected," Sylvia said. "We made it up. Evan is Arlo."

"And what happened to him?" I asked.

"He died in the ocean," Inga answered, still turned away.

I was shocked. Stunned. In my God-playing game, I had played with the truth. It was as though the truth were in the ether, residing in the cabin, and it had entered me like some grateful spirit liberated from a cast-away place of darkness.

Inga moved from the railing and went to the steps of the deck leading to the ground. She said, "I think I'll take a walk."

"That would be good," Sylvia said quickly. She nodded to me. "Don't you think so, Tyler?"

"Yes," I said. "Do you want me to go with you?"

Inga shook her head and walked down the steps and across the backyard, and then around the house.

"It's all right," Sylvia said after a moment. "We sort of planned it this way. For the two of us to be alone."

"Why?"

"Because I think you need to know some things about Inga, and about me," she answered. "You must wonder why we share this."

"I do," I admitted.

What she told me was sad.

Arlo's death was as I had imagined it—exactly. Arlo being playful. Arlo being exuberant. Arlo being foolish.

"Do you know what's so painful about it?" Sylvia said softly. "Things were so right for them, for both of them. I read a letter he once wrote to her. In it, he said he had never believed it was possible to love someone as deeply as he loved her. There was a line that I'll always remember: 'How can I be so filled with someone else and still have room for me?'"

Sylvia smiled and touched her fingers to her lips, as though feeling for the words she had repeated from Arlo's letter.

"Can you tell me of a better way to describe love?" she whispered.

"Why does she stay here?" I asked.

"The Foundation's here," Sylvia answered. "It's important to her."

"Does she believe Arlo's spirit came to see me?"

"She doesn't have to believe," Sylvia replied. "She knows it. She's never seen him, as you say you have, but she has sensed him. Many times. We've talked about it a lot." She arched her eyes over a smile. "This is an island of ghosts, you know—If you believe the stories."

"But I wonder why I could see him, and she couldn't," I said.

"Maybe he wanted you to," Sylvia answered calmly.

"Why, for God's sake?"

"You were with her, weren't you?" Sylvia said. Her eyes played over my face, watching for the reply. She added, "The first man since him, by the way. At least the first I know of. And here, in their cabin. I don't think she meant it to be, but it was a test."

"Did you believe her when she said she sensed him?" I asked.

Sylvia shook her head. "No. And I really don't believe you. I think imagination got the best of both of you. This whole ghost thing is nothing more than a tourist trap, to be honest. The seed was planted a long time ago by rumors of the ghost of Jeremiah Neal haunting the lighthouse, and every Chamber of Commerce bigwig since has added to it. It's the industry of Neal's Island—'Come, live among the spirits.' My God, one hysterical woman swore she saw the ghost of Jimmy Hoffa here."

"You think it's a put-on? All of it?"

She cocked her head curiously and studied me. "Yes. And maybe I'm wrong. Maybe Jimmy is here. Maybe he's organizing a ghost union. And maybe Arlo is floating out there in the ocean, having his back massaged by an octopus with a gentle touch. I don't know, and it doesn't bother me. Carson is a great believer, but Carson is as much hypnotist as physician and he's hypnotized himself into believing. He once told me he looked forward to death so he could frolic with his friends. I haven't been as fortunate as you and Inga and Carson, I suppose. If it happens to me, I'm sure I'll be convinced, and I'll probably become a raving lunatic about it. Until then, I don't know, and I don't think about it."

I asked, "Where did you meet Inga?"

"On the beach, at night," Sylvia answered. "It was a full moon. I was walking, as I often do when the moon is bright, and I saw her sitting on the sand, facing the ocean. I had never met her. Had no idea who she was. A drunk, I thought. Maybe a druggie. We get them occasionally. Runaways with temporary Sugar Daddies, and when the Sugar Daddy uses them up, they move on and leave the girl behind. Anyway, I went to check on her because I was afraid of her being pulled out to sea, and she looked up at me and smiled a very sweet smile and she said, 'I'm waiting for Arlo.' Of course, I knew the name because of the gossip, and I knew she had to be the woman involved with him." She paused, then added, "I also knew enough about hallucination to know what was happening to her."

I wanted to cry out. I knew the feeling well—the damnable hallucination of being lost.

Sylvia took Inga home with her, and then to Carson X. and the FullLife Foundation. The FullLife Foundation saved her, Sylvia said. Unlike me, Inga had not come purposely to Neal's Island to be made whole at a seminar conducted by the man who had founded the FullLife Foundation; the FullLife Foundation had found her on a beach and the FullLife Foundation had rescued her.

I asked a lot of questions of Sylvia, and to her credit, she answered them honestly, without hesitation.

I especially wanted to understand why Inga had ever returned to the cabin, if it contained such memories of horror for her. Before me, I mean. Two years earlier, when it all happened, when Arlo took his late show-off stroll into the lashing waters of the Atlantic and never returned. I wanted to know because I was not sure if I had the courage to return to the places Kalee and I had shared—to the field of grain, to the restaurants and the motels, to the parks. When I saw them—those places of memory—I ached.

The answer, Sylvia insisted, was Carson X. Willingham and the FullLife Foundation—the healer being in the injured. Inga had to understand that Arlo's death was not her responsibility, or her fault. She was not guilty. To end her punishment she had to do what Bloodworth was always advising me to do—face the facts, deal with the truth. With that as her goal, she moved permanently to Neal's Island, and she and Sylvia began to return to the cabin. Every day they returned. Walked the grounds, then went onto the deck, and then into the house, into the rooms. They touched the walls, the furniture, the bed where Inga had made love to me, and to Arlo. They rented the cabin for a party. Eventually, Inga could go to the cabin alone and bear the sorrow.

The only dishonesty—if it could be called that—was the story of Evan.

"The little story about Evan was not meant for Inga to deceive herself," Sylvia explained. "It was meant to satisfy people—people such as yourself—if a question of the past came up. It was—is—important for Inga to accept the truth, but that truth doesn't have to drive people away from her."

"But isn't that dishonest?" I said.

"Yes, and no," Sylvia answered. She looked at me for a long, satisfying pause, then added, "Don't we all tell gentle lies? Small ones? If we told the absolute truth at every moment, or what we believed to be the truth, wouldn't the embarrassment be unbearable?"

I tried to find my Bloodworth voice. It wasn't there. I mumbled, "Perhaps."

Sylvia had moved from her chair to sit-lean against the railing as we talked. She watched attentively for Inga, but Inga was not in sight.

"I think," she said, "that you should go find her now. Talk to her. How you respond to her will be important, but I think you know that."

"Tell me how much Dr. Willingham knows about this," I said.

A pretty smile played teasingly on her lips. "Don't worry, he doesn't know anything about this week, about the initials, or about you and Inga."

"How do you know?" I said.

"He was with me when you called. If he knew, he would have told me, because he always asks about her," she replied confidently. She added, "The Foundation does get a sizable amount of my money."

"Are you going to tell him?" I asked.

"Why should I?" she answered.

"You don't tell him everything?" I said. "Someone who means that much to you?"

Sylvia did what women often do when they are sure of themselves: she groomed. She moved from the railing and used her hands to iron down the sleeves of the sweater she was wearing. Then she said, "No, I don't tell him, or anyone, everything." The smile came back to her lips. "I told you that before." She paused. "I wouldn't tell Inga that I find you extremely sexy, and I wouldn't tell her that you're not a doctor."

I knew it couldn't last. I knew one of them would discover me. Strangely, it was a relief.

"How did you know?" I asked.

"The way you touched my breasts. It wasn't the touch of a doctor. And if you ever do it again, you should know something: when doctors examine a woman's breasts, the woman is in a reclining position, or she lifts her hands above her head."

I could feel a blush rising in my face.

"Remember what I said about absolute truth and embarrassment?" Sylvia said. "I couldn't tell you when you were examining me, but I can now: frankly, I liked it. I shouldn't have, but I did. Or maybe you knew that."

She reached her hand to touch my face.

"You're blushing," she said easily. "That's nice. You're a good man, whoever you are."

"I'll tell Inga," I said.

"That's your decision," Sylvia replied. "I won't say anything to her, or to Carson, unless it becomes necessary. It might surprise you, but I really do believe in privacy. Now, I think I should go."

I stood. She embraced me.

"Be gentle with her," she urged. "She's a very good person. You can help each other, I think."

"Maybe," I said. Then: "Are you really her friend?"

Sylvia's face brightened. She said, "I'm everyone's friend, but I'm still me. I try not to fool myself."

She turned to leave, then turned back. She asked, "Who are you, anyway?"

I answered, "I don't know. I really don't."

A small, agreeing sigh slipped from her mouth. She said, "I think that's the truth. I think you're an escaped person, hiding in someone else's borrowed name—Tyler Bloodworth. He's your doctor, isn't he? And you're here with Carson's seminar."

I nodded.

"Then there's something else I should tell you," she said. "When I came to see you, to have my breasts examined, I thought you really were a doctor. It never occurred to me you were with Carson's group, not staying here, in this cabin. It's never been used by anyone attending one of his sessions. The cabins used for the seminars are on the other side of the island. When I realized you weren't who you said you were, it didn't frighten me. It intrigued me. It still does." Her eyes flashed. She added, "Isn't it strange how things like that happen?"

I walked with Sylvia to her car and watched her drive away. She was, I decided, a complex woman, far more complex than Carson X. and probably smarter. Carson X. may exert influence over other devotees to the FullLife Foundation, but Sylvia Reeves was not one of them. Sylvia Reeves would have him on a leash that she manipulated with such unseen guile, he would never feel the tug.

I found Inga on the beach.

She was standing very still, as in a pose, her arms folded in a body hug. She was staring at the ocean, at the incessant slapping of water against the sandbar of the beach. When I approached, she turned her face to me and smiled like a child.

"Are you all right?" I asked.

She nodded, and then looked back at the ocean. She said, "He's out there, isn't he?"

"Yes," I answered. "I think he is."

"Did you like him?"

"Yes, I did," I told her. "I think he must have been a little mischievous."

A quick shudder rippled across her shoulders. A smile again flowed in her face. "Yes, he was. He enjoyed life."

"You told me Evan was a lawyer," I said. "I don't believe that was Arlo's profession. Not the man I met."

Inga shook her head. "No, he wasn't. He worked for an advertising firm."

A chill—ice, fear, something—shot through me. I had not told her that advertising was part of my make-believe about Arlo of the initials. The queasiness of guilt, of shame, bubbled in my throat.

"I think it's strange—about the initials, I mean," she whispered. "How you guessed it."

"Maybe it wasn't a guess," I suggested. "Maybe there is something—I don't know what, but something—to psychic power. Who knows?"

"Want to take a walk?" she asked.

"Sure."

We walked for a long time. I did not ask Inga to tell me about Arlo, but she did because she wanted to correct the fable she had told me earlier about Evan. There was nothing about Evan that equaled Arlo, which had made the deception easier for Inga. Hiding behind truth is not easy; truth can be as thin as a scratch. As we walked, I thought of the irony of our being together—two deceivers using tales of deceit as shields. Yet, Inga was more honest than I; she was no longer hiding.

I could relate the story Inga shared—recreate the dialogue and be amazingly accurate with it—but it isn't necessary. Let Kalee be called Inga and let me be called Arlo, and that was the story, with modifications. Her former husband was a prominent corporate executive in Richmond. She does not have children. The college-age son was, like Evan, a prop, a convenience, as Bloodworth is a convenience for me. Shamefully, I was wrong about her age. She is thirty-seven, not early forties. Pain dulls youth, I suppose.

She had met Arlo at a Halloween party given by a friend. The friend had paired them at dinner in her boy-girl seating arrangement—separating spouses to encourage merriment. That night, she knew something would happen between them. Two months later, after four lunches together, they began their affair.

"I wanted to stop, but I couldn't," Inga explained simply.

I asked how she had managed to get away to Neal's Island with him.

"That's an embarrassment now," she told me. "It was a birthday gift from my husband. Time alone. It was something we had agreed on before we married. Time alone." She looked away, over the ocean. "He even found the spot and made the arrangements. Or his secretary did."

"And you've been punishing yourself, haven't you?" I said.

"I did. Yes. At first," she answered. "I don't anymore. It was something that happened, something I have to live with. Arlo and I—" She paused.

"It's all right. You don't have to go into it," I said.

She shook her head. "I want you to know." She turned her face back to me. "We had decided that I would ask for a divorce. Arlo and I were going to be married. That's why he was playing in the ocean. It was a celebration."

246

She took my hand and began to walk away from the beach, back to the cabin.

"I'm glad you're here," she said.

There was something—strength, I think, or maybe tranquility—in the warm touch of her hand and in her look.

"How did you come to terms with everything?" I asked.

The answer was the one I expected, the one explained to me by Sylvia: Carson X. and the FullLife Foundation.

"If you believe in miracles, it was a miracle," she said, and I could not quibble with her. I had been looking for the same miracle in the click-clicking of my word-making machine and in the letters to Kalee.

I wanted to tell Inga the truth about me, yet I did not. I had more time on Neal's Island, and I had been thinking that perhaps I would stay longer than the ten days of the sessions. More time at the word-maker. More time to sort it out.

When we returned to the cabin, Inga called Sylvia to thank her and to tell her that she was all right, and then I drove her to her home, a small, well-kept house that was personable, but not crowded with haunting artifacts of a past life.

"Are you working tonight?" Inga asked.

"I have some calls to make," I lied. "Business. But that's only the early part of the evening."

She smiled suspiciously. "Sure, I know."

"I'll be free by eight. Why don't we go to dinner at Marty's?" I said. I did not know how she might feel being at the cabin after the revelation of Arlo. And I did not know how I would feel. If necessary, I would leave the session with the MOD Mob early.

"I'd like that," she answered. "But I want you to know something now, not later."

"What's that?" I asked.

"It was you I made love to, not Arlo. You."

಄

At the cabin, I turned on the word-maker and at the bottom of the letter I had written earlier to Kalee, I added:

P.S.:

When I came into the cabin a few minutes ago, the word-maker was staring at me, and I had to sit at it. I'm glad I did. I always feel better if I have talked to you. You do answer, you know. My words pop up before me like heated toast from a toaster. The blinking cursor answers me in your voice. I can actually hear it. It has a violin's sound, a sweet, perfect-pitch aria so astounding I want to leap to my feet and applaud.

I have only a few minutes before I must leave for the session, and I do not think that I will write to you again today. Carson X. gave us a hint that we may be together for an extended time this afternoon, and I will have dinner with Inga tonight. Since my earlier words in this entry, the world has changed, Kalee. Something odd is happening here. It is about other people, but I keep thinking it is about us. In so many ways, that is true: it is about us.

I love you.

Your Correspondent

22

Afternoon of the Eighth Day

It was impossible to anticipate Carson X. He was both agitator and arbiter, and his mood swings—from mellow to melodramatic—were so unexpected and fascinating they seemed to be a magician's trick. Anger pulled from a flopping sleeve. A smile blossomed into a bouquet of silk laughter at a fingersnap. Sadness poured from an empty glass. Arguments vanished in a puff of stage smoke.

I had begun to think of Carson X. not as a person, but as a movie camera circling a scene, dollying up and down, zooming in and out, framing close ups and long shots, using fades and dissolves, peeking into the scene from so many angles that it/he discovered nuances none of us could see. Cubism, the filmmakers call it, I think.

He agreed and he ridiculed. He empathized and he criticized. He embraced and he scoffed at embracing.

It was an obvious psychological maneuver: keep them on their toes, always alert, always on guard for the surprise, but surprise them anyway.

Carson X. was either a genius or he was more insane than all of us. There was not a heat-seeking missile in the world that could have followed his blazing, but tricky path.

When the MOD Mob gathered in his kitchen for our afternoon session, he held up five writing pads.

"Gentlemen," he said, "when we talked about your childhoods before, it was a miserable session. You bored me, you bored your companions, you bored yourselves. You picked at the truth but you did not tell it."

He was pacing in the kitchen, clutching the writing pads close to his chest.

"I want you to try again," he said. "I'm going to pass out writing pads, and I want each of you to write down a brief description of your childhood history as it relates to your parents. No names. Only the histories. Then you're going to fold them and put them into a box, and I am going to pass that box around and you will take one of the slips and read it. If you select your own description, you are to replace it and select again.

"When you each have the history of one of your companions, you will have five minutes to imagine being that person, and then you will tell the rest of us how that childhood has affected you. In short you are to assume the identity of that person whose name you've drawn."

Carson X.'s eyes scanned us. "Any questions?" he asked.

None of us replied.

"Good. Then let's do it," he said. He distributed the pads and pens and then sat at the kitchen counter, calmly drinking coffee, watching as we struggled with describing our relationship with our parents.

"Keep it brief," he urged.

When we finished, he moved among us, taking the folded sheets of paper and putting them into a small gift box. He shook the box. "All right, now draw one out," he instructed. "Remember, if it's yours, select again."

He moved among us, holding the box. We dipped our hands into it and removed a slip of paper. Only Menlo selected his own description. He quickly replaced it and took out another and Carson X. passed the box to Max.

I was the last to draw. The slip read: *Wealthy parents. Father in land speculation and development. Mother the queen bee of her society. They indulged me until I began to rebel, then tried to force me to "walk the line" by threatening to disown me.*

It read to me like a poor story line from one of Old Joe's soap operas. None of my four comrades fit the description, or, if one did, he had disguised it masterfully.

Carson X. waited until we all had read our selections.

"Well?" he said.

Menlo shook his head in doubt. "Why are we doing this?" he asked.

"I've never done it before, so I don't know," Carson X. said. "I hope we learn something together." Then: "Now I'm going to give you five minutes to think it over." He turned and left the room.

"Jesus," Menlo whispered.

"White boys," Barkeep said, attempting humor.

No one laughed.

Menlo stood and stretched. He walked to the window and looked out. Godsick poured another cup of coffee and spooned in sugar and stirred it slowly. His face was furrowed. Max sat at the counter and rolled his slip of paper in his hands. He seemed to be struggling with an impulse to leave. Only Barkeep seemed calm and amused. A smile toyed with his face and he wiped at it with his fingers. After a moment, he began to whistle softly, causing Max to shoot him an annoyed glance. Barkeep slid from his stool at the counter and strolled over to Miss Perfect. He touched the breast Menlo had drawn.

Carson X. returned five minutes later. "Ready?" he asked.

"I am," Barkeep replied in a spirited voice. "How does this work?"

"Read us the description, then assume that character and tell us how you've been influenced by your background," Carson X. told him.

Barkeep unfolded the slip of paper. He read: *"I am the son of an alcoholic mother and a father who was a brawler. They both worked in a factory making cars. I was left alone a lot of the time and it scared me."*

I glanced at the expressions of the men around me. None of the faces confessed to Barkeep's reading. I knew only the description was not mine.

"Go on," Carson X. urged. "As that person, what does that mean to you?"

"It means I'm screwed up," Barkeep said confidently. "It means I've got problems from the get-go, from the..." He paused, looked at Godsick, then continued, "...from the freaking cradle to the freaking grave, unless I can find some freaking way out of it." He smiled.

"And that's it?" Carson X. said.

Barkeep shrugged and tilted his head in thought. "Well, it could also mean that I'm a determined son of a bitch. One of those guys who sucks it up, puts his nose to the grindstone and makes something of himself. You know—an over-achiever. And I would guess—from knowing you guys—that's closer to the truth. Everyone of you, you've got some of that in you, or you wouldn't be here."

"Ah, good," Carson X. murmured. "What about being left alone? How did you feel about that?"

A smile again creased Barkeep's face. "Lost," he answered. "And as an adult, I'd be considerably upset if the woman I loved left me. Especially if she screwed around with my mind like my folks did." He looked around the room. "What're we supposed to do now?" he asked. "Play Guess Who?"

"I think this could become dangerous," warned Godsick.

Carson X. turned to him. "Didn't we all agree that we would share the truth?"

Godsick bowed his head in acknowledgment.

"And does it matter?" Carson X. said forcefully. "Each of you had a childhood that influenced who you are and what you suffer, because none of us can divorce our history. We all know that. Yet, it's interesting to me how each of you might interpret someone else's life, and if you see something of yourself in that revelation."

"So, we're guinea pigs?" asked Menlo.

Carson X. shrugged nonchalantly. "Well, yes, I suppose so, but if we all learn something, isn't the experiment worth it?"

A silence of uncertainty clouded the room. Carson X. was in control. He turned to look at me. "Bloodworth, you're up," he said cheerfully.

I read the selection I had pulled from the box—the well-to-do parents, the father in land speculation and development, the mother obsessed with social acceptance, the threat of disinheritance—and I said, "As this person, I'm unsure about things. I feel trapped by what's expected of me. And, well, I guess that makes me someone who's also afraid."

"Afraid?" questioned Carson X., prying with his voice. "Of what? Or of whom?"

"My mother, for one," I answered. "My mother is the most powerful person I know. If I offend her, she'll leave me. If I do what she wants me to do, I'll be safe."

Carson X. applauded. "Very good," he enthused. "Are you sure you lied about your profession, Dr. Bloodworth?"

I smiled. My answer had been a Bloodworth answer, given in a Bloodworth voice.

"And how does that make you feel about other women?" asked Carson X.

I thought about the question a moment. There seemed to be only one answer. "I don't—well, I'm not sure I could trust them," I offered. "They could be like my mother. They could love their power and their need to command."

"Ah, power and command. Great words," Carson X. sighed. He was again parading, rubbing the palms of his hands together.

"There's something else," I suggested.

"Go on."

"I would be afraid if I loved a woman too much, she might disown me." I said. "I would be afraid of being turned aside, of not being good enough."

"Good, good," Carson X. said, nodding enthusiastically. He looked at Godsick. "Let's hear from you," he said.

Godsick had pulled my name, and I tried to keep from telegraphing the discomfort of hearing him speak about my unsuccessful father, driven by a sense of inferiority that he would never understand, and about my quiet, subservient mother, and about the appointments I had to have for attention from either of them, and, still, how I knew they loved me, but often in an obligatory way.

The story deeply affected Godsick. He believed I had a need to be loved by someone who would not compromise the relationship by the greed of uncertainty or by fear. He was right. That is what I had discovered in Kalee.

"I think this person always knew he was loved, especially by his mother," Godsick continued, "but I think he's afraid of losing that love."

"If you were that person, what would it tell you?" asked Carson X.

"It tells me I would always be haunted by doubt, I think. I would believe I am loved, but I'd always need proof," Godsick said. He paused and stared at the slip of paper. Then he added, "And that can be deceiving."

"And you, Godsick, are you like that person?" Carson X. asked. "Do you think you might have been describing yourself to some degree?"

Godsick lifted his face and looked at Carson X. His expression was one of pain, or fear, or both. After a bewildered moment, he said in a soft voice, "Yes. Yes, I was."

"Interesting," Carson X. cooed. "Let's remember what you just said." He nodded to Max.

And we sat and listened to Max and Menlo read, and interpret, the slips of paper they held.

One of us had been physically abused by a hot-tempered father who worked as a chef, while his wife wept over the damnation of their life, but never tried to stop the abuse.

One of us had been the child of a father killed in the Vietnam War, whose medal-covered hero's uniform hung in a shadowbox in the living room like a shrine. That uniform, and the memory of the man who wore it, was worshipped daily by a widow who lived with the bewildered belief that no man—including his son—could possibly be his equal.

The findings of Max and Menlo repeated what we had all said: we were still those children of our environments, children who were unsure of how to be men. The women of our childhoods were either too powerful or too weak, the men too dominating or too consumed by their own lives. In each telling, we all described

255

fragments of ourselves by the ghostly fingerprints of our personalities.

"Well?" Carson X. said when Menlo finished his assessment of the Vietnam War hero and the worshipping widow.

There was a pause. Finally, Barkeep laughed uncomfortably. He said, "I don't know about the rest of you, but it won't bother me to tell you which one I am." He looked at Carson X.

"Fine," Carson X. said gently. He sat on one of the kitchen stools.

"The last one. The one Menlo talked about," Barkeep admitted. "I never really knew my father. Never saw the gentleman. He took one for the Marines a few months before the war ended, but I can tell you this..." He paused. His face flushed in anger and his voice rose suddenly. "I can tell you that I've wanted to rip that goddamn uniform off the wall a million goddamn times," he snarled. "I didn't need an empty uniform to stare at every day; I needed a man walking around in a pair of boxer shorts, sucking on a beer, somebody who'd kick my ass if he had to."

Godsick leaned toward Barkeep and touched his arm gently. "I don't know if I could feel the same way," Godsick told him. "I think I would have taken the dead father."

Barkeep turned his head to look at Godsick. "Your old man was the cook?"

Godsick nodded.

Barkeep shook his head. "Shit. Hey, I'm sorry, pal. I know guys like that. Assholes."

"Maybe they were good people when things were going right," Godsick countered. "Maybe they just had the wrong child for them."

"Bullshit," Max hissed.

256

"Why do you say that?" Carson X. asked.

"They could have had Jesus Christ as a child—and from what I know of Godsick, they came pretty damn close—but it wouldn't have mattered," Max snapped. "They were too full of themselves, too damn busy to care what happened at home. I work with a couple like that—exactly like that. I hate that attitude. Nobody's ever good enough." Max crushed the paper he held in his fist. "I've been there," he whispered.

The mood in the room was tense. We were watching Carson X., waiting for him to say something. He had his eyes closed. He looked like a man listening to the music of a great symphony. "Max, do you want to tell us?" he said after a moment.

Max swallowed hard. His eyes were moist with anger.

"I guess it's not hard to know where I fit in," he mumbled. Then: "My parents were the factory workers. They're dead, both of them. The thing I hated is how satisfied they were. They didn't care about being better, or different. They were too proud to care about it. Anybody different was stuck-up to them. Putting on airs, my mother called it. My mother, the drunk."

"Tell us how you got away," Carson X. said quietly. His eyes were still closed.

"Football," Max answered simply. "I played at a college most of you never heard of."

"Was your father violent?" asked Carson X.

"Yes," Max said.

"Do you think you're like your father?" Carson X. pressed.

Max hesitated, then answered in a quiet voice: "No."

"But you killed someone, didn't you?"

We watched Max.

"Didn't you?" Carson X. said again.

"Yes," Max admitted after a moment. "I had to. He would have killed me." He touched his chest with his fingers, as though touching the scars covered by his shirt. "And I was trying to save somebody else."

Carson X' s eyes snapped open. "And that is exactly how the brave man's sword is used," he cried. He sprang to his feet. "Killing to save." He crossed to Max and stood before him. "Max," he said urgently, "open your shirt."

Max stared at him.

"Do it, Max," Carson X. commanded gently.

Max stood and unbuttoned his shirt and pulled it open. His hands were trembling. We stared at the scars on his chest.

"Is it worth having the scars to be alive, Max?" Carson X. asked.

Max nodded.

"Yes," Carson X. thundered. "Yes, it is. Yes!" He turned in the room, his blazing eyes sweeping us. "And you will have scars—each of you," he said joyfully. "Scars in your chest, not on them. But I promise you they will be scars from living, not from dying. And having them will make you more powerful than you've ever been, just as Max is more powerful now, as a man, than he was as a tackle at a college none of us would recognize."

Carson X. did another turn in the room. His face was throbbing with ecstasy. He pulled his hands together in front of his chest and began to beat the air. "Your scars are your medals! Don't you understand that? Don't you?" He began to sing: "A-a-MEN...a-a-MEN...a-MEN...a-MEN..."

☙

I was sure Carson X. would take the stories, the short thumbnail sketches (as we called them in my world, my Atlanta world of hyperbole) and slide them under the microscope of his leaping-about mind, but I was wrong. Carson X. was in a mood to celebrate; he, at least, had learned something, and he had been seized by the inspiration of scars as medals, as proud decorations of wars fought and won on the battlefields of the psyche. He ended the session by leading us to his grand piano, where he sat and vigorously played the *Amen* song and urged us to join him in its singing until he had chased the mood of anguish from the house, and then he opened bottles of wine and we drank toasts to our break-through—a break-through that Carson X. seemed to understand better than the rest of us. As a reward, he told us, we would not meet for an evening session.

"I could dismiss all of you now, and you would be fine," he crowed. "In time, you would heal yourself. I can sense it. You're on your way to freedom."

The only two people of the group who had not claimed ownership of his written-down childhood, were Menlo and me, but comparatively speaking, our histories were boring. Vanilla. Humdrum. Tedious. We did not have the dysfunction necessary to claim a seat in the inner circle of despair.

By deduction, I knew Menlo's childhood was the story I had drawn from the box, and I was not at all surprised, though it did intrigue me. The historical image that white Southerners had of blacks almost never extended to an aristocratic society, but that had been Menlo's background and he had never doubted his place in it, yet he had no pretensions. In his easy, quiet, manner, he had

259

given me the impression that he had succeeded by his own will and with his own, carefully fashioned virtues. Still, I think he was relieved there was no discussion of his childhood. In the singing of *Amen*, he wore a glad smile and he sang with vigor. I stood beside him. I, too, sang lustily.

෮

After the session, on the drive away from the home of Carson X., I thought of my father. My father, dead at fifty-five—"run down," my mother had said to me at the funeral home, "by a truck called Work."

I had never heard her speak so bitterly, or poetically, of him, or of his obsession to do well. He had wanted to be a great man, a builder of shopping centers, a power broker in politics, a merry host at the country club for golf outings and gin games. He never achieved any of those ambitious dreams. He survived until the truck called Work ran him down.

One day, months after my father's death, my mother told me he would spend hours at night writing the names of the people he had met during the day, memorizing them as a child memorizes the facts of history for a history test.

"What he never understood was that he knew their names, but they didn't know his," my mother said sadly.

I thought it was a tragic, yet appropriate, revelation of my father; he knew the names of hundreds of people, but he never knew the name of a single friend I had. Except for Joe Youmans. Joe Youman's father, Albert, was a member of the House of Representatives from Georgia.

I also thought of Carson X.'s sermon about scars. And it had been that—a sermon, a red-faced, dancing about, shouting sermon.

The only things missing were a tambourine and a rattlesnake and a collection basket. I think he came close to converting all of us, as a roaring evangelist converts people terrified of the unknown and hungry for serenity. Or perhaps we were all merely surprised that we were so much alike, that each of us had experienced a mix of neglect and/or excessive indulgence, and that we were, as Barkeep phrased it, " ... so damned love-starved, it's no wonder we were obsessed with our women."

The last thing Carson X. had said to us as he escorted us to the door of his home was, "Gentlemen, listen to me, for I tell you the truth: You are—on this day, in this minute—a resident in the Age of Choice. Have you learned that? Have you learned that you've been tutoring yourself from your diaper days about the fickle nature of choice? Those lessons go back a long way, don't they?"

"Yes," Godsick had said softly.

"And what do we do about it?" Carson X. had asked.

Menlo had had the best reply: "Let it sink in."

23

Night of the Eighth Day

I did not call Inga and tell her of the change in my schedule. I wanted to see her, but I also wanted some time alone, some time to sort out what the MOD Mob had experienced during the afternoon session. To let it sink in, as Menlo had said.

And I wanted to think about Arlo and Inga. Was there more to the story than Sylvia or Inga had revealed?

I went to see Old Joe.

He was dozing inside the security house when I got out of my car. The closing of the door jolted him awake. His eyes swept sleepily through the windows and he recognized me approaching him. A smile wrinkled into his face like a deep erosion.

I asked, "How's it going?"

"Not much happening," he answered. "Off-season, don't nobody much come out here. How's Doc?"

"He's fine," I said. "Not bothering you, am I?"

Old Joe shook his head. "Lord, no. Glad to have somebody to talk to."

"Are the soaps over for the day?" I asked.

"One I like is," he replied with a giggle. "This old boy from some foreign country has about got hisself in a jam with one of them half-naked women."

"That right?"

"I knew what was going on," Old Joe declared. "A blind man could of seen it coming. He was messing around with this old woman and her husband showed up. They was doing it in the backseat of one of them fancy cars in the garage. Like that was

262

some big surprise. They been cutting eyes at one another for half a year."

"Sounds like you're right. He's in trouble," I said.

Old Joe giggled and wiped at his mouth with the back of his hand. "You should of heard him carry on. Started jabbering in one of them foreign tongues, like he was crazy or something. Ask me, he's about to get his ass de-ported, that's what. That's my guess. Hope he takes that old whore with him. Never did like her. She's done broke up about a dozen marriages."

I laughed with Old Joe. I thought it would be good to enjoy something as much as Old Joe enjoyed his soap operas.

"You seen any ghosts?" Old Joe asked.

"Well, I'm not sure," I said. "Could have."

"Uh-huh. Well, they out there," Old Joe assured me. "They all over the place." He glanced around, toward a strip of trees that separated the security station from the inlet. He added, in a lowered voice, "They a lying bunch, I can tell you that."

"What do you mean?"

"That's the way they have them some fun," Old Joe explained. "They'd lie to their mama and daddy. Just like a bunch of young'uns. Always making up things, playing they tricks. Can't trust them far as you could throw a mule, if you was to get your hands on one."

I thought of Arlo and his stories. "I've never heard that about ghosts," I said.

Old Joe bobbed his head vigorously. "Ask me, that's why they ghosts, why they can't just go on over like normal people. Don't nobody—the Lord, hisself, or the Devil, for that matter—want nobody that's always lying. So, they just leave them on this side, letting them play they tricks. I seen it happen. Yessir, I have."

"I'll keep that in mind," I promised.

"You do that," Old Joe said. He added, "You find out anything more about that old boy you was asking about?" Old Joe asked.

"You mean the one who drowned?"

"Yeah, that's the one."

"No. Not really," I said. "Did you think of anything else?"

Old Joe pulled from his chair and stretched. "Naw, nothing much. Only thing that come to mind was some talk."

"Talk?"

Old Joe nodded. "You know how talk is. Don't never amount to much." He cackled suddenly. "Now, ain't that something, coming from a man who don't like nothing better than talking? How it is, though. Don't nothing I say ever amount to much. The wife, when she was alive, used to turn me off just like she had one of them hearing plugs with a switch on it. I'd go on and on and after a while she'd look at me and say, 'You say something, Joe?' Used to piss me off, but, Lord, I didn't blame her. If I'd had anything worth saying, she'd of listened."

I watched Old Joe rock his head in memory and listened to his soft chuckle, and then I said, "You were saying there was some talk..."

"Oh, yessir, they was."

"You remember any of it?" I asked.

"You was asking if they was a woman, and I got to thinking about it. Some folks say they was one who had to be took off to the hospital."

"Who? Do you know?"

I saw Old Joe roll his shoulders. He cocked his head, as though listening to what he had just said, and then he shook away my question and pulled a curtain of privacy around him. He had

264

revealed more than he had intended to reveal. It was his island and the people of the island were his people. He would not betray them.

"Just some woman," he answered. "Don't think I ever got a look at who they was talking about." He reached and turned on his television. "You want to watch some?"

"I don't think so," I said.

"Come on in and pull up a seat," Old Joe urged pleasantly.

"Maybe another time," I told him. "Just thought I'd drop by and say hello."

"Glad you did," Old Joe said. "You come by anytime." He switched the channels on his set. A commercial for a detergent was playing. He focused his attention on it.

"See you," I said.

Old Joe flipped his hand in the air.

He had said enough. And he had said even more by avoiding my question.

He knew about Inga.

Sylvia and Inga had told me the truth.

At the cabin I wrote a postcard to my mother. It was a card with the picture of a cabin much like mine on it, one I had found in the dresser of the bedroom. I had lied to her about the reason for my visit to Neal's Island. A rest, I had explained. A new project to think out.

Mom—

Just a note to let you know this is a great place. You'll have to come here with me one day. I'm feeling fine. Sleeping a lot. Walking the beach. (I'll bring you some shells.) Hope you're all right. You were on my mind today. Just wanted you to know I love you.

I napped and I dreamed of Max playing football, dreamed of the power of his anger. In my dream, Max was bare-chested. His scars blazed under the lights of the football field. Other players rushed at him and he swatted them away like gnats.

On the sidelines, watching passively, was Menlo.

Menlo, letting it sink in.

Menlo, thinking of murder.

☙

When Inga opened the door of her home, I had to step back and gather my composure. I thought she was Kalee.

She had styled her hair the way Kalee's hair was always styled. It needed only the blonde to make it look identical. And I could smell Kalee's perfume, or a fragrance so similar that it fooled my senses.

She wore a pink knit-wool dress with a purple jacket. She was very pretty, very sophisticated and dignified. I felt a little uncomfortable in my slacks and pullover sweater and windbreaker—Kalee's windbreaker.

We had a quick glass of wine and then drove to Marty's—an old, refurbished home, with wicker furniture and a screened dining porch. It was past the normal dinner hour and there were only three cars in the parking lot. One of them was Sylvia's Mercedes.

"Did you know she would be here?" I asked Inga.

"No," Inga said, "but she comes here sometimes. It's one of the few places she feels welcome. The daughter of the owner is a member of the Foundation."

"Do you want to stay?" I asked.

Inga understood the question. She touched my arm gently. "It's fine," she assured me. "Yes, I want to stay. There'll be no mention of today."

Sylvia was with a man named Fred Dickey, her accountant from Beaufort. He was in his mid-fifties, tall, with salt-pepper hair that was thinning at the crown. They were about to leave when we entered. I invited them to join us for a glass of wine. A wrinkle of disapproval curled across Fred's forehead.

"We'd love to," cooed Sylvia. "We've been talking business for so long, I'm getting a headache." She looked at Fred. "You have time, don't you?"

"Sure," Fred mumbled.

Fred did not talk while we drank the wine. He sat patiently and listened. Sylvia chattered.

She said, "Dr. Bloodworth should meet Carson while he's here, don't you think, Fred?"

Fred nodded.

She smiled at me. Her smile said, "We have a secret, you and I." And we did. A half-secret, at least. She still did not know my real name.

And then she began her questions, questions that were a tease.

"Did you like being in med school?"

Me: "Not always."

"What's the oddest case you've ever handled?"

Me: "A man who believed he was George Patton."

"Do you keep up with the latest medical procedures?"

Me: "Not as well as I should, I'm afraid."

"Did you always want to be a doctor, or did you have a secret ambition, one you've never told anyone?"

It was that question that gave me a chance to squirm away from the pressure of her playfulness, or her punishment (I was not sure which it was).

I said to her, "I always wanted to be an actor."

"Really?" she replied brightly. Then she revealed something of herself I should have realized earlier. She said, "Me, too."

"Did you study theater?" I asked.

"It was my major," she enthused. She turned to Inga. "Did I ever tell you that? I did, didn't I?"

"I think so," Inga answered politely. She was not at all interested, but she pretended interest. She glanced at Fred.

"And you?" Sylvia said to me. "Did you study?"

"Like you. In college," I answered. "And I did some community plays after I started my practice, but before I had very many people ringing the doorbell."

"Ummmm, a psychiatrist as an actor. That's interesting," Sylvia said.

I shrugged and took my wine glass and drank from it, and tried to imagine Bloodworth on stage. The poor bastard would be lost if he had to play anyone other than himself, I thought. Maybe he would make a great prop, though. A piece of furniture. A hat rack. Carson X. was different. Carson X. should have been on Broadway.

Sylvia asked me to name some of the roles I had performed during my career as an actor, and I rattled off a few—Tom in *The Glass Menagerie*, Dr. John in *Summer and Smoke*, Hal in *Picnic*, Starbuck in *The Rainmaker*, Laertes in *Hamlet*. (The mention of *Hamlet* was deliberate. I wanted to say that I was more than an American mumbler on stage.) I also named *The Crucible* and *The Prime of Miss Jean Brodie* and *Bell, Book and Candle* and *Teach Me How to Cry* and *The Man*.

Sylvia was delighted. She, too, had performed in *The Glass Menagerie* as Laura and in *Summer and Smoke* as Miss Alma. Good plays, she gushed, but not as exciting as *Jesus Christ, Superstar* or *The Man of La Mancha*. She had played Aldonza in *La Mancha*, and the way she pronounced the name Aldonza— strong, thrust from the tip of her tongue—I knew it was the one role she had understood perfectly. There was fire in her eyes when she talked of Aldonza. She lifted her implanted breasts, used them to aim her words. Sitting there, in Marty's, she was Aldonza.

Inga did not notice the change in Sylvia. Nor did Fred. They were both patiently enduring us, as people always endure amateur artists.

❧

After the wine, Sylvia and Fred left and Inga and I ordered dinner—lobster for both—and it became a good, comfortable evening. We talked candidly about her recovery from Arlo's death. She told me she had been thinking of leaving Neal's Island and moving back to Richmond. "To get on with my life," she said. "To try things on my own."

She asked if I had come to the island to get away from someone.

"Why do you think that?" I replied.

She smiled. "You said a name when we were together," she said quietly. "Or did you forget that?"

I could feel the blush covering me. "You've got me," I admitted.

She smiled warmly and then said, "Why do you think people take lovers?"

I remembered something Spence had said, or maybe it was Boatwright, before his conversion to serenity: "The difference between a lover and a spouse is freedom. With a lover, there are no inhibitions, no questioning looks, no inquiries about 'Where did you learn that?' With a spouse, there's always some suspicion, some small question. And, always, you've got utility bills to talk about. What lover has ever mentioned a utility bill?"

I told Inga of the comment and she laughed. She said, "I think that might be right. It was how I felt with Arlo. Freedom. Great freedom. For a few minutes, for an hour, for a day." She gazed for a moment at the glass of cognac she was holding, then she added, "After I began seeing him, I asked some of my friends—at the right time, when we were being silly, when they would not suspect anything—I asked if their husbands were as good in bed as the lovers they had had. Do you know what they told me?"

"No," I said. "What?"

"They told me, 'No.' All of them. None of them would trade their husbands for the lovers they'd had, but all their lovers were better in bed. Isn't that strange?"

"Maybe it proves there's more to it—to being married—than sex," I said.

Inga looked at me playfully. Her smiled teased. "And what would that be?" she asked.

"The utility bills," I said.

Her laughter rang in the empty dining room.

Dear Kalee,

I had dinner tonight with Inga, and the truth is this: it was a good, charming evening, but I did not want to stay the night with her, even if, tonight, she was very much like you.

I escorted her to her home after dinner. We did not make love. She embraced me at the doorway and kissed me gently, with comfort, and told me she was comfortably tired, and I assured her that I understood. The revelation of Alro and the full meaning of the initials had been a trying experience for both of us. I suppose we both needed some alone time.

But I will see her again tomorrow night. Her friend, Sylvia, has invited us to her home for dinner. A man from Los Angeles is supposed to be there—the guest Sylvia had mentioned earlier. He's a television producer of some sort, interested in doing a short piece on the FullLife Foundation for one of the national talk shows. I'm relatively sure Carson X. won't make an appearance. At least, Sylvia—now knowing that I am here for the seminar— made an issue of saying that Carson X. disapproved of the taping and refused to have anything to do with it. "But," she told me, "it's my money that keeps the doors open. I think I have some say-so."

And, yes, she does have say-so. Believe me, Kalee, this woman has nerve that would shock you. No doubt, she would be a hit in Buckhead, among the Buckhead-ites.

I don't know how I'm going to manage the session and the dinner. It's becoming more and more difficult being two different people. Or is it now three? When I arrived here, I never thought I'd meet someone in a convenience store and become a "steady" with her over a matter of hours. It's odd. It really is. Such things simply do not happen in an ordinary life, but Inga's life has not

271

been ordinary. Nor mine. We have found some comfort in discovering one another, and that must be good. It must be.

It's late. I'm exhausted.

I want to sleep, but I am afraid. I am afraid of dreaming.

I love you.

Your Correspondent

24

Morning of the Ninth Day

My wish was granted: I slept without dreaming, or, if I did dream, it was too dark and too removed from memory to matter.

The sun was up when I awoke, bright through the bedroom windows. I could hear a single bird cheerfully whistling birdsong. The sun and the birdsong gave promise of a good day.

I took cereal and coffee at the kitchen table, then showered and dressed and, realizing I had only two more days on Neal's Island, I began the organization of leaving. It is a habit of mine. Almost compulsive. Have things in order before order is needed.

One of the things I packed away was the K-for-Kalee folder, but not before reading an entry written in anguish after Kalee's death.

if i had known you would leave me as you did,
i would have drawn a false smile across my lips
and an artificial tear beneath my eye, the way
clowns and mimes costume their faces when
they are telling their silent stories of sadness.

the ache of your leaving is in seeing you when
you are not here, when you are somewhere
far away, too far even for screams (or echoes)
or for the touches i will fling across the universe
on nights too dark to sleep without you.

when the internal clock, in its slow watch-speed,

273

tells me it is our time—our hour, our day, our
memory—i will see you. when the colors and
sounds and the quickening of that hour, that day,
drive me again to the places we met—you, waiting
there, with bright, glad voice-eyes, saying yes
in syllables of gold and green—i will see you.

when i go again to the lake and sit alone on the
quilt of cut grass, i will see you as you were—watching
red-hooded ducks swimming like ships, and pregnant
women at rest, their hands folded across their
abdomens like old men asleep in leather chairs. yes,
i will see you when i go again to the lake, when
memory again walks with me beside the lakeside,
watching fish nibbling like puppies at the surface
of the water. do you remember? a girl was there, beside
a tree, weeping, and you said, "why?" and you held
to me and said again softly, "why?" when i am alone
at the lake i will look for you where the girl stood
weeping and I will hear you saying again, "why?"
i do not know why. why are you gone from me? why?

when the flower lady offers to sell me the silk bud
of a silk jonquil, dye-colored in laughing yellow, i
will say your name aloud, ask for you like a desperate
wish, and i will see you there, there where the flower
lady sells silk jonquils and calls them forever lasting.

i will see you in the gem shops, your face and your eyes
swimming toward me out of the richly colored stones
that have been pulled from the earth and polished to fit

into palms like a rare, warm bubble. yes, in the gem
shops, among the opals and the azurites, among the
larimars and the dazzling, blue lights of diamonds,
i will see you as the eternal gift that you are.

when i go again on the late, dark walks alone, i will
see you. you will be with me and we will celebrate
the joy of the walks. stopping and holding, standing
still—absolutely still—in the center of the grand
dance of whatever and whoever moved about us,
hurrying along, never knowing we were there. never
caring. the bliss of those walks can never leave me.

but you have left me, and i have become an actor
in a stage play, making believe until it is no longer
make-believe. the tear-dot on my eye stains the
drawn-on smile. listen to the line i have
written for the leaving. listen. did you hear it?

Mid-morning, there were two phone calls within thirty minutes.

The first was from Inga, telling me she had enjoyed the evening, telling me she was fine, telling me the day and the evening had been in her needing since Arlo's death, telling me she had slept well, telling me she had had a romantic dream for the first time in years.

"Romantic?" I said, teasing her.

"Sweet, nice," she answered easily. "Anyway, I think it's progress."

"Me, too," I agreed. I could hear the bell that dangled from the door of the store jingling in the background.

"Customer," she whispered. "Don't forget the party."

"I won't," I promised.

A few minutes later, Sylvia called. She bubbled about the coincidence of seeing Inga and me at Marty's. She asked if I had been telling the truth about being an actor in college.

"Yes," I said. "I enjoyed those days."

"No wonder you can pull it off," she replied.

"Pull off what?"

"The role you're playing," she said. "You're good at it. Fred really believed you were a psychiatrist. That's the reason he didn't say very much."

"He's afraid of psychiatrists?" I asked.

Sylvia laughed. "No. Jealous. He hates Carson. Thinks I'm wasting my money on the world's second oldest profession."

"What's that?"

"Mind-bending," she answered.

"Maybe he has a point," I suggested.

Sylvia laughed again. She was in an up mood. It was in her voice, in the lyrical playfulness of her laughter. She said, "Are you telling me that Carson's failing with you?"

I hedged with the answer: "It's—it's interesting. I think I've made some progress."

"Ummmm, progress. I like that. It's a good word. Carson would be pleased. But do you think he's the reason, or could it be someone else?"

"Maybe it's everything," I answered.

"It always is," she said. "By the way, you're still planning on coming to dinner, I hope."

"Of course," I replied. "But it may be late. We do have a session tonight, unless it's canceled."

"Excuses, excuses," Sylvia crooned. "Just tell him you're not going to be there. It's your money."

"To tell you the truth, I'm not as worried about the session as I am Inga," I confessed. "I'm feeling a lot of shame over deceiving her. Maybe I should tell her the truth tonight. What do you think?"

"You keep asking that question," Sylvia said. "It's your decision. I'm sure you'll do the right thing."

"I hope so." I said. "I really hope so."

Barkeep was our lightning rod and our comic relief. Though he had suffered from his obsession, he refused to fold his tent meekly and accept his suffering without argument. Argument was part of his personality. In one moment of tension in an early session, Menlo had called him a put-down artist for a sarcastic comment he had made to Godsick. To Barkeep, it was a compliment and he had made a joke of it—a joke involving sex, of course. His jokes were always sexual in nature, always with the obscenity of a teenage boy excited by half-naked girls in cheerleader uniforms. But, still, he was funny and he was fun to be with, and all of us drew energy from him. He seemed always to set the tone for our sessions.

In the afternoon, after we had settled in Carson X.'s breakfast room for coffee, with Miss Perfect staring at us pitifully from her misshaped face with the eye patch that left her looking battered, Barkeep announced he had a disturbing experience to share: he had been awakened at three o'clock in the morning by Buck, who was restless.

"He couldn't sleep," Barkeep reported in a loud, amazed voice. "He kept jabbering away about belonging to the wrong person. Said he must have been switched at birth in the hospital by some nurse hopped-up on prescription drugs."

Carson X. waved away the easy laughter with his hand and asked Barkeep, "Did he have any evidence?"

"Nothing substantial," Barkeep answered smugly. "But, let's face it, Buck's not too substantial himself."

"Did you talk about it?" Carson X. asked, fighting to control the smirk that ached to unfold across his face.

"Well, since I was awake, I thought, all right, Buck, let's get this settled. Let's have it out."

"And?" Carson X. asked.

"Buck's got this notion that the reason I'm so screwed up has to do with not knowing when good enough was good enough. He thinks I should have stopped with Susan Todd."

"Who's Susan Todd?" asked Max.

"My first girlfriend," Barkeep explained. "Great girl. I mean, great. I still think about her from time to time."

"What happened to her?" Carson X. said.

Barkeep rolled his head and shoulders in exaggerated resignation. "Married a cop. Can you believe that? Got two or three kids. I saw her at our high school reunion a couple of years ago. She looked great, still the sweetest woman I've ever met."

Carson X. was offering seconds on coffee. He tilted the pot over Barkeep's cup and poured. He seemed to be in deep thought. After a moment, he said, "Do any of you believe your first encounter with love was, in many ways, the best?"

"It depends on what you call love," Barkeep said, wagging his eyebrows. "At that age, no sex meant no love. And I was never in bed with Susan Todd, so I was never officially in love with her."

Menlo laughed easily, a chuckle. He mumbled, "Damn."

"I've matured," Barkeep boasted. "Now I'm in love, but no sex."

If Carson X. had planned anything specific for the session, he dismissed it. The mood was too relaxed, the kind of mood I had known in the last days of certain college classes. We were in wind-down time. One more day to go.

We would talk about our first relationship with girls, about the innocence of those relationships, and Carson X. would occasionally pontificate about the importance of innocence, how innocence was essential in a healthy life. No one took him seriously. It was an afternoon for good memories, and Buck was as much in charge as Carson X.

Barkeep led us on an amusing odyssey of his weak-kneed infatuation of Susan Todd.

"God, I loved her. Couldn't talk around her. I used to stutter all the time," he confessed. "She would smile at me in school, and I would be worthless for the rest of the day. It was a miracle I wasn't put in a home for idiots."

The conversation rolled around the room, with each of us telling of our childhood experiences with girls that we thought we loved.

I told of Rachel Carrier, and of my strongest memory of her—touching her hands for the first time. I confessed that she was the first girl I kissed—under a dining room table covered like a tent with a large, white tablecloth, the kind with lace on the border.

"We were thirteen, I think," I said. "She had great, pouting lips. Don't ask me what we were doing under the table; I don't remember. I just remember the kiss. It scared hell out of me, but only for a moment."

Menlo wanted to know if I regretted not making love to her.

"No, not really," I told him. "I was overwhelmed by the kiss. The kiss was enough."

"It happened to me," Menlo said. He leaned back and gazed at the ceiling, remembering.

"You banged your childhood sweetheart?" Barkeep asked.

Menlo wagged his head. His smile became deeper, more pleasing. "I'd say it was the other way around," he replied.

And then he told us the story. The girl—Seba—had called him at his office, telling him she was in the city on a shopping trip. It had been ten years since high school, ten years since he had spoken to her.

"We talked about the usual things," Menlo explained. "Work, her kids, people we went to school with, my work. Just stuff. And then she said, in a rush: 'Look, I want to be straight with you. I've always wanted to make love to you. Always. I want you to leave your office now and come to my hotel and I want you to make love to me. Once. All I want is once.'"

"Jesus," Barkeep sighed in awe.

I asked, "Did you?"

Menlo paused before answering. A glow rested in his eyes. "Well," he said easily, "that's not like me. Maybe you guys haven't picked up on that, but most of the time, I'm pretty reserved." He glanced at Carson X. "But—yeah, I did. I almost broke my leg getting out from behind my desk. I was at her hotel in fifteen minutes, and we did make love—slow love, good love."

"And that was it?" Barkeep asked incredulously.

"That was it," Menlo answered. "One time. Haven't talked to her since that day. The world with Regina in it showed up not long after that."

"Regina? That one's easy to solve. A good hit man," Barkeep said dryly.

Menlo chuckled. He looked at Barkeep. "You know, I like you," he said simply.

"Why? I'm an ass," Barkeep replied proudly.

"Yes, you are," Menlo said, "but you're likable."

The talk drifted from Menlo's Seba to Godsick's timid confession about a girl named Arlene.

"She played the violin in the city's youth orchestra and she was shy—as was I," Godsick told us. She had become a nun. "She teaches music in a school in Minnesota," he revealed. "We still correspond. I've even thought of taking a trip to see her, maybe over Christmas."

"Nun can be spelled two different ways," Barkeep advised. He reached and punched Godsick gently in the shoulder. "But, at least you'll know what's waiting for you and Ernest—nun and none."

Godsick's face flushed under his smile.

Max's memory was of a girl named Kay Cee, and I thought of Kalee because of the rhyming sound of the names—Kay Cee and Kalee. His Kay Cee had been born in Kansas City, which was the inspiration for the name given to her by alcoholic parents who looked for happiness in absurdities. A move south, to Max's hometown, had landed Kay Cee in a trailer park near a mill village. At age thirteen, she was more woman than girl, with the promise of stunning sensuality resting in remarkably beautiful eyes. "The first fight I ever had was over her," Max said. "One of her older brothers was kidding her about me, saying she had a school picture of me put away in a book, and was always looking at it. There was nothing between us until then. After that, we became friends. Dated when we were juniors and seniors in high school. When we graduated, I went off to play football and she got a job in a dress shop, and then one day, she left. Somebody said she joined the army, but I don't know what happened. One day she was there, and the next day she was gone. She never said goodbye and she never wrote."

"Did you miss her?" asked Godsick.

Max cocked his head in thought, and then he said, "I did. Yes. I missed her." He paused before adding, "It was the first time anybody ever left me."

"Maybe you should try to find her," Carson X. suggested.

Max looked at Carson X. He nodded once. "Maybe I will. I think her brother—the one I had the fight with—still lives where we grew up."

"She could be Miss Perfect," Barkeep said in an affected whisper.

Max turned to the flip chart with the tragic drawing of a tragic woman. "I hope not," he murmured.

25

Afternoon of the Ninth Day

I had an intention of spending the afternoon alone, counseling myself, as Carson X. suggested to each of us when he dismissed the session.

"In case you haven't connected the dots, the alone time you've had since you've been here is meant to make you study your navel, so to speak," he told us. "Remember, health is in the healer and the healer is in the injured. I cannot heal you, but you can heal yourselves. Still, before healing can take place, there's always an examination, isn't there? And you must do that on your own, alone."

My intention was interrupted with a knocking at the cabin door.

It was Sylvia.

Social visit, she said.

She was dressed in faded jeans and was wearing a lime green pullover jersey that had the words Happy Camper printed in black across the front of it. She was not wearing a bra. Her nipples pressed against the word Happy and Camper like hard buttons.

She said, at the door, "Hi. Am I interrupting anything?"

"No," I told her. "I just got back from the session." I invited her in.

She explained she was on her way to Beaufort to meet her Los Angeles visitor—a man named Reuben—and because she had left early, she decided to stop by on a whim.

"I didn't see Inga's car, so I thought you might be alone," she said.

Of course she didn't see Inga's car, I thought, a little irritated at such an inane comment. She knew Inga was at work.

I made coffee and poured a cup for her and, because it was a summer-warm afternoon, we went out onto the deck and sat in the plastic-strap lounge chairs.

"I really just want to make sure you're not angry with me because of last night," she said.

"Why should I be?" I asked.

"The teasing about being a doctor. I didn't think you had said anything to Inga about it."

"Like I said this morning, I know I should," I told her, "but I'll be leaving day after tomorrow, and I didn't think there was any reason to get into it. I think it'd complicate things and I'm not sure how much more complication I can handle, or want to create. Anyway, I don't know that we'll ever see one another again."

Sylvia sipped from her coffee. "Of course, that's your decision," she said. "I'd probably do the same thing, and for the same reason."

"Reason? What reason?" I asked.

"Don't you know what you've been doing?" she answered. "You've been performing a great role. You've been an actor for almost two weeks. What great fun."

I asked why she called it fun.

"Because it is," she argued. "I do it all the time. That's why I wouldn't say anything to Inga; it'd bring down the curtain on you, and you haven't played the final act yet."

I was surprised at the rush of anger sweeping across my chest. "Is the Foundation a performance for you? Or a stage?" I asked coolly.

It didn't faze her. She smiled cheerfully. "A stage? I like that. Sometimes. Sometimes not. Aren't we both that way? Aren't all actors the same?"

I was proud of my response: "Actors may behave the same, but I think their roles are always different."

She frowned—a cute, pouting frown, a performance frown. She said, "And speaking of that, how was the session today?"

"Good," I told her. "But you would expect that, I think, or you wouldn't be supporting the Foundation."

She looked at me in the curious manner than women have when they know something another person doesn't. Her eyes were shining. Her eyes looked as though she had rinsed them in the purest of waters.

Above us, camouflaged by a clump of thin brown limbs, a bird whistled in a shrill, piercing voice, the same whistle that had awakened me earlier. The sound was so sharp and clear and loud, I could feel my body jerk in surprise. Sylvia glanced up, then turned back to me.

"I support Carson for two reasons," she said brightly. "First, I believe in what he does. I've seen it work with too many people, men and women, people like Inga. Second, it's part of the settlement."

"What settlement?" I asked.

I was not prepared for her answer, though I knew I had been led into a trap and the trap was baited.

"The divorce settlement," she said. Then she added, "Didn't Inga tell you? Carson is my ex-husband."

I'm sure I looked dumbfounded. I know I was dumbstruck.

The bird above us sang a refrain—sharp, clear, loud. A taunting sound.

Sylvia laughed merrily. "She didn't tell you, did she? I wonder why?"

I managed to mumble, "No. No, she didn't tell me."

"I can't believe Carson hasn't mentioned it," she said. "From what I understand, he uses his own experiences as examples in his men's seminars. At least I've been told that by one or two people." She leaned forward in her chair, toward me. "I should have told you myself," she added. "I just never think about it. What's done is done."

I did not want to talk about it, so I shrugged one of those it's-all-right shrugs.

And then her face blossomed suddenly. She said eagerly, "Wait. I know what he's doing. He's using one of the stories, isn't he?"

"What stories?" I asked.

"About the woman of his obsession," she answered. "What is it this time? That she was involved with a corporate pilot because she needed a fallback plan? That she ran off with the captain of a pleasure yacht? Or is it the one about losing her to a career in fashion? Or the one about the lesbian playmate?"

I smiled, remembering Inga's story about relaxing in the hot tub with Sylvia, and I wondered if that had been the inspiration for Carson X.'s story about the lesbian playmate—if, indeed, there was such a story.

I cleared my throat. "He told us about the pilot. He also told us she had become involved with one of his colleagues," I said in Bloodworth's voice.

Sylvia cackled with laughter. "Oh, I've heard that one, too," she said. "Was there a divorce involved, where the woman becomes a blimp in a Mercedes?"

"We haven't heard that part of it," I answered. "He hasn't mentioned that he had been married."

"He's editing," Sylvia enthused. "That's good. The blimp in the Mercedes was always a little offensive. But he's great, isn't he? I'm sure he used the colleague story because of you, since you were pretending to be a psychiatrist—or, at least, I assume that's your pseudo profession in the seminar."

"Yes," I told her. My face told her more.

She touched my arm with her fingers. "Don't let it bother you."

"That's not easy advice," I said.

"Why isn't it?" she asked.

"We've spent more than a few hours talking about truth," I said bitterly.

"And you think he's betrayed you with his own fibs?" she asked in a light, breezy manner.

It was, I thought, a ridiculous question. "Don't you?" I answered.

She sat back in her chair, pondering my response.

"Yes, and no," she said after a moment. "He was—and still is—obsessed with me. It gets sillier by the year, if you want to know the truth, but I was also obsessed with him. He loves me. I love him. We simply can't live together, and that bothers him a lot more than it bothers me. He has some very glaring macho traits, in case you haven't noticed. Anyway, that's the way it is. It's as trite, and as true, as that. Carson's a complex man. He has the temper and the flair of an artist, and the imagination. The way he handles our—" She smiled, then continued. "—our failure, is to have me suffer in some manner. The blimp, remember? With the yacht, I sometimes fall overboard and drown, or, at other times, I'm raped by the crew while the captain—my lover—drinks rum and cheers the performance. If he has me running off to the fashion world, I'm later arrested for stealing sketches from a famous Italian designer and passing them off as my own. The lesbian lover speaks for itself, especially when men—such as you and the rest of your group—are the audience. Men love stories about lesbians."

She paused. Her smile was radiant. Her eyes were still shining. "Forgive him his little deception," she said. "But isn't he following the same rules he set for all of you, only the flip side of it? I know the program. You are not to use your real name and real profession; all else is the truth. In his case, he gives you his real name and real profession; all else is likely to be a falsehood. And he has you calling him Carson X., doesn't he? Do you know why? X is the unknown, isn't it? He loves that—wrapping himself in the unknown." Her smile softened. "Believe me, he's really something of a miracle worker," she offered. She looked at me, studied me for a moment. "You're better, aren't you? Whoever the woman was, you're gaining some control over the hurt, aren't you?"

She annoyed me with her patronizing, yet I knew she was also right; I was finding control in my need for Kalee. I was not sure if it was the work of Carson X., or the influence of Inga and Sylvia and Arlo. Or perhaps the wisdom of Old Joe. I knew only that something was helping me.

Because I did not answer immediately, Sylvia asked again, "Aren't you better?"

"Yes," I admitted.

"And that's what matters, isn't it?" she cooed.

"I suppose so," I said. "In the long run."

"I know it is," she insisted. There was a little whimper of sorrow in her voice, a sound that she covered quickly. She stood. "I think I should be going."

We went back into the house and she took my coffee cup over my protest and rinsed it in the sink.

"You're still going to be with us tonight, aren't you?" she asked.

"Yes," I said. "I told you I would."

She looked at me with a puzzled expression. "You seem—well, almost too calm," she said. "A little like Carson. Are you all right?"

I told her I was fine. "But I do have a question," I said.

"Ask," she said.

"What did you do to handle your obsession?"

A smile eased into her face. "I found a role," she said.

"Which one?" I asked.

"Why, Dr. Bloodworth," she answered dramatically, "the one that works, of course."

"Dulcinea or Aldonza?" I said.

She laughed gaily. "Both," she said in an exaggerated stage whisper. "Both."

I wanted to tell her she would not survive the severe review of knowledgeable critics, but did not have the energy for such an argument. Instead, I said, "You might be right."

Her laugh became a smile, softly placed on her lips, in her eyes. She again reached to touch my face with her fingertips, as she had done before, and then she turned and left the cabin and drove away.

At the laptop, I wrote:
Dear Kalee,

I fashion these few words for no reason other than my need to shake them from the tips of my fingers, or to erase them from the clutter of my confused thinking.

I think that Sylvia Reeves is a bitter person.

She is bitter because she once lived with that gentle madman, Don Quixote.

And being Dulcinea is boring to someone with the restlessness of an Aldonza. Ladies of love—even those who have no charge for their service—are conquerors who have a taste for the adventure of sex. It is a hunger that never leaves them, no matter how many acts of contrition they profess or how many promises they offer to their current lovers. Give them time and they will have an accident of encounter, something quick and forgotten, another tasty treat.

And, so, I do wonder about Sylvia-Aldonza, but I cannot worry about her. Or Inga. Or Carson X. Or Bloodworth. Or anyone, but you. You, Kalee.

Here, on Neal's Island, I am learning that all people are liars. Everyone but you. I do not believe you ever misled me, not in a malicious way. I, of course, have lied, as I've admitted, and I know my companions in the MOD Mob have lied. They're men, for God's sake. It's part of their nature (our nature). Bloodworth, too. Bloodworth lies every time he tells someone buried into his soft blue sofa that he understands his or her anguish. What he understands is that their time is almost up and another hundred and fifty dollars is sitting in his waiting room, reading some magazine on psychology, or maybe the Gideon Bible. And, let's see, Sylvia has lied, certainly, because she is an actress. And Carson X. may be the Chief of Liars. Or maybe he is a better actor than Sylvia is an actress. They're perfectly matched, I'd say. Too bad it didn't work for them.

I am making progress, Kalee. I am. And making progress gives me peace.

My hand is on the hilt of the brave man's sword. It fits my grip.

I love you.

Your Correspondent

The day was still warm when I finished the letter to Kalee, the sun still swept its broom across the beach. I left the cabin and walked inland, across two streets and the dogleg of the island golf course. In the distance, on one of the putting greens used for practice, I saw Max bending over a putt, favoring his cut hand, and I remembered how pleased he seemed when he talked of Kay Cee, his childhood sweetheart. I wondered if he would search for her and, if he did find her, would he tell her about the scars across his chest. I watched his arms move through the soft stroke of the putt and from the way he stood—proud and triumphant—I knew the putt was true.

I did not have a purpose for the walk, a place to go. I only wanted to be away from the cabin, away from the word-maker that plagued me with its calling key faces, away from the lingering musk of Sylvia, away from the telephone that might fill itself with Bloodworth's voice, asking about my sanity, or even from Inga's voice, promising warmth. I wanted to be outside, where Arlo might fan my face and clear my thinking with some trickery of wind whipped up by his ghost playing.

I found myself, some minutes later, standing at Stillwater Lake, where Inga had led me. I saw egrets poised in leafless trees like the blooms of great white flowers—magnificent magnolias—

and I saw two blue herons in an air circus, and over the swaying surface of the lake, I saw fish rolling and spraying water. And then, across the lake, in the spotlight of the late sun, in the place where Inga said he would be, I saw him: I saw Lucifer, his great brown body burrowed into the matted grass. He was majestic, a king of the waters, an ancient creature hatched from an ancient egg, and staring at him, there in the sunspot, I thought I was seeing a god at rest.

A dog barked from behind me. Not a bark, really. A yapping. I turned and saw it bounce across the side of the golf course—a white terrier with black markings, ears that were like spear points. It stopped barking, cocked its head toward me and sniffed. Then it began yapping again, high-pitched and cocky.

And then I saw Old Joe Bonner quick-hobbling toward me. He called to the dog, "Stop that noise, Leo."

The dog stopped barking, then sat. I could hear it whine.

"He won't bite. All bark and no bite," Old Joe said. He cackled a laugh.

"It's all right," I told him.

"That's Leo," Old Joe said. "Named him after that lion on the tee-vee. Ain't big as a minute, but thinks he's a damned elephant." He laughed and leaned down and swept his fingers over Leo's head.

"Man's best friend," I said.

Old Joe looked up. He laughed again, again a cackle. "Better'n a woman, but when you old as I am, a woman ain't nothing but a pain. They always wanting something they don't need."

"I'll have to think about that," I told him.

"Big, ain't he?" Old Joe said, motioning toward Lucifer with his fishing rod.

"Yes, he is," I agreed.

"They was trying to kill him earlier this year."

"Why?" I asked.

"Some old ladies in a canoe come too close to him, trying to take some pictures, and he went to snarling," Old Joe explained. "Lordy, Jesus, they was a ruckus."

"They would kill him for that?" I asked.

Old Joe's head wagged rapidly. "Gotta keep the paying customers happy." His laugh skittered over the lake. "I told everybody that them old biddies was too tough to chew on, anyhow. Lucifer would of spit them out." He spat. "Just like that." He laughed again.

"Been fishing?" I asked.

"Going," Old Joe corrected. He squinted toward the sun. "Right time of day for it."

"Here, instead of the ocean?" I said.

"Can't never tell what you might catch in the ocean," Old Joe advised. "Get me a bass or two in here." He paused, turned at his waist to look behind him, toward the ocean, then he confided quietly, "Can't never tell when the fisherman might be out there. Don't like being around him."

"Who?" I asked.

"The fisherman."

"Is he a ghost?"

"Uh-huh. Yessir, he is."

"You can see him?"

"Plain as you," Old Joe declared seriously.

"What does he look like?"

"Old, like me," Old Joe answered. "Wears a raincoat and a red cap."

It was the description of the man I had seen fishing on my earlier walk, the man I had thought was Old Joe.

"Do other people see him?" I asked.

Old Joe nodded. "Some do, way they talk. Most don't know he's a ghost. I just hear folks saying things, but I don't never say nothing. What they don't know won't hurt nobody, I suppose."

"You believe in them, don't you?" I said.

Old Joe cackled again. "Ghosts? I better. I'm liable to be one soon." Then he said, "They's here. Everywhere you look. Or, don't look. Why I keep Leo with me all the time. Leo, he can sniff them out, just like they was a raccoon."

It was as though Leo heard and understood Old Joe. He lifted his ears suddenly and began a wild, maniacal barking, and then he scooted back to the safety of Old Joe.

Old Joe laughed. He ambled off, still cackling softly.

I turned back to look at Lucifer. I saw him lift his head and then begin a slow slide into the water. I watched him disappear like a submarine, saw the long crease of water fold over his body.

On the way back to the cabin, thinking of Old Joe and his island of ghosts, I realized I did not want to go to the evening session. I did not want to see Carson X. His dishonesty about the woman of his obsession was also a ghost, a mocking one.

At the cabin, I called him and told him an urgent business matter had developed and I needed to stay at the cabin for a conference call. It was a lie to counter a lie—an even exchange, perhaps canceling out the lying.

He was surprisingly pleasant.

"Perfectly fine," he said. "I'm not at all worried about you."
He paused slightly, a half-beat. "You're doing very well, maybe
better than you realize."

"You think so?" I asked.

"I know it," he replied confidently. "If the call comes early,
come on over; if not, I'll see you tomorrow. Only one more day,
you know."

"Yes," I said. I added, deliberately, "But I doubt if I'll make
it tonight. I'm supposed to go to a dinner later."

There was a hint of suspicion in his voice: "Really?"

"The woman I was with when you were taking the pictures,"
I told him. "Remember her?"

The pause was longer. "Oh, yes. Yes, I do. Well, that's—
good. I know her. She's a great supporter of my work."

"I thought so," I said. "She mentioned you. I presumed it was
because she believes I'm in the same profession."

His reply sounded brighter: "Of course. She's very pleasant.
I'm sure you'll have a nice time."

"I think so, too," I said. "I'm going with the woman who
works at the grocery—Inga."

"Oh?" The surprise was obvious.

"She's been very kind to me since I arrived," I replied.
"That's how I met Sylvia. I was shopping one day and she was
there. Inga arranged our luncheon in Beaufort."

Carson X. forced his voice to sound cheerful. "Well, that's
good. See you tomorrow, then."

He hung up without waiting for a reply.

I called Inga and told her my plans had changed, that we
could go to Sylvia's dinner earlier than I had suggested. She was
pleased. "Remember, it's casual," she cautioned. "I know Sylvia.
When she says casual, she means it. A pressed shirt is dress-up."

"I'll be appropriately scruffy," I promised.

I then called Sylvia's number. She did not answer and I left a message on her answering machine about our arrival.

Twenty minutes later, she returned my call. She was laughing. "What did you tell Carson?"

"That I was having dinner at your place. Why?"

"I just got in," she explained. "There was a message from him, asking why I'd invited you for dinner. He seemed a little miffed."

"I took your suggestion," I said. "You were right. It is my money. Anyway, I wasn't in the mood for a session tonight. I think I need the rest of the day off."

"I shouldn't have said anything earlier," she replied. "About his stories, I mean."

"No, it's all right. I just need to—to..."

"To what?" she asked.

"To start weaning myself," I answered.

"I understand," Sylvia assured me. "But I'm also glad you can come early. You'll like Reuben." Her voice became a whisper. "He reminds me of you in some way."

"He's not an actor, is he?" I asked.

"Aren't all men?" she replied. And then she laughed again.

27

Night of the Ninth Day

In one of his most impassioned and poetic lectures to me about Kalee, Bloodworth once emphasized that everything becomes clear to the person who understands what he must do.

Chaos ends, he promised.

Order reigns.

"You must understand that when everything becomes clear, everything blends, everything integrates, everything folds together when the understanding becomes real," Bloodworth explained.

Driving to Inga's home, I remembered the lecture, and I realized Bloodworth had tried to explain something that was becoming more and more apparent from the theatrics of Carson X's sessions: until we understand what we are to do, we miss much of the texture of our destiny.

For me, that texture was everywhere.

The bird I heard in early morning and heard again from the deck of the cabin when talking with Sylvia, was part of it, part of the texture—perhaps the most mystic part of it. The bird was, for me, a vagabond musician, whistling trumpet and flute and clarinet, charged by some force of wonder with announcing each new moment in the pageant of my time on Neal's Island. A vagabond bird—a wandering minstrel bird—migrating from Canada on southerly winds, taking a stopover for rest in the tree of Cabin 18, and discovering there an unexpected drama needing his music. He would stay and chirp merrily at even the shadows of what is to happen. But I knew he was there—this vagabond bird—watching and singing, and I believed he would follow me the rest of the time I was on Neal's Island, follow me until the drama ended.

The weather was also part of the texture. The weather had been warmer. It was as though summer had turned back from its flyaway and playfully slipped in to heat the air.

Bloodworth was part of it, also. It was Bloodworth who exiled me to the island to discover what I had discovered, and was continuing to discover. It was Bloodworth who had advised me, who had urged me to do this thing that I must do, and it was Bloodworth who had given me the cover-up identity to do it.

Of course, Arlo was part of it—Arlo of the dreams, Arlo alive, Arlo dead, Arlo in-between life and death. Scotch-guzzling, water-walking, astral-projecting, game-playing Arlo. A B—Boyd, not Bowers. I liked Arlo. I wasn't sure I should trust him, as Old Joe Bonner had warned, but I liked him. I wish I had worked with him. He had—has, for that matter—flair. We would have made one hell of a team for Spence, working worthless accounts. I determined to research his life—and death—when I left Neal's Island and returned to the clutter of Atlanta and to the Internet.

And, certainly, Sylvia was part of it. I had a sense that, if all this was truly my destiny, Sylvia was meant to cloud my vision, to tempt me. She was an actress, yes, and the role she was playing (without knowing she was playing it), was that of the Devil's advocate.

And Inga was part of it. She had been part of it from the beginning. I do not think I met her by accident. I think it was preordained, perhaps for both of us.

෨

When Inga and I arrived at Sylvia's home—the most elaborate on the island, according to Inga—we were greeted by Sylvia before I could ring the bell. She was dressed in a long, wrap-around skirt, a strawberry-colored sarong, and a loose-fitting white blouse low-buttoned below her neck, exposing the quivery flesh of her breasts. She had the same look she had had in Marty's: the glow of too much wine. She hugged both of us quickly, ebulliently, then ushered us inside to meet Reuben Sherwood.

If Reuben Sherwood had worn an electric-neon sandwich board announcing he was from California, he could not have been more obvious. I had seen him, or his likeness, a million times in magazines. We used to joke about it at the agency when we used a California crew for a commercial. California people are not people, Spence had declared; they are clones of themselves.

Reuben was young, perhaps in his late twenties. He wore his hair long, curled up from his shoulders. It had the carefully trained look of being fingered back from the pretentious brain massage that creative people are always giving themselves. He was dressed in California fashion—deck shoes, faded jeans, a pullover shirt, jewelry around his throat, an earring planted like a diamond seed in his left earlobe. He had sunglasses wedged across his forehead, attached to a bright orange band dangled over his shoulders. He was studio or tube tanned. His teeth were blazing white. There was a pleasant coconut fragrance about him. And he had positioned himself centerstage, on the floor, his legs crossed.

The conversation we had interrupted, according to Sylvia, was about the FullLife Foundation. I knew that Reuben was fascinated with the subject. A small recorder was on the floor, between his crossed legs, and I knew he had been aiming its microphone toward Sylvia, like a well-to-do beggar asking for well-to-do alms.

"I'm learning a lot," Reuben said pleasantly.

I did not want to be a party to the conversation, so I volunteered to be a servant, to replenish the wine and to keep the tray of hors d'oeuvres moving, person to person.

"Why, that's nice of you, Tyler," Sylvia gushed in a voice deliberately, though subtly affected. Her eyes played with me. "But I know where everything is. You can help me while Reuben and Inga get acquainted."

"I'm sure I can find things," I told her.

"No, I'll help," Sylvia insisted cheerfully. "After all, I am the hostess. And I do need to get a few things ready for dinner."

Sylvia and I went into the kitchen, which was out of view from the den. She smiled at me, and winked. Then she handed me two bottles of wine, and as I took them, she stroked her hand across my face.

She asked, "Are you disappointed in me?"

"No," I said. "Why should I be?"

"I just wondered," she replied. Then: "Are you going to help me with dinner? Inga said you're great in the kitchen." She paused. "As well as—" She paused again. "No. I'm teasing. She really only mentioned the kitchen."

"I'll be happy to help," I told her. "I don't think I belong to the conversation going on out there."

"Do what I do," Sylvia suggested. "Pretend. Be the actor. At least for a few minutes. I'll rescue you soon." She smiled sweetly. "But be careful what you say."

I returned to the den with the wine and refilled Reuben's glass and poured a glass for Inga and one for myself, and then I sat near Inga and listened to Reuben.

"It's really fascinating, all of this," Reuben enthused. "What I think we need for the segment are two things: first, we need to show—and hear from—people whose lives have been changed by the Foundation—people like you, Inga—and, then we need to tell the story of someone who has been, well, disturbed, but is finding new direction, someone in transition."

Inga whispered, "I see."

"You never have long to tell your story on a show like this," Reuben added in a serious voice. "Just a few minutes, really. It's got to happen from the get-go. We'll use a lot of visual cuts and some sound bites. It has to be quick and effective."

"I can see that. It's just that I—I don't know anything about such things," Inga confessed.

"Do you know someone who might provide that transitional character for us?" Reuben asked.

I thought, there it is: California Reuben putting it on the line. He glanced at me, and I thought again of Bloodworth and his speech about understanding what one must do. I wondered if Reuben's glance was part of the scheme of things, part of the texture of my destiny. But if he wanted transition, he was looking at it. I glorified transition. There was only one problem: I would never share it with Reuben.

Inga answered his question uncomfortably: "I'll have to think about it."

"Good," Reuben said, leaping to his feet. "Now, that's enough. I'm sure the two of you didn't come over here to be bored by my questions." He picked up his recorder and put it on a table.

There was a moment of awkwardness, of absurd, agreeing smiles, a moment of searching for something to say. I was about to ask Reuben to tell us of his experiences in Hollywood when Sylvia swept into the room.

"I goofed," she said dramatically.

"You did what?" asked Inga.

"I forgot the bread for dinner," Sylvia answered.

"Oh, we don't need it," Inga said.

Sylvia struck an exaggerated pose, like an offended Scarlett O'Hara. Her hand fluttered over her throat. "Why, ma'am, of course we do," she cooed. "We can't offer our guests dinner without the South's sustenance of life, now can we? Oh, heavens, no."

Reuben laughed. I saw his eyes dart to Sylvia's chest.

"The store's not far away," Inga said. "Want me to get some?"

"Do you mind?"

"Of course not," Inga answered. "I'll have to run by the house to get the key, but that'll—"

Sylvia interrupted her. "Here's an idea. Why don't you take my car and show Reuben that part of the island?" She answered her own suggestion. "Yes, that'll give him a chance to hear another person's voice besides mine. I'm sure I'm about to wear the poor man out, the way I've been running on since I picked him up in Beaufort. If I'm not careful, he'll get the impression that what they say about Southern women being empty-headed blather-mouths is more fact than fiction."

I thought: Amanda in *The Glass Menagerie*. Tennessee Williams would have been pleased.

"I'll drive them," I suggested.

"Don't be silly," Sylvia said, still in character. "Or are you jealous, Dr. Tyler? Are you afraid of losing your lady to this handsome young man?" She laughed Amanda's laugh. "You can help me put the finishing touches on things in the kitchen."

Inga blushed.

"I'm comfortable with anything," I said. "I'll be happy to drive them, or I'll roll up my sleeves in the kitchen."

302

Inga smiled reluctantly. "It won't take long," she said. She looked at Reuben. "You'll see the seedy side of the island."

"Nonsense," Sylvia sang. "It may be the most beautiful area, and Inga's got a wonderful home, Reuben. Really lovely. I keep telling her I'll trade places with her at the drop of a hat, but she doesn't believe me."

We walked outside to the Mercedes, listening to Sylvia-Amanda's giddy instructions about what Reuben should see and the kind of bread Inga should bring from the store. Sylvia and I watched them drive away, waving to them like children.

"You're very good," I said quietly.

Sylvia aimed a triumphant smile at me. "I know," she whispered.

We went inside and Sylvia stood at the window and watched until the Mercedes was out of sight, and then she came to me and took my hands in her hands.

"Now, Dr. Tyler Bloodworth, or whoever you are, we have a few minutes to ourselves," she said.

"To the kitchen, then," I replied.

She did not answer. She turned and led me by the hand up the stairway and into her bedroom.

"What are you doing?" I asked.

She put her fingers on my lips to stop the question, and then she directed me to her bed and forced me to sit on it. She stood before me and unbuttoned her blouse and slipped it from her shoulders. Her hard, erect breasts moved with her breathing.

"Sylvia, I think this has gone far enough. The audience left the house," I said.

She stepped to me, standing close.

"I've wanted to do this all day," she whispered. "Since I left you."

303

"Come on, Sylvia. Don't—"

"Do you really think I didn't have any bread?" she said.

She pushed me back on the bed and kissed me. I could taste the rich perfume of the wine in her mouth. I moved to stand, but her hands stopped me. Then she rolled on the bed and pulled at the tie on her wrap-around skirt and the skirt fell open. She was nude. She looked up and smiled.

"Do you think I'm betraying my friend?" she whispered.

"Yes," I answered. "You're damn right, I do."

She laughed. Her fingers reached for me, touching me expertly, moving from my face to my chest. Her fingers paused, stroked, then she moved over me, straddling my thighs. Her eyes did not move from my face.

"Do you want me?" she asked softly.

"No. No matter what you think," I told her.

"I don't believe you," she teased.

"You should," I said.

Her voice grew husky. "Who do you think I am?"

I stared at her. The look on her face was the look of command. "Aldonza," I said.

"The whore?"

"Yes."

"If you saw me on stage, would you applaud?"

"Yes."

She smiled happily. She leaned forward and kissed me tenderly, tracing her tongue over my lips, and then she rolled from me and picked up her skirt and blouse and left the room.

From outside, I heard the vagabond bird singing gaily.

When I went into the kitchen, Sylvia was at the refrigerator, again dressed, removing the makings of a salad.

She said, "What do you think? Tomatoes? Should we put tomatoes in the salad?"

"What are we having for the main course?" I asked.

"Grilled tuna," she answered. "I hope you like it."

"Very much," I told her.

She smiled mischievously. "You're a wonderful leading man. Aldonza thanks you."

"What about the FullLife Foundation?" I asked. "Does it also thank me?"

"Of course," she said brightly. "The Foundation is always happy with a healing."

"A healing? Is that what you were trying to do? Heal me?"

Sylvia broke apart the lettuce and began to rinse it at the sink. After a moment, she said, "You're being selfish. Perhaps I was thinking of myself."

"I thought you were already healed," I replied. "I thought that was why you believed in the Foundation."

She looked at me. "Healing never stops," she said. "You really need to know that. Besides, every good thing needs to be tested, doesn't it?"

"Every good thing always is, isn't it?" I said.

She laughed blithely and turned back to the lettuce. "That was a Carson answer. Maybe you've been around him too long." Her eyes flashed to me. They were shining in the same way Kalee's eyes would shine when she was happy. "Mind cutting the tomatoes? The cherry ones."

"Sure," I said, "but I'm curious: why?"

"Because I think tomatoes would be good," she answered in a light, teasing voice.

"I'm not speaking of the tomatoes and you know it," I said.

She looked at me. "Oh, I've confused you. Should I apologize for my brazen behavior?"

"It's not necessary," I replied. "I'm just curious, so I ask again: why?"

She handed me a small cutting board. "Let me answer with a question," she said. "Do you think I should be coddling you, treating you with kid's gloves, because you've had a painful experience over some woman?"

"I think it's something to consider, yes," I replied.

The teasing look, the smile of it, vanished from her face. "Whoever you are, believe me in this: the world doesn't ache for you as much as you think it should," she said. "Pity might be intense, but it's not permanent. The reason you need to get on with your life is because the world can't afford to wait around while you waste time weeping."

Her words seemed to echo, to lash at the air between us.

"And there's the other reason," she added. The smile reappeared. "I needed to know if you're worthy of my friend. That was the short-cut way of finding out."

"And?" I asked.

She did not answer. Her eyes flashed.

"You're leaving me to wonder?" I said.

"The tomatoes," she replied. "You should cut the larger ones in half."

Inga and Reuben returned shortly, and we grilled tuna, and I listened to Sylvia and Inga and Reuben talk of the FullLife Foundation, and how Reuben would structure his program to give the show balance and credibility. I fought the urge to bellow, and wished Arlo were with me. Not the ghost Arlo, but the real one, the in-the-flesh one. He, too, would have enjoyed the conversation about balance and credibility and we could have matched one another for serious nodding and expressions of awe. Reuben knew the bottom-line; he just wouldn't talk about it. The bottom-line was simple: What could be offered in slick promotions to pick up a wandering eye and make it watch whatever was on the other side of a commercial. Reuben had Sylvia and Inga eating out of his hand with his promises of balance and credibility.

☙

Inga and I left early. We returned to her home and made love in a slow and easy and tender way—the kind of lovemaking by people who are actually in love—and the joy of it left me with the sensation of being a stranger in a familiar body. I thought of Arlo, wondered if he had left me with the gift of knowing the same splendor of Inga that he had known?

She seemed to sense my confusion. She asked, as we dressed, "Are you all right?"

"More than that," I told her in a playful way. "I'm beginning to believe I've discovered a new me."

She smiled. "I know I have," she said. And then she paused and gazed at me. "I have," she repeated. "I'm not sure if it's something that's actually happening, or if I'm in a coma and having a pleasant dream. It doesn't seem possible. How long have I even known you—eight days?"

We had a cup of hot tea and talked in her living room of Sylvia and Carson X., and there was merriment in her voice. She had affection for both, yet she knew her time on Neal's Island was also coming to an end.

"I have to put all of this away," she said, "but I don't mean that I need to totally forget it. I don't. It's part of me, and always will be." She touched my hand and played her fingers over it. "I'm glad you know all of it, though. At least I don't have to pretend with you."

A rush of shame struck me. "I'm glad also," I said.

Then she asked, "When are you leaving the island?"

I said, "Soon, but maybe not for a couple of days. I should know tomorrow."

She pulled my hand to her lips and kissed it. "I'd rather not think about it," she said.

I should have told her the truth about me, and I should have told her about Sylvia, but I couldn't.

I would soon be off the island of ghosts and deceivers.

The vagabond bird sang a ballad as I walked from Inga's home to my car. I looked for him in a tree, but I did not see him. He was off-stage, in the wings, a one-throat orchestra playing a scene break.

I thought of the letter I would write to Kalee.

Maybe it would not be a letter.

Maybe it would be an SOS, clicked out behind the blinking cursor.

28

Morning of the Tenth Day

I did not write my letter of therapy to Kalee. I went to bed and slept through the night. No dreams, not even of Sylvia's performance as Aldonza-Scarlett-Amanda, or of the sweetness of Inga. Only sleep. Good, gentle sleep. The kind of sleep that comes with surgery. Counting backward one moment, unconscious the next.

Reuben Sherwood called early, waking me. He could hear the sleep in my voice and he apologized.

"It's fine," I told him. "To be honest, I don't know what time it is."

"Seven," he said. "I'm really sorry."

He wanted to make an appointment to spend a few minutes with me, a few minutes in private, he emphasized.

"Sure," I told him. "If you can make it in an hour, by eight. I've got telephone appointments starting at nine thirty." A lie, of course, but a reasonable lie. It was the last day for the group and I did not want to miss the sessions and the morning session was at 10:00.

"I can be there," he said. I gave him the address and he thanked me, again apologizing for the early call. He sounded urgent.

I made coffee and showered and dressed and waited for Reuben, wondering why he wanted to see me.

He wanted dirt, I believed, and he wanted someone with credibility—someone like a Dr. Tyler Bloodworth—to put the hex on Carson X. Just a word or two, a good sound bite with a doubtful intonation, a small thought to wrap a question around, anything to ignite controversy. Carson X. had forced us to watch the television talk show of girls who sold sex in school, and he had preached that such shows worked because they caught the country with its pants down. First-cousin incest, fat women with skinny men (and vice-versa), God and Godless, straight and gay. And Carson X. was right. Reuben would be an idiot to go back to California with anything less than controversy.

And I knew I could provide him with that, yet I also knew that perhaps I was not giving Reuben the credit he deserved. Perhaps he was a great journalist, worthy of the Pulitzer Prize. Perhaps he had pried the complete story of Inga being saved by the FullLife Foundation out of Sylvia, with Sylvia's embellished tale of Inga's new lover—me. Each morsel of the gossip would have been offered with the warning that he must keep the matter completely private. But I also knew that everyone—especially journalists—make promises with disappearing tongues. And if Reuben believed I could add to his story, he would sneak over to the cabin dressed as Bozo the Clown and doctor my coffee with anything he could get his hands on, from saltpeter to sodium pentothal. The lover of a FullLife Foundation convert should have a lot to say, especially if the Foundation is enhancing, or even interfering, with his sex life.

If that were Reuben's purpose, if he wanted to ask about Inga, I would tell him that, to my knowledge, her conversion, her transformation, had made her asexual. I would vow we had never experienced anything more intimate than the dessert we shared at Sylvia's house. I would tell him that, from my observation, Inga had attained a state of bliss so nearly perfect, she could ascend to the mountaintop with a feather-stroke push. And then I would tell him such bliss appeared to be a FullLife, money-back guarantee, and that I was pleased to give up sex to see her so content.

And there was bliss in what I saw in Inga. She was not like Sylvia, or Sylvia-Aldonza, the tease who still heard the ringing of ancient applause from thrilled theater audiences. To me, it was odd that Inga and Sylvia were friends. They were not at all alike, but, together, they were like the woman I had imagined to be Penny of P R—before I knew about the doctoring of the initials: two people in one—the queen's proper maid and the whore. It was an equation from a notebook of illusions: Inga and Sylvia were Penny.

I hoped Reuben would not ask me about Inga, and that Sylvia had not spoken to him about the initials. I hoped he only wanted to get away from the seduction of Sylvia, like a teenager who wanted to sneak off for a smoke. If that were true, I would be an acceptable excuse. And if that was what he wanted, I would let him puff away.

Dear Kalee,

Reuben Sherwood left a few minutes ago.

He was here only thirty minutes, though it seemed longer. It gives me a few minutes to be with you before I leave for the session.

(I did mention him, didn't I? Sylvia's guest. The television boy wonder with his eye on an Emmy.)

I know I am balanced on a high wire that is quivering under my feet, but some of the old me remains intact. My instincts, at least, are correct. When Reuben came to visit this morning, he did want dirt on the FullLife Foundation, as I suspected, but I could not, and would not, give him any, and he did not pressure me. I think he believed me when I told him the truth: that I had only been on the island for slightly more than a week, and that I had met Sylvia through Inga. He did not ask about Carson X., which tells me that Sylvia had not betrayed our little secret. If he had asked me, however, I would have danced around the question. Thankfully, Sylvia had also kept quiet about the initials and my ruse of being Bloodworth and of my participation in the men's seminar, and I was certain she had said nothing about testing me in the bedroom of her palatial home.

I don't think Sylvia talked about much at all. I think she was simply enjoying herself. Reuben confessed, as young California men will, that he and Sylvia had spent the night doing the deed. "Wildest woman I've ever been with," he said in awe. "Gives me a new appreciation of maturity."

And then he told me something of real interest: there are people—ex-FullLifers—who have accused Carson X. of operating a cult. Brainwashing. Some sad cases, apparently. At least one had swallowed the bullet Carson X. talked about, the bullet being from a .38. Reuben wants either to nail Carson X. to the wall, or he wants to disprove the charges. Frankly, I don't think it matters to him. He'll do what everyone in the media seems to do these days; he'll stack story against story, and the larger pile is the one he'll go with.

I wanted to tell him that he should turn his cameras on me if he is fascinated with cult following and brainwashing. When I speak your name, it is a mantra, an incessant chanting of praise and wonder.

***

*Forgive me for ***ing away.*
I need to pretend detachment, even if it does not wholly exist.

Inga called after Reuben left. She wanted to know if I was well.

I said, "Yes, why do you ask?"

"You seemed—I don't know—different last night," she replied.

"It was a different kind of night," I said.

She admitted I was right. She had talked to Sylvia, and Sylvia had gushed over how impressed she had been with me. "She said you passed the test," Inga told me. "Whatever that means."

"I think it means I didn't do anything embarrassing at dinner," I suggested. "I used the correct fork."

Inga laughed and then told me that Sylvia had agreed to be interviewed on camera by Reuben.

"I'm sure she's excited," I said.

"She does love an audience," Inga said easily.

"I can't disagree with that," I replied. I asked if she were going to be interviewed, also.

"I don't know. Reuben asked me about it. What do you think?"

"You have to decide that, don't you?" I told her.

"That's a dodge," she said.

"Yes, I guess it is," I confessed. "Sorry."

"If I do, I won't let them use my name, and maybe I'll make them distort my face and my voice," she said.

Think of that, Kalee: a disguised endorsement for the FullLife Foundation. A mask for the New Age. Such a strange recommendation for freedom.

But I don't blame Inga. She has her name(s) to protect.

***

It is amazing how close you are to me today. I cannot sit at the word-maker for long, because you are so much in me, *compelling me to stand, to pace. That is the reason for this new* ***.

When Reuben left, I thought of how easily Sylvia was manipulating him, and I wanted to call him and tell him everything, but it seemed a thought of revenge. In an odd way, Sylvia has taught me something of great value, perhaps, the most important lesson from the time spent here. She cut to the chase, Kalee. The world didn't stop spinning because I am weeping over my loss of you. I think it did slow down a bit. For me, at least. And like all mourners, I wanted it to be true of everyone. But Earth is a big rock and it needs to be chasing itself around the sun. It needs to be getting on with things, and that is what Sylvia was telling me. Certainly, she did it. She stopped her weeping and got on with it. Reuben is proof of it.

But, Kalee, I still have tears.

There, on the bench, I sensed you with me. You were standing in front of me, your back to my chest, and I was embracing you at the waist, with your hands on my arms. Remember how wonderfully we fit, standing like that? The perfume of your silver-blonde hair is still on my face.

I love you.

Your Correspondent

29

Morning Session of the Tenth Day

At the morning session, Carson X. tried to behave as though he had no interest in the dinner at Sylvia's home, but I knew he was bothered. I wondered if he had talked to Sylvia, and if he had, did Sylvia tell him about Reuben? Did she inform him that she was going to be a television star on one of the shows that had America seeking its scripted reality? I knew by the way he avoided me, he wanted to ask what had happened, but his dignity, or perhaps it was his arrogance, would not let him. He treated me instead with a slight disregard, which caused Barkeep to whisper in private, "I think he's pissed that you didn't show up last night."

"Maybe so," I said.

"You didn't miss a thing," Barkeep advised, still in whisper. "Believe me. He was off in never-never land. If it hadn't been for me, the others would have tossed him out with the tide."

Carson X. did explain to me that the evening session had focused on a discussion of the irritating traits of women. I saw smiles on the faces of the group, saw them cutting their eyes to Barkeep, saw Barkeep's smug expression of pride, and I knew it had been a lively and humorous evening, regardless of Barkeep's private assessment. I was sure he must have suggested some traits none of them had ever considered, and I regretted missing his performance.

"And, today, for this next-to-the-last time together, we're going to do just the opposite," Carson X. said brightly. "We're going to talk about the ideal woman."

Barkeep grinned. "Can't wait," he muttered. Then: "Miss Perfect?"

"Not perfect. Ideal," corrected Carson X.

"Shouldn't take long," Barkeep countered.

"I didn't say one existed, but, if one did, what would she be like?" Carson X. said.

Everyone looked at Barkeep. The match with Carson X. was on.

"She'd have the body of Cindy Crawford and the soul of Mother Teresa," Barkeep declared.

"And the bank account of Queen Elizabeth," added Menlo.

Carson X. whirled to face Menlo. "Oh?" he said in a condescending voice. "Do you think that matters?"

Menlo's face soured. "It's called a joke," he answered evenly.

"But does it matter?" Carson X. pressed.

I wanted to laugh. I wanted to go to the telephone and call Reuben and tell him to drop whatever he was doing—even if it was Sylvia—and leap into Sylvia's Mercedes and race over to Carson X.'s house. The show he wanted was being performed. I wanted to spring to my feet and shout to the group, "Look, guys, we're a bunch of fools. This miserable son of a bitch is living off the richest woman in South Carolina."

I only smiled at Carson X. A flush tinted his face. He quickly turned his eyes to Godsick.

"All right," he said. "I could argue that, but I won't. So, we have the body of Cindy Crawford, the soul of Mother Teresa and the bank account of Queen Elizabeth. Can you think of anything else?" He looked at Godsick.

"Patience," Godsick replied, after a moment.

"Ah, patience," Carson X. sighed dramatically. "A virtue." He closed his eyes and put his palms together in the pose of prayer, and he waited.

"Someone who meets you half-way," Max said.

"To keep the scales balanced?" asked Carson X., without moving or opening his eyes.

"I guess," Max answered. "Sure."

Carson X. nodded thoughtfully. He opened his eyes and stood and began to pace slowly in front of the easel holding Miss Perfect. "Anyone else?"

The suggestions began to tumble from the group, and Carson X. nodded like an accountant totaling figures in his head. He rolled his hands to motion for more, more, more. The responses were both serious and comic.

Understanding.

Forgiveness.

Great tits.

Communication.

A sense of adventure.

A nymphomaniac.

Someone with a tender smile.

Someone who cared for herself.

A mouth like Sophia Loren.

Someone who believed in surprises.

Someone who knew when to leave you alone.

"What else?" Carson X. urged.

"Honesty," I said.

Carson X. stopped pacing, but he did not look at me. "At all costs?" he asked.

"I think so," I said.

"But is that possible?"

"Probably not," I admitted. "We are talking about someone human, aren't we?"

A smirk leveled on his lips. He turned to face me.

"The woman you told us about—Kalee. Was she honest?"

"I think she told great truths," I said evenly. "And if she fibbed at all, the fibs were small ones, probably to please me."

"Would you have preferred great lies and small truths?" Carson X. asked.

"Of course not," I replied.

"Do you know the difference, Bloodworth?"

"What do you mean?" I asked.

The smirk on Carson X.'s lips curled into a haughty smile. "Couldn't you say that great lies cut like chain saws, but small lies only leave nicks?"

"But you can bleed to death from nicks, can't you?" Godsick said earnestly. "Over time, I mean. And the pain would last longer, wouldn't it?"

For a moment, I thought Carson X. was trapped. There was a flicker of uncertainty in his eyes—the same kind of flicker I had seen in Bloodworth's eyes when the question was delicate. "Too little, or too much, of anything can ultimately kill you, don't you think?" he said after a moment.

Godsick ducked his head.

"The point is, I don't believe absolute truth in all things is possible, as I explained at our first session," Carson X. continued. "And I think circumstance controls whether a truth or a lie is employed."

"Well, Doc, that sounds profound," Barkeep said sarcastically. "I think I'll have that one tattooed on my backside."

Carson X. ignored Barkeep. He began to pace again, slowly, deliberately, measuring his words by his steps. "If you have a job and you are called upon by your employer to give a particular presentation—one that he thinks is important—and on the day of the presentation you suddenly develop a migraine headache, and your employer asks you how you feel, what do you tell him? You would lie, I think. Or most people would. Most people would say, 'I'm fine. I feel great.'

"Now, you may argue that isn't a lie," Carson X. added, "and, certainly, it isn't intended to be, but it is."

"That's not what I'm talking about," I said.

"Oh?" Carson X. replied in his superior voice. "Then, why don't you tell us what you mean?"

"I mean honesty," I said. "And, to me, honesty is more than making a decision to tell the truth or to tell a lie. Honesty is being willing to correct a proposed truth or a protective lie."

"Yeah. I like that," Barkeep agreed. "That makes sense. That's the one I'm going to have tattooed on my butt."

Again, Carson X. ignored Barkeep. He tilted his head as though listening for an echo. His body rocked. His eyes narrowed in thought. Then he said, "Bloodworth's right. Honesty is being willing to correct what may or may not be the truth or may or may not be a lie. The brave man's sword is in there somewhere. When you find it—and you will—you will understand."

No one spoke. I could hear Max breathing heavily and I watched Godsick staring at the floor, remembering a moment that had caused him to ache.

"You will find it," Carson X. said, breaking the silence. "I promise you." He walked to the chart holding our portrait of Miss Perfect and touched her face, traced his finger over the outline of her lips, and then he turned back to us. "Tonight we meet for the last time. Tomorrow, you leave. Between now and tomorrow, you will use the sword." He paused. "This is what I want you to do. I want you to go to your cabins and stay there for the rest of the afternoon. Do not leave your cabin until you return tonight." He paused again, again touched the portrait of Miss Perfect. "And I want you to remember what Bloodworth has said about honesty."

He walked out of the kitchen, leaving us.

"Damn," muttered Barkeep. He looked at Menlo.

Menlo smiled and shrugged. He said, "You know, I think I just figured this out. The reason he gave us so much time off had nothing to do with our need to be alone to take stock of our madness; it had to do with him being alone to live with his."

In the cabin, I sat at the desk, before my laptop, and I opened the Document folder to write another letter. But it was not a letter for Kalee. It was for Inga.

Dear Inga,

Today, with some men I know, I talked about honesty, and when I drove away from them, I knew I had to be honest with you. Or, at least as honest as I can be at the moment—which is selfish, of course, but I beg you to understand that if I am not a little selfish now, I cannot be fully honest later.

When you asked me my name, I lied to you.

I am not Tyler Bloodworth. I am not a psychiatrist.

I know Tyler Bloodworth. He is my counselor, the reason I am here on Neal's Island. He urged me to come here, to join Dr. Willingham's seminar for men, the seminar that is supposed to cure my obsession for a woman who is, in many ways, very much like you. Yet, you are so different, it startles me.

And that is why I am writing this letter: to correct the lie I have told you.

Do you believe in destiny, Inga?

I don't think I did, not until this week.

I do now.

What else can it be? Coincidence? Jumbled odds falling in place like the icons of a slot machine? Sun signs and moon signs in perfect alignment?

No. I prefer destiny. Or, fate.

I knew I needed supplies for my stay on Neal's Island, and I stopped at the store where you work. I met you. I read your name on your nametag. I liked your name. I liked your face, the pleasantness of your eyes, the warmth of your smile, and I liked talking with you. I felt comfortable.

Why did I go into the store where you worked? Why didn't I go into the other store, the one farther in, near the docks?

Destiny. Fate.

And why did I stay in the cabin you and Arlo had used, the one that had initials carved into the deck railing, and why did I see those initials and guess Arlo's name? And why is it that you were P R?

Destiny. Fate.

I want you to understand this, too, Inga: I came to this island in anguish and with a lingering fury over an incident that, to me, was an unkind act of God.

The woman of my obsession was named Kalee. Was, Inga. Was. She died in a car accident shortly after our engagement. I needed a healing from the horror of that loss, the same as you needed your healing from the loss of Arlo. I believe that healing has been completed for you—or nearly so—and I think it has begun for me.

321

When I leave Neal's Island tomorrow, I want to be at peace with Kalee. In that way, I will always have the beauty of memory without the torment of yearning.

I believe that is what you have achieved with Arlo.

Peace.

Acceptance.

I want to be completely, fully, honest with you, Inga. And I will be. I will tell you my name, where I live, what I do, after this is over.

Please forgive me. Being with you has been one of the most joyful experiences I've ever had.

I am leaving tomorrow, but I am not leaving you.

I will return, and I will tell you everything.

I hope you will be here to listen.

I printed the letter and folded it and put it into an envelope and wrote Inga's name across the front.

30

Late Afternoon of the Tenth Day

When Billy the Kid led his gypsy deer clan across the yard, I knew it was four o'clock, or close to it. The deer traveled the island like a time-crier.

I watched them from the kitchen, watched them pausing, sniffing the air for the fragrance of the apples I had broken apart and scattered over the yard, watched them take the apple parts and nibble, watched their moon eyes blinking slowly in delight. A bird—the vagabond bird, I thought—fluttered to the ground beside a young doe, the smallest of the family, and fought with its flashing beak for a piece of the apple flesh dangling from a core. The doe stepped back, puzzled, cocked her head and looked at the bird, then moved closer to Billy the Kid.

I watched the deer and bird at feast, watched the deer wander away, watched the bird leap up under a wing-rush and fly to a perch somewhere above the roof of the cabin. I did not know why, but I thought of Spence and I went to the telephone and called him.

"Well, hallelujah," he exclaimed. "I thought you'd died or something."

"Just following orders," I said. "You told me not to call."

"How you doing?" he asked.

"Better. No. Good. I'm really coming out of it."

"Glad to hear that. Is that shrink as good as Bloodworth says he is?"

"He's—unusual."

"He's got to be if he's dealing with a fruitcake like you. When are you coming back?"

"Tomorrow," I told him. "The last session's tonight."

"If you knew what was waiting for you here, you'd throw out an anchor down there," Spence said.

We talked for a few minutes about business. Ross had landed the Dilliard account, which surprised Spence.

"They were leaning toward Elly Zingler," he confided. "But all she was doing was kissing ass—literally, I suspect. Ross showed them the campaign you put together before you left, and they pissed their pants. Wanted to know where you were."

"What did you tell them?" I asked.

"That you were institutionalized," he replied. "The idiots. They didn't believe a word I said."

I knew Spence was testing me. I knew he wanted to hear me laugh, and I did.

"Yeah, you sound better," he declared. Then, in a kinder voice: "You know, I've missed your sorry ass, boy."

"Same here, Spence," I said. "I've missed you. But I'm coming back a new man. You can bank on it. In fact, I'm going to take the clock out of the closet as soon as we hang up."

I could hear bewilderment in his voice: "What does that mean?"

I told him I would explain it later. "I just wanted you to know I'm fine."

"I hope so," he said, "but you know things like that don't go away overnight. if you need somebody to spill your guts to, I'll be here."

"Thanks," I replied. "I'm counting on it." I heard the phone click with his hang-up.

I went to the closet and took out the clock and put it in the kitchen. The digital numbers read 3:56.

ॐ

At ten minutes past four, Carson X. arrived. It was not a surprise. Something—some instinct, some voice—had warned me. Stay in your cabin, Carson X. had instructed. There had to be a reason.

He was jovial and relaxed. He had two bottles of imported water with him and I poured a glass for each of us, and we sat in the living/dining, dining/living room and talked casually about the island. I told him I had seen Lucifer and he repeated Old Joe's story of the two women in the canoe.

"We had to bring some political pressure to the table to save him," Carson X. explained. He chuckled. "A well-paid environmentalist can work wonders these days."

And then he shifted on the sofa and, when he did, he shifted the conversation from Lucifer to me.

"I want to tell you something," he said easily. "You're the only person who's ever been in one of the programs to take the name of his counselor, and that's been interesting to me."

"Why?" I asked.

"Imagination," he answered with a smile. "I keep getting the feeling that, indeed, you *are* Bloodworth. Bloodworth playing the game of games, stealing a story from some tragic client locked in a padded cell, and using that story to wiggle into my program to see how it's really done." He swirled the ice in his glass with his finger and watched me. "Are you?" he asked after a moment.

I laughed, causing Carson X. to smile. Yet, his eyes did not move from my face.

I said in a playful manner, "I like the thought, but I'm afraid I'm just an imposter."

Carson X. let his smile wiggle away. "Maybe it's just our creative minds at work," he said. "From what I've learned about you, you're highly accomplished in your field."

"I'm with a good company," I told him. "It's a business that depends on the work of a lot of people. The better they are, the better you are."

Carson X. bobbed his head in agreement. "I think that's what makes your group here so fascinating to me," he said. "Everyone participates. We don't have any mutes." He smiled. "Of course, we have one or two who would dominate if I let them." I knew he was thinking of Barkeep.

"We all have different problems and different personalities," I said. "I think we've learned that it helps to talk about it with our peers, to share some of those frustrations."

Carson X. put his glass on the coffee table. He looked at me seriously. "You know you're going to be all right, don't you?" he said earnestly.

"I think so," I told him.

"Do you know why I'm here?" he said.

"No, I don't," I answered.

"To give you the sword."

"And how do you do that?" I asked.

He stood and walked to the window and looked out to the deck. Knowing he had talked to Sylvia about me, I was certain he knew about the initials, and perhaps the appearance of Arlo.

"Do you remember what you said about honesty?" he asked.

"Yes."

"Honesty corrects a proposed truth or a protective lie. Is that what you said?"

"Yes."

He turned back to me. "I was impressed by that, and I want you to know I will appropriate it for my own use in the future, with or without your permission. It's the best definition of the brave man's sword I've ever heard." He paused, smiled. "Simple word, isn't it? Honesty. But its blade is sharper than steel."

"I—don't know how to relate that," I said.

"All of you came here with a mental block," he replied. "Something you've isolated from memory and have never been able to talk about, because to talk about it would be a confession of unacceptable failure."

"I've told you everything I can remember," I said evenly.

Carson X. shook his head patiently. "That's only partly true," he countered. "There's one other thing, something that's buried so deep you probably don't remember it. I want to hear it."

I was puzzled and suddenly angry, and I knew the anger was visible. "I don't know what you're talking about. She was killed in a car accident. I had no control over that."

"Before the accident. Tell me about that," he urged.

"I'm sorry," I said. "I really don't know what you're talking about."

Carson X. lifted his glass of water to sip from it, and then he placed it on the coffee table. He said, "Tell me about her former husband."

"Her husband?" I replied. "Why?"

He began to pace in the room, the same pacing of our sessions. "I choose men for these seminars for a number of reasons," he said. "Chief among those reasons is this: I know something about them that they refuse to acknowledge. To me, getting to that truth is exciting—or maybe I should say getting to that honesty, because in each case, with each of you, it's been a matter of correcting a proposed truth or a protective lie, as you have wisely defined it."

"What does that mean?" I asked.

He stopped his pacing and looked at me. "Max," he said. "I knew this about Max: it was he who introduced Jenny to drugs. And Menlo. Menlo's affair with his brother's wife came before the suicide, not after. He just couldn't bring himself to handle that guilt. He finally acknowledged that wanting the death of Regina is a cover-up and nothing more. Now he only has to deal with his brother's memory, and he knows his brother would forgive him, though he probably wouldn't attend Regina's funeral if she suddenly expired."

I must have had the look of shock on my face. Carson X. leaned toward me. "You do understand that you're not to share what I've just told you," he said. "If you do, I'll deny it, of course, and I'll be forced to accuse you of stealing my notes, and that could be annoyingly nasty." He smiled comfortably. "But, actually, I trust you. I think we're very much alike, and I can't dismiss this sensation that you're actually a plant for Bloodworth, if not Bloodworth, himself."

"Maybe you shouldn't tell me any of this," I suggested.

Carson X. shrugged. "You're right. I shouldn't. I just wanted you to know how unstable the mind can be when it's hiding something. Max's regret over his drug use—and it was so recreational, it could have been a flirtation with popcorn—has been near fatal. The fact that he teased Jenny into trying heroin one night at a fraternity party has become a tumor in his makeup. He had to face that truth, that honesty, and, today, he did. With Menlo, it's essentially the same."

"Why are you telling me this?" I asked.

He shrugged. "With Godsick, he was obsessed with his sin and his Anna was merely the physical manifestation of that sin. I knew him well because I'd had the same experience. Remember? I told the group about it. Like Godsick, I was obsessed with the lies, the promises. With Max, it's because I know you have concern for him. It's easy to see. I've been aware of it since Max told us his story."

I thought of Arlo's warning about Max. "Yes," I said. "I guess you could say that. He's carrying a great burden."

"Yes, he is," Carson X. agreed. "So are you."

"I've never killed anyone," I said.

"No, but you've suffered because of a killing," Carson X. countered. He swallowed from his glass. "Look," he added, "I believe Max will be fine. He had a breakthrough this afternoon. So did the others—Menlo, Godsick, Barkeep. Barkeep even wept. As irritating as that boy can be, he really is something of a jewel, and, by the way, a brilliant one. You wouldn't believe it, but he has a doctorate from Princeton, and he's wealthy enough from inheriting his grandfather's printing business to have philanthropy as his hobby."

"Barkeep?" I asked incredulously.

"Barkeep," Carson X. replied. "Remember his story of meeting Lilly at a bar, where the boss was treating everyone? I had to turn away to keep from laughing. What he said was true— mostly. He failed to mention that he was the boss."

"Barkeep?" I said again.

"Barkeep," Carson X. repeated. "But I knew he wouldn't tell everything. He's too smart for that. All of you are, and I know it. My little spiel about telling the absolute truth really applies only to perceived problems. To get to the rest of it—the whole life treatment, as I call it—is a never-ending thing. You'd have to live here. With the group, I've focused only on the blind spots I knew you had before you arrived. My duty has been to help you find them, and today Barkeep found his, as did Menlo and Godsick and Max. They all corrected a truth, or a lie. You're the last."

"And you think I've got a blind spot, too?" I asked.

"I know you have," he said gently.

"And it has to do with Kalee's ex-husband?"

His expression did not change, his eyes did not move from me. "I don't know, but you do."

"I'm lost," I said.

"Tell me about the conversation you had with her ex-husband," Carson X. said. His voice sounded distant, something from another place. "Tell me," he repeated.

I do not know why I remembered it, but I did. It was as though I had been deaf and suddenly, miraculously, I could hear again. The sensation was chilling. I could feel my body losing its strength. I tried to speak, but could not.

"Tell me," Carson X. urged gently. "I know you remember it. Take your time."

"He called me," I said weakly.

"Why?" asked Carson X.

"He said he wanted her back and he wanted me out of her life."

"And?"

"He had a deal to offer me. He would run all his company's advertising through the agency if I stopped seeing her. He had two stipulations: someone else had to handle the account and I would never contact Kalee again."

"What did you tell him?"

"I told him he was an idiot."

"Did you talk to her about it?" Carson X. asked.

"Yes," I said. "I called her immediately. She was stunned he'd done such a thing. She told me he'd been calling her for a couple of weeks, insisting on seeing her again, but she had refused. She said she'd make certain he never called me again."

"What day was that?" Carson X. said. His words were measured, each word having weight.

"Day?" I asked.

"Yes, what day was it?"

"I don't remember."

"Of course you do."

I paused and tried to focus. Carson X. sat gazing at me.

I could feel the hard pumping of my heart and the blood-heat of my face. "It was the last time I talked to her," I said. "She told me she would meet me at the club for dinner. It was the day of the surprise engagement party, the one she thought was a business dinner. But she changed her mind. She decided to go to Florida."

"The trip to Florida," Carson X. said. "Tell me about it. Who was she going to see?"

"A friend."

"Which friend?"

The question pressed against me. I knew the answer, but I did not know the reason for the answer.

"Which friend?" Carson X. asked again.

"Her former mother-in-law," I told him.

Carson X. drew in a deep breath. "There," he said softly. "Now do you know why you've been holding on to her with such a grip? Isn't it possible that your mind understood something you couldn't accept? You realized she'd gone to Florida seeking help from someone she'd been close to—the former mother-in-law with some influence over her son. Could it be you believed you were responsible for that? If you hadn't made the phone call about him,

331

she wouldn't have made the trip, and she would still be alive. Is that it?"

I could feel my head bob in answer: Yes.

"Have you found your honesty?" Carson X. asked.

Again, I bobbed my head.

"Now you can put the sword down," Carson X. said.

"How did you know about that?" I asked. "I don't remember talking to Bloodworth about it. It never seemed important."

Carson X. smiled proudly. "I'm good at what I do," he answered. "You'd really be surprised at how many questions I ask. I should have worked for the FBI." He paused to enjoy the pride of his work, and then he added, "May I ask another one?"

"Of course," I said.

"Did your agency ever handle the account?"

"No," I told him.

"Good," he whispered. "Good."

Dear Kalee,

I wish you could see me now. There is a color of health in my face. It is like the blush that used to burn in your cheeks and across your chest when you wanted to be loved. I saw it after Carson X. left from his unannounced visit, when I showered and rubbed the steam from the bathroom mirror. He is right: Health is in the healer and the healer is in the injured. I have to give credit to Carson X. and his FullLife medicine. I think what I have learned from him, and from my MOD Mob companions, is what Bloodworth has been trying to get across to me all these months, but he is too by-the-book and by-the-clock to know how simple it is.

Yet, I do believe it's as much trickery as revelation. Whatever works, works, and I have learned that distraction works wonderfully well. Yes, distraction. Find something—the buried denial I had about your reason for going to Florida—and make it the demon of madness. In short, do a shift, a re-center, a transfer. I think Bloodworth has used all those terms with me, but Carson X. made it make sense. (Time. Isn't time a distraction? Isn't that why people are always advising that time heals everything? Give it enough time and whatever bothers you will be pushed aside by something else that bothers you—or pleases you.)

And this is how Carson X. did it: He added a dollop of drama to the soup of despair, knowing that great madness is great theater. Has been since the Greeks made much of Dionysus, and Shakespeare gave us Macbeth *and* Hamlet. *I would venture that Carson X. could quote extensively from those classics.*

Anyway, it makes me wonder if the members of the MOD Mob were selected for performance potential, rather than personal need. Perhaps we have been in a play, plotted and directed by Carson X., and co-produced by Sylvia, with Inga appearing as a mature ingénue and Old Joe as a one-man Greek chorus. Could be. Yes, it could. Could be that this is being filmed from a thousand hidden cameras, and that everyone we've met is merely an actor improvising a role. Maybe it's like one of those Mission Impossible *movies, where people have rubber-formed masks they peel off to reveal the cleverness of their ruse. Maybe Old Joe and Carson X. are one and the same. I've never seen them together, so it's possible. Maybe there are four other Ingas on the other side of the island, working their way into the tender nests of need for Godsick and Barkeep and Menlo and Max, and maybe Sylvia is hosting a party a night for Reuben.*

Could be. Yes, it could.

And perhaps that is the reason we were asked to choose a pseudonym to use during our time on Neal's Island. Every playbill needs its front page listing of dramatis personae.

Theater of the Absurd, Kalee.

Yes, Theater of the Absurd.

Should I make this theory known to my fellow sufferers? I don't think so. Barkeep would insist on top billing, and by alphabetical order, he would have that right.

To other things.

It's hard to believe I began the writing of these letters only a few days ago. Harder, still, to believe I have been so obsessed with it.

I wonder how many words I've written?

Many thousands.

As I said in the first letter, I had intended the writing to be short, sweet, to-the-point.

But it has taken all these words to find the point.

And the point is, I can't say what I have to say in short, sweet words. No one can.

Excuse me. I think I will *** away for a few minutes.

***

Back. The clock informs me that it is 5:20—no, 5:21; the digital one just flopped. I have almost an hour before I must leave for Carson X's final session.

I had a glass of milk and a sandwich during my breakaway. Inga called. I told her I would call later. She seemed suspicious, but she did not question me. I don't know what I'll do later.

I have waited this day out, this slow-moving day. The sun is a dull smear of red against clouds that are as fluffy as comfortable pillows.

I also did this in my *** break: I removed your picture from my briefcase—the picture Bloodworth told me not to bring with me—and I took it to the deck and I burned it and the K-for-Kalee folder, and also the printed-out versions of the letters I have already written to you here on Neal's Island. I put them in the grill and touched a match to them, and I stood close to the grill, breathing in the smoke, taking you into me. On the picture—the one we had made in the carnival photo machine—your smile turned upward as the fire licked it. Above me, in his tree perch, the vagabond bird whistled a love song that made me shiver with joy.

I do not need the picture or the letters or the scribblings to remember you. You are in my soul, in my blood, in the eye of my memory. You will forever be with me—as we were, not as we might have been.

The one thing I have not destroyed—will not destroy—is the text you sent to me: <u>I will never leave you.</u>

I will keep those words because I understand them in a new way. You will not leave me, but I must free you. I do not want you lingering, like Arlo, in pity for what could have been. I want you to exhilarate in what was.

I put the ashes of my burning into a plastic container stored in a kitchen cabinet and I went to the ocean's edge and scattered them across the water. And then I washed my hands in the suds of the lapping tide. The water was warm. Nearby, a sea gull cried a whimper that did not sound like a sea gull. I think it was Arlo, Arlo cheering me.

Actually, Bloodworth had advised me to destroy all those physical memories of you. He has a quaint philosophy about it. Get rid of the remnants. Start anew. The mind is a far better and far safer place to store memories. The mind keeps memories on the move, dodging bullets of pain. Photographs, letters, things of that sort, keep them at a standstill, like a target with a bullseye.

I think he is right.

I wonder if Godsick and Barkeep and Max and Menlo have learned the same lesson. It's taken a long time, but I think I've got a handle on why we are alike and, yet, so incredibly unalike. We're alike, Kalee, because we've all experienced loss, yet none of us arrived on Neal's Island with the same ache, the same torment, and that makes us different. With Max, it was guilt. With Barkeep, it was vengeance. With Godsick, it was shame and remorse. With Menlo, it was also guilt and unshakable anger. And with me, it was the fear of finality—or something of that nature. With me, I'm really not certain. It is always easier to see the cause of pain in other people. There are too many mirrors in one's private life to see only one view of things.

Life. It is a mystery, is it not?

The sun has disappeared. It is dark outside.

I am dandied up in my tux, Kalee. (It was one of the strange, pre-seminar requirements: that we would bring a tuxedo.) I can see my face in the shine of my shoes. Strike up the band, boys. There'll be dancing tonight.

A post-script later, a last accounting.

After that I will coat the words of this letter with the pale blue of the Select All option under the Edit field, and I will touch the delete key (which strikes faster than the brave man's sword in the hands of a masked executioner), and it will release you to soar like a balloon that has slipped from a child's fingers. You will drift up and up and up, bobbing on playful wisps of air. And then the sky will swallow you and you will be free.

Your (Loving) Correspondent

31

Night of the Tenth Day

The last session with Carson X. and the MOD Mob was a spectacular evening. Carson X., as Barkeep put it in a surprising outpouring of praise, was, "As nutty as a New England walnut tree, but also a blue-blood genius."

What he had done for me earlier, he had done for the others, as he had boasted. He had forced us to peel away the last obstruction, the one thing none of us wanted to admit, or to remember, and he had pronounced us fit, one by one. Remarkably, no one had disagreed with him, but I think we all understood that what he did for us on our last day, he could have done on the first day. He had the answer for each of us before he accepted our application to seek healing. It simply wouldn't have been as much fun for him, and he would not have been comfortable accepting the fees we would leave in our wake.

Still, I do not know if any of it is valid, or if it is the theater I wrote about earlier in my letter to Kalee. If it is theater, the curtain will close and the house lights will come up and the audience will accept that what we have experienced is make-believe, and they will wander away to await another opening of another tale, and in the days after our stay on Neal's Island, all of us will have swallowed the bullet Carson X. talked about in his glib, confident description of his genius. In that regard, I fear for Max. Of all of us, Max seemed to be following the mood of the night, rather than celebrating it, though the look of relief did rest in his eyes. I know I will think of him often. The same is true of Godsick and Menlo and Barkeep. I will wonder if Godsick returned to his parish, or if

Menlo turned killer even after his revelation, or if Barkeep expanded his family business and opened a manufacturing operation to make signature baseball bats. I will wonder if any of us would ever truly understand what we had experienced together.

To borrow from millions who say it millions of times a day, it is what it is.

In our final session together, we did not get into the usual exchange of truth and consequences. We partied. We were all dressed formally, in tuxedos, as Carson X. had requested. Even Barkeep looked presentable. No. Barkeep looked sensational, almost as handsome as Menlo and Menlo was a fashion god. We drank moderately from bottles of fine wine, had a dinner catered by Gena's that was worthy of the finest restaurant in Charleston or Atlanta or New York, or even Menlo's kitchen. Carson X. played the piano for us. His selections were from the classics, not *Amen*, though we did sing the song a few times—in good spirits. We were awe-struck by his playing and we gave him a standing ovation. Barkeep drew fangs protruding from the lips of Miss Perfect. "The final touch," he bragged to Carson X. "You told us she would be beautiful, and now she is. Look at her," he yodeled happily. And then he ripped the sheet from the flip chart and danced with her, and Carson X. surrendered to his nagging and gave him Miss Perfect as a keepsake. Barkeep swore he would have her suitably framed and displayed as a classic example of modern art.

As the evening was winding down, we went outside and wandered the beach barefoot under the dim candlelight of a hazy moon—six men in tuxedos, two by two. I walked with Max,

Menlo with Barkeep, Godsick with Carson X. Max talked quietly of Jenny, still institutionalized, still fighting her hunger for crack cocaine, and he said again that he had been thinking a lot of Kay Cee. I told him I believed he was the kind of man to help Jenny heal her illness, yet I also encouraged him to search for Kay Cee. I said to him, "None of us know what's waiting for us around the corner, do we?"

He smiled and said, "No, I don't guess we do."

And, then, as we walked, I had a sensation—a blinding flash, a premonition—of time not yet lived. In the flash I was in a flea market and there was Miss Perfect in a broken frame, its glass dust-covered. A small price tag was tucked in one corner and the price on the tag was $25.00. The description on its tag read: *Hag from Hell*.

Max knew something had happened. He asked, "You okay?"

"Sure," I told him. "Sure." A silver light fluttered across the quivering surface of the ocean, and I thought: Arlo. I wondered if the light-flutter was a wave of leaving. Across the beach I could hear Barkeep laughing at something Menlo had said.

"You know, I like this place," Max said after a moment. "I wouldn't mind living here."

"Something tells me that part of us will still be here, even when we leave," I suggested.

Max stopped walking. He gazed at the moon. A smile slipped into his face. He suddenly seemed very much at peace.

"Great night," he said.

Max was right. It was a great night, a night of men enjoying the good company of other men. Being close. Feeling protected.

❧

When we left his house, Carson X. gave each of us a miniature pirate's sword, a novelty fish knife that is sold on the island. Its blade had a dull edge. On the handle was an advertisement: *Neal's Island, Where Memories Matter*. He told us we were leaving as brave men, not cowards, and he wanted us to have the swords as proof of it.

Menlo laughed. He said, "Just what I need."

And Carson X. advised him, "A gift is to be admired, but never used."

And then Menlo suggested breakfast together at his cabin. He wanted to cook for us, he said. Carson X. nodded an agreement, or perhaps permission, and we all told Menlo we would be there. Everyone except Carson X. An appointment, he claimed. I think he understood the MOD Mob needed to be alone, or perhaps he was preparing for his next gathering of desperate men, casting his next play.

Eight o'clock, Menlo said.

Eight o'clock, we agreed.

Carson X. embraced each of us as we left. He whispered to me, "I wish we could have spent some more time together. I think we could have learned something from one another."

For a moment I thought he was talking about psychiatry, but then I realized he meant Sylvia. I merely nodded and smiled.

I called Inga when I returned to the cabin. She was waiting for Reuben to arrive for an interview he had insisted was critical to his program.

"At this hour?" I asked.

"Sylvia put him up to it," Inga guessed. "She knows I never go to bed before midnight and that I have to work tomorrow, and apparently Reuben will be leaving earlier than he intended, so it's now or never. Personally, never is fine with me, but I can't refuse Sylvia. I'm sorry."

I told her I agreed. "Hard to deny good friends," I said.

She asked if I would call later.

"Since it's so late, I doubt it," I replied. "If not tonight, tomorrow."

In the background of sound, I heard her doorbell ring.

"I'm sorry," she said again.

"Don't be," I replied.

It was my final deception with Inga, my last act of weakness. I knew I would not call.

I knew I would go to her home the next morning while she was at work, and I would slip the letter I have written to her under her door before leaving Neal's Island. I would give her time to think and, hopefully, to understand, and then I would plead for forgiveness.

Weak men have no right to make demands; weak men can only beg.

On this night—the night before the day of leaving—I had a quaint sense of finality, of acceptance. There was only one last thing to do, a lingering promise to honor—the postscript to Kalee, though I knew it would be more than a postscript. A postscript would be too hasty, too brief, for the purpose of the writing.

Dear Kalee,

I am serene.

It has been an evening of good wine and good company, and I am mellow through and through.

I have been thinking of Bloodworth.

There's nothing wrong with him, nothing at all.

I have seen him agonize with me, Kalee. He doesn't like to show that part of his personality, but sometimes it peeks through.

In a way, it has been enjoyable pretending to be Bloodworth for the last ten days. Sylvia was right, of course. I have been playing a great role, because Bloodworth, in his own quaint way, is a great character. I hope he forgives me if he learns of my cowardly masquerade. He may even find it humorous, or pitiable. (It saddens me that psychiatrists have such strict codes about mixing and mingling with their subjects. I would like to be Bloodworth's friend, to have lunch with him, to invite him for a game of golf or racquetball. Maybe even have a laugh or two over how he's faring with his other clients.)

Do you think Bloodworth and I are alike, Kalee? I do. Yes, I do. In many ways, we are so much alike, we could be same person, as Carson X. suggested.

He. Him. Me. I. We. Us.

***

*Excuse me for the ***. I had a sorrowful flutter of regret, but over Inga, not Bloodworth. There is always a victim of deception, and she is mine. I have treated her badly and I would like to make amends, yet I am not sure what I have done is forgivable. I hope my letter to her offers some understanding. She is a remarkable person.*

Kalee, Kalee.

How odd this is.

I am more at peace than I have been in years. Everything is clear, as Bloodworth had promised, so incredibly clear I do not know if I am sane or insane. When everything is incredibly clear, it can be confusing, Bloodworth once told me, yet it is the light-path to understanding.

I hear the sweet flute voice of the vagabond bird, singing a soft, mesmerizing song from the limb of a tree that looks like a giant bonsai.

And I hear the words you once breathed against my face: "Something within me believes we will always be together."

And we will, Kalee. We will.

In memory.

Memory is our Galaxy, our Universe.

Strange. The vagabond bird has stopped singing. I wonder if he has flown away. Are you with him, Kalee? Are you riding his wings?

Yes, I think so.

It must mean this is over, this forever-letter.

I am well, if not yet completely healed. I have learned that healing does not come with the spit of lightning and the clap of thunder. Healing comes in the balm of tender moments, with the voice of whisper.

I promised to free you, but how do I do that? How? Do I say I love you? Is that enough? I do not want to think of those words—I love you—as mumbo-jumbo. You know that I love you, yet we both know I must free you. I promised I would write these final words, this eulogy of yearning, and then I would click on the delete key and these words would vanish and you would be free. Yes, that is what I promised, isn't it? The words, then, must be special. I want the words that free you to be both a cry of anguish and a song of joy.

You died in rain.

And these are the words I hear when I think of that death-rain:

Il pleure dans mon coeur.

The French poet Paul Verlaine wrote those words.

Do you know the translation, Kalee?

Verlaine said Il pleure dans mon coeur means this: It rains in my heart.

It's a sad thought, isn't it? Beautiful words, but a sad thought.

Yes.

Without you, Kalee, it rains in my heart.

Without you.

Sans vous.

Sans vous il pleure dans mon coeur.

Without you it rains in my heart.

No matter what happens to me in time to come—the good and the bad of it—you will always be the wish I could not have, but cannot forget.

Listen, Kalee. Listen.

This is how I free you, with words that have the taste of God's wafer on my tongue:

Sans vous il pleure dans mon coeur.

344